THE PROW BEAST

Also by Robert Low

The Whale Road
The Wolf Sea
The White Raven

ROBERT LOW

The Prow Beast

HarperCollins*Publishers*

HarperCollins*Publishers*
77–85 Fulham Palace Road,
Hammersmith, London W6 8JB

www.harpercollins.co.uk

Published by HarperCollins*Publishers* 2010
1

A catalogue record for this book
is available from the British Library

ISBN-13 978 0 00 729855 6

Set in Sabon by Palimpsest Book Production Limited, Grangemouth, Stirlingshire
Printed in Great Britain by Clays Ltd, St Ives plc

To my daughter Monique –
all the treasure this
father needs

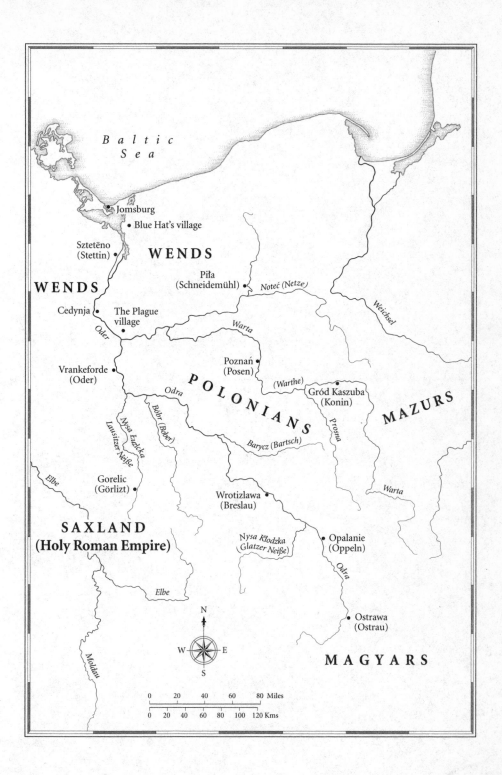

Baltic Sea

• Jomsburg

• Blue Hat's village

Sztetěno
(Stettin) •

WENDS

WENDS

Piła
(Schneidemühl) •   *Noteć (Netze)*

Cedynja •

The Plague
village •

Oder

Warta

Weichsel

Vrankeforde
(Oder) •

Poznań
(Posen) •

P O L O N I A N S

(Warthe)

Gród Kaszuba
(Konin) •

Odra

Böhr (Bober)

Prosna

M A Z U R S

Lausitzer Neiße

Nysa Łużicka

Barycz (Bartsch)

Elbe

Gorelic
(Görlizt) •

Wrotizlawa
(Breslau) •

Warta

**SAXLAND
(Holy Roman Empire)**

*Nysa Kłodzka
Glatzer Neiße*

Opalanie
(Oppeln) •

Odra

Elbe

Ostrawa
(Ostrau) •

Moldau

N
W E
S

M A G Y A R S

0   20   40   60   80 Miles
0 20 40 60 80 100 120 Kms

The prow-beast, hostile monster of the mast
With his strength hews out a file
On ocean's even path, showing no mercy

Egil Skallagrimsson

AUSTRGOTALAND, 975AD

The sun stayed veiled behind lead clouds streaked with silver. The rain hissed and the sea heaved, black and sluggish as a walrus on a rock, while a wind dragged a fine smoke of spray into my eyes.

'Not storm enough,' Hauk Fast-Sailor declared and he had the right of it, for sure. There was not enough of a storm to stop our enemies from coming up the fjord with the wind in their favour and that great, green-bordered sail swelled out. On a ship with a snarling serpent prow that sail looked like dragon wings and gave the ship its name.

The oars on the *Fjord Elk* were dipped, but moving only to keep the prow beast snarling into the wind that drove the enemy down on us; there was no point in tiring ourselves – we were crew-light, after all – while the enemy climbed into their battle gear. When we saw their sail go down would be the time for worry, the time they were ready for war.

Instead, men kept their hands busy tightening straps and checking edges, binding back their hair as it whipped in the wind. All of Jarl Brand's lent-men from *Black Eagle* were here, save six with Ref and Bjaelfi who were herding women and weans and thralls away from Hestreng hall and up to

1

the valley, with as much food and spare sail for tentage as they could carry. Away from the wrath of Randr Sterki and the snarlers on *Dragon Wings*.

I hoped Randr Sterki would content himself with looting and burning Hestreng, would not head inland too far. I had left him wethers and cooped hens and pigs to steal, as well as a hall and the buildings to burn – and if it was the Oathsworn he wanted . . . well, here we were, waiting for him at sea.

Still, I knew what drove Randr to this attack and could not blame him for it. I had the spear in my throat and the melted bowels that always came with the prospect of facing men who wanted to cleave sharp bars of metal through me but, for once, did not wish to be elsewhere. This was where I had to be, protecting the backs of mine and all the other fledglings teetering on flight's edge, from the revenge of raiding men.

Men like us.

Gizur, swinging down from stay to stay through the ranks of men, looked like a mad little monkey I had seen once in Serkland, his weather-lined face such a perfect replica that I smiled. He was surprised at that smile, considering what we faced, then grinned back.

'We should ship oars, Jarl Orm, before they get splintered.'

I nodded; when the ships struck, the oars on that side would be a disaster to us if we left them out. There was a flurry and clatter as the oars came in and were stacked lengthways; men cursed as shafts dunted them and now I saw the great snarling prow of *Dragon Wings* clearly, heard the faint shrieks and roars, saw the weapon-waving.

I was watching them flake the sail down to the yard when two of Jarl Brand's lent-men shoved through our throng, almost to the *Fjord Elk*'s prow, nocking arrows as they went, stepping over bundled oars and shoving folk aside. They shot; distant screams made our own men roar approval – then curse as an answering flight zipped and shunked into the woodwork. One of the bowmen, Kalf Sygni, spun half round

2

and clutched his forearm where a shaft was through, side to side.

'Missed that coming,' bellowed Finn, hefting his shield as he moved to the prow, clashing ring-iron shoulders with Nes-Bjorn, who was headed the same way; they glared at each other.

'I am Jarl Brand's prow man on the *Black Eagle*,' Nes-Bjorn growled.

'You are not on the *Black Eagle*,' Finn pointed out and, reluctantly, the big man gave way, letting Finn take his place. Across on *Dragon Wings* his counterpart, hero-warrior of his boat, stepped up, mailed, helmeted and carrying a shield, but nothing better than a ship-wood axe.

They had the sail down and the oars shipped, leaving *Dragon Wings* with enough momentum to crash on us, rocking the *Elk* sideways to the waterline, staggering men who had been unprepared for it. Randr's crew howled and axes clattered over our side, causing men to duck and raise shields – the axe-owners hauled hard at the ropes ringed to the shafts, pulling the hooked heads tight to the inside of the *Elk* with their iron beards, clinching us close as lovers.

A man screamed as his leg went with such a pull, trapping him like a snared fox against the side while he beat and tugged. Holger, I remembered dully as he screamed his throat out in agony. His name was Holger.

An arrow skittered off the mast and whipped past my head; I wore no ring-coat, for I was not so sure I could wriggle out of it in time if I fell overboard. Botolf, who stood on my right, heard me curse and grinned.

'Now you know what it feels like,' he yelled and I laughed into his mad delight, for it was a long-standing joke that Botolf had never found a ring-coat big enough to fit him. Then he threw back his head and roared out his name; Randr Sterki's men shrieked and howled; the sides of the boats clashed and men flung themselves forward while the locked ships groaned and rocked.

The worst thing about battle, after a few bloodings drive away the first fears of it, is that it is work. The stink and the horror, the belly-wrenching terror and savage hatred of it were all things I had grown used to – but the backbreaking labour of it was what always made me blench. It was like ploughing stony ground, where the stones rise up and try to hit you and the whole affair leaves you sick and tremble-legged with exhaustion. The one good part about being jarl was that you did not sink into the grind of it, at least not all at once – but you had to stand like a tree in a boiling flood and seem unconcerned.

I stood rock-still and guarded by Botolf's shield, watching the *Dragon Wings* crew pile forward in a rush, dipping both ships almost into the water with their weight. They struggled and hacked and died on the thwart-edges, my picked men darting in to cut the ropes that bound us together, or shoot out the men on *Dragon Wings* whose task it was to haul us tight.

They were red-mouthed screamers, Randr Sterki's crew, waving spears and axes, garbed in leather and some in no more than makeshift breastplates of knotted rope. They had helms of all kinds, none of them fine craftings, and waved blades as notched as a dog's jaw – even Randr Sterki's ring-mailed prow man wielded no better than an adze-axe. Yet they had the savagery of revenge in them and that made the arm strong and the edge sharp.

Randr stood and roared out unheard curses in the middle of his ship, in the middle of a group as unlike the men round them as sheep-droppings in snow. They made my knees turn to water, those men whose eyes stared and saw nothing, who wore only thick, hairy hides over their breeks, who champed flecks of foam onto the thicket of their beards and hefted weapons with an easy skill and arms blood-marked with strength runes. Some of them, I noted, had swords, well-worn and well-earned.

'Bearcoats!' yelled Botolf in my ear. 'He has bearcoats, Orm . . .'

Even as he spoke I saw them, all twelve of them, stir like a wolf pack scenting a kill. Bearcoats – berserker – had been

4

no part of Randr Sterki's crew before. Where had he got them from? My mouth went dry; I saw them snarling and howling, slamming into those of their own side who did not see them in time to get out of the way.

The first of them, tow-haired, tangle-bearded, reached the side and howled out to the sky, then hurled himself over on my men before the cords of his neck had slackened; they hacked at him with the desperate fury of those too trapped to run. The rest of the pack began to follow and Randr Sterki urged them on with bellows from the middle of his ship, his face red and ugly with rage and battle.

'We shall have to kill Pig-Face,' panted Nes-Bjorn, suddenly on my other side, pointing to Randr. If he was cursing at having been left behind by Jarl Brand to serve with us on this seemingly bad-wyrded day, his cliff of a face did not show it.

'First stop the bearcoats,' I pointed out, as calmly as I could while watching Tow-Hair carve his way towards me, trailing blood and screams; Botolf hefted his shield and byrnie-biter spear and braced himself on his one good leg. I raised my own sword a little, as if only resting it lightly on one shoulder, while my throat was full of my heart at the sight of a berserker slashing a path straight to me.

'Ach,' said Nes-Bjorn with a dismissive wave of his bearded axe. 'We have our own man for that.'

At which point came a growling grunt from behind me, so like the coughing charge-roar of a boar that I half-spun in alarm. Then a half-naked figure with skin-marks of power and an axe in either hand launched straight over the heads of my own men, scattering them as he clattered into the howling bearcoat. Tow-Hair went down in a bloody eyeblink and the axes flailed on in Stygg Dusi's fists, his carefully applied skin-marks streaked with blood, as he hurled himself in a bellowing whirl of arms and legs and axes over the side and into the crowded *Dragon Wings*. Men scattered before him.

'Stygg Dusi,' Nes-Bjorn pointed out and split a feral grin

as the man by-named Shy Calm howled and chopped and died hard in the middle of the enemy ship.

'There are twelve of them,' I offered and Nes-Bjorn scowled.

'Eleven now – no, ten, for Stygg has done well. Have you a point to make, Jarl Orm of the Oathsworn, or are you just after showing your skill at tallying?'

Then he elbowed men aside to reach the prow, where Finn, gasping and exhausted, had been forced to step back, ropey strings drooling from his mouth. The *Dragon Wings* prow man was nowhere to be seen.

I listened and watched as Stygg Dusi served out the last seconds of what the Norns had woven for him from the moment he slithered wetly into the world. Everything he had done had led to this place, this moment, and I raised my sword to the life he honoured us with, almost envied him in the certainty of his place in Valholl. *Not yet, but soon*, I was thinking, the old message we gave to all the dying to take with them to those gone before. Very soon now, it seemed.

The last rope was cut; Kalf Sygni, with the arrow still through his forearm, managed to shoot the last rope-hauler and the ships drifted apart from the stern, so that the prow beasts bobbed and snarled, almost seeming to strike out at each other. Men from both crews, trapped on the wrong boat, tried to fight their way to a thwart edge and leap for it.

Everything after that became a blur to me. I remember shoulder-charging a man, sending him flying into the water and it was only when he floundered there that I saw he wore a bearcoat. Finn loomed up, shook slaver and blood from his face, then launched back into the mad struggle, roaring curses and insults.

Hauk Fast-Sailor went down under the frenzied, raving chops of a wet-mouthed trio of bearcoats; Onund Hnufa went over the side, blood streaming from a cut on his head, and a man bound in knotted rope came at me, so that I had to kill him. By the time I looked, Onund had gone and I did not know if he had surfaced or not.

6

Something small and dark flew at the prow and Nes-Bjorn batted it contemptuously to one side. Flame engulfed him. Just like that. One minute he was roaring invites for someone to face him, the next minute he was enveloped in flame, a pillar of fire staggering about the prow. He fell back and men shrieked; one scrambled away screaming and batting at the flames on his leg, but that only caused his hands to flare. Another flung away a flaming shield, which hit the water and sank – but the water continued to burn in a circle.

'Magic!' yelled a voice, but it was no rune-curse, this. I had seen it before and the second little pot smacked into the *Elk's* prow and burst into flames exactly as Roman Fire was supposed to. I watched the flames leap up the proud horns of Botolf's carving, saw ruin in them even as the frantic crew of *Dragon Wings* saw those same flames leap to their own ship. Then Botolf yelled out that there was a second ship.

A second ship. Roman Fire. Bearcoats. These had been no part of Randr Sterki before now. I blinked and stared, my thoughts wheeling like the embers of my burning ship while men struggled and slipped and died, raving curses.

'Orm – on your steerboard . . .'

I half-turned into a wet-red maw, where spittle skeined like spume off a wave. He had a greasy tangle of wild hair and eyes as mad as a kennel of frothing dogs, while the axe in his hand seemed as big as a wagon tree. I swung and missed, felt my sword bite into the wood of the mast, where it stuck.

I got my shield in the way a little, so that his axe splintered it and tore it sideways, out of my finger-short grasp. His whole body hit me then and there was a moment when I smelled the woodsmoke and grease stink of his pelt, the rankness of his sweat. My hand was wrenched from the hilt of my trapped sword.

Then there was only the whirl of silver sky and dark water and the great, cold plunge, like a hot nail in the quench.

ONE

Six weeks before . . .

The year cracked like a bad cauldron, just as winter unfastened its jaws a little and the cold ebbed to drip and yellow grass. Those from further south would say it was March and spring, but what did they know? It was still winter to us, who counted the seasons sensibly.

In the northlands we also know what causes the ground to move: it is the pain-writhing of Loki, when Loki's wife has to empty her bowl, leaving her bound husband in agony, his face ravaged by the dripping poison of the serpent for the time it takes her to return and catch the venom again. The gods of Asgard gave dark Loki a hard punishment for his meddlings.

His writhings that year folded the cloak of the earth to new shapes with a grinding of stones, and great scarred openings, one of which swallowed an entire field close to us, kine and all.

A sign from the Aesir, Finn said moodily, echoing what others thought – that we should be back on the whale road and not huddled on land trying to be farmers. It was hard to ignore his constant low rumbling on the matter, harder still to put my head down and shoulder into the loud unspoken stares of the rest of them, day after day.

Odin had promised us fame and fortune and, of course, it was cursed, for he had not warned us to beware of what we sought so fiercely. Now that we had it, there was no joy in it for raiding men – what point raiding, as Red Njal grumbled, if you have silver and women enough? Nor was there any joy in trying to forsake the prow beast and cleave to the land, digging it up like worms, as Hlenni pointed out.

I heard them and their talk of the crushing wyrd of Odin. Others, still claiming to be Oathsworn, had wandered off into the world, with promises to be back at my side if the need arose, the old Oath binding them – *We swear to be brothers to each other, bone, blood and steel, on Gungnir, Odin's spear, we swear, may he curse us to the Nine Realms and beyond if we break this faith, one to another.*

I accepted their promises with a nod and a clasping of hands, to keep the Oath alive and them from harm, though I did not expect to see any of them again. Those who remained struggled with the shackles that kept them from following the prow beast. They plodded grimly through winters in the hope that better weather might bring a new spark to send them coldwards and stormwards. It never seemed to flare into a fire of any fierceness, all the same.

The only ones who no longer moaned and grumbled were Botolf and Short Eldgrim, the first because he was no good on a raiding ship with one timber leg and, besides, had Ingrid and a daughter he cared more about; the second had no clear idea half the time of where he was, the inside of his head knocked out of him in a fight years before.

Finn had bairned Thordis in the fever that followed our return, silver-rich and fame-rich, and now she cradled their son, Hroald, in a sling of her looped apron. Finn looked at the boy every day with a mix of pride and misery, the one for what every father felt, the other for the forging of another link in a chain that chafed, for Thordis hourly expected a marriage offer.

On the other hand, when I looked across at Thorgunna and she let me know with her eyes that her own carrying was fine, there were no words, no mead of poetry that described how I felt at the news. It was a joy doubled, for she had lost a bairn before this and to find that it had not broken Thorgunna as a mother was worth all the silver Odin had handed us.

Yet the dull haar of disappointed men hung over Hestreng, so that the arrival of young Crowbone in a fine ship brought heads up, sniffing eagerly at his fire and arrogance like panting dogs on a bitch's arse.

Crowbone. Olaf Tryggvasson, true Prince of Norway and a boy of twelve whose fair fame went before him like a torch and was so tied in with my own that swords and axes were lowered, since no-one could believe Crowbone had come to raid and pillage his friend, Orm of Hestreng.

He sat in my hall rubbing sheep fat into his boots, the price you pay for being splendidly careless and leaping off the prow of a fine ship into the salt-rotting shallows.

I had not seen him in three years and was astounded. I had left a nine-year-old boy and now found a twelve-year-old man. He was sharp-chinned and yellow-haired, his odd-coloured eyes – one brown as a nut, the other blue-green as sea ice – were bland as always and his hair was long enough to whip in the wind, though two brow braids swung, weighted with fat silver rings woven into the ends. I was betting sure that the one thing he wanted, above all else, was to grow hair on his chin.

He wore red and blue, with a heavy silver band on each arm and another, the dragon-ended jarl torc of a chief, at his neck. He had a sword, cunningly made for his size, snugged up in a sheath worked with snake patterns and topped and tailed with bronze. He had come a long way in the three years since I had freed him from where he had been chained by the neck to the privy of a raider called Klerkon.

I said that to him, too, and he smiled a quiet smile, then answered that he had not come as far as me, since he had started as a prince and I had come to being jarl of the legendary Oathsworn from being a gawk-eyed stripling of no account. Which showed what he had learned in oiled manners and gold-browed words at the court of Vladmir.

'A fine ship,' I added as his growlers, all ringmail and swagger, filed in to argue places by the hearthfire. He swelled with pride.

'*Short Serpent* is the name,' he declared. 'Thirty oars a side and room for many more men besides.'

'*Short Serpent*?' I asked and he looked at me, serious as a wrecking.

'One day I will have one bigger than this,' he replied. 'That one I will call *Long Serpent* and it will be the finest raiding ship afloat.'

'Is Hestreng ripe for a *strandhogg*, then?' I asked dryly, for already the fame of this boy was known in halls the length of the Baltic, where he had been hit-and-run raiding – the *strandhogg* – all year.

Crowbone only grinned and shook his head so that the rings tinkled. Then I saw they were not rings at all, but coins with holes punched through them and Crowbone's grin grew wider when he saw I had spotted that. He fished in his pouch and brought out another, a whole one, which he spun at me until I made it vanish in my fist.

'I took it and its brothers and cousins from traders bound for Kiev,' Crowbone said, still grinning. 'We will choke the life from Jaropolk before we are done.'

I looked at it – a glance was all it took, for minted silver was rare enough for me to know all the coins that whirled like bright foam along the Baltic shores. It was Roman, a new-minted one they call *miliaresion* and silver-light compared with other, older cousins that spilled out of Constantinople, which we called Miklagard, the Great City. The ones Crowbone had braided into the ends of his hair were gold *nomisma*, seventy-two to a Roman pound and, I saw, with the head of Nicepheros on them, which made them recent – and one-quarter light.

I said this as I spun it back to him and he grinned, suitably admiring my skill. He had skills of his own when it came to coinage, all the same – backed by the ships and men of Vladimir, Prince of the Rus in Novgorod, he had ravaged up and down the Baltic to further the cause of his friend against Vladimir's brothers, Jaropolk and Oleg. They were not quite at open war, those three Kievan brothers, but it was a matter of time only and the trade routes in their lands were ravaged and broken as a result.

That and the lack of silver from the east that made Crowbone's coin rare – and light – also made any trade trip there worthless unless you went all the way down the rivers and cataracts to the Great City. I said as much while Thorgunna and the thrall women served platters and ale and Crowbone grinned cheerfully, uncaring little wolf cub that he was.

A shadow appeared at his elbow and I turned to the mailed and helmeted figure who owned it; he stared back at me from under his Rus horse-plume and face-mail, iron-grim and stiff as old rock.

'Alyosha Buslaev,' declared little Crowbone with a grin. 'My prow man.'

Vladimir's man more like, I was thinking, as this Alyosha closed in on Crowbone like a protecting hound, sent by the fifteen-year-old Prince of Novgorod to both guard and watch his little brother-in-arms. They were snarling little cubs, the Princes Vladimir and Olaf Crowbone, and thinking on them only made me feel old.

The hall was crowded that night as we feasted young Crowbone and his crew with roast horse, pork, ale and calls to the Aesir, for Hestreng was still free of the Christ and mine was still the un-partitioned hall of a raiding jarl – despite my best efforts to change that. Still, as I told Crowbone, the White Christ was everywhere, so that the horse trade was dying – those made Christian did not fight horses in the old way, nor eat the meat.

'Go raiding,' he replied, with the air of someone who thought I was daft for not having considered it. Then he grinned. 'I forgot – you do not need to follow the prow beast, with all the silver you have buried away under moonlight.'

I did not answer that; young Crowbone had developed a hunger for silver, ever since he had worked out that that was where ships and men came from. He needed ships and men to make himself king in Norway and I did not want him snuffling after any moonlit burials of mine – he had had his share of Atil's silver. That hoard had been hard come by and I was still not sure that it was not cursed.

I offered horn-toasts to the memory of dead Sigurd, Crowbone's silver-nosed uncle, who had been the nearest to a father the boy had had and who had been Vladimir's *druzhina* commander. Crowbone joined in, perched on the high-backed guest bench beside me, his legs too short to rest his feet like a grown man on the tall hearthstones that kept drunk and child from tumbling in the pitfire.

His men, too, appreciated the Sigurd toasts and roared it out. They were horse-eating men of Thor and Frey, big men, calloused and muscled like bull walruses from sword work and rowing, with big beards and loud voices, spilling ale down their chests and boasting. I saw Finn's nostrils flare, drinking in the salt-sea reek of them, the taste of war and wave that flowed from them like heat.

Some of them wore silk tunics and baggier breeks than others, carried curved swords rather than straight, but that was just Gardariki fashion and, apart from Alyosha, they were not the half-breed Slavs who call themselves Rus – rowers. These were all true Swedes, young oar-wolves who had crewed with Crowbone up and down the Baltic and would follow the boy into Hel's hall itself if he went – and Alyosha was at his side to make the sensible decisions.

Crowbone saw me look them over and was pleased at what he saw in my face.

'Aye, they are hard men, right enough,' he chuckled and I shrugged as diffidently as I could, waiting for him to tell me why he and his hard men were here. All that had gone before – politeness and feasting and smiles – had been leading to this place.

'It is good of you to remember my uncle,' he said after a time of working at his boots. The hall rang with noise and the smoke-sweat fug was thicker than the bench planks. Small bones flew; roars and laughter went up when one hit a target.

He paused for effect and stroked his ringed braids, wanting moustaches so badly I almost laughed.

'He is the reason I am here,' he said, raising his voice to be heard. It piped, still, like a boy's, but I did not smile; I had long since learned that Crowbone was not the boy he seemed.

When I said nothing, he waved an impatient little hand.

'Randr Sterki sailed this way.'

I sat back at that news and the memories came welling up like reek in a blocked privy. Randr the Strong had been the right-hand of Klerkon and had taken over most of that one's crew after Klerkon died; he had sailed their ship, *Dragon Wings*, to an island off Aldeijuborg.

Klerkon. There was a harsh memory right enough. He had raided us and lived only long enough to be sorry for it, for we had wolfed down on his winter-camp on Svartey, the Black Island, finding only his thralls and the wives and weans of his crew – and Crowbone, chained to the privy.

Well, things were done on Svartey that were usual enough for red-war raids, but men too long leashed and then let loose, goaded on by a vengeful Crowbone, had guddled in blood and thrown bairns at walls. Later, Crowbone found and killed

14

Klerkon – but that is another tale, for nights with a good fire against the saga chill of it.

Randr Sterki had a free raiding hand while matters were resolved with Prince Vladimir over the Klerkon killing, but when all that was done, Vladimir sent Sigurd Axebitten, Crowbone's no-nose uncle and commander of his *druzhina*, to give Randr a hard dunt for his pains.

Except Sigurd had made a mess of it, or so I heard, and Crowbone had grimly followed after to find Randr Sterki and his men gone and his uncle nailed to an oak tree as a sacrifice to Perun. His famous silver nose was missing; folk said Randr wore it on a leather thong round his neck. Crowbone had been wolf-sniffing after his uncle's killer since, with no success.

'What trail did he leave, that brings you this way?' I asked, for I knew the burn for revenge was fierce in him. I knew that fire well, for the same one scorched Randr Sterki for what we had done to his kin in Klerkon's hall at Svartey; even for a time of red war, what we had done there made me uneasy.

Crowbone finished with his boots and put them on.

'Birds told me,' he answered finally and I did not doubt it; little Olaf Tryggvasson was known as Crowbone because he read the Norns' weave through the actions of birds.

'He will come here for three reasons,' he went on, growing more shrill as he raised his voice over the noise in the hall. 'You are known for your wealth and you are known for your fame.'

'And the third?'

He merely looked at me and it was enough; the memory of Klerkon's steading on Svartey, of fire and blood and madness, floated up in me like sick in a bucket.

There it was, the cursed memory, hung out like a flayed skin. Fame will always come back and hag-ride you to the grave; my own by-name, Bear Slayer, was proof of that, since

I had not slain the white bear myself, though no-one alive knew that but me. Still, the saga of it – and all the others that boasted of what the Oathsworn were supposed to have done – constantly brought men looking to join us or challenge us.

Now came Randr Sterki, for his own special reasons. The Oathsworn's fame made me easy to find and, with only a few fighting men, I was a better mark to take on than a boatload of hard Rus under the protection of the Prince of Novgorod.

'Randr Sterki is not a name that brings warriors,' Crowbone went on. 'But yours is and any man who deals you a death blow steals your wealth, your women and your fame in that stroke.'

It was said in his loud and shrill boy's voice – almost a shriek – and it was strange, looking back on it, that the hall noise should have ebbed away just then. Heads turned; silence fell like a cloak of ash.

'I am not easily felled,' I pointed out and did not have to raise my voice to be heard. Some chuckled; one drunk cheered. Red Njal added: 'Even by bears,' and got laughter for it.

Then the hall was washed with murmurs and subdued whispers; feasting flowed back to it, slow as pouring honey.

'Did you come all this way to warn me?' I asked as the noise grew again and he flushed, for I had worked out that he had not been so driven just for that.

'I would have your Sea-Finn's drum,' he answered. 'If it speaks of victory – will you join the hunt for Randr Sterki?'

Vuokko the Sea-Finn had come to us only months since, seeking the runemaster Klepp Spaki, who was chipping out the stone of our lives in the north valley. Vuokko came all the way from his Sami forests to learn the true secret of our runes from Klepp and no-one was more surprised than I when the runemaster agreed to it.

Of course, in return, Klepp had Vuokko teach him his *seidr*-magic, which was such that the little Sea-Finn was already well-known. Since *seidr* was a strange and unmanly thing,

16

there were whispers of what the pair of them did all alone up in a hut in the valley – but muted ones, for Klepp was a runemaster and so a man of some note.

Vuokko, of course, was an outlander Sami sorcerer and not to be trusted at all, but it seemed folk were coming over the sea to hear the beat of his rune-marked drum and watch the three gold frogs on it dance, revealing Odin's wisdom to those brave – or daft – enough to want to know it.

I saw Thorgunna, serving ale to Finn, Onund Hnufa and Red Njal, three heads close together and bobbing with argument and laughter. She smiled and the warmth of that scene, of my woman and my friends, washed me; then she gently touched her belly and moved on and the leap of that in my heart almost brought me to my feet.

'Will you hunt down Randr, Sigurd's bane, with me?'

The voice was thin with impatience, jerking me back from the warmth of wife and unborn. I turned to him and sighed, so that he saw it and frowned.

The truth was I had no belly for it. We had gained fame and wealth at a cost – too high, I often thought these days – and now the idea of sluicing sea and hard bread and stiff joints on a trip even across to Aldeijuborg made me wince. Even that was a hare-leap of joy compared to sailing off with this man-boy to hunt round the whole Baltic for the likes of Randr Sterki.

I said as much. I did not add that I thought Randr Sterki had a right to feel vengeful and that Crowbone had played a part in fuelling the fire on Svartey.

I heard the air hiss from him and there was petulance as much as disappointment in that, for young Crowbone did not like to be crossed.

'There is fame and the taste of victory,' he argued, pouting into my twist of a smile.

I already had fame, while victory, when all is said and done, tastes as blood-foul as failure – which was the other side of the spinning coin in this matter. He scowled at that, his eyes reflecting me to myself – what I saw there was old and done, but it was the view from a boy of twelve and almost made me chuckle. Then Crowbone found himself and smiled blandly; more signs of the princely things learned from Vladimir, I saw.

'I will have the drum-frogs leap for me, all the same,' he said and I nodded.

As if he had heard, Vuokko came into the hall, so silently that one of the younger thrall girls, too fondled by these new and muscled warriors to notice, gave a scream as the Sea-Finn appeared next to her.

Men laughed, though uneasily, for Vuokko had a face like a mid-winter mummer's mask left too long in the rain, which the wind-guttered sconces did not treat kindly. The high cheekbones flared the light, making the shadows there darker still, while the eyes, slits of blackness, had no pupils that I could see and the skin of his face was soft and lined as an old walrus.

He grinned his pointed-toothed smile and sidled in, all fur and leather and bits of stolen Norse weave, hung about with feathers and bone both round his neck and wound into the straggles of his iron-grey hair.

In one hand was the drum of white reindeer skin marked with runes and signs only he knew, festooned with claws and little skulls and tufts of wool; on the surface, three frogs skittered, fastened to a ring that went round the whole circle of it. In his other hand was a tiny wooden hammer.

Men made warding signs and muttered darkly, but Crowbone smiled, for he knew the *seidr*, unmanly work of Freyja though that magic was, and a Sea-Finn's drum held no terrors for a boy who saw into the Other by the actions of birds. I wondered if he still had some more of the strange stories he had chilled us all with last year.

'This grandson of Yngling kings,' I said pointedly to the Finn, 'wants a message from your drum on an enterprise he has.'

The Sea-Finn grinned his bear-trap grin, as if he had known all along. He produced a carved runestick from his belt and then drew a large square in the hard, beaten earth of the floor – folk sidled away from him as he came near.

Then he marked off two points on all the sides and scraped lines to join them; now he had nine squares and folk shivered as if the fire had died. In the middle square, the square within a square, he folded into a cross-legged sit and cradled the drum like a child, crooning to it.

He rocked and chanted, a deep hoom in the back of his throat that raised hackles, for most knew he was calling on Lemminki, a Finnish sorcerer-god who could sing the sand into pearls for those brave enough to call on him. The square within a square was supposed to keep Vuokko safe – but folk darted uneasy looks at the flickering shadows and moved even further away from him.

Finally, he hit the drum – once only – a deep and resonating bell of sound coming from such a small thing; men winced and shifted and made Hammer signs and I saw Finn join his hands in the diamond-shape of the *ingwaz* warding rune as the gold frogs danced. No man cared for *seidr* magic, for it was a woman's thing and to see a man do it set flesh creeping.

Vuokko peered for a long time, then raised his horror of a face to Crowbone. 'You will be king,' he said simply and there was a hiss as men let out their breath all at once together, for that had not been the enterprise I had meant.

Crowbone merely smiled the smile of a man who had had the answer he expected and fished in his purse, drawing out his pilfered coin. He flicked it casually in the air towards Vuokko, who never took his eyes from Crowbone's face, ignoring the silver whirl of it.

I was astounded by the boy's arrogance and his disregard – you did not treat the likes of Vuokko like some fawning street-seer, nor did you break the safety of his square within a square while he was in the Sitting-Out, half in and half out of the Other, surrounded by a swirl of dangerous strangeness.

Crowbone had half-turned away in his proud, unthinking fashion when the scorned *miliaresion* bounced on the drum, the tinkle of its final landing lost in the thunder it made. He turned, surprised.

'What was that sound, Sea-Finn?' he demanded and Vuokko smiled like a wolf closing in.

'That was the sound of your enterprise, lord,' he replied after a study of the frogs, 'falling from your hand.'

After that, the feasting was a sullen affair coloured by Crowbone's morose puzzlement, for now he did not know what the Sea-Finn had promised. Most of his followers only recalled the bit about him becoming king in Norway, so they were cheered.

I stood with Crowbone on the sand and dulse two days later, while his men hefted their sea-chests back on the splendid *Short Serpent* and got ready to sail off.

He was wrapped in his familiar white fur and a matching stare, waiting to see if terns or crows came in ones or twos, or went left or right. Only he knew what it meant.

'All the same,' he said finally, clasping my wrist and staring up into my gaze with his odd eyes, 'you would do well to join me. Randr Sterki will come for you. I hear he is sworn to Styrbjorn.'

That was no surprise; Styrbjorn was the brawling nephew of my king, Eirik Segersall. Now just come into manhood, he had designs on the high seat himself when Eirik was dead and sulked when it became clear no-one else liked the idea.

Foolishly, King Eirik had given him ships and men to go off and make a life for himself and Styrbjorn now prowled up and down off Wendland on the far Baltic shore, snarling and making his intentions known regarding what he considered his birthright. Someday soon, I was thinking, he would need a good slap, but he was only a boy. I almost said so to Crowbone, then clenched my teeth on it and smiled instead.

I saw Alyosha hovering, a mailed and helmeted wet-nurse anxious to see his charge safely back on the boat. I widened my smile indulgently at Crowbone; I was arrogant then, believing Oathsworn fame and Odin's favour shield enough against such as Randr Sterki and having no worries about Styrbjorn, a youth with barely seventeen summers on him. I should have known better; I should have remembered myself at his age.

'Have you a tale on all this?' I asked lightly, reminding Crowbone of the biting stories he had told us, a boy holding grown freemen in thrall out on the cold empty.

'I have tales left,' he answered seriously. 'But the one I have is for later. I know birds, all the same, and they know much.'

He saw the confusion in my face and turned away, trotting towards the ship.

'An eagle told me of troubles to come,' he flung back over his shoulder. 'A threat to its young, on the flight's edge.'

The chill of that stayed with me as I watched *Short Serpent* slither off down the fjord and even the closeness of Thorgunna under my arm could not warm it, for I was aware of what she carried in her belly and of what her sister cradled in her arms.

Young eagles on the flight's edge.

TWO

The sun clawed itself higher every day; snow melted patch by patch, streams gurgled and I started to talk earnestly about joint efforts to harvest the sea, of ploughing and seeding cropland and how Finn could borrow my brace of oxen if he liked.

He looked at me as if I was a talking calf, then went back to drinking and hunting with Red Njal, while Onund Hnufa and Gizur went to make the *Fjord Elk* ready for sea and Hlenni Brimill and others fetched wood for new shields and pestered Ref to leave off tinsmithing nails against rust to put a new edge on worn blades.

After the feasting night for Crowbone, Finn had come to me and asked if the Oathsworn were going raiding after Randr Sterki, though he knew the answer before I spoke. When I confirmed it, he nodded, long, slow and thoughtful.

'I am thinking,' he said softly, as if the words were being dragged from him by oxen, 'that I might have to visit Ospak and Finnlaith in Dyfflin, or perhaps go to find Fiskr in Hedeby.'

The idea of not having Finn there made me swallow and he saw my stricken face. His own was a hammer that nailed his next words into me, even though he said them with a lopsided grin.

22

'It is either that or challenge for the jarl's seat.'

Well, there it was, the fracture cracked open and visible. I bowed my head to it; the curse of Odin's silver right enough.

'I will stay for one more season and, if the raiding is good, it may change my mind. If not, I am thinking it best to leave, Orm.'

This would be the third season and, I was thinking, a remarkable feat of patience for the likes of Finn. Yet I was no more certain that this raiding season, which involved a long, uncomfortable voyage up and down the Baltic and sometimes into the mouths of a few rivers, pretending to trade and looking for something to steal, would be any better than the last two. There was seldom anything worthwhile for the Oathsworn, who were choking on all they already had. Yet they trained daily, making shieldwalls and breaking them, fighting in ones and threes, showing off and honing their battle skills. The lure of the prow beast, as the skalds had it, still dragged us all back to the dark water.

Now Finn wanted more jarl-work from me and threatened either to leave or take over. I could only nod, for words were ash in my mouth. After that, the promise of summer sunshine was ominous.

The women bustled the grime and stink out of Hestreng's buildings and took clear joy in drying washing in the open air; Cormac and Helga Hiti tumbled about on sturdy legs, shouting and playing.

Into this, just after the *blot* offerings for the Feast of Vali, a ship slid up the fjord to us. I knew about it two hours before it arrived, which pleased me – I had set two thralls to watch in shifts and suffered Thorgunna's waspishness over it.

'A waste of work,' she declared, while she and Ingrid and two female thralls hurled sleeping pallets out. 'They could be beating the vermin out of these.'

'I would rather know who is coming to me,' I answered, 'than have dust-free sleeping skins.'

'Tell me that when next your backside is chewed by a flea,' she spat back, blowing a wisp of hair which had fought free of her head-cloth down onto her nose. 'And if I am doing this, I am not making butter – you will feel differently when you have to choke on dry bread.'

From this, I knew she was happy that winter was over and that she had life in her – life I would rather see grow than be burned out if Randr Sterki arrived and we did not know of it. I said as much and had her snort back at me but when word came of this ship, I saw her stiffen and turn and start chivvying thralls and Ingrid to fetch the children, gathering them to her like a hen with chicks.

I let her for a while, though I knew it was no threat; the sail was large and plainly marked with Jarl Brand's sign and unless someone had taken *Black Eagle* from him intact – as unlikely as wings on a fish – then it was himself coming up the fjord.

He came up showing off, too, the sail flaked down and the oars bending as his men made *Black Eagle* cream through the sea. Then, at a single command we all heard as we stood watching on the shore, the oars were lifted clear and taken in until only a quarter of their length was left.

Along this sprang a figure, dancing and bouncing from stem to stern; we all cheered, knowing it was probably his prow man Nes-Bjorn, called Klak – Peg – because he was shaped like one, having oar-muscled shoulders, but skinny hips and legs. He could walk the oars with those skinny legs, all the same, swinging from one side to the other on a loose line.

The crew were equally skilled and slid the thirty-oar *drakkar* neatly to the stone slipway, where the *Fjord Elk* was propped up, with scarcely a dunt on its gilded side. Men spilled ashore then, shouting greetings to those who went to meet them. Thorgunna sighed, scattered the children and roared for thralls; there were sixty new mouths to feed and precious little left in the stores.

She stopped scowling, all the same, when she found what Jarl Brand had brought. He came off smiling, as usual, bone-white as he had always been, wearing a gold-embroidered black tunic trimmed with marten, fine wool breeks that flared over kidskin boots and his neck and arms heavy with amber and silver.

At his side trotted a boy as white as Brand was and people stared for he was Cormac's double, only older, at least five; Aoife kept her head meekly down and said nothing. On Jarl Brand's other side was a strange little man dressed in a black serk to his toes, young, moon-faced and glum.

'My son,' Brand declared gruffly, indicating the sombre, white-haired boy. 'I bring him to you to foster.'

That took my breath away and I was still struggling to suck more in when he indicated the moon-face on his other side.

'This is one called Leo,' he said. 'A Greek monk of sorts, from the Great City.'

I shot Jarl Brand a look and he chuckled at it, shaking his head so that his moustaches trembled like melting icicles.

'No, I am not turned to the White Christ,' he replied. 'This Greek is sent by the Emperor to take greetings to our king. I picked him up in Jumne.'

'Like a sack of grain,' agreed the man with a slight smile. 'I have been stacked and shipped ever since.'

It took me a moment to realise he had spoken Greek and that Jarl Brand had been talking Norse, which meant this Leo knew Norse and also that both Jarl Brand and I understood Greek. Jarl Brand chuckled as I brought Thorgunna, introduced her and had her take Leo into the hall.

'Watch him,' Brand said, tight into my ear as the monk reeled away from us, his legs still on the sea. 'He is more than a monkish scribbler, which he does all the time. He is clever and watches constantly and knows more than he reveals.'

I agreed, but was distracted by what was now unloading

from *Black Eagle* – two women, one young and fat with child, the other older, almost as fat and fussing round her like a gull round a chick.

Jarl Brand caught my stare and grunted, the sound of a man too weighted to speak.

'Sigrith,' he said, pulling me away by the elbow. 'Fresh returned from visiting her father, Mieczyslaw, King of the Polans, and near her dropping time – which is why we are here. King Eirik wants his son born in Uppsalla.'

I blinked and gawped, despite myself. This was Sigrith, splendid as a gilded dragon-head, no more than eighteen and a queen, yet young and bright-eyed and heavy with her first bairn; she was just a frightened child of a Slav tribe from the middle of nowhere.

'The fat one is Jasna, who was her nurse when she lived with her people,' Jarl Brand went on, miserably. 'I am charged with bringing them to the king, together with whatever the queen unloads, safe and well.'

'That's a cargo I could do without,' I answered without thinking, then caught his jaundiced eye. We both smiled, though it was grim – then I noticed the girl at the back. I had taken her for a thrall, in her shapeless, colourless dress, kerchief over what I took to be a shaved head, but she walked like she had gold between her legs. Thin and small, with a face too big for her and eyes dark and liquid as the black fjord.

'She is a Mazur,' Jarl Brand said, following my gaze. 'Her name turns out in Slav to be Chernoglazov – Dark Eye – but the queen and her fat cow call her Drozdov, Blackbird.'

'A thrall?' I asked uncertainly and he shook his head.

'I was thinking that, too, when I saw her first,' he replied with a grunt of humour, 'but it is worse than that – she is a hostage, daughter of a chief of one of the tribes that Mieczyslaw the Pol wants to control to the east of him. She is proud as a queen, all the same, and worships some three-headed god. Or four, I am never sure.'

26

I looked at the bird-named woman – well, girl, in truth. A long way from home to keep her from being snatched back, held as surety for her tribe's good behaviour, she had a look half-way between scorn and a deer at the point of running. Truly, a cargo I would not wish to be carrying myself and did not relish it washing up on my beach.

However, it had an unexpected side to it; Thorgunna, presented with the honour of a queen and a jarl's *fostri* in her house, beamed with pleasure at Jarl Brand and me both, as if we had personally arranged for it. Brand saw it and patted my shoulder soothingly, smiling stiffly the while.

'This will change,' he noted, 'when Sigrith shows how a queen expects to be treated.'

His men unloaded food and drink, which was welcomed and we feasted everyone on coal-roasted horse, lamb, fine fish and good bread – though Sigrith turned her nose up at such fare, whether from sickness or disgust, and Thorgunna shot me the first of many meaningful glances across the hall and fell to muttering with her sister.

Since the women were full of bairns, one way and another, they sat and talked weans with the proud Sigrith, leaving Finn and Botolf and me with Jarl Brand and his serious-faced son, Koll.

The boy, ice-white as his da, sat stiffly at what must have been a trial for one so young – sent to the strange world of the Oathsworn's jarl, ripped from his ma's cooing, yet still eager to please. He sat, considered and careful over all he did, so as not to make a mistake and shame his father. At one and the same time it warmed and broke your heart.

There was no point in trying to talk the stiff out of him – for one thing the hall roared and fretted with feasting, so that you had to shout; it is a hard thing to be considerate and consoling when you are bellowing. For another, he was gripped with fear and saw me only as the huge stranger he was to be left with and took no comfort in that.

27

In the end, Thorgunna and Botolf's Ingrid swept him up and into the comfort of their mothering, which brought such relief to his face that, in the end, he managed a laugh or two. For his part, Jarl Brand smiled and drank and ate as if he did not have a care, but he had come here to leave me the boy and, like all fathers, was agonising over it even as he saw the need.

Leo the monk had seen all this, too, which did not surprise me. A scribbler of histories, he had told me earlier, wanting to know tales of the siege at Sarkel and the fight at Antioch from one who had been at both. Aye, he was young and smiling and seal-sleek, that one – but I had dealt with Great City merchants and I knew these Greek–Romans well, oiled beards and flattery both.

'I never understood about fostering,' Leo said, leaning forward to speak quietly to me, while Brand and Finn argued over, of all things, the best way to season new lamb; Brand kept shooting his son sideways glances, making sure he was not too afraid. 'It is not, as it is with us in Constantinople, a polite way of taking hostages.'

He regarded me with his olive-stone eyes and his too-ready smile, while I sought words to explain what a *fostri* was.

'Jarl Brand does me honour,' I told him. 'To be offered the rearing of a child to manhood is no light thing and usually not done outside the *aett*.'

'The . . . *aett*?'

'Clan. Family. House,' I answered in Greek and he nodded, picking at bread with the long fingers of one hand, stained black-brown from ink.

'So he has welcomed you into his house,' Leo declared, chewing with grimaces at the grit he found. 'Not, I surmise, as an equal.'

It was true, of course – accepting the fostering of another's child was also an acceptance that the father was of a higher standing than you were. But this bothered me much less than the fact that Leo, the innocent monk from the Great City and barely out of his teens, had worked this out. Even then, with only a little more than twenty years on him, he had a mind of whirling cogs and toothed wheels, like those I had seen once driving mills and waterwheels in Serkland.

He also ate the horse, spearing greasy slivers of it on a little two-tined eating fork. This surprised me, for Christ followers considered that to be a pagan ritual and would not usually do it. He saw me follow the food to his mouth and knew what I was thinking, smiling and shrugging as he chewed.

'I shall do penance for this later. The one thing you learn swiftly about being a diplomat is not to offend.'

'Or suffer for being a Christ priest in a land of Odin,' interrupted Jarl Brand, subtle as a forge hammer. 'This is Hestreng, home of the Oathsworn, Odin's own favourites. Christ followers find no soil for their seed here, eh, Orm?

'Bone, blood and steel,' he added when I said nothing. The words were from the Odin Oath that bound what was left of my *varjazi*, my band of brothers; it made Leo raise his eyebrows, turning his eyes round and wide as if alarmed.

'I did not think I was in such danger. Am I, then, to be nailed to a tree?'

I thought about that carefully. The shaven-headed priests of the Christ could come and go as they pleased around Hestreng and say what they chose, provided they caused no trouble. Sometimes, though, the people grew tired of being ranted at and chased them away with blows. Down in the south, I had heard, the skin-wearing trolls of the *Going* folk took hold of an irritating one now and then and sacrificed him in the old way, nailed to a tree in honour of Odin. That Leo knew of this also meant he was not fresh from a cloister.

'I heard tales from travellers,' he replied, seeing me study him and looking back at me with his flat, wide-eyed gaze while he lied. 'Of course, those unfortunate monks were Franks and Saxlanders and, though brothers in Christ – give or take an argument or two – lacking somewhat in diplomacy.'

'And weaponry,' I added and we locked eyes for a moment, like rutting elks. At the end, I felt sure there was as much steel hidden about this singular monk as there was running down his spine. I did not like him one bit and trusted him even less.

Now I had been shown the warp and weft of matters there was nothing left but to nod and smile while Cormac, Aoife's son, filled our horns. Jarl Brand frowned at the sight of him, as he always did, since the boy was as colourless as the jarl himself. White to his eyelashes, he was, with eyes of the palest blue, and it was not hard to see which tree the twig had sprouted from. When Cormac filled little Koll's horn with watered ale, their heads almost touching, I heard Brand suck in air sharply.

'The boy is growing,' he muttered. 'I must do something about him . . .'

'He needs a father, that one,' I added meaningfully and he nodded, then smiled fondly at Koll. Aoife went by, filling horns and swaying her hips just a little more, I was thinking, so that Jarl Brand grunted and stirred on his bench.

I sighed; after some nights here, the chances were strong that, this time next year, we would have another bone-haired yelper from Aoife, another ice-white bairn. As if we did not have little eagles enough at the flight's edge . . .

In the morning, buds unfolded in green mists, sunlight sparkled wetly on grass and spring sauntered across the land while the Oathsworn hauled the *Fjord Elk* off the slipway, to rock gently beside *Black Eagle*. Now was the moment when the raiding began and, on the strength of it, Finn would go or stay; that sank my stomach to my boot tops.

It was a good ship, our *Elk* – fifteen benches each side and no Slav tree trunk, but a properly straked, oak-keeled *drakkar* that had survived portage and narrow rivers on at least two trips to Gardariki.

All the same, it was a bairn next to *Black Eagle*, which had thirty oars a side and was as long as fifteen tall men laid end to end. It was tricked out in gilding, painted red and black, with the great black eagle prow and a crew of growlers who knew they had the best and fastest ship afloat. They and the Oathsworn chaffered and jeered at each other, straining muscle and sinew to get the *Elk* into the water, then demanding a race up the fjord to decide which ship and crew was better.

Into the middle of this came the queen, ponderous as an Arab slave ship, with Thordis and Ingrid and Thorgunna round her and Jasna lumbering ahead. As this woman-fleet sailed past me, heading towards Jarl Brand, Thorgunna raised weary eyebrows.

The jarl had his back to Queen Sigrith as she came up and almost leapt out of his nice coloured tunic when she spoke. Then, flustered and annoyed at having been so taken by surprise, he scowled at her, which was a mistake.

Sigrith's voice was shrill and high. Before, it might have been mistaken for girlish, but fear of childbirthing had sucked the sweetness out of it and her Polan accent was thick, so her demands to know when they were sailing from this dreadful place to one which did not smell of fish and sweaty men, had a rancid bite.

If Jarl Brand had an answer, he never gave it; one of my lookout thralls came pounding up, spraying mud and words in equal measure; a *faering* was coming up the fjord.

Such boats were too small to be feared, but the arrival of it was interesting enough to divert everyone, for which Brand was grateful. Yet, when it came heeling in, sail barely reefed and obviously badly handled, I felt an anchor-stone settle in my gut.

There were arrow shafts visible, and willing men splashed out, waist deep, to catch the little craft and help the man in it take in sail, for he was clearly hurt. They towed it in; two men were in it and blood sloshed in the scuppers; one man

31

was dead and the survivor gasping with pain and badly cut about.

'Skulli,' Brand said, grim as old rock, and the anchor-stone sank lower; Skulli was his steward and I looked at the man, head lolling and leaking life as the women lifted him away to be cared for.

Brand stopped them and let Skulli leak while he gasped out the saga of what had happened. It took only moments to tell – Styrbjorn had arrived, with at least five ships and the men for them, clearly bound for a slaughter against his uncle's right-hand man, to make a show of what he was capable of if things did not go his way.

Jarl Brand's hall was burning, his men dead, his thralls fled, his women taken.

The black dog of it crushed everyone for a moment, then shook itself; men bellowed and all was movement. I saw Finn's face and the mad joy on it was clear as blood on snow.

While Thorgunna and Thordis hauled Skulli off and yelled out for Bjaelfi to bring his skill and healing runes, Brand took my arm and led me a little way aside while men rushed to make *Black Eagle* ready. His face was now as bone-coloured as his hair.

'I have to go to King Eirik,' he declared. 'Add my ship to his and what men I can sweep up on the way. Styrbjorn, if he is stupid, will stay to fight us and we will kill him. If not, he will flee and I will chase him and make him pay for what he has done.'

'I can have the *Elk* ready in an hour or two,' I said, then stopped as he shook his head.

'Serve me better,' he answered. 'Call up your Oathsworn to this place. Look after the queen. I can hardly take her with me.'

That stopped my mouth, sure as a hand over it. He returned my look with a cliff of a face and eyes that said there would be no arguing; yet he cracked the stone of him an instant later, when he shot a sideways glance to where Koll watched, round-eyed, as men bustled. I did not need him to say more.

'The queen and son both, then,' I replied, feeling the sick dread of what would happen if Styrbjorn sent ships here, for it would take time to send out word to the world that Hestreng needed the old Oathsworn back. Jarl Brand saw it, too, and nodded briefly.

'I will leave thirty of my crew – I wish it were more.'

It was generous, for the ones he had left would break themselves to run *Black Eagle* home, with no relief. It was also a marker of what he feared and I forced a smile.

'Who will attack the Oathsworn?' I countered, but there was no mirth in the twist of a grin he gave, turning away to bawl orders to his men.

There was a great milling of movement and words; I sent Botolf stumping off to bring the thirty of Jarl Brand's crew. They stood forlorn and grim on the shore as their oarmates sailed away – but there was none more cliff-faced and black-scowling than Finn, watching others sail away to the war he wanted. Then I gathered up Botolf's daughter, little red-haired Helga, and made her laugh, as much to make me feel better as her. Ingrid smiled.

Jasna waddled up to me, the queen moving ponderously behind her, made bulkier still by furs against the chill.

'Her Highness wishes to know what *blot* you will make for the jarl's journey,' she demanded and her tone made me angry, since she was a thrall when all was said and done. I tossed Helga in the air and made her scream.

'Laughter,' I answered brusquely. 'The gods need it sometimes.'

Jasna blinked at that, then went back to the queen, walking like a loaded pack pony; there were whispers back and forth. Out of the corner of my eye I saw Thorgunna scowling at me and in answer I carried on playing with the child.

'This is not seemly,' said an all-too familiar voice, jerking me from Helga's gurgles. The queen stood in front of me, mittened hands folded over her swollen belly, frowning.

'Seemly?'

She waved a small hand, like a little furred paw in the mitten. Her face was sharp as a cat's and would have been pretty save for the lines at the edges of her mouth.

'You are *godi* here. This is not . . . It has no . . . *dignitas*.'

'You sound like a Christ follower,' I answered shortly, putting Helga down; she trundled off towards her mother, who gathered her up. I saw Thorgunna closing on us, fast as a racing *drakkar*.

'Christ follower!'

It was an explosion of shriek and I turned my head from it, as you would from an icy blast. Then I shrugged, for this queen, her young and beautiful face twisted with outrage, annoyed me more and more. I was annoyed, too, to have forgotten that the Christ godlet had been foisted on her father and his people; like the rest of them, she resented this.

'They also confuse misery and prayer,' I managed to answer and heard a chuckle I recognised as Leo. Thorgunna bustled up, managing to elbow me in the ribs.

'Highness,' she said to Sigrith, with a sweet smile. 'I have everything prepared – what do men know of sacrifice?'

Mollified, the queen allowed herself to be led away, followed by Jasna, who threw me a venomous glare. The ever-present, ever-silent Mazur girl followed after, but paused to shoot me a quick glance from those dark eyes; afterwards, I realised what had made me remember it. It was the first time she had looked directly at anyone at all.

At the time, I heard a little laugh which distracted me from thoughts of the girl and turned my head to where Leo watched, swathed in a cloak, hands shoved deep inside its folds.

'I thought traders of your standing had more diplomacy,' he offered and I said nothing, knowing he had the right of it and that my behaviour had been, at best, childish.

'But she galls, does she not?' he added, as if reading my mind.

'Even less soil there than here for your Christ seed,' I countered. 'Even if you get to the court. Your visit to Uppsalla is proving a failure.'

He smiled the moon-faced smile of a man who did not think anything he did was a failure, then inclined his head and moved off, leaving me with the last view of *Black Eagle*, raising sail and speeding off into the grey distance.

I felt rain spot my neck and shivered, looked up to a pewter sky and offered a prayer to bluff Thor and Aegir of the waves and Niord, god of the coasts, for a good blow and some tossing white-caps. A storm sea would keep us safe . . .

I rose in the night and left my sleeping area, mumbling to a dreamy Thorgunna about the need for a privy, which was a lie. I stepped through the hall of grunting and snores and soft stirrings in the dark, past the pitfire's grey ash, where little red eyes watched me step out of the hall.

The sharp air made me wish I had brought a cloak, made me wonder at this foolishness. There was rain in that air, yet no storm and the fear of that lack filled me. Dreams I knew – Odin's arse, I had been hag-ridden by dreams all my life – but this was strange, a formless half-life, a *draugr* of a feeling that ruined sleep and nipped my waking heels.

Never before or since have I felt the power of the prow beast on a raiding ship as it locks jaws with the spirit of the land – but I felt them both that night, muscled and snarling shadows in the dark. Even then, I knew Randr Sterki was coming.

Yet the world remained the same, etched in black and silver, misted in shreds even in the black night. A dog fox barked far out on the pasture; the great dark of Ginnungagap still held the embers of Muspelheim, flung there by Odin's brothers, Vili and Ve. Between scudding clouds, I found Aurvandill's

Toe and the Eyes of Thjazi after a search, but easily found the Wagon Star, which guides prow beasts everywhere. The one on Randr's ship would be following it like a spooring wolf.

There was a closer light from the little building that housed Ref's forge, a soft glow and I moved to it, drawn by the hope of heat. A few steps from it, the voices halted me – I have no idea why, since they were ones I knew; Ref was there and Botolf with him and the thrall boy, Toki.

Ref was nailing, which was a simple thing but a steading needed lots of them and he clearly took comfort in the easy repetitive task; he took slim lengths of worked bog-iron, flared one end and pointed the other, two taps for one, four for the other, then a plunge into the quench and a drop into a box. Even for that simple task, he kept the light in the forge dim, so that he could read the colour of the fire and the heated iron.

Toki, a doll-like silhouette with his back to me, worked the bellows and hugged his reedy arms between times, chilled despite the flames in his one-piece *kjartan* and bare feet, his near-bald head shining in the red light.

The place had the burned-hair smell of charred hooves, braided with the tang of sea-salt, charcoal and horse piss. In the dim light of the forge-fire and a small horn lantern above Botolf's head, Ref looked like a dwarf and Botolf a giant, the one forging some magical thing, the other red-dyed with light and speaking in a low rumble, like boulders grinding.

'That dog fox is out again,' he was saying. 'He's after the chickens.'

'That's why we coop them,' Ref replied, concentrating. Tap, tap. Pause. Tap, tap, tap, tap. Plunge and hiss. He picked up another length.

'He won't come near. He is afraid of the hounds,' Botolf replied, shifting his weight. He nudged Toki, who pumped the bellows a few times.

36

'Why is he afraid?' the boy asked. 'He can run.'

'Because the hounds run slower but longer and will kill him,' answered Ref. 'So would you be afraid.'

The boy shivered. 'I am afraid even in my dreams,' he answered and Botolf looked at him.

'Dreams, little Toki? What dreams? My Helga has dreams, too, which make her afraid. What do you dream?'

The boy shrugged. 'Falling from a high place, like Aoife says my da did.'

Botolf nodded soberly, remembering that Toki had been fathered by a thrall called Geitleggr, whose hairy goat legs had given him the only name he had known – but none of the animal's skill when it came to gathering eggs on narrow ledges. His mother, too, had died, of too much work, too little food and winter and now Aoife looked out for Toki, as much as anyone did.

'I like high places,' Botolf said, seeking to reassure the boy. 'They are in nearly all my dreams.'

Ref absently pinched out a flaring ember on his already scorch-marked old tunic and I doubted if his horn-skinned fingers felt it. He never took his eyes from the iron, watching the colour of the flames for the right moment, even on just a nail.

Tap, tap, tap, tap – plunge, hiss.

'What are they, then, these dreams of yours, Botolf?' Ref wanted to know, sliding another length of bog-iron into the coals and jerking his chin at Toki to start pumping.

Botolf tapped his timber foot on the side of the oak stump which held the spiked anvil.

'Since I got this, wings,' he answered. 'I dream I have wings. Big black ones, like a raven.'

'What does it feel like?' Toki asked, peering curiously. 'Is it like a real leg?'

'Mostly,' answered Botolf, 'except when it itches, for you cannot scratch it.'

'Does it itch, then?' Ref asked, pausing in wonder. 'Like a real leg?'

Botolf nodded.

'Did some magic woodworker make it so that it itched?' Toki wanted to know and Botolf chuckled.

'If he did, I wish he would come back and unmake it – or at least let me scratch. I dream of that when I am not dreaming of wings.'

'Does no-one dream of proper things any more?' Ref grumbled, turning the bog-iron length in the coals. 'Wealth and fame and women?'

'I have all three,' Botolf answered. 'I have no need of that dream.'

'I dream of food most often,' Toki admitted and the other two laughed; boys seldom had enough to eat and thralls never did.

'Sing a song,' Ref said, 'soft now, so as not to wake everyone. Pick a good one and it will go into the iron and make the nails stronger.'

So Toki sang, a child song, a soft song of the sea and being lost on it. The wave of it left me stranded at the edge of darkness, icy and empty and wondering why he had chosen that of all songs and if the hand of Odin was in it.

I had heard that song before, in another place. We had come ashore in the night, blacker than the night itself with hate and fear, unseen, unheard until we raved down on Klerkon's steading on Svartey at dawn – a steading like this, I remembered, sick and cold. Only one fighting man had been there and he had been easily killed by Kvasir and Finn.

Things had been done, as they always were in such events, made more savage because it was Klerkon we hunted and he had stolen Thorgunna's sister, Thordis. He was not there, but all his folk's women and bairns were and, prowling for him, I had heard the singing, sweet in the dawn's dim, a song to keep out the fear.

38

I heard it stop, too. I had come upon the great tangle-haired growler who had cut it out of the girl's throat with a single slash, his blade clotted with sticky darkness and strands of hair. He had turned to me, all beard and mad grin and I had known him at once – Red Njal, limping Red Njal, who now played with Botolf's Helga and carved dolls for her.

Beyond, all twisted limbs and bewildered faces, were the singer's three little siblings: blood smoked in the hearthfire coals and puddled the stones. The thrall-nurse was there, too, forearm hacked through where she had flung up her arms in a last desperate, useless attempt to ward off an axe edge. Red Njal was on his knees in the blood, rifling for plunder.

There were shouts then, and I followed them; outside lay a plough ox still dying, great head flapping and blood bubbling from its muzzle, the eyes wide and rolling. Across the heaving, weakly thrashing body of it, as if on some box-bed, three men stripped a woman to pale breasts and belly, down to the hair between her legs, while she gasped, strength almost gone but fighting still.

Her blonde braids flailed as her head thrashed back and forth and two of the men tried to hold her, while the third fought down his breeches and struggled to get between her legs. She spat crimson at him and he howled back at her and smacked her in the mouth, so that her head bounced off the twitching flank of the ox, which tried to bawl and only hissed out more blood.

They panted and struggled, like men trying to fit a new wheel on a heavy cart, calling advice, insults, curses when the ox shat itself, working steadily towards the inevitable . . . then the one between her legs, the one I knew well, lost his patience, unable to hold her and rid himself of the knee she kept wedging in his way.

He hauled a seax from his boot and slit her throat, so that she gug-gug-gugged on her own blood and started to flop like a fish. The knee dropped; the man stuck the seax in the ox and his prick in the woman and started pumping while the others laughed.

The boy came from nowhere, from the dark where he had seen it all, from where he had watched his mother, Randr Sterki's wife, die. He came like a hare and snatched up the seax, while the man pumped and pumped, gone frantic and unseeing and the woman gurgled and died beneath him.

My blade took the back of the boy's skull clean off, an instant before he brought the seax down. I watched the back of his head fly in the air, the hair on it like spider legs, the gleet and brain and blood arcing out to splash the dying woman's last lover, who jerked himself away and out of her, gawping, his prick hanging like a dead chicken's neck.

'Odin's arse . . . well struck, Orm. That little hole would have had me, liver and lights, for sure.'

Grinning, Finn hauled his breeks up and grabbed his seax from the boy's gripping hand, so that, for a moment, it looked as if the lad was raising himself up. But he was dead, slumped across his mother and Finn spat on him before stumping off into the dark . . .

'Why are you standing out there?'

The voice raked me back to the night and the forge. All the heads had turned towards me and Botolf chuckled. Toki, half-turned, was bloodied by the forgelight and, for a moment, I saw the face of the boy I had killed. Toki was the same age. Too young to die. Yet Randr's boy would have killed Finn – had once laughed as he helped his mother scrape Crowbone's head raw, then chain him to the privy as punishment for running away. What the Norns weave is always intricate, but it can be as dark and ugly as it is beautiful.

'Listeners at the eaves hear no good of themselves,' Botolf intoned. Toki dropped from his perch, breaking the spell.

'Sleep comes hard,' Ref grunted, 'too many farters and snorers in the hall.'

40

We all knew that was not the reason I was here, but I went along with the conspiracy, grunting agreement.

Ref, seeing the flames change colour, lifted his head. 'Back to the bellows, boy,' he called, but Toki kept staring – he pointed behind me, away into the dark land where I had set watchers and fire.

'What is that light?' he asked.

I did not need to turn, felt the sick, frantic heat of that warning beacon though it was miles away. When I spoke I stared straight at Botolf, so he would know, would remember what he had been told of Klerkon's steading on Svartey.

'That light is men who kill bairns and fuck their mother on a dead ox,' I said, harsh as a crow laugh.

'Men like us.'

Men like us, following their prow beast up the fjord in a ship called *Dragon Wings*, grim with revenge, hugging a secret to them with savage glee, for they did not want a fair fight, only slaughter.

You can only wear what the Norns weave, so we sent everyone else off into the mountains and worked the *Elk* out to meet Randr Sterki. Men struggled and died screaming battle cries and bloodlust there on the raven-black, slow-shifting fjord; the prow beasts bobbed and snarled at each other as men struggled and died in the last light of a hard day – and both sides found the secret of the Roman Fire that burns even water.

THREE

HESTRENG, after the battle

The vault of his head was charred to black ruin and stank, a jarring on the nose and throat but one which had helped bring me back to coughing life. My throat burned, my chest felt tight and my ears roared with the gurgle of water. It was night, with a fitful, shrouded moon.

I blinked; his hands were gone, melted like old tallow down to the bone and his scalp had slipped like some rakish, rat-fur cap, the one remaining eye a blistered orb that bulged beneath the fused eyelids, the face a melted-tallow mass of sloughed brow and crackled-black.

'Nes-Bjorn,' said a voice and I turned to it. Finn tilted his chin at the mess; the claw of one hand still reached up as if looking for help.

'Three ladies, over the fields they crossed,' he intoned. 'One brought fire, two brought frost. Out with the fire, in with the frost. Out, fire! In, frost!'

It was an old charm, used on children who had scorched or scalded themselves, but a little late for use on the ruin that had been Nes-Bjorn.

'Came out of the sea like one of Aegir's own *draugr*,'

42

Finn added. 'Fire had seared his voice away and most of the breath in him. The gods alone know what kept him walking. I near shat myself. Then I gave him The Godi, for mercy.'

He raised the named sword in question and now I saw the raw-meat gape round the throat of the thing that had been Nes-Bjorn, while the wind hissed sand through the shroud of stiff grass, bringing the scent of salt and charred wood with it. Something shifted darkly and slid into a familiar shape that grinned at me and dragged me to sit upright with a powerful hand.

'You swallowed half the fjord,' rumbled Botolf cheerfully. 'But you have bokked most of it up now, so you should be better.'

'Better than the others,' Finn added grimly, crouched and watchful and Botolf sighed and studied the thing next to him, while the sand pattered on it and stuck. It looked like driftwood.

'Aye – poor Nes-Bjorn Klak will never run the oars again after this.'

I came back to the Now of it, realised we were somewhere in the dunes to the east of Hestreng. The charred wood smell came again, stronger on the changing wind and Finn saw my nose twitch.

'Aye,' he said, grim as weathered rock, 'the *Elk* is burned and gone and good men with her. All of them, it seems to me, save us.'

'I saw Hauk fall,' I croaked and Botolf agreed that he had also seen Hauk die.

'Gizur, too,' Finn added mournfully. 'He held on to the steerboard and told me he had made this ship and he would die with it. He did, for I saw at least two spears in him as I went over the side.'

'Red Njal? Hlenni Brimill?'

Finn shrugged and shook his head. Botolf said, brightly: 'Onund lives. I saw men drag him off up the beach.'

Finn grunted. 'He will not be long delayed to a meeting

43

with Hel herself then, for they will kill him for sure. That Roman Fire . . . it even spread to *Dragon Wings* and they had to beach it to throw sand on it. They tried water and that only made it worse.'

I struggled to sit up and to think, while the deaths of the Oathsworn were like turning stones, milling the sense and breath from me. Gizur and Hauk . . . ten years I had known them. And Hlenni Brimill and Red Njal, who had struggled through the Serkland deserts and the frozen steppe. All of them had sought out Atil's treasure and thought they had won fair fame and fortune . . . truly, that hoard was cursed.

'Roman Fire,' I said hoarsely and Finn spat.

'Fucking Greeks-Who-Call-Themselves-Romans,' he said bitterly. 'Who else would make a fire that burns even water?'

'Bearcoats,' I added and turned to where his eyes gleamed in the dark. My throat burned with sea water, making my voice raw.

'When did Randr Sterki get them?' I asked. 'Bearcoats don't roll up to the likes of him and announce they are his men until death – and not twelve of them. And you cannot buy pots of Roman Fire in some market, like honey, neither.'

'What are you saying, Orm?' Botolf demanded. 'My head hurts and my friends are gone, so I am no good with riddles tonight.'

'What he means is that there is more to this,' Finn growled savagely. 'More than Randr Sterki and his revenge.'

Botolf stirred, then shook his head.

'Perhaps. I am thinking only that we have become what once we raided.'

No-one spoke, but the memories slithered to us, slime-cold and unwelcome and Botolf, who had not been there but had heard some of it, let his massive shoulders slump. He looked at me, eyes white in the darkness.

'I wish you had not spoken of the woman and the dead ox. Things were clearer to me out on the whale road, when

44

we followed the prow beast and everything we owned was in a sea-chest.'

Finn's head came up at the reference to the woman and the dead ox and he looked from me to Botolf and back. Then he grunted and hunched himself against the cold memories.

'Well, we have fame, land, women and bairns,' he spat angrily. 'Odin's gifts. Should we spurn them, then, because of what we are?'

Botolf shrugged. 'What we were,' he corrected sullenly. 'Now we are the ones raided and our women are likely to be humped on a dead ox.'

'Be dumb on that,' Finn savaged. 'What do you know? Look at you. You do not even possess the thought-cage of a mouse. Where would you be without Hestreng? Without Ingrid and little Helga Hiti, eh? That is your wyrd, for sure, and running back to the whale road after the prow beast will not change what we are now, nor what we once did. Aye – and may do again, for I know myself to be a vik-Norse, until they burn me up as a good Odinsmann.'

I was astounded; Finn, above all others, had been the one muttering and raging against the shackles of land, women and bairns. Botolf sulked at Finn's rage, not knowing that it was because Finn was the humper in the story of the woman and the dead ox. Finn, for all his bluster, was aware that it was that, in part, which had brought Randr Sterki down on us – aware, also, of the threat to little Hroald, the son he did not know what to do with.

'You should not say such things to me,' Botolf muttered. 'About not having the thought-cage of a mouse.'

'Just so,' agreed Finn poisonously. 'I take it back. You do have the thought-cage of a mouse.'

'Enough,' I managed to say at last and then coughed and spat; pain lurked, dull and hot in my chest. 'I am thinking we will not have thought-cages at all, if we do not act. I am thinking Randr Sterki will not be content with claiming a

45

victory over the Oathsworn and stealing some chickens and pigs. Not a man who brings bearcoats and Roman Fire with him.'

'Aye, right enough,' agreed Botolf, mollified by what he saw as Finn giving in.

'What do we do, then, Orm?' Finn asked. 'It will be a sore fight whatever you decide.'

I shot him a look, for he did not even try to hide the cheerful in his voice. I did not like what we had to do. We had to find out what was happening and to do that someone had to get close. Since there was no flaring fire, the great longhouse was not burned and that was because Randr and his men were using it – so someone had to sneak into the hall and find out what all this was truly about.

They looked at me in the dark, one whose idea of stealth was not to roar when he charged, the other who was half a bench; it was not hard to work out who had to be the fox.

Finn handed me his seax, as if to seal the bargain.

No starlight. A limping moon that stumbled from cloud to cloud, driven by the same wind that whipped the tops off waves and drifted sand through the grass. We moved, soft as roe deer towards the shadowed bulk of Hestreng hall and the lights scattered about.

For all his size and lack of leg, Botolf could move quietly enough and the sand muffled the thump of his timber foot, while Finn crept, shoulder-blades as hunched as a cat's. We stopped, licking dry lips and sweating like fighting stallions.

The harsh stink of burned wood hit me and I saw the looming shadow, lolling like a dead whale, slapped with soothing waves – *Dragon Wings*, beached and blackened along half its length. Botolf made a bitter laugh grunt in the back of his throat at the sight and we moved into the lee of it, where the wet char stink was worst and the shadows darkest.

Beyond, rocking at its tether near the slipway, was the second ship. I did not recognise it.

I sat down to pull off my sodden boots and handed them to Finn – then we froze at a sharp, high sound. I knew that sound well, that mating fox shriek of frantic fear; someone was being hard-used by pain.

I looked at Finn, then Botolf, then slid towards Hestreng hall, feeling the wet wool of my breeks chafe and tug, the sand sliding under my feet, sharp with shell and shingle. My ankle burned, as if it had one of Ref's hot nails through it; an old injury, like the stumps of my missing fingers, which itched maddeningly; I knew what Botolf meant about his leg.

I found what I sought and made sure no-one was in it – then I climbed on to the lean-to roof of the privy and up on to the hog-back hall roof. My soles were stabbed by wooden slates I was willing not to crack or creak as I crabbed across it to where the crossed gables with their dragon-head ends snarled blindly up into the night.

There I paused, shivering as the wind keened through my wet tunic, yet sweating. Then I grabbed one of the dragon-heads and swung over into the dark, square pit of the smokehole, just wide enough to take me in onto a beam. Voices growled up through the blue reek that told me the pitfire was still lit.

It was a strangeness, this having a smokehole at either end rather than in the middle and had been done by the previous master of the Hestreng longhouse, a Dane, before he had backed the wrong side. The twin holes had merits – sucking reek the length of the hall and high into the rafters, killing vermin and smoking hanging meats, for one – but none better than letting me slide unseen into the shadows along the roof-trees.

I slithered in, surprised at what it took to squeeze silently through; I had not realised the breadth of shoulder on me and was still a skinny boy in my head. Just as well, or I would have been too afraid to even try this.

The voices were louder, the blue reek stung my eyes; someone had opened the further door, driving the pitfire smoke up, spilling it out of the hole at this end. I touched the hilt of the seax sheathed in my lap and fought to keep my breathing shallow, while my heart pounded and my throat and eyes stung; it had been a time since I had done anything this foolish or daring.

Up in the ash-tainted dark, I perched like a raven on a branch and looked down into the fire-lit dimness, edging forward slightly, one hand on the cross-beams over my head for balance. Below me hung whalemeat and cheeses and fish, smoke-blacked and trembling on their lines; I stepped more softly still – then froze, smelling the mouth-wetting scent of roasting meat wafting in from the outside breeze.

Nithings. Odin curse them to the Nine Hells. They were spit-roasting my brace of oxen in my own cookhouse and, at last, I was bitten by the sense of loss of what was mine. I had some fifteen male thralls somewhere, most of them scattered into the night, shivering and weeping – those oxen cost more than twelve of them to buy and more than all fifteen to keep.

That was because they turned more land than harnessing fifteen thralls to a plough – and now they were greasing the chins of hard raiding men. I tried not to think of it, or of the times I had done it to others, or the dying ox in a yard on Svartey. Instead, I squinted down into the fetid dim of the hall.

I saw a huddle of men and had a heart-leap at the sight of them; two were Red Njal and Hlenni, not dead, but sitting with their arms clasped under their raised knees, wrists bound. Another was Onund, naked and strung up by the thumbs, gleaming with sweat and streaked with darker, thicker fluids. A fourth lay smiling two smiles and seeping blood through cloth wrappings; Brand's luckless steward, Skulli, whose throat had been cut in his sickbed.

There was litter scattered, what was left after men had

48

plundered the place, and I felt a cutting pang at the sight of eider feathers sprayed like snow; Thorgunna's favourite pillows, which she would mourn.

There was a man I did not know sitting on a bench with an axe and a sword nearby. He chewed bread, which he tore idly from a chunk, and he was smeared with black – wet char-wood, I was thinking, from where he had fought a fire earlier. There was the red line of a helmet rim on his forehead and brown marks on his nose from the noseguard iron-rot.

There were two more. One was a Svear by his accent, with a striking black beard, streaked with white so that he seemed to have a badger on his face. His hair was also black and iron-grey, with a single thick brow-braid on the right side, banded in silver. He was naked from the waist and his right arm, from wrist to shoulder all round, was blue-black with skin-mark shapes and figures – a tree, I saw, and gripping beasts among others.

I knew him from the old days and he had been less salted then. Even if I had not, the skin-marks revealed him as Randr Sterki, for it was well-known that he had adopted this shield-biter perversion, which was said to be magic, for strength or protection or both. If I had been in doubt of who it was, there was the leather thong round his neck and, swinging on the end of it across the matted hair of his sweat-gleaming chest, was Sigurd's silver nose.

He strode to the pitfire and shoved a cooled length of iron back in it, then turned to the second man, who watched him with his hands on his hips and a sneer on a clean-chinned face with a neat snake moustache. His yellow hair was caught up in a thong and a braided one round his brow kept any stray wisps off his face. With his blue tunic and green breeks and silver armrings, it was clear he liked himself, this one, while the inlaid hilt of the sword at his waist told me he was probably master of the second ship. I did not know him at all, but he spoke with a Dane lilt.

49

'This will not serve,' he told Randr Sterki. 'We are wasting time here.'

'My time to waste,' Randr Sterki answered, sullen as rain-cloud, working the length of iron deeper into the coals of the pitfire.

'No,' said the other impatiently. 'It is not. It belongs to Styrbjorn, who has charged us both with a task.'

'You did not get your men killed and your ship all but burned to the waterline, Ljot Tokeson,' Randr Sterki bellowed, whirling on the man. 'I beat the Oathsworn in battle, not you . . . and somewhere around here is Orm Bear Slayer's silver to be dug up, his women to be taken and himself . . .'

He paused and snatched up the sword from the table; the bread-eater shied away as the careless edge whicked past his ear.

'I have his sword,' Randr hissed. 'I want the hand that wielded it.'

I did not know this Ljot Tokeson, but he was clearly one of Styrbjorn's men and one with steel in him, for few men gave Randr Sterki a hard time of it, especially when Randr had a blade in his hand – my blade, I realised, rescued from the *Elk*.

Ljot slapped his hand on the bench, with a sound like a wet drum.

'Not all your men fought and died, Randr Sterki,' he harshed out. 'Three bearcoats died. Three. My brother had those twelve with him for four fighting seasons without loss and you have lost three in a day.'

The wind seemed to suck out of Randr then and he slumped down on a bench and took up a pitcher, scorning a cup to drink; ale spilled down his chest and he wiped his beard with one slow hand.

'They fought hard, the Oathsworn,' he admitted. 'That Roman Fire did not help.'

'Then you should not have lost your head and thrown it,' Ljot growled. 'You lost more of your own men to it than the

Oathsworn did. It was given as an expensive gift, to make sure you succeeded in what Styrbjorn sent you to do.'

Randr licked his lips, his eyes filled with screaming men and burning sea.

'I did not know what it would do . . .'

'Now you do,' interrupted Ljot, sneering. 'And if you do not want the same fate for yourself, it would be better if we did what we came to do. For my brother will tie you to a pole and hurl Roman Fire at you until you melt like ice in sunshine if we fail.'

There was a long and terrible pause, broken only by the sound of Onund breathing in bubbling snores through what was clearly a broken nose. I wondered who this Ljot was and who the brother – it was not Styrbjorn, that much I did know. Then Randr stood up.

'I will send scouts out. We will find what we seek.'

The tension flowed out of the taut line that was Ljot and he forced a smile.

'There will be time enough for all this,' he said softly, waving a hand that took in the bound prisoners and the hung Onund. 'The important thing is . . .'

'Fuck yourself, Ljot Tokeson,' Randr spat back. 'When you have lost all you hold dear, come and speak to me of the important thing.'

He slammed out of the door in a blast of rainwind that swirled the blue reek of the hall, stinging my eyes. In the blur I saw the back of the boy's head shattering in a spray of blood and bone while his mother drowned in her own blood on the arse of a dying ox. All he held dear . . .

The man at the table looked up sourly from where he was idly rolling bread into little pills.

'His thought-cage is twisted, that one,' he growled at Ljot. 'Still – has Randr Sterki the right of it? About this buried silver?'

'They say the Oathsworn robbed a tomb of all the silver

in the world,' Ljot growled back scornfully, 'which is clearly a lie, since I myself wear silver armrings.'

'All the same,' the other said and Ljot shook his head wearily.

'Just watch them, Bjarki,' he spat. 'Fall asleep and I will gut you.'

I saw what Ljot did not as he turned to leave – the narrow-eyed hate at his back. Even before the hall door clattered shut, this guard Bjarki was on his feet and moving to the pitfire and the iron in it.

'No good will come of this,' growled Red Njal from where he sat, seeing which way the wind blew. 'Shameful deeds bring revenge, as my granny used to say.'

Bjarki ignored him and hefted the iron, wincing when it burned his fingers; he searched round for something to wrap round it, deciding on the good fur off my high seat.

'Your chance to speak will come,' Bjarki said to Red Njal, moving like a wolf towards Onund. 'Now,' he added, with a gentle sigh, 'let us hear you speak with a silver tongue, hump-back. No more screams, just a place name will do. Between us, as it were.'

He had his back to me when I gripped the beam and swung down on it, my legs slamming into his shoulder-blades. He shot forward into the upright beam to Onund's left, the crack of his forehead hitting it like the sound of a falling tree. Worse, for his part, was that he was brandishing the hot iron at the time and it was rammed between his face and the pillar.

He scarcely made a sound all the same, for the blow had laid him out and he crumpled, a great red burn welt from left eyebrow to right jawbone, across his nose and one eye, which spat angry gleet. Blood trickled from a great cut on his head and the hot iron hissed and sizzled on his chest; his tunic smoked and flames licked.

I got off my backside and kicked the iron off him into the fire, then had to rescue the wrapped fur. A good fur that, white wolf and not cheap – I said as much as I took up my sword and turned to cut Red Njal and Hlenni Brimill loose.

'Remind me never to borrow a fur from you without asking,' Hlenni said, rubbing his wrists and standing up stiffly. He kicked Bjarki so that his head rattled back and forth.

'Little Bear,' he sneered, which was what *bjarki* meant and was a name you gave a child, not a grown man. 'A pity only that he was laid out before he felt the heat of that iron.'

'Just so,' panted Red Njal, struggling with Onund's bonds. 'Help me here instead of gloating or we will all feel the lick of that heat – pray to the gods if you must, but carry a keen blade, as my granny used to say.'

I gave Red Njal the seax and hefted the familiar weight of my sword as I opened the door cautiously, expecting at least one guard outside. There was nothing – then a bulk moved, darker than the shadows; fear griped my belly and I had to fight not to run. I smelled him then, all sweat and leather and foul breath and I knew that stink well.

Finn.

'You took so long I came to find you,' he rasped hoarsely, gleaming teeth and eyes in the dark. 'I saw folk leaving and thought to chance matters. What did you find?'

I said nothing, but heard him grunt when he saw Hlenni and Red Njal, Onund half-carried, half-dragged between them.

'This way,' he said, as if leading them to clean beds in a dry room and we shadowed into the night, from dark to dark like owls on a hunt, every muscle screaming at the expected bite of steel, every nerve waiting for the shout of discovery.

Somewhere out on the pasture, where the hall was a dim-lit bulk in the distant dark, we stopped, while I put my boots back on. We headed towards the north valley, prowling and fox-silent.

All the time, circling like wolves in my head, was what had passed between Randr Sterki and Ljot – and, when those wolves put their muzzles on weary paws, the old dead rose in their place, leering and mocking me.

FOUR

It rained, a fine mirr that blotted out the stars, so that we fumbled along, panting like dogs and stumbling. I led the way, hoping more than knowing, into the wet dark where trolls leered and *alfar* flickered at the edge of vision.

A darker shape against the black; I froze. Finn stumbled into the back of me, almost knocking me over and rain dripped off our noses as we stuck them close to each other to hiss in whispers.

'What is it?' he hoarsed out and, even as he asked, I knew. 'The stone. Our stone . . .'

Slick and rain-gleamed, the great stone, half-carved with Klepp's handiwork, half-painted by Vuokko the Sea-Finn, was as large as our relief and we hugged it close, delighting in the wet-rock smell of it, for it meant we were at the entrance to the valley.

Nearby was a hut, once the home of the horse-herder thralls, now Klepp's *hov* until it grew too cold to work stone. Dark as a cave, of course, because he would be gone, with Vuokko and Thorgunna and Thordis and all the others, heading further up the valley to the foothills of the mountains.

'Ruts,' said Finn suddenly, catching my sleeve and guiding my hand to the wet ground. The scar and the smell of new-turned soil gave truth to it; ruts, where a cart had passed, maybe more than one.

'At least they are safe,' I muttered and we moved after the struggling figures carrying Onund into the shelter of the dark hut.

It was a rough affair, for use in the summer only and made of low split-log walls and roof-turfs and daub. Inside was the smell of leather and iron and oil, the cold-tomb smell of stone dust and the harsh throat-lick of paints.

'How is Onund?' I asked of the shadows grunting him down, panting with the effort.

'Heavy,' growled Hlenni Brimill sourly.

'Babbling,' added Red Njal and I moved closer to the wheezing bulk of Onund, wishing I had light to see how badly he was hurt.

'Bairn,' he bubbled through his broken nose. 'Bairn.'

'He's been saying that since we cut him down,' muttered Red Njal, wiping his own streaming face. Botolf stumbled over something and cursed.

'Hist, man!' Finn spat hoarsely. 'Why don't you bang on a shield, mouse-brain?'

'I was looking for a horn lantern,' came the sullen reply. 'Some light would be good.'

'Aye – set fire to the hut, why not?' Finn cursed. 'Why have our trackers fumbling in the cold and wet and dark when we can lead them right to us?'

Botolf rubbed his shin sullenly. 'Why is it always the real leg that gets hit?' he demanded. 'Why not the gods-cursed wooden one . . .?'

I wanted quiet and hissed it out, for there were sounds outside I did not like; movement, someone blowing snot and rain off their nose, the suck of hooves lifting from muddy ground.

Finn's eyes gleamed and he slid away from me, out into the night; we crouched in the hut, waiting and listening.

Three, I worked out. Maybe four. And a horse, though not ridden.

'A hut,' said a voice. 'At least we can get dry.'

'Perhaps a fire . . . butcher the horse and have a decent meal, at least,' said another.

'Oh aye – tell them all where we are, eh, Bergr?' rumbled a third. 'Before you go in that hut, Hamund, I would scout round and make sure we are alone.'

'Of course we are alone,' spat the one called Hamund. 'By the Hammer, Bruse, you are an old woman. And if we are not to eat this spavined nag, why did we bring it, eh?'

'We will eat it in good time,' Bruse answered. They were all hunkered down in the lee of the hut, no more than an arm's length and the width of a split-log wall between us.

'I will be pleased when Randr Sterki is done with this,' muttered Bergr. 'All I want is my share, enough for a farm somewhere. With cows. I like the taste of fresh milk.'

'Farm,' snorted Hamund. 'Why buy work? A good over-winter in a warm hall with a fat-arsed thrall girl and a new raid next year, that will do for me.'

'I thought you were scouting?' Bruse grunted and Hamund hawked in his throat.

'For what? They are far from here. Everyone is far from here. Only the rain is here – and us. Who are these runaways anyway? A hump-back more dead than alive, I heard, and a couple of survivors from a battle we won, no more. Hiding and running, if they have any sense. The rest of them will be half-way over the mountains and gone by now. We should take what loot we can and leave.'

'Go and scout – one of them is Finn Horsehead,' Bruse answered, straightening with a grunt. There was a pause, then the sound of splashing and a satisfied sigh as he pissed against the log wall.

'Finn Horsehead?' muttered Bergr. 'Of the Oathsworn? They say he fears nothing at all.'

'I can change that,' sneered Hamund.

'Pray to Odin you never meet him,' Bruse said, adjusting his stance and spurting in little grunts, his voice rising and fading – talking over his shoulder, I was thinking. 'I raided with him, so I know. I saw him rise up and walk – walk, mark you – towards a shieldwall on his own and before he got there it had split and run.'

'I know,' said the voice and I knew, as I knew my own hands, that it was right in Bruse's ear, a knell of a voice, tomb-cold and deep as a pit.

'The others said it was my ale-breath. What do you think, Bruse?'

The splashing stopped. Everything stopped. Then Bergr whimpered and Hamund yelped and everything was movement.

'The ice will not be cleaved from within,' Red Njal grunted, 'as my granny used to say.'

So we rose up and hit the door at a fast run as the screams and chopping sounds began.

By the time we got there, the work was done and Finn, flicking blood off the end of The Godi, stirred one of the three bodies with the toe of his muddy boot.

'I do not recognise him,' he said, frowning. He looked at me. 'Do you know him?'

The man – Bruse, I was thinking, because his breeks were at his knees – was bearded, the blood and rain streaking his face and running in his open, unseeing eyes. I did not know him and said so. Finn shrugged and shook his head.

'He knew me, all the same,' he grunted. 'Seems a pity that he knew me so well and I did not know him from a whore's armpit. Does not seem right to kill such a man on a wet night.'

Botolf lumbered up, clutching a rope end attached to a halter and a horse fastened to that. It limped almost in step with him and Finn laughed at the sight. Botolf, mistaking it for delight at his find, beamed.

'Well, all that talk of horse-eating made me hungry. Now that they are dead, we can have a fire and cook this beast.'

I moved to the horse's head and had it whuff at me, for it knew me well and I knew it – a young colt, a good stallion in the making, whose brothers still charged up and down the valley. I ran a hand down the offending leg, felt the heat and the lump on the pastern; not spavined at all, just ring-bone from a kick and not too badly injured at that. He was under-nourished – as they all were after the winter, rough-coated and stiff with mud – but not bound for a platter just yet. I said so and wondered why the night and Odin had brought this horse to me at all.

Botolf scrubbed his head in a spray of rain and frustration.

'He is done,' he argued. 'What – are we to wait until he drops dead?'

'He will not drop dead. Some decent grass and a little atten-tion and he will be fine,' I told him, then looked Botolf in his big, flat, sullen face. 'If he does die, all the same, it will be in this valley, when his time has come and for more reason than to provide a meal.'

'Odin's arse,' Finn growled. 'I am not usually agreeing with mouse-brain – but this is a horse. Do you think he cares much how he dies?'

Odin cared and I said so.

Botolf growled and yanked the halter harder than he needed, jerking the colt's head after him as he plootered through the rain to the hut. Finn shrugged, looked at me, looked at the horse, then at the sprawl of dead bodies, which was eloquence enough.

'Well,' he growled, 'at least we can load Onund on the beast – unless your darling pony is too poorly for that?'

I ignored the dripping sarcasm and the matching rain. Onund would not help the colt, but it would not harm him badly if it was only for a little while.

'What makes you think it will be a little while?' Finn

countered, looking up from looting the corpses. 'We cannot stay here until light – more of these may come. If we move in the dark, we will travel in half circles, even if we are careful. It could take all night.'

We would not travel in half circles and I told him so; we would easily find our way to Thorgunna and Thordis, bairns, wagons and all, in an hour or less.

'Another Odin moment, Bear Slayer?' he asked, grunting upright and wiping bloody hands on his breeks. 'Have the Norns come to you in the dark and shown you what they weave?'

'Look north,' I told him, having done so already; he did and groaned. The faint red eye of a fire, certain as a guiding star, glowed baleful in the rain-misted dark.

'What are they thinking?' Finn growled.

'I was thinking,' Thorgunna said, 'that bairns needed food and everyone else needed some dry and warm. I was thinking that thralls have run off in panic and, with nowhere to go, will be looking to find us again in the dark.'

She looked up at me, blinking. 'I was thinking,' she added, trying to keep her voice from breaking, 'that menfolk we thought dead might not be and would want to find a way home.'

I held her to me and felt her clutch hard, using her grip instead of tears. Across from me, Ingrid held Botolf and he patted her arm and rumbled like a contented cat.

'I said Thorgunna was a deep thinker,' Finn lied cheerfully, while Thordis clutched his wet tunic so tightly it bunched and squeezed water through her knuckles. 'Was I not saying that all the way here, eh, Orm?'

They swept us up and swamped us with greetings and warmth and pushed food at us. Onund Hnufa was gathered up and wrapped and cooed over, while I laid out the tale of the fight to the flame-dyed faces, grim as cliffs, who gathered to listen.

'Nes-Bjorn,' muttered Abjorn, who led the six men left out of the crew Jarl Brand had lent me. 'Someone is owed a blow for that.'

'Gizur and Hauk,' added Ref, shaking his head. 'By the Hammer, a sad day this.'

Finn went off to look at his sleeping son and Botolf went to his daughter, leaving Hlenni Brimill and Red Njal to expound the tale; the hooms and heyas and wails rose up like foul smoke as I moved from it into the lee of a *wadmal* lean-to, where Thorgunna bent over Onund. Bjaelfi sat with him.

'Can he speak?' I asked and Bjaelfi shook his head.

'Asleep, which is best. He was hard used with hot irons.'

Thorgunna saw me frown and asked why, so I told her that I thought Onund had something to say that would cast a light on all this.

'I thought it simple enough,' she replied tightly. 'Randr Sterki is come to visit on us what once we visited on him.'

I shot her a look, but she kept her head down from me, fussing pointlessly with a cowhide for Onund's bedcovering. She had been there on Svartey when we raided Klerkon, but waiting with the ship while we hewed the place to rack and ruin. We were urged on by that cursed little Crowbone, I said and she lifted her head, eyes black as sheep-droppings.

'Don't blame it all on that boy,' she spat. 'I saw then what raiders were and never wish to see it again. It was not all that boy.'

No, not all, she had the right of it there. There had been raiders too long caged, who sucked in a whiff of blood-scent started by Crowbone, and went Odin-frenzied with it. When all was said and done with it, it was a *strandhogg*, like many others – a little harsher than most, but blood and flame had been our lives for long enough and it was only, I was thinking, that we now were the victims that made the matter of it here in Hestreng so bitter.

None of which answered the mystery of why Styrbjorn's man was here alongside Randr Sterki, nor why bearcoats and Roman Fire had been given to the enterprise. I laid that out for Thorgunna, too, and watched her sit heavily, folding her hands in her lap as she turned it over in her head.

'Styrbjorn wants what he has always wanted,' she said eventually, rising to fetch spoon and platter, busying herself with the things she knew while her mind worked. She filled a bowl with milk-boiled beef and handed it to me absently, then fetched a skin of *skyr* – thick fermented cow's milk thinned down with whey – for me to drink.

'Have we brought away enough?' I asked and she shrugged.

'Anything that was ready to hand and easily lifted,' she answered. 'Food. Three wagons and the horses for them. Shelters and wood for fire. Goats for milk for the bairns. This and that.'

I nodded and ate the beef, watching her rake through her only rescued kist, picking out items to show me. Two spare over-sarks, one in glowing blue, both patched and re-hemmed with braid more than once. A walrus-ivory comb, carved with gripping beasts. A whetsone. Some small stoppered pots with her ointments and face-paints. A walrus-skin bag with a roll of good cloth in it, snugged up in the dry because it had many little pockets sewn into it, all of them stuffed with carefully wrapped spices and herbs.

I nodded and smiled and praised, knowing she mourned for what was left behind – fine bedlinen and cloaks and clothes and food stores. It would all be looted and the rest burned before things were done with; I did not mention her eider-down pillows.

'Where will we go?' she asked suddenly, her voice tight with a fear she tried hard not to show.

'Over the mountains,' I said, making it light as I could. 'Down to Arne Thorliefsson at Vitharsby. There is a *seter* of his, a summer place, just over the high point on the far side

– it will not be occupied this early and will give us some shelter.'

We would need it by then, for the way was thawed just enough to be a sore, hard climb at the best of times, never mind the frantic haste we would need to put distance between us and what pursued.

Arne was a good tarman and had three sons, the two youngest needing their lives sorted, since only the eldest would inherit. The younglings were tired of the filthy, backbreaking work of rendering pine root resin into tar for fresh boat planks and Arne would help on the promise of them joining me, the raiding jarl, when the time came.

'Hlenni Brimill went there last year,' Thorgunna said suddenly, remembering, 'when we bought the tar for the *Elk*.'

The *Elk*, now burned and sunk with Gizur and Hauk and all the others floating down and down to the bottom of the black water fjord. I chewed slowly, the beef all ashes in my mouth. Raiding jarl my arse; no ship, no hall and no future if Randr and his bearcoats had their way.

Thorgunna brought me flatbread and sat while I tore chunks off and stuffed it in, trying to look as if I relished eating, but glad of the *skyr* to wash down the great tasteless lumps, my throat too filled with the fear of those bearcoats. Somewhere in the questing dark they prowled, waiting for the scouts to bring them news. Then they would be unleashed on us.

'Will they stop then, when we reach the other side of the mountains?' she asked, as if reading my thoughts.

I did not know. I did not think so. I was thinking only death would stop Randr Sterki – but Styrbjorn's man, this Ljot, wanted something else and I did not know what it was and that part I mentioned to her.

Thorgunna hauled a cloak round her shoulders as the rain-chilled air smoked her breath into the night.

'Styrbjorn is King Eirik's nephew and so his heir,' she answered, slowly working it through her head. 'He was so until he became such a ranter and raver that he was thrown out for his pains. But he still is heir and will be king if Eirik dies.'

'Aye, maybe,' I said, forcing a final swallow. 'Though more than few will not like the idea much. Anyway, he is young yet, though it seems he does not want to wait to be king.'

'He will not be at all,' Thorgunna answered meaningfully, 'if Eirik has a son.'

There it was, like a cunning picture of little tiles seen too close up; step back from it and it swam into view; Queen Sigrith. Styrbjorn wanted Sigrith – well, he wanted the child she carried and he wanted it dead.

Thorgunna watched my mouth drop like a coal-eater and then she rose, taking me by the hand. I followed her through the bodies huddled round the fire or close together under shelters, dank with misery. In one of the wagons lay a bulky, moaning figure and, squatted next to her like a bull seal, was Jasna, stroking and crooning soothing balm into the groans of the other.

'How is she?' asked Thorgunna and Jasna raised her pudding face, jowls trembling, and patted the sweat-greased cheeks of Queen Sigrith.

'Not good. No easy birth. Soon, little bird, soon. All the pain will be over and then a beautiful son, eh . . .'

I looked wildly at Thorgunna, who said nothing, but led me a little way away.

'The queen will birth, in a day, perhaps less.'

It was as good as an axe to the hull of all our hopes, that simple phrase; there would be no swift moving from here, banging her about in the back of a cart and, soon, we would have to stop entirely until the bairn was birthed. I thought I heard the bearcoats roar their triumph to the wet-shrouded moon.

Botolf added another log to the fire as Aoife collected wooden platters, Cormac locked to one hip and nodding, half-asleep.

63

Thorgunna came to me with dry breeks and tunic and serk, made me strip and change there and then, taking my sea-sodden boots to be rubbed with fat.

I sat next to Finn, sticking my bare feet closer to the flames as he cleaned the clotted blood from The Godi. The rain spat on the *wadmal* canopy and hissed in the fire just beyond it. Ref came up, carrying my sword; I had not even realised I had let it go, probably when Thorgunna hugged me.

'Not too bad,' he said cheerfully. 'There's a great notch out of it and I cannot grind it out, for it is all of the edge metal from that part.'

Then his face changed, like a sudden squall on a mirror fjord.

'Cannot grind it out properly anyway,' he added with a sigh. 'My forge is gone and all the tools with it.'

He handed it to me and I looked at the v-notch he pointed to. The sliver was in the mast of the *Elk*, for sure and I told him so. We all went quiet then, thinking of the black fjord and the sunken *Elk* and our oarmates, rolling in the slow, cold dark with their hair like sea-wrack.

'We should make *blot* for them,' Finn said and Abjorn came up at that moment, with little Koll at his heels.

'I have set watchers,' he told me from the grim cliff of his face, then jerked a thumb at the boy behind him. 'Like me, young Koll wishes news of his father.'

'I have none,' I answered, feeling guilty that, of all the fledglings who had occupied my thoughts, the one I had been charged with fostering had not been one of them. I signalled him closer and he stepped into the light and out of the rain, the firelight on his face showing up the white of him and the grit of his jaw, making a fierce light in his pale eyes.

'You are safe here,' I said, hoping it was true. 'Your father, once he has dealt with Styrbjorn, will come and help us defeat these nithings. Until then, we will get a little damp and have an adventure in the mountains.'

'My mother . . .' he said and I felt a stab, felt foolish. Of course . . . he had heard at the beach how Styrbjorn had dealt with all his family. Ingrid swept in then, gathering the boy into her apron and making soothing noises about honey and milk and sleep, for it was late.

I looked round the fire then, at all the expectant faces – Klepp Spaki, the blank, strange mask of Vuokko, the droop-mouthed Ref, bemoaning the loss of his forge and tools, Red Njal and Hlenni and Bjaelfi, staring at me across the flames, faces bloody with light and hoping for wisdom.

And there, in the shadows, no more than a pale blob of face, was Leo the monk.

'Roman Fire,' I called to him and he stepped forward, all the faces turning from me to him.

'So I heard,' he answered, arms folded into the sleeves of his clothing. 'Though we call it Persian Fire. Sometimes Sea Fire.'

'No matter what you call it,' I spat back into his plump smile, 'it is never let far from the Great City. Nor into the hands of such as Styrbjorn. I had heard it was a great crime to do so.'

'Indeed,' he replied sombrely. 'The ingredients of what you call Roman Fire were disclosed by an angel to the first great Constantine. It was he who ordained that there should be a curse, in writing and on the Holy Altar of the Church of God, on any who dare give the secret to another nation.'

He paused and frowned.

'Whether this is giving the secret is a matter for debate – the likes of Styrbjorn could not learn how to make it from what he has been given. However, such an event is cause for concern among many departments of the Imperium, where such weapons are strictly regulated.'

Concern? Burned ships and dead men were more than concern and I bellowed that at him. The rage gagged in my throat, both at his diffidence and the implication that the northers were barbarians too stupid to find out the secret of

Roman Fire from weapons handed out like toys to bairns. It did not cool me any to know he was right in it, too.

He nodded, smooth as a polished mirror and seemingly unconcerned by my glaring.

'Indeed. I would not be surprised if certain of those departments took steps to find out what has happened to their missing amounts.'

'Such as sending someone to find out?'

He inclined his head, face blank as an egg.

'I would not be in the least surprised.'

I watched him for a moment longer, but nothing flickered on it, no firm sign that he was the one sent to find out. He was young – not in the way we counted it, but certainly in the way the Great City did – but I suspected he had been sent and that made him a man to be watched. In the end, I broke the locked antlers of our eyes, turning to tell everyone that Styrbjorn had sent warriors here to end the life of Sigrith and the child she carried in her belly, so that he would remain sole heir to the high seat of the Svears and Geats.

The women grunted, while the men stayed silent. I did not say anything about why Randr Sterki had – I was sure – begged Styrbjorn to be the one to take on the task; those who remembered what we had done on Svartey did not need reminding of it. I told them all we would move north, across the mountains, as soon as it was light enough to see, trying to keep my voice easy, as if I was telling them when we would sow rye and in what field that year.

Afterwards, when others had rolled into skins and cloaks, I sat with Finn listening to Botolf snore – alone by the fire, for he had given his space beside Ingrid to Helga and Aoife and the other bairns, for better warmth. In the dark, I heard Aoife cooing softly to Cormac to soothe him – beautiful boy, she said. Where's my lovely boy, white as an egg, then?

'If it comes to it,' Finn said eventually, 'I will fight Randr Sterki.'

'Why you?' I countered and he shrugged and looked at me, half-ashamed, half-defiant. The memory of him humping away at the dying wife of Randr Sterki slunk sourly between us.

'I killed his boy,' I said sourly. 'So it should be me. Red Njal, I am remembering, killed others of his family. Perhaps we should take it in turns.'

Botolf woke himself with a particularly large snore and sat up, groaning and wiping sleep from his eyes.

'Odin's arse . . . my shoulder and back hurt. I hate sleeping on the ground in winter.'

'A hard raiding man like you?' snorted Finn. 'Surely not.'

'Shut your hole, Finn,' Botolf countered amiably, sitting up and wincing. 'The worse thing is the itch in my wooden leg.'

There was silence for a moment; a last log collapsed and whirled sparks up.

'What are we going to do?' demanded Botolf suddenly.

'About what? Your itching log-leg?' I asked and he waved his arms wildly in all directions.

'All this. The queen and weans.'

'We take them to Vitharsby and then east to Jarl Brand,' I told him.

'Just like that?' Botolf snapped. He rubbed his beard with frustration. 'Hunted by toad-licking wearers of bear and wolf skins? And at least a ship's crew of hard raiders? With a woman about to pup and half the bairns in the country?'

'One of them your own,' Finn pointed out poisonously. 'Another is mine. Do we begin throwing them over our shoulder as we run, then? We will start with Helga Hiti.'

I saw Botolf's face twist and frown as he fought to work all this out, only succeeding in fuelling more anger.

'What do you think we should do?' I asked and it was like throwing water on a sleeping drunk. He blinked. He blew out through pursed lips and surfaced with a thought, triumphant.

'We ought to leave the queen and ride off with our own,'

he declared. 'We could go to Thordis' place, which will be Finn's when he marries her. What are the fate of kings and princes to us, eh?'

It was astounding. I remembered Jarl Brand had said something of the same when we were in Serkland, only it was about the back-stabbing in high places that went on in the Great City. It never stopped amazing me, the things that stuck in Botolf's thought-cage.

'She is our queen,' Finn growled, flailing with one hand, as if trying to pluck the words he needed out of the air. 'We have to protect her. And Thordis' steading is only a short ride from Hestreng – if it was not behind the hills here, you could probably see it burn.'

I looked at him, but if the thought of everything he might one day own going up in smoke bothered him, he did not betray it by as much as a catch in his voice. Botolf flung his arms in the air.

'Protect the queen? Why? She would not give the likes of me the smell off her shit,' he grunted sourly. 'And how do we protect her? There is barely a handful of us.'

'We are Oathsworn,' Finn declared, thrusting out his chin. 'How can we do anything else but guard a queen and the heir to the throne of Eirik the Victorious?'

There was silence then, for fair fame had closed its jaws and even Botolf had no answer for the grip of them. We were Oathsworn, Odin's own, and would die before we took one step back, so the skalds had it. Not for the first time I marvelled at how fame had shackles stronger than iron to fasten you to a hopeless endeavour.

'Might be a girl,' Botolf offered sullenly and I shook my head. Thorgunna had done her hen's egg test and it had come up as a boy, no mistake. I said as much.

'Ah well,' Finn said as Botolf continued to glower. 'Perhaps you have the right of it, Botolf. I never did care much for wealth and glory; after all, we have all we need, though rebuilding Thordis' place – if it is burned and if I wed her – will be expensive and all gold is useful.'

He stretched, winked at me where Botolf could not see and farted sonorously.

'Anyway,' he went on. 'Once I have a ship under me I am a happy man – so perhaps we should tether the queen here like a goat and head for safety.'

'Aha!' Botolf declared triumphantly, looking from me to Finn and back. Then he frowned.

'What wealth and glory?'

I shrugged, picking up from Finn as he looked wickedly at me from under his hair, pretending to wipe a scrap of fat-rich fleece carefully up and down The Godi.

'The usual stuff,' I said. 'Meaningless to the likes of us, who have silver and fame and land enough already.'

'I have no land,' Botolf growled and I felt a pang of shame, for I had known this was a fret for him, since Ingrid constantly nagged and chafed him over it, wanting him to be first in his own hall rather than just another follower in mine. That was why I had mentioned it.

'Oh, aye,' I said, as if just realising it, then shrugged. 'Still. We would have to bring the queen and bairn safe back to King Eirik before he showered us with rings and praise and odal-rights on steadings – after all, it is his first-born and the heir to his wealth and lands. What would he not give for such a safe return? But – too dangerous, as you say. Better to cut and run, pick up the pieces of our old lives once these hard raiders have gone.'

There was silence, broken only by the rain hissing in the dying fire and the snores of the sleepers nearby.

'Would they really give us land?' Botolf asked after a while.

'Aye, sadly, for we are men of the sea, after all,' Finn replied. 'Still – skalds would write whole sagas about you.'

'Fuck that,' Botolf grunted. 'I have such sagas already. You cannot graze goats on a saga. And for a man of the sea, Finn Horsearse, you are talking of steadings readily enough.'

He was silent for a moment and I decided enough was enough; somewhere, through the rain mist, dawn was racing at us. I half rose and Botolf looked up and spoke.

'Do you think we can win against *ulfhednar*?' he asked suddenly. Finn laughed, quiet and savage; I sat down again, chilled by the term, which was used for madmen in wolfskins.

'Have we ever been beaten?' Finn demanded.

Botolf considered it for a moment, then stood up, nodding and serious.

'Then you are right. We are Oathsworn. We never run from a fight and this is our queen. I am with you, for sure. Now I am off to a warm bed, if I can squeeze in between bairns.'

Finn watched him stump off into the dark beyond the fire and shook his head wearily.

'By the Hammer – there are stones with more clever than him.'

We both knew, all the same, that all Botolf had needed was an excuse to do what he already knew to be right, to have someone persuade him to it.

Then Finn turned to me, sliding The Godi back into the sheath.

'Do you think we can beat them?' he asked.

We had to. It was as simple as that. I said so and he nodded, rising and heading off for his own bed, leaving me with fire-shapes and weariness.

Thorgunna, when I went to her, was awake, sitting hunched up and wrapped in blankets and almost under the wagon in which the queen of all the Svears and Geats groaned and gasped. Nearby, Kuritsa huddled under a cloak – not his own, I fancied – under the canopy and out of the rain and his black eyes watched me arriving. He was a thrall and his name meant 'chicken' because, when I had bought him, he had a shock of hair like a cock's comb before it was cut to stubble.

'No-one sleeps tonight,' I said, trying to be light with it. Thorgunna pulled me down beside her, tenting me under her cloak and blankets, giving me her warmth. Her head was heavy on my shoulder.

'Kuritsa just arrived,' she said. 'The two who ran off with him are still missing and Kuritsa does not know where they are. But he killed a man, he says.'

That was news and I sat up. Kuritsa sat up, too, looking warily at me from out of the cave of his face.

'You killed a man,' I said to him and he nodded uneasily; I was not surprised at his wariness, since thralls found with weapons were almost always killed outright.

'I took his little knife and killed him,' he said, almost defiantly. 'Then I took his bow and shot at his friend, but it was dark, I was hasty and I am out of the way of it. I missed.'

He produced the bow and three arrows, thrusting them towards me, his square, flat-nosed face proud. He grinned.

'I was not always a thrall,' he said. 'I hunted, in my own land.'

I looked at him; he was thin, dark-eyed, dark-haired and far from his own lands, somewhere in the Finnmark – yet he had a tilt to his close-cropped chin that would have had him beaten if matters were different. I told him to keep the bow, that he would need it sooner or later.

Kuritsa blinked at that, then smiled and held the weapon to his chest as if it warmed him.

'They hunt in fours,' he offered suddenly. 'One of the *ham-ramr* and three with him, tracking and offering him their shields. I had the favour of gods when I found two trackers and no *ham-ramr*.'

I looked at him; the word *ham-ramr* was an interesting one, for it was used on a man who changed his shape in a fit that also gave him great strength and power. Small wonder, then, that all the thralls had run off screaming – and more power to this one, who had not. Yet Thorgunna muttered under her breath, something about the direness of arming a thrall.

71

'You should sleep,' I told her and had back the familiar scorning snort.

'I am too old to enjoy cold nights and wet ground,' she replied. 'Still – this will make your son into a raiding man, for sure, since it seems that is all his lot.'

I ignored her dripping venom and put my hand on her belly then, feeling the warmth, fancying I could feel the heat of what grew in it. I thought, too, about what it would feel like to lose what was snugged up in the harbour of that belly – and the belly, too. All hopes and fears buried in the earth, given to Freyja and, with them, a part of me in that cold, worm-filled ground.

What was left, I was thinking, would be a *draugr*, a walking dead man, with only one thought left – revenge. Like Randr Sterki. I knew he would never stop until he was killed.

'Do you have a plan?' Thorgunna demanded.

'Stay alive, get to Vitharsby, then to Jarl Brand.'

'Death holds no fears for me,' she said suddenly. 'Though I am afraid of dying.'

'You will not die,' I said and felt, then, the rightness of what had to be done. She looked at me, a little surprised by the strength and depth of my voice; I was myself, for I thought a little of Odin had entered into it, even as he placed the thought in me as to what to do next.

FIVE

Dawn was whey and pewter, sullen with the promise of rain, and we were packed and moving even before it had slithered over the mountains we had to cross.

Jasna levered herself out of the wagon the queen lay in alongside bairns and supplies, for we had little room for those who could not walk or keep up; looking at the fat thrall-woman I was not sure she would manage with all that weight on her splay feet, but, if she felt the pain of trudging, nothing showed on her broad scowl of a face. The Mazur girl swayed alongside her, a skald-verse of walking, as if to show the fat woman in even worse light.

'Let us hope that Jasna can keep up,' grunted Thordis venomously, a squalling Hroald sling-wrapped round her. 'The horses will be grateful the longer we keep her out of a wagon.'

'And the walking will melt her,' added a smiling Ingrid, popping Helga into the wagon, where Cormac already sat, gurgling, Aoife looking after all of them and the soft-groaning queen. The cart lurched; the queen moaned.

'She will not suffer that long,' muttered Jasna to me in her harsh attempt at Norse. 'This first birthing time is bad for her. My little Sigrith cannot eat anything but sweet things and I have been feeding her hot milk and honey all night.'

I wondered if it had been spoon and spoon about. Precious little chance of that from now on, I thought, turning away to where Finn and Botolf stood with the limp-footed stallion. Little Toki was there, holding the head of it, for he had a way with horses – and, to my surprise, so was Abjorn and the other five men of Jarl Brand, all ringmailed and well-armed. Abjorn had his helmet cradled in the crook of one arm and a stone-grim look on his face.

'We will come with you,' he said, then looked from one man to another and back. 'There is something we must ask.'

I did not like it that they were all here and not with the struggling column, grinding a way up the mountain pass road – but what we were about to do would not take long.

There was little ceremony. We climbed a little way, to where a flat stone sprawled up above the road and into the realm of the *alfar*; whom some call Lokke; men hissed now and then when something flickered at the edge of their vision, or when the sun glimmered in a certain way on water, for they knew that it was Lokke, the Playing Man, the *alfar* no-one ever saw properly – or wanted to.

I kept my heart on my wish and my head up to the sky, away from the glitter of unnatural eyes in the moving shadows. My business was with Odin.

I drew the sword – a good blade, but not the nicked one rescued from the *Elk*. That was Kvasir's old blade and I would not be parted from that willingly, yet this was still a good sword which we had taken from the men we had killed near our rune stone and so a rich gift for Odin. I heard the men breathe out heavily, for it was known that the *alfar* did not care for iron, as I plunged it in the soft, brackened turf in front of the stone. Toki brought the limping stallion up to me.

It snuffled in the palm of my hand hopefully, but found nothing and had little time for the disappointment of it; I plunged a sharpened seax into the great pulse in its neck and heard it squeal and jerk, the iron stink of blood adding to the fear. It kicked and reared and Toki and I hung on to it, our weight forcing it still until the pulse of blood grew weaker and the stone and the sword blade dripped and clotted with it.

Men yelled out, fierce shouts of his name to draw Odin's attention; Finn moved in and took the sharpened seax, began cutting off the rear haunches – all Odin wanted was the blood and the blade, he had little need of all the meat and the *alfar* needed none at all, nor clothing. Finn skinned it, too, waiting properly until I had made my wish aloud.

It was simple enough – a life for a life. Let everyone else survive this and take life from me, if one were needed. Men hoomed and nodded; I felt leaden at the end of it, for Odin always needed a life and there was never enough blood and steel to sate One-Eye.

'So,' Botolf said, 'that was why you did not want to eat the horse. Deep thinking, Orm. I should have known better.'

'A bad thing,' growled Finn, 'to bring your doom down on your own head.'

'Randr Sterki will not stop until he is dead or we are,' I answered; he knew why, above all the others and shrugged, unable to find the words to speak to me on it.

Abjorn stepped forward then, with a look and a nod to the men behind him.

'Jarl Orm,' he began. 'We wish to take your Oath.'

I was dumbed by this; Finn grunted and found the words which were dammed up behind my teeth.

'You are sworn already, to Jarl Brand,' he pointed out and Abjorn shifted uncomfortably, with another glance to the men behind him for reassurance.

'He gave us to Jarl Orm,' he countered stubbornly. 'And Jarl Brand is almost brother to Jarl Orm.'

'He lent you,' I offered, gentle as a horse-whisperer, not wishing to anger him. 'Not gave.'

'For all that,' Abjorn pushed, his chin jutting out. 'We have all agreed to ask – Rovald, Rorik Stari, Kaelbjorn Rog, Myrkjartan, Uddolf and myself.'

As he said their names, the men stepped forward, determined as stones rolling downhill.

'This is foolish,' Finn said, pausing in his flaying of the horse. 'Jarl Brand will be angered by it and with Jarl Orm for agreeing to it. And what if they come to quarrel, what then? Who will you fight for?'

'We will leap that stream when we reach it,' Abjorn replied. Finn threw up his hands; a gobbet of fat flew off the end of the seax and splattered on the turf.

I knew why they wanted to take the Oath. They needed it. They had heard that Odin favoured the Oathsworn, held his hand over them and with all that snapped at their heels they needed to know that hand cradled them, too.

So I nodded and, stumbling like eager colts with the words of it, with the stink of fresh blood and the gleam of *blot*-iron in their eyes, they took it.

We swear to be brothers to each other, bone, blood and steel, on Gungnir, Odin's spear we swear, may he curse us to the Nine Realms and beyond if we break this faith, one to another.

Afterwards, laden with horse meat – the head left on the stone for the birds to pick – we went back down to the path and hurried to catch up with the others.

Abjorn and the new-sworn men were cheerful, chaffering one to the other and with Botolf and even Toki, when they would not usually have looked twice at a scrawny thrall boy. They were so happy I felt sorry for them, knowing how the smell of blood and iron appeals to One-Eye even as the happy plans of men do not.

An hour later, the *ulfhednar* caught us.

I did not hear or see them at all, having my shoulder into the back of the rearmost wagon, my whole world taken up by the pothole the left rear wheel had sunk into and not wanting to have to unload it to get it out again. The rest of the column was further ahead, round a bend and out of sight.

So, with Botolf alongside, Finn and Kuritsa on either rear wheel and little Toki trying to get the sagging-weary horses to pull, we strained and cursed and struggled with it. Somewhere up ahead, round the next bend, the others laboured on.

'Give them some whip!' bawled Finn.

'The fucking trail is too hard for this,' Botolf grunted out and he was right; I had no breath to argue with him anyway.

Then Toki yelled out, a high, piping screech and we all stopped and turned, sweating and panting, to see the four men come round the bend behind us in the trail. It was moot who was more surprised by it.

'Odin's arse . . .'

Finn sprang for The Godi, sheathed and in the wagon; Botolf hurled after his axe, which was in the same place, but all I had was my seax and that was handy, snugged across my lap. But Kuritsa, who had said he had been a hunter in his own land, showed that he had been a warrior, too.

Three of the men wore oatmeal clothing, carried spears and axes and shields, but the fourth was big as a bull seal and had the great, rain-sodden bearcoat that marked him. He whirled and gestured; one of the others started to run back and Kuritsa sprang up on the top of one wheel, balanced and shot – the man screamed and pitched forward.

The bearcoat roared at another, then hefted his shield in the air, caught it by one edge and slung it, whirling in a one-handed throw that sent it spinning at us, like a wooden platter hurled by a woman gone past reasonable argument. Kuritsa, nocking another arrow, did not see it until it hit him, knocking him off the wheel before he could make a sound; he hit heavily and lay gasping for breath and bleeding.

We watched the messenger vanish round the bend and the

bearcoat straightened slowly, hefting the bearded axe in one hand. The last man stood slightly behind him, licking his lips.

'I am Thorbrand Hrafnsson,' the bearcoat bawled out in a hoarse voice, spreading his arms wide, the great tangled mass of hair and beard matted so that his mouth was barely visible. His eyes were two beasts peering out of a wood.

'I am a slayer of men. I am a son of the wolf and the bear,' he roared.

'I,' said the man with him, 'am not eager for this.'

He backed away, shield up but sword hand held high and empty. Thorbrand never even turned round when he spat a greasy glob of disdain.

'I am known as a killer and a hard man, from Dyfflin to Skane,' he bellowed, pointing the axe at us. 'I am favoured by Thor. And you are Finn Bardisson, known as Horsehead, the one the skalds say fears no-one. And you are Orm Bear Slayer, who leads the Oathsworn and who found all the silver of the world. I see you.'

'You will not see us for long,' said Finn, hefting The Godi and stepping forward. 'And if you have heard anything of us at all, you will know you are not as god-favoured as we are.'

'What about me?' demanded Botolf angrily. 'I am Botolf, by-named Ymir. I am Oathsworn. What about me?'

'You can be last to die, One-Leg,' answered Thorbrand, 'because you are a cripple.'

Finn and I moved in swiftly then, just as Botolf bristled like an annoyed boar and we balked whatever he had intended, shouldering him to one side, then moving right and left as Thorbrand flung back his head and howled out a great frothing cry.

Then he went for Finn, but it was a feint, for he suddenly cut back and, only having a little seax and closing on him with it, I was caught flat-footed on muddy scree – so much so that I skidded on my arse, which saved me; the axe hissed at what would have been hip height, save that I was on the ground. It thundered past my nose, big as a house and the wind of it fluttered my braids and beard.

Scrabbling away, I saw Finn dart past, slashing; Thorbrand, slavering madly, eyes red as embers, half fell, then turned like a bull elk at bay. Finn stopped and watched; Thorbrand started a run, but the leg was tendon-cut and would not work – he fell on one knee and rose up. Marvelling, I saw no blood and it was clear he felt no pain, but the leg would not work properly and Finn sauntered, thinking the man was finished. A normal man would have been.

He was *ulfhednar* and Finn should have known better, as I said later. Thorbrand simply hirpled forward in two great one-legged leaps and Finn, yelping, managed a block before Thorbrand's bearded axe hooked The Godi, trapped it and flung it out of his hand.

Now Finn was weaponless and Thorbrand, like the bear whose hide he wore, growled and lurched, dragging one leg behind him, but closing fast on the hapless Finn.

I sprang forward, was hit by what seemed to be a boulder and bounced sideways, my head whirring; Botolf stumped down on the bearcoat and was almost on him when Thorbrand heard, or sensed it and whirled round, axe up, the slaver trailing from the edge of his mouth.

'Cripple, am I?' roared Botolf and grabbed the swinging axe in both hands, tearing it free, as if ripping a stick from a wean. 'Now we are even matched.'

He flung the axe away from him. The great, stupid rock flung the axe away, then closed with Thorbrand as if it was some friendly wrestle at a handfasting. Finn scurried to find his sword and I sat up, trying to stop the world rocking and lurching as if we were all on a boat at sea.

They strained; Botolf suddenly took a step back and swung, the crack of his fist against Thorbrand's ear loud as a whip – but the man was *berserk* and felt nothing, which fact Finn roared out as he picked up The Godi.

'Feel this, then,' grunted Botolf and he gripped and wrenched, so that Thorbrand was spun sideways, the great bear hide ripping free from him and left in Botolf's hands. He flung it to one side.

'Stand clear,' yelled Finn, hefting The Godi.

'Stand back,' warned Botolf and went after Thorbrand, who had rolled over and over and now sprang up, as well as his useless leg allowed.

'No bearcoat now,' Botolf said, spitting on his palms. 'More bare arse. Now we are evenly matched, skin to skin, leg to leg.'

Thorbrand was madder than ever, a slavering wolf who howled out his rage from a corded throat and launched off his one good leg, straight at Botolf, who half knelt and took the rush of it in both hands, one at Thorbrand's crotch, the other at his throat.

Then he straightened, the muscles on him bunching so that it seemed they would split, lifted the kicking, screaming madman in the air, half-turned him like a haunch on a spit and brought him down on his knee, the one which had wood four inches below it, anchored to the ground as strong as any bone.

The crack was a tree splitting; I thought it was Botolf's leg until he levered Thorbrand off him. The man still slavered and howled, but not even his head moved, for the back of him was splintered and he was only voice now.

'I am Botolf, by-named Ymir, strongest of the Oathsworn, on one leg or two,' Botolf panted and spat on Thorbrand. 'Now you know that, so you know more.'

Finn moved in and mercifully silenced the raving screams, while I climbed wearily to my feet. The remaining man, pale and wary behind his shield, stood and said nothing, which showed that he was sensible and braver than his lack of fight seemed to suggest.

There was silence, save for panting, ragged breathing – then Finn moved to Thorbrand's axe, picked it up and handed it to Botolf.

'Your prize,' he said. 'Next time, try not to throw it away.'

Botolf reversed it, using it as a stick to lever himself upright; I saw blood on his breeks and pointed it out. He shrugged.

'His, I think. He did not hit me.'

He hirpled off to the cart, while Finn and I watched him go.

'His great heart will be the end of him,' muttered Finn softly, still breathing hard and we remembered the other times the giant had saved us. Then we looked at the last man, saying nothing until he swallowed into the silence of it, which must have been grinding his courage away.

'I am Hidhinbjorn,' he said, eventually. 'I came at the request of Ljot Tokeson, to tell this Thorbrand what has happened.'

'Tell us,' I grunted and the weight of the shield was suddenly too much for him, so that he took a knee, resting his elbow – and still behind cover, I saw, which showed cleverness.

'We had news from up the fjord. Styrbjorn fought his uncle King Eirik and Jarl Brand. Brand is sore wounded, but Styrbjorn is defeated and fled, so this enterprise is finished with, says Ljot.'

'That is news, right enough,' growled Botolf, trailing back from the cart. He looked at me and added: 'Kuritsa is dunted, so that it will hurt by morning, but he is alive and not too done up.'

I nodded; the bowman had done well, thrall or not.

'This Thorbrand,' Finn was saying, 'knew all this?'

The man nodded and shifted uncomfortably. 'The bearcoats find Randr Sterki more to their liking than Styrbjorn.'

That did not surprise me; Randr Sterki was not about to give up his revenge and the bearcoats would want something out of this mess. Hidhinbjorn saw that I understood and got wearily to his feet.

'There is one, Stenvast by name, who has said that killing the queen and the bairn in her will rescue this venture. That way, he says, they keep faith with Pallig Tokeson, who is their sworn lord.'

81

This Pallig was clearly Ljot's brother and one with a weight of silver to afford so many bearcoats. I did not think he would be smiling at the way they were vanishing, all the same – unless someone was handing him buckets of money to make sure Styrbjorn had his due. King Eirik would hesitate to have the troublesome boy parted from his head if he was, in fact, his only heir; but I wondered how sorely Brand was wounded, for if his eyes were in the least open, Styrbjorn would die for what he had done and Brand would apologise to the king afterwards.

Hidhinbjorn stood, taut as a strung bow, for he clearly thought he would have to fight, but I was bone-weary and blood-sick. To my surprise, it was Finn who waved The Godi casually at him to go away.

'Next time we meet, Hidhinbjorn,' he growled, 'it had better be in a friendlier setting, or I will tear off your head and piss down your neck.'

Hidhinbjorn acknowledged it with an unsmiling nod and put his back to us, which was brave and polite, rather than edge away. When he had vanished round the bend, I realised I had been holding my breath and let it out.

'Aye,' growled Finn, fishing out a rag to clean The Godi. 'It has been an awkward day – and there is light left in it yet.'

Back at the cart, Kuritsa was sitting up and wheezing, his chest bared to show a livid bruise where the shield rim had struck. He breathed in rasps and winced, so that I thought something might be broken there and told him to get in the cart, that we would take him to Bjaelfi.

'That was a good shot with the bow. We will have to promote you, from chicken to eagle,' I added and Toki chuckled.

'Well,' growled Finn, 'rooster at the very least.'

And we laughed, so shrill and brittle in the pewter day that little Toki was as deep-voiced as any of us, all bright with the relief of survival.

Yet the blood on Botolf's breeks was wet and the stain grew as we ground up the track to join the other carts. When Ingrid saw it her hand flew to her mouth and she called out for Bjaelfi, then huckled her big husband off, while little flame-haired Helga stood, solemn eyed, thumb in her mouth.

The others crowded round, wanting to know what had happened and, for a moment, the faces swam as if under-water and I wanted badly to sit. Thorgunna saw it and chided me in out of the rain and I sat down, listening to it stutter off the canvas; it came to me then that they had not progressed far and had made camp while it was still light.

I told them what had happened while Aoife and Thordis tended to Kuritsa, who was looked at with new, grudging admiration – but it was the news of Styrbjorn's defeat which occupied them most.

'At least the wee bairn is safe,' said a familiar voice and Onund Hnufa shuffled painfully forward. 'I kept trying to warn you, but all that my mouth would make was "bairn".'

I felt a flood of warmth, as if I had stepped in front of a hearthfire.

'I see you, Onund,' I told him. 'It seems you are not so easily killed, then.'

He acknowledged it with a wry smile, but you could see that they had used him hard, for he was gaunt and his face was marked from the burns, still dark, raw-red under the grease the women had salved him with; the hump that gave him his by-name seemed sharper and higher than before on his shoulder.

'They wanted to know of buried silver,' he said. 'As well you told no-one, for another lick of that hot iron and I would have told them all they needed.'

'One who sees a friend on a spit tells all he knows,' Red Njal agreed, 'as my granny used to say.'

'At least one of those who licked you with it felt the heat of it,' growled Finn and told him of the man called Bjarki.

83

'Small reward,' Onund answered, 'for the loss of Gizur and Hauk.'

I remembered them, then, as a trio, each a shadow to the other and felt Onund's loss with a sudden keen pang.

'Gizur would not leave the *Elk*,' Hlenni Brimill threw in. 'Since he had made it, he said.'

Onund grunted. 'He made some of it, but no ship is worth a death.'

That, from such a shipwright, surprised me and he saw it in my face.

'I built the *Elk*,' he said. 'There was more of me in that ship than any of the others. But I can build another.'

'Heya,' said Finn, grinning. 'Once this is done with, I shall help.'

Onund, with a flash of his old self that made me smile, raised his eyebrows at the thought and made Finn laugh out loud.

'The whole matter of this should be done with now, I am thinking,' offered Klepp Spaki hopefully, but Vuokko, his ever-present shadow, gave a little high-pitched bark and told us all that he had asked the drum and it spoke of loss, keenly felt.

That clamped lips shut, sure as a hand on the mouth; I saw Thorgunna's lips tighten and her face take on that blank look, which I knew meant that she dared not speak for fear of tears. The others, of course, tried not to look me in the eye; they all knew the *blot* I had promised Odin for their lives.

Then Abjorn stepped forward, wiping the drizzle of rain from his face; behind him, the others new-promised as Oathsworn gathered like pillars, their ring-coats dark with rain, streaked here and there with the blood of iron-rot.

'If you have it right,' he said, 'then there are eight bearcoats only.'

'And Randr Sterki and his men,' Finn pointed out, hunching down to pitch some small sticks into the guttering fire.

'Randr Sterki may be a fighter, but his men are nithings,' I said.

'Still,' said Finn, wryly, 'eight bearcoats is enough.'

Abjorn shrugged. 'These bearcoats belong to Pallig Tokeson, who is jarl in Joms these days and this Ljot we have seen is his brother, so they are thrown into the enterprise on behalf of Styrbjorn. I am thinking they may not pursue it now. I am thinking that we should be pushing on. I am thinking that the queen is still in danger and that we will stay here and guard the path – me, Rovald, Rorik Stari, Kaelbjorn Rog, Myrkjartan and Uddolf.'

'They must not have the babe,' Jasna spat and I knew who had put them up to this. They looked at her, slab-faced men with braids and eyes grey as pewter and jingling at the brim with hopelessness, for they knew they were no match for eight bearcoats.

I said as much. I said also that we would all go on, together, for there was more chance with numbers.

'We will not go on in much of a hurry,' Thorgunna said at the end of all this and jerked her head at the covered cart, where Jasna and the silent hostage-girl sat beside a lump of coverlet that moaned.

'How bad?'

Thorgunna shook her head, which was answer enough. So we were stuck here then, until the birth; I looked around at the place and found Finn doing the same. It was a fattened part of the trail, with a branch turning to the right, leading into an even more tortured scar in the mountains. There was a bridge not far along that part, raised by a mother to her sons, so said the stone by it, for once there had been fine tall pines at the top, which was the highest point overlooking the fjord.

Now there were only wind-stunted trees, twisted and useless and the trail had always ended there, dribbling out like drool from a drunk's mouth. There was a way down the other side, but rough travelling even for a man on foot, so carts and bairns and women and fat thralls would never do it.

Finn and I looked at each other and knew what each thought – this was no great place for us to fight. I moved to him then as the gathering broke up into muttering twos and threes and he scrubbed his face furiously, a sure sign of his confusion.

'Well?' I asked.

'Well what?' he countered, scowling, his beard scrubbed into a mad fury of spikes.

'Do you think we can win?'

He stopped then, for he knew I would not voice that out loud when there was more than just him to hear it.

'Well,' he growled. 'I am no stranger to woman-killing, as you keep wanting to tell me, as if it was something to be shamed at. All the same, I have never killed a bairn that had no proper life and I am reluctant to begin.'

'Kill one to save us all?' I answered, with a wry smile, for this thought had been running like spate-water in me. He grinned, then spat.

'It is not about numbers – one or a hundred bairns, it would still be a price worth paying for such a reward as the life of wee Helga and the boy Hroald, whom I have acknowledged as mine. It is about what is right and what is not. He may be a great king, this fledgling eagle. Who can say what wonders he may bring about?'

I laughed with the sheer, surprising delight of him and pointed out the other side of the coin; that he would most likely turn out to be another Harald Bluetooth.

'If I thought that,' he growled, 'I would kill it before the head appeared between the mother's thighs.'

We were smiling, then, when Botolf limped up, towing Ingrid and Bjaelfi in his wake. Behind them, I saw the Greek, Leo, allowing Koll to lead him by the hand towards us.

'How is the leg?' I demanded and Botolf waved an answer away, hauling Helga up high in the air, so that she shrieked with delight and bone-haired Cormac stood, wanting the same but older and so too proud to ask. When Botolf hoisted him up, he shrieked his delight all the same, but Botolf grunted with pain.

Bjaelfi gave me a look and I moved to him, so he could tell me, soft and low.

'I cut too little from the bone,' he said tersely. 'I warned him not to go back to lifting carts with the pony in them, but Botolf is Botolf.'

I remembered it well, the hot, fetid boat heading into the hard-pull of the Middle Sea up to the Great City, Botolf delirious with wound-fever, rolling great fat drops of sweat. Bjaelfi, sheened like some mad black dwarf in a cave, kept cutting and sewing, so that there was skin to wrap round and stitch for a stump, with the blood washing in the scuppers.

'I think the skin is splitting round the stump-bone,' he added bleakly. 'If it does, he will not be able to have such an end in the socket of a wooden leg, clever harness or no.'

I looked at Botolf, standing tall, Cormac held giggling and wriggling to the sky. The big man would not like being reduced to the crutch he had endured once before, while the stump healed. He would not like that at all.

Koll broke in just then, his high-pitched voice querulous and demanding.

'Tell me if what this priest says is true, Jarl Orm, for you have been to the Great City. That people live in halls set one on top of the other.'

I looked at Leo and answered his bland smile, then nodded.

'Just so,' I replied. 'And they have marvellous affairs built for no other reason than to throw water into the air, for the delight of it. And they eat lying down. Much more besides – I shall take you there when all this is done with.'

'If we live,' the boy answered, suddenly grim. 'Leo says the bearcoats are better warriors.'

Leo spread his hands in apology. 'A careless remark. I had

heard such warriors were to be feared because they had no fear of their own.'

'They will find some when they meet us,' I answered and Toki, appearing sudden as a squall, declared that Kuritsa would shoot them all with his bow. The man himself, wheezing still, but grinning, agreed from a little way away and Finn chuckled.

'By the time this is all done away with,' he declared, 'we will have to give Kuritsa a new name, I am thinking. And put Prince at the head of it.'

'Hunter will be title enough,' Kuritsa replied and I marvelled; already it was hard to tell this man from the droop-headed, silent thrall he once had been. 'I can shoot an arrow for miles and still hit true. Even round a corner. Such a thing once saved my life.'

Koll and Toki, bright-eyed and struck silent, watched him. Finn, grinning, sat down and others gathered. Kuritsa, lean-faced, shave-headed, hirpled to the wagon and sat heavily by the wheel.

'Before I was taken, in my own lands, I was set upon by the Yeks, a tribe who hated us. They were many and I was one and was, I admit it, hunting in their lands – so what do you think happened?'

'You were killed, for sure,' chuckled Botolf, leading Helga and Cormac to where they could listen, 'for there are times when you work like a dead man.'

'Not as dead as some, I am thinking,' answered Kuritsa smartly. 'I was lucky. I had my own bow with me, one I called Sure in my own tongue. Sometimes the power of that bow frightened me, for I lost many arrows and sometimes wondered whether one that vanished from my sight hit a friend in the next village, or a king in another country. It took me a time to get the grip of that bow, but after a while, I could hit a fat deer as far as I could see it – though I might have to turn half-round if it were a pair rutting, to be sure of hitting the deer and not the stag.'

Finn laughed out loud at that one, slapping his thigh with delight, then waved Kuritsa to go on, while the others, child and man both, listened open-mouthed.

'Well,' Kuritsa said, 'I spotted an elk far off – so far off it was no bigger than a tiny beetle and I pointed at it, so that the skin-wearing trolls of Yeks stopped and looked while I nocked an arrow in Sure and took aim. I waited until the tail twitched out of sight over the hill, then I shot – allowing for the breeze and a touch of snow in the air.'

Botolf and Finn collapsed at this point, howling and wheezing. I could make out, between the grunts and snorts, the words 'allowing for the breeze' and 'snow in the air'. Kuritsa, haughty as a jarl, ignored them.

'I persuaded those Yeks to go over the hill, with me as prisoner, on the promise that if they had elk meat at the end of it, I could go free. They agreed, for it was on their way and it took the best part of the rest of that day to walk it – but there was the elk, my arrow in him and dead. They were delighted at having the horns and the meat and so let me go.'

'A fine shot,' Finn said eventually, spluttering to halt. Kuritsa shook his head sorrowfully.

'It was that moment when I knew I was cursed – not long after, of course, the gods allowed me to be captured and taken into slavery. I have not shot such a long shot since.'

'Why?' demanded Botolf. 'Did your gods order it?'

Kuritsa sighed. 'No, my own failing eye and hand. I had aimed for the heart and there was that old bull elk, gut-shot in the worst way. I was ashamed.'

'Yet you shot today,' Toki pointed out into the chuckles following that and Kuritsa shrugged.

'Not so long. At that range I can shoot the balls off a clegg.'

'Do cleggs have balls, then?' Koll demanded, frowning and Kuritsa, serious and unsmiling, shook his head.

'No horsefly has any when I am around with a bow.'

It was good laughter, washing away the lurking horrors of

89

eight bearcoats and lasted well into the rattle of skillet and cauldron, while the sun staggered out from behind clouds and showed me the rain, small-dropped and fine as baby hair.

It was a good evening and you would not think we were hunted folk at all, so I thanked Freyja for that moment of goddess-peace.

Of course, it did not last until morning.

SIX

I woke to screams and fire, scrabbling for a sword and cursing the sleep out of me; then a soft voice I knew well told me to put on a tunic and stop shouting.

Thorgunna squatted by a goat, working the teats relentlessly into a bowl. It was dark, but there were fires everywhere it seemed and the place bustled with movement and purpose; somewhere, a woman moaned and then yelled aloud.

'Why are you milking a goat in the dark?' I asked, still stupid with sleep and Thorgunna, grunting with the effort of bending, jerked her head in the direction of the yelps.

'Her waters broke. I need the milk to bathe the bairn in.'

The mother-to-be appeared a second later, out from where she had been moved for more comfort, which had banished me and all the other men to find sleep and shelter where we could. She moved ponderously, splay-legged, held up by Aoife on one side and Thordis on the other.

'She has no strength,' Thordis hissed. 'She needs a birthing stool.'

'Aye, well,' grunted Thorgunna, sharp as green apples, straightening with the bowl of milk held in the crook of one arm. 'It was a thing I forgot in all the confusion of finding things for food and shelter in a hurry, with my husband's enemies at my heels.'

I shrugged into my tunic, seeing the fires lit in a circle to keep the *alfar* at bay, for there is nothing those unseen, flickering creatures like better than stealing a newborn wean and leaving one of their own twisted wee horrors.

Ingrid appeared, dripping blood from her hands and the other women fell back a little in deference. She came up to the moaning Sigrith and clasped her rune-cut, bloodied palms on the queen's joints, to give her strength and ease. I knew Ingrid was Hestreng's *bjargrygr*, the Helping Woman for all the steading's births, which role had some *seidr* work in it, too; Thorgunna and her sister, I knew from old, had no *seidr* in them at all.

'Jasna . . .' moaned the queen.

'We cannot support her and deliver the bairn,' Thordis insisted. 'Especially at the last.'

I knew this was when the mother got on her elbows and knees, the bairn delivered from behind. Ingrid moved busily, undoing knots and loosening straps and buckles where she saw them, another spell to ease the birth. The women's hair was also unbound, tucked into their belts at the waist to keep it out of the way.

The queen moaned and sagged. 'Jasna,' she said.

'I have a birthing stool,' Ingrid said, then waved to the shadows and all heads turned as Botolf stumped into the middle of the fires, grinning. Thorgunna and Thordis looked at each other; no men were allowed at a birthing by tradition and usage.

'Oh, I am half a bench,' grunted Botolf, sitting himself on a sea-chest, 'so half of me is not here at all. The other half will close my eyes if you like.'

He hauled the queen to him, holding her in powerful arms, her legs splayed over his knees, her head resting, intimate as a lover, on his great chest.

'You'll ruin those breeks,' Thorgunna said wryly and Botolf chuckled.

'I could take them off.'

There was a chorus at that and, suddenly, the queen, sheened face raised, muttered: 'Not seemly. I will buy you a new pair, Birthing Stool.'

'That's better, my pet,' Ingrid said, sure that her palm-carved runes were working. 'A little pain and sweat and then the joy of a son.'

'Jasna . . .' whispered the queen.

'Will someone rout out that fat cow Jasna from her sleep?' bellowed Thorgunna angrily.

Ingrid looked pointedly at me. I realised I was not welcome in the circle of fires and backed off hastily, while Botolf crooned softly to the bundle in his arms and Ingrid raised her arms and started a muttered prayer-chant to Freyja.

Beyond, where men were, seemed darker away from the fires and I almost fell over Finn and Abjorn, talking urgently with each other.

'Banished, were you?' chuckled Finn. 'Just as well. No place for a man, that. I pity the stupid big arse who is now high-seat for a birthing queen.'

I told Abjorn to send out watchers and he nodded, his face grim and grey in the dark.

'Those fires . . .'

He let it trail off, for there was little need to voice it all. Those fires were a sure beacon and I could see the hunting packs of bearcoats and Randr Sterki's skin-wearing trolls slithering through the dark towards us.

'There is worse,' growled Hlenni Brimill, looming out of the dark, dragging a squirming figure by the hair; the Mazur girl yelped as he swung her into the circle of us.

'That fat cow of a thrall woman is dead,' he declared. 'When I went to get her, she was cold and stiff – and this one made a bolt out from under the wagon she was in.'

I blinked. Dead? Jasna?

We went to the wagon in a crowd, the Mazur girl dragged back with us and yelping whenever Hlenni jerked her savagely by her hair. Bjaelfi was climbing out, rubbing his chin and spreading his hands.

'She is dead, right enough,' he announced. 'Not a mark on her I can see – but it is hard enough in torchlight. Perhaps daylight will let me know more.'

'Not a mark,' muttered Red Njal from over Bjaelfi's shoulder. 'That is *seidr* work, if ever I saw it. Her hand will wag above her grave, as my granny used to say.'

Desperate eyes raked the girl, who felt them and struggled until Hlenni jerked her hard and she shrieked. An answer came from the dark, from where the fires blazed and I had had enough of it all.

'Let her go, Hlenni,' I said and he reluctantly opened his fist; the girl sank to the ground, then stood, with a visible effort. She squared her shoulders and looked at me, chin out, eyes dark and liquid as a seal. I felt a lurch in my stomach, for I had seen such looks before on women and all of them had been rich in *seidr* and had done me no good with it.

'Drozdov,' I said. 'Is that your name?'

'What they call me,' she answered, her Norse of the eastern type and further bent out of shape by her accent; those eyes were fixed on mine, swimming at the brim but not spilling over.

'Chernoglazov,' I remembered and she nodded, then said, 'Yes, lord,' before Red Njal had lifted his hand to correct her.

'Did you kill her, then?' I said, waving one hand at the dark, dead bulk in the wagon.

'No . . . lord. Someone came in the night. I heard her make little noise and then silent. I stay hidden.'

'Someone came?' demanded Finn, the scorn and suspicion reeking in his voice.

She turned those dark, seal eyes on him. 'A man, I think. Silent.'

'What did he do, this silent man?' I asked and she frowned and shook her head.

'Something,' she answered, then the frown disappeared and her face turned to mine like a petal to the sun. 'Lord.'

'I knew it was not good,' she added. 'So I hid.'

Yes, she would be good at hiding by now, good at staying out of the line of sight and the strong light. Finn looked at me, then at Bjaelfi and shook his head.

'Was she armed?' I asked Hlenni and he shook his own shaggy head, reluctantly.

'You looked?'

He nodded, then added sullenly: 'No blade is needed with *seidr*, Jarl Orm.'

A scream split the night and made us all start.

'Odin's hairy balls,' Finn swore, then swallowed another, for it was not good to malign the gods while the Norns were so close, weaving a new life out of the Other.

'Shave the hairs from your arm,' muttered Klepp Spaki fearfully.

I looked at the girl again, all wet eyes and defiance in the tight-strung little body. I told Hlenni to watch her the rest of the night, in turns with Red Njal. In the morning, I promised, Bjaelfi, Finn and I would look at the body and find out what had happened and that I was no stranger to *seidr* and worse.

They had heard the Oathsworn tales – some of them had been there when they were made – so they went off, muttering, to huddle in the damp dark and listen to Sigrith pant and shriek a new bairn into the world.

It took a long while; I dozed until wakened with a shake on my toe, came up with a seax in my fist – which was why Thorgunna, clever woman, had shaken only my toe and stayed clear of a swinging blade. She knew all the men were tight-wound and likely to be armed and leaping from sleep.

95

'Done,' she said wearily and I blinked in the light of her flickering torch; beyond it, the dawn was a thin smear.

'A boy,' she added. 'Healthy and loud. The mother is alive, too, which is good.'

It was good; too many first mothers died giving birth and, in the clearing round the dying fires, I saw the weary, gore-handed women and the blanket-wrapped bundle that was Sigrith. Botolf, a little way away, stretched stiffly and gave me a smile and a wave as I came up, the rest of the men behind me save for those on watch.

'That was a bloody affair,' he growled, moving slowly and shaking his head. 'Odin's arse, lads, I have stood in shield-walls that had less hard work in them and less blood and shit and fewer screams.'

'Take off those breeks,' Ingrid said to Botolf, bustling forward with a fur bundle which had a squashed red face nestled in it. Underneath, I knew, each limb would be linen-wrapped to keep it straight and fine, having been washed in hot milk and salt. His little mouth was a sticky bud, for the women had rubbed honey in his gums, to promote appetite.

'First,' said a waft-soft voice and we stopped, staring at Sigrith, 'since you did most to bring him into the world, Birthing Stool, you can name him. His father says he is to be Olaf.'

Botolf stopped and scrubbed his beard with confusion, pleased and embarrassed in equal measure. Ingrid handed him the bundle and he played the father, raising it to us over his head, standing proud and tall in his slathered breeks as he called us all to attend.

'Heya,' he bellowed. 'This is the son of King Eirik the Victorious. This is Olaf, Prince of the Svears and Geats.'

We stamped and cheered and there was more than duty in it, for that bairn had come to be the focus of all our lives and we watched as Ingrid handed it to Sigrith – watched, too, as she took it back moments later, when the exhausted slip of a girl fell asleep.

I was remembering that surviving the birthing was only the first step and that making it through the days that followed it were fraught for mothers. Too many of them died and I felt a stab deep in me when Thorgunna came up to stand beside me, all bright with the promise of our own child.

'It went hard with her,' she said quietly to me, as people murmured themselves into a new day. 'She needs quiet and rest and a wet-nurse, for she cannot feed the wee soul properly herself.'

'Will he die then?' I asked, alarmed, seeing the whole of our efforts crumbling. She shook her head and gave me one of her black-eyed, pitying looks.

'Of course not – the idea. We can feed him, as we do kids and calves with no mothers.'

That I knew well enough, for I had done it myself with a foal I favoured, using a sheep's bladder as a teat and a little drinking horn full of milk. It was an awkward, messy business and I said so.

'That is children all over,' she answered and clasped her belly as she leaned into me. I nestled her there for a moment or two, patting her absently while my mind raced on how there was unlikely to be a fast remove from here and my eyes scanned the lightening day for signs of bearcoats. I could feel them, like hot breath on the back of my neck.

She felt it in me and leaned away from me then, was about to speak when Toki bounded up in his breathless way, saying Bjaelfi wanted me.

I knew where he would be and there were others gathered round that wagon. Hlenni had laced the hands of the seal-eyed Mazur girl with a thong and tied it to his own wrist. Red Njal, Klepp, Vuokko and others gathered, while Bjaelfi knelt beside the corpse in the wagon bed.

'Well?' I asked, hauling myself in. Bjaelfi said nothing, simply drew back the wool cloak that covered her and pointed.

There was nothing but the blue-white dead flesh, the

grey-streaked hair . . . and the trickle, thin as a slug trail and dried so that it seemed black in the new light of a day. It had run almost to her jawline and tracked back, curling a little, to where a drop had dried and crusted on one lobe.

'The only mark on her,' Bjaelfi said, loud enough for all to hear. 'A flea-nip on an earlobe.'

The word leaped from head to head. *Seidr*. No Norse killing that. Gunnhild, Mother of Kings, was said to have been able to arrange such deaths, secret and stealthy in the night, shapeshifting to further the cause of her ambitious sons all over Norway.

I sat back on my heels, turning the coin of it over and over in my mind's fingers, testing the worth of what I worked out. A deadly fleabite? Even Gunnhild, noted shapechanger that she was, had never slipped into the body of anything so small. Or that killed so easily.

This was no *seidr*. This smacked too much of a place where poison needles settled more quarrels than blades – the Great City. I jerked up then, cursing, shouting orders that were far too late. In a moment, it was confirmed – Leo the priest had gone.

'And his sharp little needle with him,' growled Finn, when I told him what I had been thinking. He smacked an open hand on the side of the wagon, making it rock. 'Turd.'

'I am having trouble thinking this one out,' confessed Hlenni, looking from the Mazur girl to me and back again. Finn leaned over, his little eating knife flashed and cut the thongs; the girl rubbed her wrists and Hlenni scowled.

'He killed Jasna thinking it was Sigrith,' I said, working it out in my own head as I spoke. Thorgunna had moved the queen, but the little Greek had not known that and, in the dark, had felt softly along the bulked shape of what he believed to be a pregnant woman and stuck his needle in her ear, quick and sharp and away into the night, so that she scarcely made a yelp. A grunt, a scratch at another of many little bites – and then the long sleep of death. Poor Jasna, dead of her own fat belly.

'I might as well still be in the dark,' growled Bjaelfi, confused, 'since now I know how it was done and by whom, but not why a monk from the Great City would want Queen Sigrith dead.'

Because the Great City had backed Styrbjorn and the monk had been sent, not to find out who had supplied Roman Fire, but bringing it to make sure the enterprise went off, then slithering himself to the side of the target, just in case. I had no idea why the Great City wanted Styrbjorn as king of the Svears and Geats, but that was the way they worked and I knew it well.

Once, I had been at the sacking of the Khazar city of Sarkel by Sviatoslav, Prince of Kiev, and he had been given engineers by the Great City. He needed them to help him knock that fortress down because it had been built for the Khazars by engineers of the Great City. They were a snake-knot of plots, were the Greeks who called themselves Romans in Constantinople.

Now Styrbjorn had failed, so the whole enterprise seemed doomed and the leader of it fled – but not to ruin if he was still the only heir to the high-seat. His uncle would think twice about having him killed in that case and where bearcoats seemed to be stumbling, a silent, grim little Greek with poison thought he could do better. Thankfully, he had not.

'Aye, well, you would know, for sure, Orm,' Onund Hnufa said, lumbering out of the sour-milk dawn to hear me lay out the length of this for folk to measure. 'I have seen and heard you dealing with the Great City and it is a marvellous thing how you can fathom the way their minds work, right enough.'

Everyone agreed with it, with nods and hooms.

'So perhaps you can be after telling me this, then,' Onund added. 'Why has this Greek taken little Koll with him?'

SEVEN

It was a fine bridge, as long as two tall men, wide enough for a wagon to pass over and made of good stone. Beneath it, the river that had cut the gorge burbled and sang to itself, while the green-mossed stones of the mountain flashed with quartz and trickled with silver water. Jewels of the Mountain King, Finn said, in a skald moment.

We were like that, standing there waiting, for I was thinking that this was where the Norns' weave came to an end for me. I had offered a life to Odin and I knew One-Eye would take his sacrifice. Provided he kept to his part of the bargain, I told myself, it was worth it.

Still, life was sweet and seemed sweeter still, standing there, waiting for the bearcoats to come, with the clouds piled up like snow and a sea-swallow, ragged by the wind and yet swooping for the sheer joy of it, grating a shriek that scoured a sky as blue as a newborn's eye.

That, too, made my heart leap painfully into my throat; I would never live to see the son Thorgunna carried. Yet, if Odin held to his part, another babe would find a life, the bairn Botolf carried in the crook of his arm, stumping his unseen way up to the headland overlooking the fjord.

A scramble down the other side and he was safe. A hard

scramble for a man with two good legs, as Finn pointed out when we made this plan, never mind one who was half a bench, with the thought-cage of a mouse and a wean under one arm. He said this where Botolf could not hear it, all the same.

'And a boy with him, too, dragging a goat,' I added, trying to make light of it. Toki, hearing the word 'goat', looked up, beaming, and gave his charge a pat between the thick horns.

Finn grunted his answer to that, then Botolf himself came up, his broad face braided in a smile, the babe wrapped up so warm it looked no more than a bundled old cloak held against his chest.

'Here,' said Thordis, shoving a bag at Finn. It was a good waterproofed walrus-hide bag and he peered in it, thinking to find food and warm clothing. Instead, he found linen squares and moss.

'Am I expected to eat this, woman?' he grumbled and she slapped him smartly on the arm.

'No,' she answered, but less tartly than she might have, since she was afraid for him. 'You are expected to use it on the bairn's arse, to keep it clean. From the state of your own breeks, it is a lesson you should learn for yourself, too, before we are wed.'

Finn grunted as if hit at this last and those closest laughed, the too-hearty laughs of those straining to find humour. Botolf slung a similar bag over one shoulder, with all that was needed to feed the sleeping prince, then turned and grinned at Toki and his goat.

'Ready, wee man?' he demanded and Toki, trembling with the excitement of it all, nodded furiously, then scowled as Aoife, winking on the brink of tears, dragged him into an embrace.

'Look after my little hero,' she demanded of Botolf and he patted her shoulder. Then he turned to the wagon and the figure in it, propped up on pillows and pale as winter wolfskin.

'Take care of my son, Birthing Stool,' said the queen in a voice with no more in it than wind.

101

'He will be safely delivered,' Botolf promised and Finn, hearing the firm resolve in his voice, shook his head at the memory of the man who had so recently wanted to leave queen and wean both and run for the hills.

It had seemed a fair plan in the cold light of dawn; take the bairn, leave the queen, confuse the enemy and split them. It was the queen's bairn they wanted, so the rest of the women and weans might be left alone, considering there were men willing to fight and nothing to be gained taking them on. Well – only for those who wanted bloody revenge and I was hoping the bearcoats would not think fit to join in with that. Meanwhile, we could take the little prince to safety, getting a headstart and travelling fast and light.

'With a goat?' demanded Finn.

'What milk will you find to feed a bairn?' countered Thorgunna. 'And Toki is to goats what Botolf seems to be to that wee prince.'

At which the big man grinned, for it was a strange sort of almost-*seidr* he had and he was not ashamed of it at all. The newborn prince wailed, no matter who cooed or shushed or rocked him – even his too-weak mother – until he was placed in the fat-biceped crook of Botolf's arm, where he closed his eyes and went silently to sleep.

Red Njal and Hlenni Brimill came up and we clasped, wrist to wrist. I had already made them swear to do all in their power to recover little Koll from wherever he had gone and told them I suspected the one called Ljot Tokeson would get him, for he was Styrbjorn's man.

The only reason for the Greek to have taken Jarl Brand's son was to use him as a hostage against Brand and so against King Eirik.

Randr Sterki would not give the snap of his fingers for Koll, or the new little prince of the Svears and Geats; it was vengeance he wanted and he would keep after Thorgunna and the others with what was left of his men – but the bearcoats would not,

102

or so I hoped. The bearcoats would come after us and the bairn, in the hope of rescuing the whole endeavour at the last.

That's what I told them and they nodded, millstone-grim and silent. I did not tell them of the vicious gnawing in my heart and belly at what I had done to Koll. Too taken up with everything else, I had been happy to have him cared for by the women – and grateful for the soft, consoling words that the priest seemed to be offering him. My words, they should have been – but I was too busy with the work of protecting him to notice how he had strayed into danger.

Some foster-father me, and now I was thinking I would never find out if I might have improved on the task, for him or me, or both, would be dead soon.

Others came up and said their farewells, so that I was glad to leave in the end, away from the weight of their sadness. Their faces, pale blobs of concern in the whey-light of dawn, looked at me with that hard, miserable stare I had given others I knew I would never see again.

But it was only Thorgunna's face, stricken and *skyr*-pale, that stayed with me all the way to the bridge.

It was a fine bridge – Finn said so. Narrow enough for two men to hold against many.

So Botolf looked at us, from one to the other, the babe crooked in his arm and one hand on the head of Toki.

'Bone, blood and steel,' Finn said and gave him the bag of arse-wrappings. Nothing more was said, just a nod and a clasp for each of us, wrist to wrist, then Botolf turned abruptly and hirpled over the bridge, Toki and the unwilling goat trotting behind him.

Botolf did not look back, yet I knew he was seeing us there and would see us for the rest of his life, standing on that bridge and not dead. Like Pinleg, long ago, dying under a shrieking pack of swords on a beach, allowing us to sail safely away – if we did not see his death happen, then perhaps he was fighting there still.

103

'That is that, then,' Finn said, when the big man and the boy and the goat had vanished. He peered over the side of the bridge, as if checking for trolls, then hauled out The Godi and inspected the edge.

'Your doom is not on you,' I said to him, though my bowels were water as I spoke it. 'You should go with him.'

Finn cocked one eyebrow, looking at me from under the tangle of his hair, which he refused to tie back – it revealed that he only had one good ear, the other mangled in a fight.

'Who knows what the Norns weave?' he replied with a shrug. 'This could be my day or not – but you cannot hold this bridge alone.'

He grinned.

'Bone, blood . . .' he began.

'. . . and steel,' I finished.

He took off his sheath and shed his cloak, for he did not want them tangling his legs in the fight. He checked the straps on his helmet and put it on, hunched his shoulders a few times to settle the rust-streaked ring-coat he wore, for it was not his own, then sat, leaning back against the stone of the bridge, while the water splashed and sang.

I envied him and hated him in equal measure; Finn, the man who feared nothing. How could he not tremble and find a great spear in his throat that made it impossible to swallow? Frothing madmen in skins would come after us and he had the wit to imagine what would happen. But all he did was open a lazy eye and wonder who Assur had been.

It was the inscription, weathered and lichen-streaked, on the grey stone by the bridge – *Helga, ThorgæiRs dottir, systir SygrøðaR auk þæiRa Gauts, hun let giæra bro þæssa auk ræisa stæin þænna æftir Assur bonda sinn. SaR waR wikinga warðr mæð Gæiti. Siþi sa manr is þusi kubl ub biruti.*

'Helga, daughter of Thorgar, sister of Sygrida and Gauts and others, she had this bridge made and this stone raised after Assur, her husband. He was an oathsworn guard with

104

Gauts. Let him practise *seidr*, the man who this monument destroys.'

'A good curse, that last – see, it is written as if in warning to anyone who desecrates the monument, but also that the monument itself will destroy. A good runesman, that.'

'A well-thought-of man, this Assur,' I noted, seeing the power of the runes there. Only his name survived, but this Assur would be remembered for as long as stone and we knew he had a loving wife and sisters, who thought enough of him to make runes for him.

'A sworn man, like us,' Finn noted and grinned. 'Good place to die, then, under a monument to a sword-brother.'

I was not so sure – a silly stone bridge leading to nowhere. Fitting, all the same, for the life we had led. Finn scowled when I blurted this out.

'Once it led to the best trees for miles around,' he pointed out. 'Good pine for ship planks and resin. No matter the place – we stand defending the back of a prince and what could be more fitting for the famed Oathsworn of Orm Bear Slayer than that? Besides, even now, it is a place of beauty.'

Once, I wanted to point out to him gloomily, it had been the famed Oathsworn of Einar the Black, save he was now dead – so where did it get him? But Finn had the right of it about the place and I raised my head to the sun and the joyous sea-swallow and the clouds like snow. Below, life bubbled in a stream, which started with the melting of snow in the mountains, flowing and merging out to the warm sea, where the sun sucked it up and dragged it back over the mountains to fall as snow again.

The Norns' loom of life; I drank it in, sucked it in like a parched man with water.

Then Finn slid to his feet and said: 'They are here.'

They came loping up the rough path to the bridge and stopped; two men, spear-armed and without armour or helmets, though they had shields and I saw knives at their belts. They stopped, wolf-wary at the sight of two ringmailed warriors, well-armed and shielded.

Randr's trackers, I was thinking, and Finn agreed, with a derisive spit in their direction. I would have added one of my own if I had had any water in my mouth.

They crouched a little, the two men, and one looked over his shoulder. In a moment, three other men appeared and I felt Finn shift a little, settling himself behind his shield; the bearcoats were here. Three only – I wondered where the others were.

One was tawny-haired, with a massive beard plaited in at least four braids, heavy with fat iron rings. Over stained clothing that had once been fine, he had a stiff-furred cloak – a boar skin it looked like to me – and he carried a sword with a deal of silver on it, but a blade notched as a dog's jaw.

A second wore the pelt of a wolf, the head and top jaw over his leather helmet, the paws tied on his chest, so that when he lowered his head and loped up, it raised the hairs on my arms, for he looked like a wolf on its hind legs – but the two swords he carried, one in either fist, were his true fangs.

The third wore ringmail and a bearcoat, had a dark beard cut short and his hair braided tight and coiled – a careful man, then, who did not want anything for an enemy to grab. He carried a long axe and I did not like the look of this one at all, knew him for their leader by the way the other two glanced at him, looking for instruction.

He stopped then and rested one hand casually on the top haft of the long axe, resting his chin lightly on the inch or so of wood above the bitt. It was as if he was meeting old friends.

'Stenvast, they call me,' he called out. 'I see you.'

'Ingimund,' bellowed the tawny one, slapping his sword on his shield. 'Son of Tosti, son of Ulfkel, son of Floki Hooknose of Oppland. I fear no man.'

Finn sighed, as if weary.

106

'I am Finn Bardisson of Skane,' he replied, just loud enough to carry the distance between them, 'and I can change that.'

'Randr had the right of it, then,' Stenvast said. 'Three men, a boy and a goat – milk for the bairn, was it?'

'Aye,' agreed Finn easily. 'He is a sharp one, that Randr. He will cut himself one day – or someone will. He should have sent more of you, all the same. This is not a little insulting.'

'Best if you stand aside,' Stenvast said, 'but I see you will not do that.'

'I am Guthrum,' the wolfskin said to me. 'You are Orm, leader of the Oathsworn. I see you and have come to take your life.'

'Three men guard my life,' I answered, hoping my voice did not sound hoarse with fear, 'Odin, Thor and Frey. None may harm me, unless he is greater than they.'

He made a sign against that old charm and I laughed at him, but my top lip stuck to my teeth and I hoped he had not seen that.

We stood and waited and that was part of what little plan we had; they were *beserker* and so a strange breed, having a power that made folk afraid, which fear fed the power. Some, like Pinleg, could summon it in an eyeblink and others needed time, needed to pace like trapped animals and growl and work up to it, believing they were sucking up the strength and speed of the skins they wore. It was said that others licked the strange slime off the backs of toads, or drank bog myrtle brews, but I had not seen any of that myself.

Let them do what they will, we had agreed, for every minute we held them at the bridge was a stride or two more for Botolf and Toki.

'I say the boar will get to it first,' Finn growled at me, without looking away from his man. 'An ounce of silver says he will go piggy-eyed and charge before any of the others.'

I should have taken his bet, for it was the wolf-skin who reached his power first, throwing back his head and howling

107

it out – then he came at me, all blinding hand-speed and fast shuffle, so that I fell back a little and heard the blades score down my shield and shriek off the boss. All I could manage in return was a half-hearted wave of my blade, then he was bounding back, crouching and boring in again.

Like a wolf, I thought. He attacks, low and fast, trying for the soft spots, trying to disable and bring me down like a bull elk . . . but you needed a pack for that. One was not enough and I cut him badly on his third attack and he bounced back, looked at his forearm and shook his head, grinning with foam-smoked lips. There was no blood and no pain – and no focus in his mad eyes when he came at me again.

There were clangs and grunts and yells from my left but I dared not look – but a flicker on my right made me half-turn my head; Stenvast slid past me and, for a moment, I thought he was going to take me from behind and felt a shriek of terror at the thought of two of them. Then Guthrum slithered in again, blades whirling and I had to block and cut and dance with him.

'Finn . . .'

It was a stupid, desperate call and might have been the death of Finn if he had been a lesser fighter – but he did not turn his head, simply cursed and yelled back that he was a little busy at the moment. Stenvast vanished over the bridge and up the trail.

Guthrum howled and leaped and bounced and I cut back at him when I could, but knew the best I could do was hang on and not let him kill me. My breath rasped and wheezed loud in my ears under the helmet; a blade scored the ring-mail sleeve of my sword-arm, another spanged off the hilt of my sword.

He bored in again, a high cut that I barely blocked with the shield; it sliced slivers off the edge and scored along under the rim of my helmet above one eye, so that I saw, for a glimmering moment, the pits in the blade-metal and the change

108

in colour where core met cutting edge. I stumbled back, felt the coping stones of the parapet on the backs of my thighs and twisted desperately to one side, not wanting to go over.

There was a great, soft roaring in my ears and the world went black, then red. I felt a blow on my belly, thought to myself, well, there is the soup-wound, no pain yet but here it comes, the death and the offering to Odin, make it quick, One-Eye . . .

Light flashed, red-smeared. A great, filthy finger poked me in the eye and Finn's face loomed, streaked with sweated rust from under his helmet. The hand came again, with a rag in it, and he wiped my face.

'Nasty wee cut, Bear Slayer. Lots of blood, but no real damage. Good scar, though, which will make women swoon and men back off.'

I struggled upright. Finn handed me the blood-soaked rag and sank down on one knee; one sleeve was bloody at the forearm and three men were dead behind him.

'What?' I said, shaking the red mist from my eyes and the inside of my head.

'Aye, all dead,' Finn answered cheerfully. 'That wolf man included, unless he can survive a long drop and a dookin in the river below us. Neat trick that, Bear Slayer – I thought he had you until you turned him off the bridge.'

I blinked and got up on shaky legs, looking round.

'I did not turn him,' I said. 'At least, I did not mean to. At least, I do not think I meant to.'

'Do not fash,' Finn replied, getting off his knee and wincing as he did so, holding his ribs.

'He got you one then,' I noted and Finn snorted.

'Not that bladder Ingimund – I killed him in a heartbeat, but then had to knock his legs out from under him, which is the way of these mouth-frothers. No, it was those goat-fucking spearmen who caused me trouble.'

I did not doubt it; two spearmen who knew the work,

109

acting together on a single enemy, was the worst thing a warrior could face – other than an archer in a place too high to reach.

'Aye,' Finn agreed, scowling. 'I took a poke which would have burst me if it had not been for that ringmail. Battle-luck that I was the same size as Red Njal – but, look you, I will have to pay him for it now.'

He stuck fingers in the shredded hole and waggled them; we grinned and then laughed and clasped each other.

Alive. Enemies dead and us alive – Odin had not claimed me yet. I had forgotten that he liked to play with his prey, like a cat does. I felt my legs shake then and had to sit; I did not know how Finn felt no fear and said so.

'I was too afraid even to run,' I added, half-ashamed, half-defiant, but Finn grinned and clapped me on the shoulder.

'There,' he grunted. 'Now you have the secret of it.'

Too afraid even to run. I looked at him, wondering if it was true, or just Finn being Finn. Then the memory of what had happened on the bridge flooded in, leaping me to my feet.

'Stenvast,' I said and Finn scowled.

'Aye.'

We hirpled off up the trail, leaving the bridge and the dead and the gathering crows. The cut started to bleed again, running with the sweat into my eye and stinging it, so that I had to shake it away in fat, scarlet drops.

It started to rain.

Toki told us what had happened, half-awed by it, half-shaking. We found him right at the top of the headland, where the trail ended on a scarp of rock, like the scalp of a bald man. Once, there had been trees here, but overcutting had taken them and the rain, without the bind of root, had washed away the top soil; what trees were left clung here like stray hairs, gnarled and stunted by the wind.

Beyond, the trail to safety led down into the last stands of thick pine on a slope too steep to cut trees, but it was clear that Botolf and Toki had just started down it when Stenvast came up on them. The way Toki told it, in his wide-eyed child's way, this giant had appeared, waving a big axe and bellowed at Botolf to stop.

Botolf had handed the bairn to Toki, telling the boy to be fast on his way down. The giant, said Toki, made to cut him off, but Botolf moved to block it.

'He only had a seax,' Toki said, then half-sobbed. 'It was not fair.'

'What happened then?' asked Finn, looking round; I knew he searched for bodies, but there were none, which was a puzzle. The rain fell, shroud-soft and silent and the slate-blue fjord was white-capped in the background. The bairn squalled in Toki's arms and I took it from him.

'I wanted to go,' Toki said with a sniff. 'But I could not move and the goat would not move and the wean was greetin' fit to burst . . .'

'What happened with Botolf and the giant?' I asked gently, settling down beside him. I pulled the hood of his *kjartan* up against the rain and the goat nuzzled, trying to get under his armpit, so that he took it and stroked its muzzle, absently.

'The giant told Botolf to stand aside and that his name was Stenvast and that he had come for the bairn. Botolf said his name was Botolf and he would not get the bairn and then the giant looked at Botolf a little, sideways, the way Thorgunna looks at Finn sometimes when he has done something un-expected, like fetch the milk unasked. Then he asked if this was the same Botolf, the cripple who had broken the back of Thorbrand Hrafnsson and Botolf said he had snapped the spine of a man, but that Stenvast must be mistaken, for he was no cripple and then the giant . . .'

He stopped, hiccuped and shivered and I patted him while

Finn prowled, scrubbing his beard furiously, which he did when things did not tally up for him.

'What then?'

Toki scrubbed his red eyes.

'The Giant Stenvast said to Botolf that he was a man who had come up leg short and blade short against a better one and that he had the brain of a beetle if he had the idea he was going to win this fight. But Botolf grinned and wagged one finger and said that was your first mistake, I have the thought-cage of a mouse, not a beetle, for a good friend said so.'

Toki stopped and looked at me, brow furrowed, face streaked with tears and snot.

'I did not understand this,' he went on and I told him it did not matter. He hiccuped.

'The giant did not understand it either,' he went on. 'He whirled his axe and cut and Botolf stopped it with his seax, but he could not leap out of the way and the giant cut the other way and it hit Botolf in the leg, his wooden one, so that it snapped and he pitched on the ground. The giant said now you are a cripple and Botolf got on one good leg and he turned and winked at me.'

My heart froze, for I knew that wink. Toki blinked and tears spilled.

'He said I was to watch out for wee Helga and when she was older, tell her he was sorry her da was not there, but a prince got in the way. Then he said to the giant, you have the bettering of me right enough, for you have a longer blade and a stronger leg, but there is something I am betting sure I can still do that you cannot.'

Toki stopped then and the tears spilled to the brim of his wide, bright little eyes.

'What was it that Botolf could do, then?' demanded Finn, still scouring everywhere with his eyes, looking for blood or bodies and finding none.

112

'Fly,' said Toki and I felt the world fall away from me in a dizzying rush, as if I had been carried up on wings myself. I heard a groan, which was me, found myself blinking at the ground.

'He leaped off his good leg,' Toki said, 'and took the giant in the belly with his head and they both went over the edge. I saw Botolf spread his arms. He had wings. Black ones.'

Toki stopped and bowed his head and the tears fell, soft as rain.

'I was sure he had wings.'

My belly had dropped away, leaving a black void filled with loss – I remembered Vuokko saying it: 'a loss, keenly felt'. I had thought, in my arrogance, that it would be me.

Finn, his eyes desperate, looked from me to Toki and then out over the headland to the fjord. He made a half move, no more than a step, towards it, as if to hurl himself over.

'Arse,' he said, in a voice thick with grief. 'Stupid, stupid, stupid great arse.'

'He will come back,' Toki said, but his voice was uncertain. 'He dreamed sometimes he had big black wings, like a raven he said and I saw them. I am sure I saw them.'

Finn peered out over the headland, as if to find Botolf hanging grimly by a fingernail a few feet down, which is how the skalds would have it. Instead, he shaded his eyes with a hand and then half-turned to me.

'A ship is leaving the fjord,' he called and I moved to his side; it was Ljot and his crew, rowing hard for the open water. That meant only Randr Sterki was left.

'Why is he leaving, I wonder?' Finn asked. I did not care, it was what he had on board that worried me – one Greek monk and my *fostri*.

'He will fly back,' said Toki, dragging us back to why we stood at the edge of the cliff in the first place, so that the loss crashed in like a huge wave. I handed him the squalling bairn and gathered the pair of them to me as the sun burst out like a wash of honey, turning the fine rain to a mist of gold.

We all saw it, then, the great arch of Bifrost, the rainbow bridge which only appears when a hero is crossing to Valholl.

So we knew Botolf was not flying back.

EIGHT

The way of it, as Randr Sterki told everyone, was like this: you throw your weapons in the dirt and Orm Bear Slayer does not get hurt. Of course, what he did not add were the words 'for the moment', but everyone knew that – knew, also, that throwing down their weapons would not be the end of the matter, only the beginning.

So, rightly, Red Njal and Hlenni shook their heads and shot glances of misery at me, tied up and held by a savage snarler whose face was a great stone cliff set against me.

'The wolf and the dog,' Red Njal shouted hoarsely, 'do not play together, as my granny used to say.'

True though it was, I had been hoping his granny had something useful on my predicament. Finn and Toki and me had surfaced from our grief on the bald mountain and it was clear to both Finn and me what had to be done next, so it it did not take much talk. He and Toki, goat and precious-as-gold bairn went one way, to safety. I turned back, for I could not leave the women and weans to bear the brunt of Randr Sterki and the remaining bearcoats alone – anyway, I had made my promise to Odin.

Perhaps it was he, then, who walked me past the fly-buzzing heaps on the bridge, back up the water-runnelled trail a way, round a bend, round another – and into the scores of heads, turning in amazement.

Like a nithing into the middle of Randr's men, where I was grabbed and trussed like a stupid sheep.

Beyond stood a line of ringmail pillars, shields up and ready – Rovald, Rorik Stari, Kaelbjorn Rog, Myrkjartan and Uddolf, with Abjorn in their middle, while Red Njal and Hlenni, with only shield and helmet, hovered behind them. Two bodies lay at their feet and a third a little way off, an arrow in one eye showing that Kuritsa had not boasted about his prowess idly.

'Heya,' I called out. 'The child is safe – Finn is with him and Toki. The bearcoats they sent are dead . . .'

The blow whirled stars into me and I half-fell; someone yelped out a scream and I found the legs of the man who had hit me, followed them upwards to the face, a braided twist of hate.

'Another peep, Bear Slayer,' the man growled, 'and I will fill your mouth with your own teeth.'

'Where is Botolf?'

I heard the half-scream and knew, without looking, that it was Ingrid. I never took my eyes from that face of hate.

'Crossing Bifrost,' I bellowed and he hit me. Even ready for it, I managed only to deflect the blow a little and felt my nose crunch, the pain shrieking in so that I found myself, blind with tears and snot and blood, open-mouthed and gasping for air on my hands and knees. The wailing that went up from the women at the news of Botolf was more painful still.

'Leave that, Tov,' snarled a voice. 'I want him undamaged.'

Gradually, I blinked back into the blurred world and the noise of keening women. Now all that remained was to stand like a decent sacrifice and die well, so I hauled myself into the pain, spitting out the blood that flowed down the back of my tortured nose. The cut on my forehead had opened, too, and I had to flick the blood out of my eyes, which caused my nose to throb.

116

'The Giant Ymir is gone, then? One less,' bellowed Randr Sterki, at his own men as much as mine, I realised.

'The cost was high,' growled a voice – one of the remaining *ulfhednar*, I realised. 'Stenvast now is dead.'

It came to me then that half his crew were too new for this, had not been on Svartey and were not driven by the revenge of the others. Half was half a chance . . .

'Still many of us left,' I called out hoarsely, the force of the words inside my head making my nose scream with new pain. Randr whirled and thrust a sword – my sword – under it.

'You have the right of it, for sure,' he said and viciously tapped upwards so that my head burst with the red light of pain and new tears sprang to blind me.

'Tell them to throw down their weapons.'

'So you can slaughter them?' I managed to cough out and shook my head, which was a painful mistake. 'No bargain for them there.'

'No bargain anywhere,' howled Tov, trying to fist the side of my head and missing. 'You took my woman and my wealth, you hole – I will rip off your balls . . .'

There was a slap of sound and Tov yelped; Randr lowered the sword, scowling.

'Think yourself lucky I used the flat,' he spat. 'I told you to leave off with all that.'

Tov glowered back, barely held by the last shreds of a leash of fear; soon, I thought, it will part and he will spring at Randr like a ship down a slipway. All it took was that last push . . .

'There is a bargain, all the same,' I yelled out, trying to ignore the stabs of pain each word lanced in my head. 'Moonlit-buried silver, blood-price enough to end this feud.'

That brought heads up; everyone there knew the Oathsworn tales, particularly the one about finding all the silver of the world. Even allowing for the lies of skalds, that left silver enough for any man's dreams.

'There is not enough silver to end this,' Randr bellowed

117

back, then heard the mutterings that ran through the wolf pack behind him and whirled to face it. In an eyeblink, he saw them fracture, into those who thought there was enough silver and those who wanted blood only.

'Stenvast is dead,' growled the same bearcoat who had spoken before. 'There is little left for us here and some of the Oathsworn's famed silver seems a fair price.'

'I will tell you where you can find it,' I offered, driving the wedges deeper. 'If you agree that it is finished and we each go our ways.'

'You bitch-licking turd!'

The shriek came from Tov and he launched himself at me, all screaming and clawed fingers, seeing his revenge tremble on the brink of failure.

It was reflex from Randr, no more than that, the savage, sudden burst of anger from a jarl with too many problems all at once and disobeyed once too often; my sword whicked past my own ear and cut Tov's throat out of him in a vomit of blood that splashed me as he thumped on the road.

There was a frozen moment of stillness, broken only by the sound of Tov's blood trickling to a whisper and sliding in tendrils through the rain-water.

Then uproar and yells and argument. Fights started and Randr bellowed and laid about him with the sword. I saw Abjorn and the others look at each other, sizing up the chance of taking the fight to the enemy while they were so fractured and, for a moment, was frantic they would do it.

In the end, the bearcoats, bristling and growling in a group tight as a fist, brought order where Randr failed – and faster than the Oathsworn could make their minds up; I heaved a sigh of relief.

There was a brief, muttered argument, then Randr stalked angrily at me, badger-beard trembling. Two men were with him, one of them a wild-bearded giant of a bearcoat who announced himself as Skeggi Ogmundsson.

'Tell where the hoard is,' Randr said, jerking his head at the men. 'They will go to it. If it is not there, you will die when the news is brought back.'

'If it is?' I countered, my voice thick with blood and pain, sounding strange and faraway in my ears.

He looked into my tear- and blood-streaked face and sneered.

'We will take it and sail away. You and your whelps may have your lives for now.'

The 'for now' did not escape me. I knew he would not agree to forever, so I nodded and told what I knew.

Standing there for the time it took the men to go all the way to it and back was a long, long day. No-one spoke much, nor gave up their positions, nor rested their arms save in shifts. Randr's men lit a couple of fires, but they had precious little fuel and they soon went out while, from the direction of the carts, I smelled smoke and soup, heard the grumbles from Randr's hungry men and would have smiled, save that the muscles would not work for the trembling in them.

Then it rained again and the shadows slid and darkened. Men broke out what cloaks they had, or pulled their clothing tighter round them as the cold gnawed them. My nose throbbed and I had to stand open-mouthed as a coal-eater, because I could not breathe through it.

Then, suddenly, one of the men was back, lurching up the trail. Men stood; excitement drove out hunger and cold and they waited.

'Well, Hallgeir?' demanded a cold-eyed Randr.

'Silver,' said the man, scarcely able to speak. 'Great piles of it – look.'

He thrust out a hand and men crowded to it; in the charcoal dim, the soft glow of coin and silver torc sucked the breath from them with a hiss. They looked at the handful, seeing it in dragon heaps.

'Well,' said Randr, straightening. 'Now we have the silver.'

119

'Untie me,' I said and he laughed, a crow-snarl laugh that let me know it was not about to happen.

'There is another matter . . .' Hallgeir said, trying to thrust himself through the crowd that wanted to see, to touch, part of the fabled hoard of the Oathsworn.

Scowling, Randr turned, impatient at being thwarted from killing me, which was his next act, I knew. Odin was about to get his sacrifice. Make it quick, AllFather, I was thinking, while part of me was gibbering and wanting to flee rather than stand there like an ox at a *blot*.

'Where is Skeggi Ogmundsson?' demanded a voice.

Before anyone could speak, something flew out of the shadows, whirling like a stone. It smacked wetly on the ground and rolled towards Randr, who stepped back from it; all hackles were up when they saw it was the bloody ruin of a wild-bearded head.

'There was a grey gull.'

The voice came out of the darkness, down the trail from where the head of Skeggi the bearcoat had come. A piping voice, not yet broken.

A boy's voice.

Heads turned and voices stilled; I saw Randr Sterki's face just then and it was white round eyes which flicked briefly with fear, like Hati the moon goddess hearing the howl of the devouring wolf which pursued her.

'That is the other matter,' Hallgeir sighed, wearied with resignation. His hand fell to his side and the silver in it dropped, unregarded by anyone, to the rain and the mud.

Crowbone stepped to where men could see him. He wore a ringmail coat made for his size and carried a spear in either hand, was bareheaded so that his coin-weighted braids swung, and he did not look like a mere boy. Alyosha, as ever, was at his shoulder and, behind, the creak and shink and breathing of ringmailed men, gleaming faint and grey in the twilight, was a cliff at Crowbone's back.

120

My legs sagged; now I knew why Ljot had been rowing so hard for the open water – to avoid Crowbone coming up. That Ljot had not informed Randr Sterki of it told a great deal.

'There was a grey gull,' Crowbone said, stepping closer and shouting less. 'A raiding gull, who lived high on a cliff, on the flight's edge. A king of gulls, whom men called Sterki – Strong – and who laughed at those same men and stole their fish and shat on them for fun.'

There were nervous sniggers, for they had all suffered that. Meaningful looks were shot at Randr Sterki, who shared the same name as this gull and at whom the tale was clearly aimed. I saw men sidle sideways, away from the rest; the last of the bearcoats, I was thinking.

'I need no talk of gulls,' Randr began, but Alyosha, only eyes showing in the helmet of his face, made a little gesture with a big axe that spoke loudly. The bearcoats stopped moving.

'Better listen,' I offered. 'Better one of little Prince Crowbone's sharp stories than the sharper alternative.'

Randr licked his lips; the alternative stared back at him from all the faint faces behind Crowbone's back. Yet here was the boy who had turned his hate on all Randr had held dear. Here were all his enemies, all those he wanted revenge on and he hovered on the sheer cliff of wanting to hurl himself at them. He also knew, in the little part of him not blinded with red mist, that he would fail and that leash held him a little yet.

'This king of gulls had an egg, a fine egg,' Crowbone said, after a pause during which the silence became painful as my nose. 'He knew it would hatch to be a fine son to replace him in his time and he left his fine gull-wife to sit on it while he flew away in search of food.

'When he returned, he found his gull-wife with her neck broken and the fine egg gone and he knew, at once, that it

121

was the blacksmith who had done it. He had shat on the smith many a time, stolen the fish right from the fingers of his children – and he knew the smith could climb any cliff.'

'Speak up,' yelled Ref from where the fire burned. 'I think I know this man.'

There were soft laughs, but they had no mirth in them and Crowbone went on, level and firm and slow, in his rill-clear voice.

'The gull-king knew at once that the blacksmith must have taken it. So he went to the man and demanded that he give the egg back. But the smith pretended it was just a shrieking bird flying round his head and waved the gull-king away.

'The gull-king was heartbroken and flew about looking for help. On the way he met a pig, and asked him to root up the carrots of the smith who had stolen his egg, to make him give it back.

'The pig grunted once or twice. "No, not I," he said and walked away.

'The gull-king then met a hunter, who bowed politely and asked why the mighty lord of gannets was so distressed. The bird said: "Will you shoot an arrow at the pig who would not root up the carrots of the smith and make him give me back my stolen egg?"

'But the hunter shook his head. "Why should I? Leave me out of this."

'The gull-king wept tears of pure bile and flew on till he met a rat, who also asked why he was in tears. The gull-king said: "Will you gnaw and cut the bowstring of the hunter who would not shoot the pig who would not root up the carrots of the smith and make him give back my egg?"

'The rat squeaked once, then twice, then promised to do it – but ran away instead.'

'Heya,' yelled a voice from the dark. 'I know that rat.'

'I wed her,' yelled another, which brought grim laughter

and calls for silence equally. Crowbone waited until the silence again became painful, then continued.

'Next, the gull-king met a cat and asked her to catch the rat who would not cut the bowstring of the hunter who would not shoot the pig who would not root up the carrots of the smith and force him to give back the egg he had stolen.

'The cat licked her whiskers once, then twice, then said she would rather mind her own business and ran off.

'The poor gull-king was beside himself with anger and grief. His wails attracted the attention of a passing dog, who asked what was bothering the mighty gannet. He asked: "Will you bite the cat who would not catch the rat who would not cut the bowstring of the hunter who would not shoot the pig who would not dig up the carrots of the smith who stole my egg?"

'The dog barked once. "No, not I," he said and ran away.

'The gull-king's wails grew louder and louder. An old man with a long white beard came that way and asked the screaming bird what the matter was. He said: "Grandfather, will you beat the dog who would not bite the cat who would not catch the rat who would not cut the bowstring of the hunter who would not shoot the pig who would not root up the carrots of the smith who has stolen my egg and will not give it back?"

'This greybeard shook his head at such foolishness and went his way. The gull-king, in desperation, next went to the fire for help and asked it to burn the white beard of the old man, but the fire would not do it. Next the gull-king went to the water and asked it to put out the fire which would not burn the beard of the old man who refused to beat the dog who would not bite the cat who would not catch the rat who would not cut the bowstring of the hunter who would not shoot the pig who would not root up the carrots of the smith who had stolen his egg and would not give it back.

'But the water just gurgled and refused to help Sterki the gull-king.

'Frantic and furious, the gull-king swooped down on an

ox, demanding that it stir up the water which would not put out the fire which refused to burn the beard of the old man who would not . . .

'But the ox did not even wait for the explanation; it lowered its massive head and went back to chewing.'

Crowbone paused, as if to take a longer breath and those who knew the way of it stirred, for here was the closure of the tale; no-one moved or spoke.

'Then,' said little Crowbone, 'the gull-king spotted a flea on the arse of the ox, who also asked what was troubling the mighty Sterki, king of gulls.

'The gull-king, who would never have even noticed such a creature before, sprang eagerly up and bowed. "O flea! I know you can help me. Will you bite the arse of the ox for not stirring up the water which would not put out the fire which would not burn the beard of the old man who would not beat the dog who would not bite the cat who would not catch the rat who would not cut the bowstring of the hunter who would not shoot the pig who would not root up the carrots of the smith who stole my egg and will not give it back?"'

At which point there were admiring noises about Crowbone's feat of memory, from those who did not realise he was not the boy he appeared.

'The flea,' said Crowbone, ignoring them, 'thought about it for a moment, then said: "Why not? Here I go." And he crawled right up the arse of the ox and bit, which made the beast dash into the pool of water and stir it up. The water splashed and began to put out the fire, which went mad and burned the white beard of the old man, who beat the dog, who ran after the cat and bit her. The cat caught the rat, who had to gnaw the string of the hunter's bow before she was freed. The hunter tied on a new one and shot an arrow at the pig, who went and rooted up the carrots of the smith.

'"Aha, aha!" shrieked the gull-king in triumph and the

smith, looking ruefully at the remains of his carrot patch, shrugged and said: "You have succeeded, right enough, Sterki."

'The gull-king swooped and laughed. "Then hand back my egg," he screamed. The smith blinked once and blinked twice.

'"Is that what this is all about?" he asked and shook his head. "I ate that egg for breakfast days ago."'

There was silence as the story echoed to a close. Men shifted, not liking the ending much.

'Take the silver,' Crowbone said softly. 'Your egg is gone, Randr Sterki, and all your long revenge will not bring it back.'

There was silence, broken only by the hissing wind and the sibilance of shifting feet.

'I should have killed you when I caught you running off,' Randr said bitterly and Crowbone stepped closer, a spear in each hand and his voice sharper than either of them.

'Instead,' he said, his voice suddenly deeper than before, 'you gave me to Klerkon's woman, to beat and chain like a dog outside the privy. Instead, you had your woman and boy shave me with an edgeless seax. You let Kveldulf put his wean in my ma's belly and then kick the life out of both of them when it suited him. And laughed.'

Randr blinked and shook his head, as if trying to drive that away like an irrelevant fly – but it would not quit him and he had no answer to it. Slowly, he nodded once, then twice. Behind him, men shifted and muttered and then a bearcoat threw back his head, howled and lurched at Crowbone. The gods alone know why, for there was no profit or sense in it, but those skin-wearing droolers seldom fight for either, though fighting is all they know.

It was like watching a cliff fall on a mouse – yet Crowbone did not even flinch, merely looked up, half-spun and threw with both hands. Two spears smacked the man, one in his chest, the other in his right thigh and he went pitching forward on his nose. Alyosha stepped forward smartly and axed his

125

throat open, knowing a pelt-wearer was not dead until he was really dead.

Someone – from Randr's own men – gave an admiring 'heya' even as the victim curled and writhed round the spears, like a hooked worm; the last trio of bearcoats, trembling on the brink of summoning power, looked at each other – and all their skin-magic soaked away, so that they seemed to wrinkle and sag like empty *skyr*-bags.

'Courage is not hacksilver, to be shut always in a purse,' Red Njal growled, seeing this. 'It needs to be taken out and shown the sun, as my granny used to say.'

'Finish this,' Hlenni called out, but I saw Crowbone's warning eye and held up a stopping hand.

'Enough has been done, one to the other,' I said. 'Take the silver you have dug up and let that be blood-price for any loss. Let this be an end.'

Randr's face was smeared with twisted hate, yet he backed away then, into the maw of his men, hauling Hallgeir with him; one by one at first, then in groups, they sidled round the half-hidden men of Crowbone and slithered into the shadows, heading for my silver and safety.

Alyosha let out his breath with a sharp sound as the last one vanished and my own men rushed forward to free me.

'Good throwing,' Alyosha declared, but Crowbone frowned, looking at the dying man with disdain.

'Too weak in the left hand,' he answered. 'Both spears were meant to go in his chest.'

In later life, Crowbone perfected throwing spears with both hands at the same time and it served him well, but this first attempt was timely enough for me, I thought, as eager hands untied me. I managed to get that out to him before Thorgunna's embrace drove the air from me entirely.

Crowbone's scowl vanished.

'Aye, it was timely at that,' he answered brightly, as if realising it for the first time.

'You should have finished Randr Sterki,' Hlenni pointed out and, even washed by the safe and loving press of friends and those who held me dear, I could feel Randr's hate and wondered why the boy had not pressed the fight.

'He still has Sigurd's nose,' I said to him.

'Your sword also,' he replied, then lost the grin and sighed. 'I would have, but . . .'

Right there and then I heard the crack as his voice broke to manhood. He cleared his throat and looked bewildered for a moment or two, then spoke on, his voice breaking on every second or third word, to his annoyance.

'I came short-handed to the feast. Alyosha was concerned.' Then he motioned, so that a mere ten men stepped forward from the shadows behind him. If Randr had decided to fight, Crowbone and his men would almost certainly have gone under. Alyosha peeled off his gilded, face-mailed helmet, puffing out sweat-sheened cheeks and grinning from behind a damp beard.

'We left too many men with *Short Serpent*,' he declared and shot Crowbone a sharp, sideways look that made it clear whose fault that had been; the boy loved his ship too much. Crowbone ignored him and held out his small fist; I clasped him, wrist to wrist and heard his voice, rising and falling like a ship on a bad sea.

'I will take back Sigurd's nose one day, from off the stump of Randr Sterki's neck,' he said, trying to growl and only half succeeding. 'But all is done with for now.'

The grin returned, making it clear who I had to thank for it. Somehow, I knew there would be a price to pay for that – if Odin let me live that long.

'Will he be done with this now that he has your silver?' Red Njal asked and I remembered Randr's hate-mask of a face. My look told him all he needed to know.

Still, we were free of danger for now, so that people clapped each other on the shoulder, or hugged one another, smiling and the children, caught up in the moment, laughed and danced. But the joy of it was soured by the weeping for Botolf – and, later, the great red glow which I knew was Hestreng hall burning, a last spiteful act that told me Randr had not finished yet with his hate.

'That and your silver loss,' Crowbone mused, watching the red glow, 'must be a sore dunt – but I saw the state *Dragon Wings* was in and it comes to me that those burned strakes will maybe leak him all the way to the bottom of the Baltic, *weregild* silver and all.'

I said nothing. The one child not laughing was red-faced, flame-haired Helga Hiti, wailing because her mother wailed for Botolf – yet it was still birdsong to me, as was every other voice I heard, for they were alive and safe and I said as much, so that the new man that was Crowbone nodded soberly.

'Fitting, then, for that old tale,' he said and, through the pain of Thorgunna spooning the blood clots from my tortured nose, I managed to tell him that I owed him for the telling of it, which made him grin. The grin broadened as Thorgunna and her sister told me to be still and to weesht and stop behaving like a bairn while they tortured my neb further.

Through the tears I saw Crowbone, too pleased to take the news of it blandly, as an older prince would do. He managed to stammer out that nothing was owed between friends and I am sure he meant it, seeing the baleful red eye turning Hestreng to ashes and Randr Sterki running off with my wealth.

Well, that was one moonlit burial and, though it was the largest amount of Atil's cursed silver, it was not the only hoard of it; only a careless man piles all his wealth in one hole. I kept my teeth shut on that matter around Crowbone, all the same, for it is a doubly-careless man who boasts of such cleverness.

Anyway, if I had opened my mouth at all, only foul curses would have come from it at what Thorgunna and her sister were doing to my nose, which would have left me with cold oatmeal and a turned back for weeks. With everything else, that would have been a mountain weight on my shoulders.

The air was a sharp breath of ash and snow around Hestreng hall on the day we trundled back to it. A ribcage of wet, black timbers it was, collapsed on itself like a dead beast and a light rain sifting down like tears to turn the ground round it to black mud.

'I am sorry for it,' said the queen, coming up behind Thorgunna and Aoife and me as we stood, stilled by the loss, while the others poked about and cried out when they recognised the remains of something they had once known well.

'Aye,' agreed Crowbone, though too young to make his pretended sombre look work. He had seen too much of this – done a deal of this himself – up and down the Baltic to be truly moved by a tragedy that was not his to bear. It came to me then that I had done the same, in my time.

'I shall have men and timber sent,' the queen said, 'when I am home.'

I remembered Finn telling Botolf about what a king such as Eirik would do for those who saved his little prince and hoped the big man heard this now in Odin's hall, enough to nod and smile at it all, standing proud and tall on two good legs.

Thorgunna and Thordis embraced, then bustled off to choke their tears in ordering folk about, to set up what shelters and cooking fires we could; Ingrid, red-eyed, chivvied Helga away from the ruins of Hestreng hall, too late to prevent black streaking her dress and face.

'At least the bairns are safe,' Red Njal offered, trying to be bright. 'And if you need silver . . . well, I have most of my share in a secret hole. Hlenni Brimill, too.'

I felt the warmth of them then, felt the other side of that cold Oath we had sworn when we had followed the prow beast and owned no more than could be safely stowed in a sea-chest. I told him I still had my own secret hole, at which he nodded as if he had known it all along. Then he clapped me on the shoulder and went off to help sort matters out; the old yard of Hestreng rang with noise and bustle, just as if it was not burned.

Yet not all the bairns were safe. Somewhere, out on the slow-heaving grey-green water of the whale road, Jarl Brand's son shivered and hoped.

NINE

It was an island humped like Onund's shoulder, where green slopes ran down to meet sand, then water; on a day of bright sunshine and birdsong it would have been a pretty place to be, but on this day, with what we had come for and the rain in our faces, it had no charm.

On the shore were buildings, mean as sties most of them, but others large and prosperous-looking, with carved wooden doorways and thatched roofs. In the quiet curve of this cluster of houses lay a series of wharves, like spokes on a half-wheel, where ships were tied up; more vessels were run up on the beach not far away and most were the solid, heavy riverboats the Slavs call *strugs*, carved from a single tree. The others were fat trading *knarrer*, but the only raiding ship other than the one I stood on was hauled up for careening; I knew it at once as Ljot's ship.

'Look at them run,' laughed Ospak, pointing and a few others joined in, harsh with the excitement of it all. They were all the newer crew, who had never been anywhere; the old hands hardly looked up.

There was a clanging noise from the solid fortress, a square of fat timber piles, their sharpened points softened by age and moss, with square towers at each corner and flanking the gate. I had taken the prow beasts off, but the settlement swarmed like an anthill and the alarm was sounding in the fortress which glowered over it.

'Send a man to the prow,' I said to Crowbone. 'Unarmed and without byrnie. Let him stand there with his arms out and weapon-free, to show we mean no harm.'

He acknowledged it with a small nod and passed it on to Alyosha, who cut a man from the pack and sent him. So far, so good – but having Crowbone and his crew as Oathsworn was like walking on the edge of a seax; I would not have done it had it not been for Jarl Brand and Koll.

Jarl Brand had been the only one not at the feast King Eirik gave for the safe return of his queen and his son. As Finn had said, once we had done with our greetings, that was not because Brand was lacking the strength or grit for it, but just because he had a wounded face that would put folk off their eating.

Not that everyone at the feast, where King Eirik presented his son, had an appetite; too many of the guests were strange company for that.

There were Christ priests, a gaggle of them from the West Franks and the Saxlanders of Hammaburg, all gabbling about baptisms and chrism-loosenings while glaring at each other and trying to make sure they had no horse meat in their bowls.

Then there was Haakon of Hladir, ruler of Norway which he had from the hand of Denmark's King Harald Bluetooth and which hand he was now trying to bite. Bluetooth, not quite a broken-fanged dog, was snarling back and so Haakon was seated at King Eirik's left, looking for help and smiling politely through the teeth he had to grit every time he heard Crowbone called 'Prince of Norway'.

Eirik himself, though crowned king of the Svears and Geats, still had troubles up and down his lands and Bluetooth had designs on them that he was not about to give up, so any enemy of Bluetooth was a friend of King Eirik and Haakon had been handy for the fight against Styrbjorn.

Then, astoundingly perched in the guest bench, was Svein, Bluetooth's son, who had also helped against Styrbjorn, though he was scarce older than that cursed youth. Young enough, in fact, not have fleeced up the chin-hair that would give him his famed by-name in later life – Forkbeard – he was here to annoy his da, for he wanted more say in Danish matters and Bluetooth had no liking to let him.

Then there was Crowbone, fresh broken to manhood and following Queen Sigrith with his dog-eyes. For her part, she was dressed in a blue so dark it was almost black, trimmed with white wolf and dripping with amber and silver, every inch the queen she wanted to appear, pleased with herself for presenting a son to her king, rich and ripe with life because she and the boy had survived the affair. Better still, of course, was her man's acceptance of little Olaf, for he had not been near the birth himself as was proper and that was a matter doubled when kings were involved.

So she knew the effect she had on the new man that was Crowbone and revelled in the power of it while spurning him, as you would a little boy, with witty flytings wherever possible.

Some trader had brought a talking-bird all the way from Serkland, a green affair with a crown of blood and Haakon had bought it for show. It sat, hunched, with its feathers falling out and miserable from the cold and dark of the north as well as the lack of proper food – the thrall weans kept trying to feed it flakes of fish, as if it was a gull.

'It speaks,' Svein called, trying to make himself a presence, 'in that tongue they use in Serkland.'

Then he turned to me, a twisted little smile smeared on his face and called out the length of the table: 'Orm Bear Slayer, you speak some of that. What does it say?'

It gave the proper response to a greeting in the Mussulmann tongue, as well as phrases such as 'God is great' and 'There

133

is no god but Allah and Muhammad is his prophet' and so people oohed and aahed when it seemed that I chatted amiably to the bird. My standing, fame-rich already, was confirmed and it was clear from his scowl that Svein had not meant that to happen. Nor, it seemed, was Haakon any happier and he did not like me to begin with because of my closeness with young Crowbone. I could not blame him for that – he was king in Norway and sitting a few careful benches down from a boy claiming to be the true prince of that land.

'Perhaps the Bear Slayer can use this gift to command the return of his *fostri,* Koll Brandsson,' he said nastily and smiled a sharp-toothed grin. I marked it, pretended disinterest and continued to tell the thralls charged with caring for the bird that it needed berries and nuts, should be kept out of the cold and put in the sun, when it actually shone.

Then, eventually, I turned into his smile and ignored it, looking at King Eirik instead.

'A marvellous bird,' I told him. 'Seldom seen in these parts and so doubly strange that Jarl Haakon here has come into possession of it.'

'Strange?' Eirik asked.

'Aye,' I mused. 'I know Gunnhild is old and fled from Norway – but her *seidr* is still strong enough.'

The smile died on Haakon's face; panic and fear chased over it like cat and dog and he looked wildly from me to the bird and back again. He had ousted Gunnhild, and the last of Bloodaxe's sons, from Norway five years ago – they had fled to Orkney and were causing trouble there – but he feared the witch Mother of Kings still. She was reputed to be able to take the shape of any bird and fly through the Other, far and wide, to perch and listen to plots and plans.

'Such *seidr,*' I added, lightly vicious as the kiss of a fang, 'has no effect on me.'

Which, because they had heard all the skald tales of the witches I had supposedly killed and the scaled trolls and all the rest, was a boast accepted easily by the company and they laughed, though shakily.

As a result King Eirik had the bird removed from the feasting hall and Haakon watched it all the way out of the room; later, I heard he had it thrown to his deerhounds and felt sorry for that, even though I knew the bird would have died soon anyway.

One other watched that bird leave the room. I had forgotten that Crowbone had developed his way with birds because of Gunnhild's reputation; she, of course, had hunted the young Crowbone after killing his father to get the throne Haakon now sat on. It was that which prompted Crowbone to do what he did next, I am sure of it, for he always acted on the signs birds offered up to him and there was no more singular bird than that blood-headed talking one from Serkland.

'If you go after Koll Brandsson,' he whispered to me, ashen-faced, 'I will take your Odin Oath and follow you.'

I blinked at that; the idea of Crowbone as one of the Oathsworn was one I did not wish to think about at all for the dangers in it – but there was no easy way to refuse it, especially when it became clear that I needed him.

That was after the feasting was done and the real business commenced. King Eirik promised thralls and timber and men who knew how to build, as well as fat ships to transport all of this and supplies enough to see Hestreng through the lean time of summer to the first harvest.

'I cannot spare fighting men,' he added, frowning, 'nor raiding ships, for I am battle-light in both and my right arm is felled for now.'

Eye to eye and alone in his closed room in the prow of the hall, he leaned closer, blood-dyed by torch glow. His neat-trimmed beard was faded red-gold and under the hat he wore for vanity he was bald save for a fringe round his ears. His feasting horn of mead was elsewhere; now he toyed with a blue glass goblet of wine and had offered me some, but I stuck with an iron-banded horn of nutty ale. Clear heads are best when dealing with kings – besides, my head hurt enough from the scar on my forehead and my blood-clotted nose to add wine fumes to it.

'The Greek monk, Leo, has taken Koll as hostage and sailed with Ljot Tokeson,' he said, pinching salt on bread to rid himself of the cloy of mead in his mouth. 'Ljot is brother to Pallig Tokeson and Styrbjorn is with them both.'

Pallig, Lord of Joms. King Eirik looked at me with rheumy eyes and saw I knew the name, then waved a hand and sighed.

'I know, I know – Styrbjorn is a young fool and will need to be punished – but he is my nephew and still has uses. I want him returned to me.'

I did not think Styrbjorn would want to return until he was sure of mercy rather than wrath and I said so.

'Just so,' Eirik said, looking at me. 'So when you go to get your *fostri*, you may like to carry my mercy with you and let him know of it.'

'Jarl Brand, lord?' I asked, as bland and polite as I could make it. King Eirik stroked the neat trim of his beard and scowled.

'It will sit hard with him, but he has placed his hands in mine and I will pay any blood-price for his losses at the hand of Styrbjorn, who is kin, after all.'

So there it was – King Eirik wanted Styrbjorn around, for his son was a bairn and bairns are fragile wee things; Styrbjorn was the only other heir he had. It came to me that Brand might not suffer it as lightly as King Eirik thought – what was the blood-price for a dead wife and the hostaged son of someone as powerful as Jarl Brand? Not enough if it was my wife and bairn.

He saw something of that in my face and, to my surprise, laid a friendly hand on the length of my forearm.

'You are a good man, Orm Bear Slayer,' he said slowly, as if picking his words from a chest of coins and wanting all the whole ones. 'You have silver-luck and fame-luck and men follow you for it, for all that your birthing was awkward. You have served me well these past years.'

He paused and I said nothing, though it smacked me like a blow, the fact that a king thought my birthing awkward; if he did, then others thought the same.

The fact of it is that, in the north, knowing who fathered a child to an unmarried woman was important enough to have its own law. According to it, the old Bogarthing Law, a woman was asked the father's name at the point of labour and, if she stayed silent, the child was considered a thrall from birth. If she named a man, he became 'half-father' and had responsibilities to the child.

My mother, of course, had married Rurik while filled full with me and he had claimed fatherhood. The truth was that another, Gunnar Raudi, had been the seed of me and was thought dead. By the time he returned, I was born and my mother dead of the strain of it – so I had avoided thralldom by the merest whisper of Rurik's breath. All of which made the awkward matter the king spoke of.

He looked at me and took a breath; I braced for more daggers to come.

'I would not do you offence,' he went on, 'but for those reasons and some others you will never be more than a little jarl and, for all your women and weans and sheep and horses, never a landsman farmer.'

He stopped, studying me carefully to see my reaction and the air in the room became as still and thick as a curtain. I kept my face bland and my hands on the table where he could see them; the truth was that he had the right of it, for sure, and though the blood was in my face, I could not do anything other than admit it by a silence like the stillness of rock.

'You follow the prow beast,' Eirik went on, 'taking the Aesir with you out onto the whale road. Here on the land . . .'

He paused again and waved his glass to encompass his

kingdom, slopping wine on his knuckles. 'Here on the land, matters are differently done. Like the Christ priests at my table.'

'I saw them,' I gritted out.

The king nodded, sucked wine from his hand and sighed.

'They come from the Franks and Otto's Saxlanders and snarl at each other,' he said. 'Do you know why, Jarl Orm?'

'They like to argue about their Tortured God,' I answered and he blinked and smiled gently.

'Aye, just so – and not so. What think you of the Christ Jesus?'

I gave him the answer I gave all who asked me that – I have never met the man. Then I added that I would say nothing more, for it was not a good thing to malign the Tortured God in a place thick with his priests and Eirik shifted a little on his bench at that.

'They come and snarl at each other and smile at me because there is more to this White Christ matter than worship,' he said eventually, then leaned forward a little, as if imparting some great secret.

'They are always the first men to come. What follows is a binding among kings. Alliances, wealth and power,' he hissed. 'There are Frank priests and Saxland priests and even ones from the Englisc, all looking to bring their White Christ to my lands rather than suffer someone else to bring the White Christ here. They offer much in return for a dip in water. That is kingship.'

'They offer a white underkirtle,' I answered flatly, 'or so I had heard.'

Eirik's smile was lopsided and wry. 'Kings do a little better – though sometimes I am thinking the prizes glitter well, but are not worth all the kneeling and praying they say has to go with it.'

'So much the better for kicking them all out and offering a sacrifice to Odin for having the clever to do it,' I answered stubbornly, more sharply than I had intended, but Eirik simply squeezed my forearm and shook his head sorrowfully.

'Out on the whale road that may seem clear,' he answered and, in that moment I saw he envied the thought of that and realised the true burden of the crown he wore.

'So – you have Christ priests looking to prise you away from the Aesir,' I growled, irritated with the maudlin king, more so because he was right in what he said. 'What has this to do with the matter of Styrbjorn?'

King Eirik blinked and drank some wine.

'You are a clever man,' he said. 'You know it was this Leo who brought the silver that let Styrbjorn buy Pallig, Ljot and their bearcoats. You have yet to ask yourself the why of it.'

I blinked, for he had it right and I felt the blood flush to my cheeks at this, as sure a sign of being a little jarl as he had claimed. King Eirik nodded.

'All the Christ priests here are from the West,' he said. 'No Greek ones, the ones who cross their chests the opposite way. Vladimir of Novgorod has no Greek ones at his court either, which makes us friends. His brothers do, which makes them my enemies.'

I saw it then, in a sudden churn of belly and mind. Vladimir of Novgorod, facing off against his brothers Oleg and Jaropolk, was for the old gods of the Slavs, though he tolerated Christ worshippers for his grandmother had been one. His brothers had priests of the Greek type swarming all over them, but Vladimir did not care for those monks much.

This was the Great City at work. Vladimir stood in the way of their turning all the Rus to the Greek Christ – and so to the will of Constantinople – so it would try to oust him using his brothers. King Eirik, of course, had sent warriors to help Vladimir, so the Great City would prefer it if that changed. Enter Styrbjorn.

He saw I had worked it out at last and sighed.

'I am thinking Styrbjorn's failure makes him useless to

them now. They will try another way. I may even have to accept that monk Leo back at my court, offering me rich gifts to turn my eyes away from Vladimir. Or a secret death in my wine or food. What they cannot force they will try to buy or kill.'

I felt pity for him then, this man who would be king, who had to bend and twist himself into unnatural shapes to make his arse fit the seat of it. I drank to take the taste away, but that only made it worse.

'Go to Pallig Tokeson, where the monk Leo has fled,' Eirik said. 'If Pallig sees there is no trade to be had other than my friendship for the boy's return, he will give your *fostri* back,' King Eirik said. 'If he has any clever in him at all.'

There was much said about Pallig Tokeson but excessive clever was not part of it. He controlled Joms, which the Saxlanders called Jumne and the Wends, Wolin. There were other names for it, but the skalds – gold-fed by Pallig, no doubt – sang silly tales of the warriors of Joms, who never took a step back in battle and who all lived in a great fortress, where no women were allowed. For all that his men were no Northmen at all, but Wends, he had enough of them to be a dangerous man – and still had some bearcoats, which I mentioned.

'Styrbjorn himself will help,' King Eirik declared, 'for he will want me to know how sorry he is for all that has been done and so will put himself at some risk to make Pallig see sense.'

The fact that I was putting myself at risk, of course, was neither here nor there, it seemed. I still did not think Brand would be so amiable about matters and was surer still after Finn and I went to see him, later in the night.

Brand had taken an arrow in the face, to the right of his nose and just below the eye. It had been a hunting arrow, which was wound-luck for him, for the shaft sprang free and left the head, which was not barbed. Normally, a hunter would cut the valuable arrowhead out of the animal and use it again

– but now it was driven six inches deep through the cheek and into the back of Jarl Brand's skull.

Ofegh, they called Jarl Brand. It was a good by-name for him and meant 'one whose doom is not upon him', though a man with four eyes would be hard put to see that in the face that turned to Finn and me. His main wife, Koll's mother, was dead and his own life was down to a single strand of Norn-weave, it seemed to me.

In the light of a fat, guttering tallow his bone-white hair was lank and stuck to his yellowed face by sweat, but his eyes were still hot and fierce and his wrist-clasp strong. He had what seemed to be a tree growing from his face, though it turned out to be thin, stripped withies of elder, dried and stitched into silk marked with suitable runes, though they were not our own sort.

This was to widen the wound down to where the arrow-head was and, once the healer – a Khazar Jew – was certain it was deep enough, he would insert some narrow-point smithing tongs and take the thing out. Until then, there was only the great, raw-wet lipless mouth of the widened wound and endless agony, which had carved itself on Brand's face, shaved clean for the first time I had known him.

'Bad business,' Brand said in a voice mushed with pain; the withies waggled as he spoke and the Khazar fussed with cleaning probes made from flax soaked in barley, honey and what looked like the pine resin tar we used on fresh ship planks. It stank.

'Aye – it looks a sore one, right enough,' I answered, which seemed inadequate when I could see Brand's back teeth and his tongue waggle as he spoke. He waved one hand as if chasing a fly.

'My son,' he said. 'That priest.'

'I will get him back,' I answered and he closed his eyes briefly, which was a nod, I worked out, the real thing being too painful for him. So was talking, but he did it.

'The king will help. Styrbjorn.'

He meant he was owed by the king for what Styrbjorn had done. I told him what the king had said about him helping to free Koll and being brought back as if nothing had happened at all.

Jarl Brand blinked his blink.

'Kingship,' he mushed, which was answer enough, I now knew.

Men appeared suddenly, quiet and shuffling, bareheaded and twisting their hands – Rovald, Rorik Stari, Kaelbjorn Rog, Myrkjartan and Uddolf, with Abjorn at their head.

'Nithings,' Jarl Brand hissed and would have said a lot more if it had not been agony for him to speak at all. Instead, he waved a hand and sent them off, droop-headed and shamed, dismissed from his service – and into mine, of course.

'Take care of them,' he growled at me and twisted his face in what tried to be a smile, but failed for the pain of it. Then he flapped his hand again and a man appeared holding a sheathed sword. Brand took it and handed it to me.

'I hear,' he said, pain gritting his teeth between the words, 'Randr Sterki took yours. Take this. Get your *fostri* back.'

Then he looked at me, pale eyes lambent with meaning.

'Use the blade well, as I would,' he forced out and gripped my hand like a raven's claw.

It was his own blade and so a rich offering doubled. The hilt was worked with carved antler horn and silver, the sheath whorled and snaked with gripping beasts in fine leather. The gift-price of it did not go by me – I knew he wanted me to bury it in Styrbjorn – nor did his phrase: 'Get your *fostri* back.'

Not his son. My *fostri*. My responsibility, my shame for losing him and my shame doubled if I did not get him back unharmed. I had known that and knew also that Brand was just cutting the runes of it clearly, like a prudent father, so I allowed no offence, bowed politely, took the sword and left,

142

thinking to myself that it did not matter, that nothing mattered to a man as wyrded with doom as myself.

I hoped Odin might hold off enough to let me save Koll, all the same – and kill Styrbjorn, if possible. I brooded on that, sitting under the prow beast as it carved across the slate-water to the mouth of the Odra, saying nothing much and aware that folk were looking at me. I remembered, years before, we had all looked at the Oathsworn's old leader Einar the Black in much the same way, when we were sure his doom was on him and so on all of us, too.

I spoke with Finn on it all, partly because I had to charge him with some of the task if Odin decided to take his sacrifice sooner rather than later. I wanted to mark it out clearly for him to follow – but this was Finn.

'Get the boy back. Kill Styrbjorn. I need no tally stick for that,' he growled.

I sighed. 'Get the boy back, but kill Styrbjorn carefully. Remember – Jarl Brand wants him dead. King Eirik wants him alive. Both have power over the ones we leave behind us.'

Finn scrubbed his beard with frustration, but he nodded, blinking furiously. I spent the rest of the time trying not to pick the itching scar on my forehead, blow bloody snot out of my aching nose and brood on how Finn, a man who thought a quiet, subtle killing was not screaming a warcry and leaving your named sword in the corpse, would carry off the death of Styrbjorn if it fell to him. Or, for that matter, how I would.

Heading into the maw of Pallig Tokeson and his Jomsvikings did not help. The Joms *borg* was feted far and wide as a powerful fortress of sworn brothers, the best fighting men around, but that was all skald-puffed mummery; the reality was a moss-pointed square of timbers with a clanging alarm and a mad scramble of ragged-arsed Wends.

We backed water beyond long arrow range and waited,

143

me standing in the beastless prow with my arms held out, until I was sure they had seen us and the peace-signs we made. Then I had the ship rowed beyond the main wharves, where Hoskuld, called Trollaskegg – Trollbeard – brought us to the beach with almost as neat a movement as Gizur or Hauk might have done.

The mar on it was a hard bang against the shingle, but Crowbone beamed, for the ship was *Short Serpent* and most of the sailing crew was his. They had all sworn the Oath, of course, but I knew the braiding of us together was a loose affair so far.

'Is it not the finest ship afloat?' he yelled, bright with the excitement of it all and his men, used to his ways, laughed with him.

Onund Hnufa snorted.

'You do not think so, Onund Hnufa?' demanded Crowbone sharply – then took an involuntary step backwards as the great bear-bulk of the shipwright loomed over him, the hump on his back like a mountain. Onund did not have to use the word 'boy', for his whole body and voice did that for him.

'You had this ship from Vladimir in Novgorod,' he rumbled and Crowbone managed to squeak that he had the right of it. Onund grunted. Men paused in spilling over the side, armed and ready.

'It was not a question,' he went on. 'It is an old ship, left there long ago, when Novgorod was more known as Holmgard – in my grandfather's day, I am thinking. Maybe the crew sold it, for it was damaged and it is certain Slavs repaired it – look there. The original ribs of it are good oak, but several have been replaced and the oak is poor quality and cut too thick. Where those have been placed makes the ship less of a snake in the water, too stiff, like a wounded old bull.'

We looked; Crowbone gawped.

'Planks were also replaced – see there?' Onund growled. 'The original rivet holes were burned all the same size – good

144

work, from folk who knew and had pride in their skill – and so the rivets fit tight. The new ones were badly done and some of the holes are too big, so they leak. You need to pine resin it fresh, inside and out. Not oak resin, which will crack when the ship moves. You need to replace the oar-strap – it is loose and the steer-oar does not answer quick enough to the helmsman's hand. That's why we dunted the beach so hard.'

He paused. No-one spoke, but Hoskuld was nodding.

'Anything else?' Crowbone demanded bitterly, recovering himself.

'Teach your crew and your helmsman better,' Onund said and there were growls at that from the men formed up on the shingle, so he rounded on them like some angered boar and they all shrank back a little.

'Who is it that keeps dragging the boat out of the water on rocks and gravel? The keel is no doubt scarred and there is no avoiding that – but any sailor with the least clever in him knows to lift the steer-oar off. It is worn nubbed and splintered from such dragging – my teeth look better.'

And he snarled blackly at them to prove the point, while Abjorn and Uddolf and the others who had sailed *Black Eagle* nodded agreement, which did not endear them to the men of *Short Serpent*. With the few old Oathsworn, there were three crews here, not one; that would have to change, I was thinking.

There was shamefaced silence, then Crowbone opened his mouth to speak – and I used the moment. I may not have had what King Eirik thought of as jarl-greatness in me, but I had enough to know the timing of such a thing.

'While we are talking with Pallig here,' I said to Onund, 'replace the oar-strap. The rest will have to wait until we can beach her and sort it out – at which time the crew, I am thinking, will be carrying the steer-oar as if it was their own bairn.'

There were wry chuckles at that and Crowbone, furious at

145

being interrupted, opened and closed his mouth; I was aware, somewhere behind me, of Alyosha, watching and listening. He said nothing, for I was leader here, even if Crowbone had not realised it yet.

'I am sure Crowbone here will want you to build his next ship, Onund,' I added with a light laugh. 'When he is king in Norway. He plans to call it *Long Serpent* and make it the biggest boat in the world.'

'I will be long dead by then,' grumbled Onund and that raised a louder laugh; Crowbone's mouth was working like a dying fish, but I was spared mentioning it by the arrivals from the fortress, moving along the shingle in an ungainly half-trot.

They were ring-coated, helmed and armed with shield and spear, about a dozen led by Ljot, who wore only coloured clothing and a green, fur-trimmed cloak, so I relaxed a little, for this arrival had been the awkward moment and it seemed to have passed off well enough.

'Olaf, son of Tryggve,' he said politely, bowing to Crowbone, for he had fixed his eyes on the boy and the rest of us were just well-armed retainers, he thought. 'Welcome to Jomsburg.'

'Olaf Tryggvasson thanks you,' I said, before Crowbone could get his mouth working. 'Jarl Orm of Hestreng is come to the Joms *borg*.'

Ljot finally saw me and jerked his head to me and back to Crowbone, confused; he had seen and recognised the ship and made assumptions from that. I nodded and grinned a wolf grin at him. Finn slung his shield on his mailed back and gave a bark of laughter.

'Aye – here is your worst nightmare, Ljot,' he snarled. 'Crowbone is now one of the Oathsworn of Jarl Orm of Hestreng. We have come for our property.'

Ljot gaped and stuttered a bit, then looked at me with narrowed eyes.

146

'If you plan trouble here,' he began and I waved a silencing hand. Finn chuckled.

'No trouble,' I answered, 'but this is for Pallig's ears, not all these.'

Ljot glanced round at the ringmailed and gawping growlers he had at his back, Wends mostly, with a scattering of those tribal trolls who always gather round trade places. He nodded and led the way up to the *borg* proper, off the beach and tussocked grass and on to the raised half-log walkways.

I called Finnlaith over, just before I fell in behind them all.

'Keep these thieves off the ship,' I told him. 'And keep the girl hidden.'

He nodded, then scowled. 'Why we have her is not clear to me, sure,' he grunted. 'She is a strange one and no mistake.'

I had no quarrel with him on that and said so, which made him grin. Then he called up his Irishers, Ospak among them and I heard them chaffer and bang shields together, as if they had won a good fight, as we went off after Ljot.

I was glad of Finnlaith and Ospak, old Oathsworn who had arrived at Hestreng while Finn and I were with Jarl Brand. They had come 'for the raiding' and heard in Hedeby that there was trouble at Hestreng.

They had left Dyfflin some time ago and arrived on a trading *knarr* owned by someone who knew me and trusted that the half-a-dozen mad Irishers with their bearded axes and strange gabble were unlikely to cause harm to him or his cargo.

'A timely arrival,' Finnlaith had said, once beams and wrist-grips had been exchanged, 'for sure. It is a sad thing, so it is, to see Hestreng reduced to ashes.'

Then he had brightened a little and said that now that the Ui Neill had arrived, the war against those who had done it could commence and made out that he had come all the way from Dyfflin just for that.

The truth, of course, was that the Irisher lands were in flame – again – and the Ui Neill were not getting the best of it.

Meanwhile, the Norse in Dyfflin laughed at the Irishers quarrelling over who was king of the dungheap, when they controlled the trade and so the wealth.

'But sure,' Finnlaith had added, when he had finished bewildering me with all their names, 'we will go back presently and sort this Brian Boru lad out.'

Meanwhile, he was back with his old oarmates, enjoying the *craic* at the entrance to the Odra and thinking it a good day, even with the rain sifting down on him, because he had friends, a bearded axe slung on one shoulder, a handful of silver in a pouch under his armpit and the prow beast telling him where to go.

I envied him as we clattered over the slick walkways through the town, all smells and curious people, to where the buildings thinned until there were only a few scattered round the meadow. Mounded above it, the Joms *borg* itself squatted like a troll moody over his lost bridge.

Finn nudged me as we went, pointing out the forge and the mill – and the Christ church, where a priest, his brown robe caught up between his legs to make short, baggy breeks, worked a patch of vegetables, looking up only once at us. Most of the folk we saw, including the leather-clad guards on the gates, were Wends.

Pallig waited at the threshold of the hall, surrounded by three women; the youngest – barely a woman at all – he presented as his wife and a thumb-sucking boy he proudly announced was Toke, his son.

'No women allowed at all,' Finn whispered scornfully to me and then laughed at the lies of skalds.

I had expected a different look to Pallig, for his brother was of a good height with no belly on him and reasonable in his looks, making the most of them with his neatness. All of which made his name – Ugly – a joke. Pallig, on the other hand, was sow-snouted, bald save for a straggling fringe of dirty flax and had a paunch that trembled like a new-shelled egg yolk.

Ale was brought and bread and cheese. Crowbone sat apart, chatting animatedly to Pallig's wife and, after a scowl or two, Pallig decided that he was too young to bother with. We sat on benches and Pallig, beaming and jovial, hooked one knee over the arm of a high seat and spread his hands expansively. No-one was fooled; he and the cat-wary Ljot were ruffled by the arrival of the Oathsworn and, for all his bluster, Pallig was not sure he could handle such trouble if it came to a fight.

Still, he played a tafl game of being unconcerned.

'Welcome to my hall, Orm of Hestreng,' he announced. 'The Oathsworn fame has travelled far and wide and is almost as great as my own. It is an honour to have you here.'

Then, unable to resist it, he peered at me and gave a little laugh. 'You look a little battered – was it a rough crossing?'

I said nothing, for the high seat he was on, like a perilously perched pig, had the familiar carving on the back, of Thor arrogantly fishing for the World Serpent. He saw me look and smiled, for it had all been planned that way.

'You admire my high seat? It is very fine.'

'I know it well,' I answered. 'It belonged to Ivar Weatherhat until recently. Then my arse was on it until Ljot came to Hestreng.'

Pallig feigned surprise.

'Then you must have it back,' he declared expansively.

I shook my head and his smile wavered a little, for refusal had not been in his design. But I knew how the game was played and had shoved words around the board with better men than him.

'Keep it,' I countered. 'For Ivar had it and was burned out of all he had and I had it and enjoyed the same luck. The Norns, as they say, weave in threes. I can always get another seat.'

'Once you get another hall,' Ljot offered, with a dangerous sneer that made Pallig shoot him a hard look. I felt Finn shift a little beside me, to ease his hilt nearer his hand.

149

'Oh, that is being built,' I said lightly. 'It will be finished by the time we return to Jarl Brand with his *fostri*, the boy Koll whom your man Leo took.'

The brothers exchanged looks then, no doubt remembering – as I had intended – the Oathsworn tales of unlimited silver. Then Pallig, in an attempt to counter this unexpected move, slathered a vicious smile on his face and waved one hand. Men came forward – two of the bearcoats I had last seen sidling away to burn Hestreng, I noticed – and Styrbjorn between them. He was pale, but smiling and wore good coloured clothing and his hands were unbound, though he had no more than an eating knife on him.

'Orm Bear Slayer,' he acknowledged with a nod. Pallig watched my face and, finally, I turned into his pouched gaze.

'King Eirik would like Styrbjorn returned to him,' I said. 'He is confident you will not oppose him in this.'

Styrbjorn laughed, showing too many white teeth.

'I am sure my uncle would like me to walk into his mouth and be eaten,' he replied, 'but, as you see, I am among friends.'

Pallig said nothing and even Styrbjorn was not convinced by what he said so confidently.

'The king speaks of mercy and forgiveness,' I said. 'He will pay *weregild* to Jarl Brand for what was lost. He swears no harm will come to you.'

Styrbjorn's whole body seemed to sag a little, then he straightened, beaming.

'Well – so it is, then,' he declared to Pallig. 'A king swears it, so it must be true.'

There was silence and Styrbjorn blundered on into it, like a ram in a thicket. 'I will put myself at the mercy of my uncle and king, so bringing this affair to an end. You have my thanks, Pallig, for your hospitality.'

There was a heartbeat of silence, then Pallig broke contact with my eyes and looked at Styrbjorn, as if just noticing that he was there at all.

'I can see that you have served your purpose,' he growled. 'So now you have, it would be best if you stayed silent. Better still if you waited somewhere else for the grown men to finish their business.'

Crowbone could not stifle a snort of delight at Styrbjorn's look, which was ugly and red, tight around the eyes and mouth. He drove to his feet, clattering over the bench; the ringmailed men on either side of his shoulders clamped him with hands hard as wolf bites, so that Pallig waved them to be still.

'You forget who I am, Pallig,' Styrbjorn said, his mouth twisted and wet. 'You would do well to remember it.'

'Who are you?' Pallig challenged. 'Nephew to King Eirik, no more than that. If he wishes you back and swears not to kill you, then he is a fool – and a fool is easily parted from money. Will he pay to have you back, do you think?'

He looked at me as he spoke, but I made my face a cliff and, with a scowl, he turned back to Styrbjorn.

'You are a nithing boy, with no men and less ships and such battle luck as to attract none. Besides, the Great City has disowned you.'

Everyone was too occupied in marvelling at the colours Styrbjorn was turning in his rage to notice the real import of that last bit, but I did. While the bearcoats hauled the youth off, I pilled some bread idly and thought matters through.

Leo the monk was gone.

It came to me then that perhaps King Eirik and I and everyone else had woven the tapestry of this in the wrong colours. After a while, I asked: 'So, where did the Greek monk go, then?'

Pallig frowned for a moment, then glanced at Crowbone. He was wondering, no doubt, if tales of little Olaf's bird-magic were true and that, somehow, the monk's arrival and departure had been seen by some *seidr*-possessed crow on a branch. Crowbone grinned at him and I saw the realisation flash in Pallig that he had been the one to give it away, like a bad move in a game of tafl.

'Gone back to the Great City,' he said, scowling. 'Down to Ostrawa and into the Magyar and Bulgar lands.'

The old Amber Road; I had not thought that trail still existed and Ljot, while his brother fumed at his slip and poured ale to cover his annoyance, explained that it was not much of one, not for boats unless they flew, nor carts. Pack horses could make it and men with small loads, so it was usually little stuff that got carried that way – amber and furs, or the cargo that carried itself, slaves.

'Small boys and monks?' asked Crowbone. Pallig managed a laugh.

'Aye, probably slaves by now, or dead. They went together and the monk hired some men – Sorbs – as guards.'

So there it was. Pallig had not been the final destination of the fleeing Leo. The little turd of a monk was heading for home, though it was unlikely he would ever reach it, as Finn pointed out.

'Sorbs,' he said and would have spat if there had been anywhere to do it without offending. Pallig cocked an un-apologetic eyebrow.

'What is this monk to me now?' he said. 'He came, he invited us to fight for Styrbjorn and he came back when all had failed. I do not expect him to return in a hurry to invite us again. He took the boy with him, thinking to use him to control Jarl Brand and through him influence King Eirik since Brand is his right arm, as everyone knows.'

He stopped and laced his hands across the trembling belly, frowning.

'This Styrbjorn business was ill-paid. It is not good to have such a stain on your fame,' he grumbled and looked at me. 'You know how it is, Jarl Orm – this is just red war and the way such matters are done. Having poor battle luck is bad for the fame at Joms.'

'Perhaps you will think differently, when such red war visits you one day,' I told him and watched his eyes narrow.

'Perhaps,' he said. 'I am sorry you were caught up in this and for your losses. I want no trouble from you. I will pay blood-price for what was done at Hestreng and it is this – I will permit you to leave and tell King Eirik that he can have that useless lump Styrbjorn if he offers me a fair price. Then you should go back to Hestreng, fasten the peace-strings on your hilt and be grateful the Northmen of Joms are not turning out on you.'

This was enough for Finn, who leaned forward with his face as hard and ugly and grim as a hidden rock in a sound.

'You wobbling nithing,' he began. 'All your Northmen are Wendish trolls and never saw a decent vik . . .'

Before I could act, Crowbone laid a quiet hand on Finn's arm, which made the man blink from his rage and look round. The boy shook his head and smiled; Finn subsided like a scrap-fed hound, to my amazement.

The spell of it broken, I stood up and nodded.

'As to Styrbjorn,' I said with a shrug, 'you may do as you see fit – but when we leave we will go upriver, not down.'

Ljot shook his head and Pallig made a pig-grunt of sound.

'Not good,' Ljot said, then smiled a rueful, apologetic smile. 'Look you – I know Jarl Brand's boy was taken and that he was your *fostri*, so it will sit hard with both of you. The boy is gone, all the same – almost certain dead or a slave of the Sorbs or the Wends or the Pols, which is all the same thing. That monk was a chief of the *gestir* of the Great City's emperor, but it will make no difference – those skin-wearing trolls along the river are all supposed to be Christ men, but they will kill him, just the same.'

Gestir, he had said. Well, it had been obvious enough, but it was good to have it said out loud. There are two kinds of oathed men in a king's hall. The first are the great louts, like those standing guard at Pallig's door. The second are the *gestir*, clever men who can spy and make trade agreements and treaties and more. Leo the monk, it seemed, was one of them, working for the emperor in Constantinople and so a man of considerable skills – among them, I was sure, the ability to deal with skin-wearing trolls along the Odra.

'Besides,' Pallig grumbled. 'I do not want you going upriver. You will cause upset in a boat like that and interrupt the trading.'

He dipped one finger in his ale and drew a wet, wiggly line on the table.

'Here is the Odra, flowing south from the mountains beyond Ostrawa to us in the north. It is a frontier land. Here we are at the mouth of it, where are the Wends, who you call trolls and the Saxlanders call Wilzi and others call Sorbs. There are many small tribes of them, on both banks of the river, but most are subject to the Saxlanders on the west.'

He stopped and sucked his wet finger while we all peered at the wiggly line as if it were about to come alive on the table and snake along it.

'On the east bank are more Wends and Sorbs and such, but also the Pols of Miesko, who are coming north pretty fast – only last year they beat the Saxlanders at Cidini which is very close to us. Now the Saxlanders and Pols glare at each other across the river and the trade on it is a *fud*-hair away from being ruined.'

He frowned and wiped the wiggly snake away with a sweep of one hand, breaking the spell on us.

'No-one will want to see a raiding boat such as yours on the river,' he added. 'Otto's Saxlander forts on the west bank will think I sent you up to cause trouble. The east bank has Pol forts who will think the same.'

'Not that you will get that far,' added Ljot, almost beaming with the finality of it, 'for there are other tribes, who will eat you.'

No-one spoke for a long heartbeat, then Pallig cleared his throat and spread expansive arms.

'Well, there is the way of it,' he said, then beamed. 'I would not wish you to sail away from here feeling less than well-treated so I invite you and the young Prince Olaf here to be feasted in my hall tonight.'

I agreed and smiled, which was hard work on the cheek muscles since I was working against a lot of scowl. There was the arrogance of these brothers, the problem of Styrbjorn and how to free him and, worst of all, the thought of what the Polanians – the ones the brothers scornfully called 'Pols' – would do if they found the Mazur girl they thought safely hostaged in a foreign land with the daughter of their king.

Not for the first time, I wondered what Vuokko had seen in his drum later on that feast night for the return of Eirik's bairn. The Sea Finn had appeared out of the shadows like some nightmare, just as Finn and I were picking our way in the salt-tanged dark to see Jarl Brand.

'I have called it and the drum has spoken,' he told us in his rheum-thick accent. 'It says to take the Mazur girl.'

With three runes to speak with it might have said more, but I had gone to Sigrith in the night, half-ashamed at doing it just because of the Sea Finn's drum, and asked her to let me have Blackbird, whose real name was Dark Eye. She, even knowing the worth of the girl to her father and where I was headed, did so, as she said, 'for the loss of her Birthing Stool'.

Now Blackbird was stowed like baggage on *Short Serpent* and as nagging as a broken nail in my mind as we clumped back down to the ship, where Finnlaith and Alyosha were growling at men to get them loading supplies.

They crowded round, wanting to hear what had been said and by whom, so I laid it out for them.

'Take these Joms bladders now,' growled a big Swede called Asfast when I finished.

'Burn them,' snarled Abjorn, 'as Ljot burned Hestreng.'

'Ljot did not burn Hestreng,' Rorik Stari pointed out. 'It was Randr Sterki who did that.'

There were rumbles for and against charging up and cutting them down, calls for blood and fire. There were also growls about going upriver at all, for there was little in it that raiding men could see.

So I put them on the straight course of that simply enough.

'There are two matters that must be done,' I told them. 'One is to free Styrbjorn, for King Eirik's sake.'   ·

Finn grunted, but said nothing, for only he and I knew that it was also to kill him, for Jarl Brand's sake, though neither he nor I had worked out a way to make a square out of that circle.

'I am also going after my *fostri*,' I added, 'for it is my honour and good name here. You may follow if you choose, but will break your Oath if you do not. The only other way is for one of you to become jarl.'

That silenced them, so much so that I was sure they could all hear the bird-fluttering beating of my heart at the idea of one of them challenging me for the dragon-torc of jarl. Fame, that double-edged sword, held them at arm's length, for this was Orm, single-handed slayer of white bears, killer of scaled trolls, who had once won a *holmgang* with a single stroke and only recently had fought and killed berserkers, two at a time.

Yet they were sullen about it and a broad-faced growler called Gudmund could not let the bone of it loose.

'Pallig does not want us to go upriver,' he offered moodily.

'So?' spat Red Njal, fanning the flames of it. 'Who is Pallig Tokeson to tell the Oathsworn of Orm Bear Slayer where they can go or not?'

'He is kin to Harald Bluetooth,' Crowbone offered brightly. 'The wife he took pains to introduce us to is Bluetooth's daughter and the sister of the Svein who was at King Eirik's feast.'

He stared into the astonished faces, then innocently up into mine and I knew now what he had been doing, while seeming to play the eyebrow-batting boy with the womenfolk.

Bluetooth was not a name you ignored lightly, as Gudmund persisted. Finn spat and pointed out that we had been ignoring Bluetooth for years, had stolen his ships and killed his men and were none the worse for it, which cheered everyone, for they knew we were going upriver, no matter what.

Then Onund cleared his throat, which he always did before he said something important and we all stopped, thinking it would be ship talk and being as wrong as a two-headed cow.

'If it is such a bad thing to be going upriver, for the trouble it will cause the brothers of Joms,' he rumbled thoughtfully, 'I am wondering why they let Randr Sterki and his dogs go up?'

TEN

Having hurled the axe of that into the middle of us, the hunchback laid out the saga of how he had found out about Randr. While we spoke with Pallig, he had gone off to find decent wood to fix the steerboard and quickly found an entire steerboard, in good condition, which he thought was ship-luck.

A few traders further on, as he looked for just the right cut of ash wood to make an elk prow for the ship – Crowbone shifted and scowled at that part of his tale – he had found good nails and ready-cut ship planks, far better quality than he would have expected in a place such as Joms. Then a trader said it would be better to have a whole prow rather than go the trouble of carving one and showed Onund one he had.

'So I asked him where he had it from,' Onund told us. 'I had to be firm with him, too, for he was reluctant. I picked him up by the heel and hung him for a while until he spoke and we concluded the business. I was pleased to have done it with no violence.'

That got him chuckles and I wished there was no feasting that night, for I wanted to be away as fast as supplies could be loaded, if for no other reason than to avoid the results of Onund's firmness with a trader.

In the end, Onund was shown the source of the snarling dragon prow he knew well – we all knew well. On the far side from the settlement, wallowing half-in, half-out of the weak Baltic tideline, stripped to the ribs and the keel and the charred strakes no-one wanted, was what was left of *Dragon Wings*.

'We should go to Pallig and his brother,' Finn growled after this news was out, 'and use your little truth knife on them.'

Those who knew of the truth knife, which whittled off body parts until the victim stopped lying, agreed with relish and I felt the little, worn-handled blade burn where it nested in the small of my back. It had belonged to Einar the Black once and had served me as well as it had him, but there was no need for it now.

'Randr Sterki had ship-luck to make it this far,' I pointed out. 'He would be coming to have it out with Ljot for leaving him and I bet he had more men bailing than rowing by the time he ran *Dragon Wings* ashore here.'

They nodded and growled assent to that.

'What of the hoard they had from you?' demanded Finn of Onund and the hunchback shrugged, a frightening affair.

'If he did not take it with him, then it is scattered through the settlement,' he answered. 'And so lost to you, Orm – these *rann-sack* pigs took every last rivet from the wreck.'

There would be no hoard found, I was bitter-sure, for Randr would have used some of it to buy supplies and one of those tree-carved riverboats. The rest would be either with him or buried secretly and I had no doubt a deal of it went to Pallig, for no balm soothes like silver.

'Why is he going upriver at all?' Finn had asked. That one was easier still; to get Koll and the monk. The monk, in Randr Sterki's hate-splintered eye, either owed money or blood or both and the boy was my *fostri*. He would want the boy alive, would know I was coming after him with Crowbone. All his enemies, sailing straight towards the revenge he was not yet done with.

'He did not take the lesson from your last story,' I said to Crowbone and he shrugged.

'I will tell him a harder one, then,' he growled back and everyone laughed at his new, deep voice, so that his cheeks flushed. He looked at me, those odd eyes glittering like agate.

'I have a thought on how to get Styrbjorn away,' he said, then inclined his head in a gracious little bow.

'If my lord is pleased to hear it,' he added and folk chuckled. I heard Finn mutter, though, and did not need to hear it clearly to know what he was saying: that boy is older than stones.

'A prince's wisdom is always welcome,' I said and he grinned his sharp-toothed mouse grin and then laid it out. It was a good plan, put him at the centre of matters and at no little risk – which was what the fame-hungry little wolf cub wanted – and gave the skill and strength of it to Finn. I looked at Finn after Crowbone had finished.

'Can you do this?'

Finn's grin was the same one seen an instant before fangs closed on a kill and folk chuckled at so eloquent an answer with not a word spoken.

It seemed less of a good plan in the flickering red roar of Pallig's feasting. He sat on my high seat flanked by two big men in ringmail and helms who scowled at having to miss the best of the feast because of this duty. Pallig beamed greasily while his men growled and gorged and threw bones at one another, or grabbed the female thralls who stumbled in with platters of mutton boiled outside in a stone-lined pit heated by rocks.

I sat on a bench directly across the pitfire from Pallig, horn-paired with Crowbone for the feasting. None of my own men were here and Pallig knew why – they were with the ship, pointedly kept there because I did not trust him. I had already noted that, while Pallig's women were clustered round him, there was no sign of Ljot, nor of the two bearcoats, last of the beasts, it seemed. Styrbjorn, his mouth in a thin, tight

160

line, sat clenched in on himself on a lower bench and far enough away from the door that he could not make a run for it if he chose.

A skald had been wintering here, a man with a lean face and a body thin as gruel. His name was Helgi and he claimed the by-name of Mannvitsbrekka – Wisdom-Slope – though it was clear any deep thinking he had was long since slid away, for he persisted in trotting out the same old stuff he had most likely been giving them for months. Even the commands of Pallig failed to stop men deep in their ale from flinging bread and bone at him.

Crowbone looked at me with his odd eyes and grinned his mouse grin. Then he stood up.

'I have a tale or two,' he said.

Silence fell almost at once, for the marvellous tales of this man-boy were fame-richer than my own supposed heroics. Graciously, Pallig waved a hand for him to continue.

Crowbone told tales of Dyl U'la-Spegill, which was perfect for the audience he had. They were old tales and still told today, for the laughter in them. Dyl U'la-Spegill is sometimes a youth, sometimes an old man and his very name is as much a whispered mystery as runes; there were those present, I saw, who fancied Crowbone was Dyl U'la-Spegill himself and I could not have refuted it if asked, for he held them as if enchanted.

'Once,' Crowbone said into the silence, 'there was a man down on his luck – we shall call him Ljot – who was given a piece of bread. Hoping this was a sign from Asgard's finest, he went to the market stalls and begged, thinking some meat or a little fish would go well with his bread. They all turned him away with nothing, but Ljot saw a large kettle of soup cooking over the fire. He held his piece of bread over the steaming pot, hoping to thus capture a bit of flavour from the good-smelling vapour.'

Folk chuckled – those, I was thinking, who knew how it felt to be that hungry. Pallig glared them to silence.

'Suddenly the owner of the soup – let us call him Brand – seized the unhappy Ljot by the arm and accused him of stealing soup,' Crowbone continued. 'Poor Ljot was afraid at this. "I took no soup," he said. "I was only smelling it." "Then you must pay for the smell," answered Brand. Poor Ljot had no money, so the angry Brand dragged him before his jarl.'

'Is that where Ljot has gone, then?' shouted someone and I knew Finn's voice when I heard it. Pallig snarled a smile into the laughter that followed and Crowbone went on with his tale.

'Now,' he said, 'it so happened that Dyl U'la-Spegill was visiting with this jarl at the time and he heard Brand's accusation and Ljot's explanation. "So you demand payment for the smell of your soup?" he asked as the jarl struggled to come to a decision on the matter.

'"I do," insisted Brand.

'"Then I myself will pay you," said Dyl and he drew two silver rings from his arm and juggled them in his hand so that they rang – then he put them back, much to Brand's annoyance.

'"You are paid," Dyl told the man. "The sound of silver for the smell of soup."'

They laughed and thumped the tables at that one and, hidden by the noise and uproar, Finn slid to my side briefly and nodded, then rolled his shoulders.

'They will choose the bearcoat called Stammkel, the one they call Hilditonn – War Tooth,' he said quietly to me. I did not ask him if this would be a problem.

'Once,' Crowbone began again, 'Dyl U'la-Spegill lay in the shade of an ancient oak tree, thinking as he always did, on the greatness of the gods and the mightiness of Odin.'

There was a loud throat-clearing sound from down the table, where the Christ priest sat and, for a moment, all heads turned to him, so that he flushed at being the centre of such attention.

'God will not be mocked,' he offered and Crowbone shrugged.

'Then let him sit elsewhere,' he replied, which brought laughter – though muted, for there were more than a few Christ men here. Pallig craned a little to look down the benches at the priest, who drew in his neck a little and, after a pause, the jarl turned his poached-egg eyes back to Crowbone and beamed.

'Go on, little man,' he said expansively, 'for this is better stuff than we have had for some time.'

At which the skald scowled.

'Dyl,' Crowbone began, 'considered the wisdom of Odin – and then questioned whether it was indeed wise that such a great tree as this be created to bear only tiny acorns. Look at the stout stem and strong limbs, which could easily carry, say, fat marrows that sprout from spindly stems along the ground. Should the mighty oak not bear such as a marrow and the acorn creep in the mud?'

'I have often thought so myself,' the skald interrupted desperately, but voices howled him down.

'So thinking,' Crowbone continued, 'Dyl went to sleep – only to be awakened by an acorn that fell from the tree, striking him on his forehead. "Aha," he cried. "Now I see the wisdom of One-Eye – if the world had been created according to Dyl U'la-Spegill, I would have been marrow-killed for sure."'

Crowbone paused and stared at the priest.

'Never again did Dyl U'la-Spegill question the wisdom of Odin,' he finished and the hall banged tables and hooted; a few bones flew at the priest – in a good-natured way and Pallig stood and held up his hands for silence, planning no doubt to lay into them for treating the priest so poorly. Just as the wobbling-bellied jarl opened his mouth to the silence, he broke wind noisily.

Folk sniggered and Pallig went white, then red. Crowbone cleared his throat a little and spoke into the embarrassment.

'There was once a jarl who farted dishonour to himself forever,' he began and Pallig's face had thunder on it – but there were enough drunks in the hall to cheer stupidly at another Crowbone tale, so he sat back down, silent and dangerously black-browed.

'It was at his own wedding,' Crowbone went on. 'The bride was displayed in all her gold to the women, who could not take their eyes off her for the jealousy. At last the bridegroom was summoned to stand by her side, while the *godi* stood ready with his blessing hammer.'

At this point, the priest stood up and made the sign of the cross and there were as many who joined in as those who hooted. Say what you like about Christ priests, say they are as annoying as a cleg-bite in summer, say they have minds so narrow it is a wonder anything can live there – but never say they are afraid. I seldom encountered one who had no courage.

Crowbone favoured him with a look until the priest had finished and was sitting. Then he cleared his throat and went on with his tale.

'The jarl rose slowly and with dignity from his bench,' he said and then paused, looking round the breathless company.

'In so doing,' he went on portentously, 'he let fly a great and terrible fart, for he was overfull of meat and drink. It was a Thor-wind, that one, a mighty cracking.'

'I think I know this jarl,' shouted someone, anonymous in the dark and Pallig shifted in his seat a little, then braided his scowl into an uneasy smile. Crowbone waited a little, then went on.

'Of course, it was a great insult to the bride and her kin and, in fear of blood-feud and the ruin of a good day and dowry, all the guests immediately turned to their neighbours and talked aloud, pretending to have heard nothing.

'The mortified jarl, in that instant, was so overcome by shame that he turned away from the bridal chamber and as if to answer a call of nature. He went down to the courtyard,

164

saddled his mare and rode off, weeping bitterly through the night. In time he reached Dovrefell, went on across it to the very snows, where he sacrificed the horse and lived among the Sami for years.'

'Safe enough there,' observed a growler morosely, 'since they are all expert breakers of wind in that country.'

He was hissed to silence and Crowbone went on with his tale.

'Finally, this unlucky jarl was overcome with longing for his native land – like that of a lover pining for his beloved it would not be denied, though it nearly cost him his life. He sneaked away from the Sami without taking leave and made his way alone and dressed in the rags of a seer, enduring a thousand hardships of hunger, thirst and fatigue, braving a thousand dangers from trolls and wyrm and *draugr*. He eventually came to his old home and, eyes brimming with tears, walked among the houses of it, unknown, pretending to be an old seer of no account.'

Crowbone paused; there was not a breath of sound.

'He was delighted with being home,' he went on, 'thought of announcing himself and abjectly grovelling in apology for his foolishness in running away for so trivial a reason, no doubt forgotten a day or two after it had happened. Just as he had made up his mind to do just that, he passed a hut and heard the voice of a young girl saying, "Mother, tell me what day was I born on, for there is an old seer outside and I want him to tell my fortune."

'The mother did not hesitate. "My daughter," she said, "you were born on the very night the old jarl farted." No sooner had the jarl heard these words than he rose up from the bench and fled for the last time, for his fart was now a date that would be remembered for ever and ever.'

The laughter was long, though Pallig had to force his out. For all that, he peeled off an armring and tossed it regally to the young Crowbone, who caught it deftly. The skald's head drooped like a wilting stalk, seeing his own riches melt from him.

'Good tales, well told,' he announced. 'If you continue the same way, I will give you the one off my other arm.'

Crowbone laughed, then looked sideways at me a moment and I nodded.

'I have no more tales of momentous farts,' he said to the assembled company; a few of them groaned in mock disappointment and Crowbone held up one hand with the ring in it.

'I could tell of Thor fishing for the World Serpent,' he said slowly, looking pointedly at Pallig, whose back rested on that very carving. He shifted nervously and caught my eye – I hoped my old high seat dug splinters in him.

'On the other hand,' Crowbone went on slowly, 'tales of strength like that are best witnessed at first hand. Happily, we have one of the Oathsworn here with such Thor strength.'

On cue, Finn stood up and spread his arms wide as if to embrace them all, turning left and right and into as many jeers as cheers – though the jeers were muted, for most had heard of Finn's fame.

'I am Finn Horsehead from Skane,' he declared, jutting out his badger-beard. 'When I fart, walls tumble. Dragons use my pizzle to perch like birds on a branch.'

I watched Pallig, saw his eyes slide to one side and jerk his chin at a thrall, who immediately got up and went outside. Now comes the hard bit, I thought.

'So – a feat of strength, then, Finn Horsehead,' Pallig declared, grinning in a twisted way, vicious as a rat in a barrel. 'Arm wrestling perhaps?'

'With you, Jarl Pallig?' Finn asked and managed to put enough sneer in that to make Pallig flush and start half out of his seat. Then he subsided and worked a smile back to his face.

'My champion,' he announced and, as if magicked up, the man himself came into the hall, bringing all the heads round. Breath hung, suspended and frozen.

He was ring-coated, of course, with a helm worked in silver and he had to duck coming under the lintel. With him came a long axe, mark of a Chosen Man of the jarl's retinue and he carried it as easily as a child does a stick.

'Stammkel War Tooth,' Pallig announced and the hall rang with cheers from all his oarmates. Pallig looked at the great flat, stolid face of Stammkel, framed by a wild tangle of ribbon-tied beard like flame and the fancy helmet he wore, all silver and dented iron.

'This is Finn Horsehead of the Oathsworn,' Pallig went on. 'He wishes to arm wrestle you.'

Stammkel grunted and peeled off his helmet, so that a great shock of red hair sprang up like a bush. Finn regarded him up and down, then turned back to Pallig.

'Some mistake, surely,' he said. 'Is the father not available?'

The hall liked that and showed it with catcalls and table thumping. Stammkel may have glowered and narrowed his eyes, but it was hard to tell in that face. His voice was clear enough, all the same.

'Arm wrestling is hardly a fair contest with this one,' he rumbled, then stared straight at Finn out of the red tangle of his face. 'I would kiss one of Odin's Daughters with him, but I fancy he would be afraid of her lip.'

I felt my bowels drop, for this had not been the plan; Finn did not so much as blink. Into the silence that followed came the sound of Pallig clearing his throat.

'So be it,' he said – then I forced myself to stand, for it was always best to keep moving forward, even if your plan was askew. Pallig looked at me in some confusion.

'A wager,' I said lightly, 'to make matters more entertaining.'

The hall growled and hoomed and thumped tables in agreement, so that Pallig had to agree, though he did not like it much, beginning to see a trap and not yet sure where to put his feet to avoid it. Too late, I was thinking – and sprang it.

'Him,' I said, pointing to Styrbjorn, 'when Finn wins.'

Pallig, too late to back out of it, looked from the sullen youth to me and back again. Then he stared at Stammkel, the great long axe clutched like a honeycomb in a bear's paw. Finally, he smiled and settled back in my old high seat.

'What will be my reward, then, when your man loses?' he demanded and I tried not to hesitate, or draw in a breath as I laid a hand on the jarl torc round my neck. Scarred, notched, it was a mere twelve ounces of braided silver – burned silver, which meant that it had been skimmed of impurities when molten – yet it was the mark of a jarl and, moreover, of Jarl Orm of the Oathsworn. A prize I knew Pallig could not resist; I was right, for he licked his lips and demanded that they bring Odin's Daughter into the hall.

A Chosen Man carried it in, after a moment or two of delay which, I worked out, was involved in blowing the dust and cobwebs off her for she had not been used in a time and the reason for that sat in a brown robe, scowling disapproval from under his tonsure.

The Chosen Man laid her on a bench; folk drew back in a ring and Odin's Daughter lay there, smiling, gleaming, naked and ornate.

It was a *blot* axe, a great heavy single-bit, worked with intricate knot-patterns, skeined with silver and gold. Such axes are never used for fighting – they are over heavy and ornamented for that work – only in sacrifices to Odin, hence the name. You can put such an axe head on any shaft you prefer and most are the length of a man's arm from fingertip to elbow, easy for a *godi* to handle without making a mess of the work.

Odin's Daughters, they call them, only half in jest, for Odin's daughters are the Valkyrii, which translates as Choosers of the Slain and so also were these axes, some of them named. This had no name, but was a slender and tall daughter of

Odin lying on the table for all that. Four times the length of a man's arm from fingertip to elbow and thick as a boy's wrist, this long axe was seldom used for sacrifice work in these Christ days, but was still the mark of the Jomsviking jarls and carried by a Chosen Man, to be raised aloft in the heat and dust of battle to show that the jarl still stood fast. There was only one other more powerful than this and that had belonged to Eirik Bloodaxe of Jorvik – but that was lost when he went under treacherous enemy blades.

Pallig wobbled out of his chair, holding up a length of red silk ribbon for everyone to see, then fastened it round the rune-skeined shaft, a forearm's length from the bottom. He stood back and raised his arms.

'Who wishes the first kiss?' he demanded and Finn, rolling his neck and shoulders, looked at the impassive Stammkel, grunted and moved forward to take up the smooth, polished ash length in both hands.

Men drew further back as Finn then stepped up onto a bench and moved to the end of the table. It shifted slightly and Crowbone, being nearest, leaned forward on the other end, to keep it from tilting – a brave move, since it put him danger-close to the affair. Everyone else, I saw, had drawn far back and Pallig had moved swiftly back to the high seat.

Perched on the edge of the table like a bird – to add balance to strength and prevent any excessive bending to compensate for lack of wrist power – Finn took a breath or two and hefted the axe to feel the weight of it. I caught his eye, then, across the heads and down the length of the table and he flicked a grin through the great beard of his face.

He took the shaft, just below where the ribbon was tied and raised it in both hands, arms outstretched and locked at the elbow. Then he raised it higher and began tilting it down to his upturned face, blade first, until, with hardly a tremor at all, the power of his wrists lowered the razor edge of it to his lips.

169

There were a few cheers as he did so, then he leaped off the table and offered the shaft to Stammkel. He took it, climbed onto the creaking table and did the same; men roared and thumped on wood as Pallig stepped forward and, careful to let everyone see, lowered the ribbon by a hand-span.

That is kissing Odin's Daughter. Each time the ribbon creeps to the end of the shaft, the axehead grows heavier and harder to control. Drunks or fools do this at feasts with ordinary long axes and rarely come out of it without scars, or bits of nose and lip missing.

The silence grew with each soft slither of the ribbon down the shaft until, at last, there was no room to grip with both hands and everyone held their breath, for this was where it started to get interesting and desperate. I was sweating, now, for I had seen Stammkel at work and he and Finn were like a pair of plough oxen, perfectly matched and moving in step. I was no longer as sure as I had been when we had made this plan based on Finn's arm-wrestling skills.

Finn took the axe in his right hand and, with a look left and right at the pale, upturned faces gleaming in the red-dyed dark, he raised the one arm and slowly, slowly, tilted the axe head down. Sweat gleamed on his forehead, I saw – but the blade touched his lips, no more. There were no cheers, simply the exhaling of held breath, like a wind through trees.

Stammkel stepped up, hefted the axe and the flame-beard of him split in a grin that curdled the bowels in me. I knew he would do it and with ease – the great roar that went up when he did made the rafters shake and I saw Pallig settle back in my high seat, stroking his thin beard and smiling.

The way it worked now, of course, was that the pair kept doing it until exhaustion set in and a wrist failed. Finn had other ideas and he winked at me, that old Botolf wink that dried all the spit in my mouth.

Then he climbed on to the table and took Odin's Daughter in his hand. His left hand; folk made soft mutterings, like

170

moths searching in the dark. A fighting man was almost always right-handed and that was his strong hand – Finn had raised the stakes.

He lifted the long shaft until the pitfire gleam slid carefully along the winking edge of it, then slowly lowered it to his face, turned like a petal to rain, like a child to a mother. I saw it waver, just once and had to clench hard to keep my bladder in check. Then he kissed it – a harder kiss than before, perhaps, but not hard enough to draw blood.

There were a few cheers at this, for even Pallig's men knew skill and strength when they saw it and Finn dropped to the beaten-earth floor of the hall and offered the axe back to Stammkel, his face impassive as a wrecking reef.

The big warrior took it, scowling – was that uncertainty in his eye? I grasped at that straw as I watched him climb on to the table edge and take the axe in his left hand. He hefted it for a moment or two and frowned – my heart gave a great leap at that. He was unsure; he did not have the strength of wrist in his left!

Finn thought so and grinned up at him, trying to add to the pressure. Hesitant, uneasy, Stammkel raised the axe high – and it wavered. Folk who saw it groaned and Finn's grin widened, so that Stammkel saw it.

Then, to my horror, the red beard opened in a laugh. Stammkel raised the axe higher still, tilted it and brought it smoothly down, kissed it lingering and gentle, then straightened and lowered it to the floor.

'You should know, wee man,' he said to Finn, 'that I fight with two bearded axes, one in either hand, for the fun in it.'

The roars and howls and thumping took a long time to subside, by which time I was slumped like an empty winebag; I saw Pallig look at me and the triumph was greasy on his face.

I saw Finn's face, too and was more afraid of that, for it had turned granite hard, with all the laughing in it that a cliff has. He took the axe from Stammkel and paused. Then he swept up the other one, Stammkel's own long-axe, and leaped onto the table end.

My heart was hammering so hard I was sure those nearest could hear it. Finn stretched his arms out, an axe in both hands – and one heavier than the other, which made matters nigh impossible, I was thinking – then looked down at Stammkel, whose face showed only mild interest and appreciation.

'A good kiss needs two lips,' he said and raised the axes high.

I hoped the skald was watching, for if anything the Oathsworn ever did deserved a good saga-tale then Finn's kissing of both Daughters at once was one. He brought them down and I had to grind my teeth to keep from crying out when the left one – Stammkel's own axe – wavered left and right. Then it settled and both Odin's Daughters, delicate as maidens should be, kissed Finn's lips.

Now there was uproar. I found myself bawling out myself, all dignity lost as Finn dropped lightly to the floor and grounded the butts of both axes.

Stammkel – give that warrior his due – nodded once or twice as the uproar subsided, for folk knew legend-making when they witnessed it and none wanted to miss the word-play in it.

'You kiss well,' Stammkel said, 'for a boy. Here – let me show you how such matters are done when a man is involved.'

He was bordering on arrogance, so much so that I fretted. He could not match this, surely? No sane man would try.

Yet I knew, from the moment he measured the different weights with little bounces of his wrists, that he would do it. The cold stone of that settled like ballast in my belly – where did we go from here?

Crowbone knew it, too. I only realised that when I saw his blond head come up as Stammkel raised the axes high and the hall began to ring with the rhythmic thumping of fist and ale cup to the sound of his soft-shouted name – Stamm-kel, Stamm-kel, Stamm-kel.

It was at the point where he started to shift the axes to his face that Crowbone sat up a little straighter – no more than that, as if to see better, as if craning in a boy's eagerness to witness this supreme feat of strength and skill.

The weight came off the table and it trembled a little, dipped slightly under Stammkel's bulk. Stammkel wobbled. The right-hand axe, the true Odin's Daughter, wavered. He almost recovered it, but it was lost – the harsh, unforgiving, ornate weight dragged it down and, with a sharp cry, Stammkel jerked his head to one side and sprang down in a clatter of falling axes. Blood showed on his face.

Finn was at his side in a blink, looked, raised a hand and smeared the blood from the man's stricken cheek. Then he grinned and clapped Stammkel on the shoulder.

'Aye,' he said. 'A nice cheek scar. A name-wound, that.'

Stammkel looked at Pallig's thunderous scowl. Then he looked across at Crowbone and my heart fluttered like a mad, trapped bird. Finally, he looked into Finn's beaming face and I waited for the accusations, the fury, the blood that would flow. I groaned – this was not how it was supposed to be.

Instead, to my shock, I saw Stammkel nod once or twice, as if settling something to himself.

'Next time, Finn Horsehead,' he said and I saw Finn's eyes narrow – then realised he had not seen what Crowbone had done, saw also that Stammkel knew this, too.

I wiped it from me as I stepped forward and looked hard at Pallig, then at the hunched figure of Styrbjorn, blinking stupidly.

'Mine,' I said and waved the youth to my side. He came, rat-swift and too stunned to even offer pretence of dignity.

'Good contest,' I said to Stammkel and dared not look him in the eye – but Crowbone, the cursed little monster, smiled so sweetly at him I felt I had to bundle him away before even Stammkel cracked.

Outside, in the cool of a night-wind washed with the promise of rain and the smell of wrack and salt, we moved steadily away from the hall, down towards the shore and the rest of the crew. My back creeped; I could hear the mutterings and feel the heat of hate on it from the hall we left, but I would not turn round to see.

'That went well,' Crowbone offered, his voice moon-bright in the dim.

'Shut your hole,' I growled at him, which brought me a puzzled look from Finn, but he was too occupied in carrying the torch that lit our way and herding the stumbling Styrbjorn, who had recovered himself a little and was beginning to make whining noises about his treatment and who he was.

'Did you think simply to leave here?'

The voice was a thin sliver out of the dark and we came to a halt at the sound of it. Then Ljot loomed and, behind him, a handful of figures, dark with ringmail and intent. One, I recognised with sag of my knees, was the last bearcoat.

'I have imposed on your hospitality too much,' I managed and Ljot's smile was a stain on his face.

'I was told not to allow you to go upriver,' he went on gently and the soft snake-hiss of his sword coming out of the sheath was sibilant in the shadows. 'Now I will also relieve you of the burden of Styrbjorn. I am surprised that you thought you could get away so easily, Orm of the Oathsworn. There is too much arrogance in that.'

I nodded to Finn, who raised the torch even higher, as if to see better.

'Not arrogance,' I answered into the planes and shadows of his flickering face and jerked my chin. 'Planning.'

The shink-shink sound of ringmail made him half-whirl, then back to me.

'Is that an escort you are having there, Jarl Orm?' called a familiar voice. 'Or do we have to axe off their heads and piss down their necks?'

I looked at Ljot, his lip-licking face pale under the ornate helm and horsehair plume.

'Your choice,' I said easily. 'What answer do I give Ospak and the rest of the Oathsworn?'

I was so sure of Ljot I was already starting to move round him, sure that he did not have the balls to do this. Bearcoats, though – you should never depend on those mouth-frothers for anything sane.

This one had a head full of fire and howling wolves, for he brought them all out in a hoiking mourn of sound that made me jerk back. Then he flew at the pack of us.

Out of the side of one eye I spotted Finn, hauling his Roman nail from his boot with a wide-mouthed snarling curse while, beyond him, Styrbjorn dived for the shadows and rolled away. Out of the other, I saw Crowbone leaping sideways, fumbling for the only weapon he had, an eating knife.

Ahead, though, was only the great descending darkness of the bulked bearcoat, rank with the stink of sweat and ale and badly-cured wolfpelt. Too slow to move, or reach for the eating knife at my belt, I was caught by him, but his wolf-mad eagerness undid him, for he crashed into me, too close to swing the great notched blade he had.

I clutched at him and we went over, crashing to the ground hard enough to make us both grunt and to drive the wind from me. He scrabbled like a mad beast to get away and stand, find room to start swinging, but I was remembering the fight between Hring and the berserker Pinleg, when the latter had gone frothing mad and chopped the luckless Hring into bloody pats; I clung to this bearcoat's skin like a sliding cat on a tree trunk.

He roared and beat me with the pommel end, each blow wild, so that I felt the crash of it on my shoulder, then one that rang stars into me and scraped the skin down my face. I tasted blood and knew the end was on me, for I could not hang on any longer.

Light burst in me at the next blow and my head seemed far away and filled with fire and ice. Then something rose up from the depths, a dark and cold and slimed something; for all I knew it well, Brother John's dark Abyss, I opened myself like lovers' legs to it, licked the fear and fire of it. Polite, that feral snarl of a place, it asked me at the last, winking on the brim of dark madness.

'Yes,' I heard myself say and opened my eyes to where the pallid pulse of the bearcoat's throbbing throat nestled against my chin. I felt the harsh kiss of his beard on my lips.

Then I opened my mouth and savaged him.

They peeled me from the dead man not long after, but I knew nothing of it. Ljot was dead, with Finn's Roman nail in his eye and the rest of his men were slashed bloody and pillaged swiftly, for the uproar had caused the rest of the hall to spill out like disturbed bees.

It was the sight of me chewing the throat out of a berserker that had done it, Finn claimed later to the awe-struck Oathsworn. Ljot and his men had hesitated on the spot at seeing that, so killing them had been simple. Then we had all run for the ship and the river, Styrbjorn included.

I knew nothing of it for a long time, only that my body ached and my head thundered and I felt sick and slathered inside. I had felt the toad-lick of the berserk once before, when I had fought Gudlief's son after he had killed Rurik at Sarkel; I had lost the fingers off my left hand without even knowing it.

At least then I had fought decently with sword and shield and put the madness of it down to excessive grief, for I had thought Rurik my father until he told me the truth two heart-beats before he went to Valholl.

This time, though, there had only been the dark madness and the small-bird pulse of his throat, the taste of his blood in my mouth and the flood of his fear when he knew he would die.

I had enjoyed it.

ELEVEN

Perched as high as he could get, arms wrapped lovingly round the prow beast, Red Njal peered out ahead, looking for the ripple of water that told of hidden snags. He did not try and speak, for the wind took words and shredded them, as it flattened his clothes to his ribs and whipped his hair and beard, so that it looked as if it grew out of one side of his head only.

The oars bowed, the crew grunted with effort, eyes fixed on the stroke men – no-one beat time, like they did on Arab and Greek ships; what would be the point in sneaking up on a *strandhogg* raid while hammering a drum?

We were not silent, all the same. *Short Serpent* crabbed, rattling and creaking, up the wide river, which was stippled by that chill lout of a wind, bulling over the floodplain like a rutting elk, sweeping and swirling down the river, crashing through the fringing of trees on both banks.

I stood on the mastfish and smiled and grinned at the rowers, who had stowed their ringmail; half of them were naked to the waist and sweating hard despite that wind and because of it, too – it circled and beat sometimes on the steerboard, sometimes running into the teeth of the prow beast. The wind and the current meant hard work at the oars.

'We should lay up and wait for the wind to change,'

Crowbone said in his cracked bell of a voice, hunched into his white cloak. I had no doubt that was what he would have done and had the men thank him for it and toast his name in the ale he would no doubt have broken out. Truth was, I would have done it myself if he had not mentioned it, but now he had and so I ignored it – and that made me irritated at myself.

'We stop when I say,' I answered shortly and, after a pause, the white-swathed figure stumbled to where he could sit and brood. I glanced at him briefly as he went and caught the eye of Alyosha, watching as always; he irritated me also.

'Something to say, Alyosha?'

He raised his hands in mock surrender and grinned.

'Not me,' he said. 'I am charged by Prince Vladimir to watch the little man and see he comes to no harm. There is no part in that which tells me to interfere when he is being taught the ways of the real world. He took the Oath like everyone else, save me and Styrbjorn, and now he must settle with it.'

I eased a little, half-ashamed at myself for being twitched as a flea-bitten dog. Crowbone had held to his promise at King Eirik's feast and the whole crew with him, not a few bewildered to be taking such a binding Oath, but all of them awed by the fact that, having done so, they were now part of the fame that was the Oathsworn.

As *godi*, I did what was expected with an expensive ram and the whole business was done properly and drenched in blood – much to the annoyance of the competing Christ priests and King Eirik's embarrassment at having such a ritual done in front of them.

We swear to be brothers to each other, bone, blood and steel, on Gungnir, Odin's spear we swear, may he curse us to the Nine Realms and beyond if we break this faith, one to another.

Simple enough for a mouse-brain to remember and harder to break than any chains, even the one that bound Loki's cursed son, the devouring wolf Fenrir. Yet two handfuls of Odin oath-words were stronger.

At the time, Finn growled and grumbled at the business, certain that Crowbone would get someone from his crew to challenge me for jarlship of the Oathsworn and try to take over. He and Hlenni Brimill, Red Njal and others started taking bets on who it would be, the favourites being Alyosha and the half-sized, black-haired Yan, by-named Alf because, it was said, he was so fast in his movements that you only ever saw him flicker out of the corner of your eye, like one of the *alfir*.

Yet, that day, the day I thrust the challenge into all their faces, the memory of my mouth clotted with the throat of a berserker was still young and no-one had stepped forward; now the bets were all off.

Alyosha had told me straight away that he would not take the Oath, for he was service-bound to Vladimir and, besides, his gods were proper Slav ones. Yet he would come with us, for he was charged with looking after Crowbone – and, truth was, half the crew who sailed with Crowbone only did so because they knew Alyosha guided Crowbone.

Crowbone's men were all free Svears who had fought for King Eirik until released to find blade work with Vladimir. They had followed Crowbone for the plunder in it – and because Alyosha was there to make the sensible decisions – and thought there would be buckets of silver now that they were in the famed Oathsworn of Orm Bear Slayer.

Styrbjorn, of course, had not been given the offer to take the Oath – and was now dragged along with us whether he liked it or not; it was clear he did not like it at all.

'You can stay in Joms,' I had said to his scowl, 'but Pallig may not be as friendly as before and may work out that keeping you as a hostage is a waste of food and ale; Eirik might be daft enough to pay to have you back, but Pallig may not have the patience for it. You are safer with us – unless, of course, you trip over that petted lip and fall in the water.'

179

Finn, of course, had not been able to suppress a look and laugh at that, for he knew the truth of why we had rescued Styrbjorn and only wondered why the youth was still alive at all. So, I suspected, did Styrbjorn – and the truth of it was that the bearcoat's throat was still so uppermost in my mind that it stole any stomach I had for red-murdering the boy.

He came with us all the same, wary as a wet cat and dragging his heels, a hand on the hilt of his eating knife – Eirik had sent him a fine sword, as proof of his forgiveness, but I had it snugged up in secret – and nursing all his grievances to him until he could pay everyone back.

I was thinking he would run for it first chance he got and was in two minds whether to let him or not, for if some skin-wearing tribesman killed him along the Odra, I could hold up my hands to the king and honestly say it was no fault of mine.

It was clear now that any who had designs on jarl matters were still stunned by what I had done and, taken with all the other legends that swirled round me, were too afraid to speak up – even Crowbone, who might have tried it, for all his size and lack of years.

The truth of it all was clear to me and worse, of course, than Finn thought. Crowbone did not need to challenge me for the jarl torc. He knew the Oath bound us all, as it said, one to another; if it meant he had to sulk in the stern now and behave himself, one day he would call on us and we would be reeled in like fish in the net of that Oath, to go and help win him a throne in Norway. That I had stuck myself in that net was what irritated me, for I needed Crowbone's ship and his crew.

All day we rowed and I took my turn at the oar like everyone else, so that I ached by the end of the day, a hot bar from shoulder to shoulder and my arse rubbed raw on my own sea-chest. Yan Alf saw it when I squatted over the lee side for relief and laughed.

'Orm is truly a great jarl,' he yelled. 'Look – he even prepared for a coming fog by making a beacon.'

They hooted and slapped thighs at the sight of my arse which, if it glowed like it felt, was indeed a fair light in a mist.

'I went into a red forest,' Bjaelfi intoned, waving a wax-sealed little pot. 'In the red forest was a red house and in the house was a red table, and on the table was a red knife. Take the red knife and cut red bread.'

But I refused Bjaelfi's potent charm against the rash on my cheeks, since it was accompanied by an offer to smear salve on the affected part. The men, enjoying the sight of their jarl so put out, hooted and guffawed and slapped themselves and each other, which was, I knew, as good a way as any of braiding them together. Unlike them, though, I could not put the bearcoat's throat behind me.

I caught sight of Crowbone watching me, appraising and not the least put out. Another lesson learned for him, I thought, for I was no more than one of the spears he practised with each time we made landfall, throwing them with either hand and getting better all the while.

At night we lit fires and ate horse beans and bread, the bought stuff first before it got too moulded. After a week of this there were moans, which did not surprise me. Those with the skill wanted to hunt, Kuritsa among them.

'If I eat any more horse beans,' he grumbled, 'I will blow the boat up the mountains to where this river begins.'

I said anyone who fancied it could hunt and saw the delighted looks among those who saw a way out of rowing; folk were even doing it in their sleep and elbowing their neighbours on the cramped boat.

Then I reminded everyone of the Redars and Czrezpienians, the Wengrians, Glomacze, Milczians and Sorbs, all of whom would be pleased to find Northlanders hunting their lands and would surely offer proper hospitality.

181

'With a stake up the arse,' Finn added and Red Njal flung back his head and laughed, the cords of his neck standing out.

'*Gefender heilir,*' he intoned a moment later, '*gestr er inn kominn.* Greetings to the host, a guest is come.'

'*Hvar skal sitja sja? Mjok er bradr, sa er brondum skal, sins um freista framr* – Where must this one sit? He is very impatient, the one who must sit on the firewood to test his luck,' Styrbjorn finished and those who knew the old Sayings Of Odin howled with laughter at their own cleverness.

That was the night I tried to talk sensibly with the Mazur girl. She was sitting, quiet as a hare and her eyes, those dark, seal eyes, were never still. They looked large and brimmed with fluid in her thin face, too big for it, too big for the small shoulders over which she had drawn a cloak given to her by Queen Sigrith, too large certainly for the legs that came out of the oatmeal-coloured shift and ended in small, clumpy turn-shoes, another gift.

For all that, the great hairy Svears and Irishers raised their brows and rolled their eyes at her, watching her when they could while she stared at nothing, like a little carving of wood. At night, I had men I could trust guard her, Finnlaith and Ospak usually; she was young and small but these were vik men and if some had not humped a dying woman on a dead ox it was only from lack of opportunity. They would hump a knothole if the mood took them.

I sat beside her and smiled. Her eyes flicked to my face and she said nothing; I saw the heads of the rowers we sat behind twisting themselves off to try and see what the jarl was up to.

They knew the girl was no thrall, was highly prized and that I had told them all to keep away, no talking to her, no hands on her or, by the Hammer, I would tie those who did to a tree with their pricks hanging and leave them for the Sorb women.

182

'I hope you have some comfort and are not afraid,' I said slowly, knowing her Norse was poor; I could speak neither Wend, nor Polanian, which she might know and certainly not Mazur. 'You are worried about why I have brought you, no?'

'No.'

The reply was flat and soft, surprising enough to make me blink, but her face did not change and the eyes, those eyes, were deep as a fjord. I felt there was some old wisdom gliding in the dark water of them; for a stabbing moment I was reminded of Hild, the mad woman who led us all to Attila's hoard and, at the same time, caught sight of Crowbone, a shadowed shape looking at me, though his face was all darkness and I could not see his eyes.

Something about that disturbed me – but, then, I was all disturbance, like a cat in a high wind, fur-ruffled this way and that and made uneasy and twitched. Having your doom laid on you will do that. Ripping the throat from a man with your teeth will do that.

'You are not worried?' I managed and she shook her head.

'No. You brought me because the flatfaced one with the drum told you to. You brought me because the Polanians will want me and you might have to bargain with them. It is dangerous; they will certainly try and take me by force when they find out.'

She had not missed the mark of it, right enough and spoke it in a detached way, as though it concerned someone else. The other fact of it was that, no matter what, she would not get back to her people, far to the east of the Polanians. Yet I was sure she clutched the hope of that tight to her.

She looked at me with her wood-carved look, then dropped those swimming eyes, saying nothing more.

'Well,' I said, though it was like pushing boulders uphill, 'you have listened and watched, I am thinking. Now I need you to talk.'

I needed her to tell me of the river, for we had no guide.

183

I needed to know where it narrowed, or shallowed, what settlements of size were on it and whether they could be trusted and where the Saxlander and Wend forts were. Further up still, I needed to know of the Polanians and what lay even beyond them, up to where the river stopped being navigable by a boat such as *Short Serpent*.

'The river runs for days,' she answered, 'it runs for weeks. Forever. Here, where it is wide and slow are Wends, on both sides, but they do not live near the river unless there is high ground. They keep sheep and cattle and do not farm much, because the river floods.'

She paused and her mouth twisted.

'They are sheep and cattle themselves, who do not fight.'

That was good to know, but beyond it Dark Eye was not much use. There was a Wendish settlement called Szteteno further up, where two rivers met and made almost a lake, with islands in the middle. Saxlanders were there, too.

Beyond that – and by the time you could just shoot an arrow from a good bow to reach the far bank – there would be thicker woods and higher ground on either side. The river shallowed once that she could remember, at a place the Slavs called Sliwitz and the Saxlanders Vrankeforde – Free Ford – and there they had built a big log fort.

There were fur and amber traders there, she remembered, but mostly slavers, for both the Wends and the Polanians raided each other and sold the captives as slaves. Beyond that, further into the mountains, was a place called Wrotizlawa but Dark Eye had never been there. The only settlement either of us knew north of that was the end of the Amber Road, Ostrawa.

'I was young when they took me down this river,' she added defiantly, seeing my look of disappointment and I nodded and acknowledged it with a rueful smile.

'This ford – is it passable upriver by boats?'

She frowned. 'The riverboats are hauled over it by long lines from the bank, but they take everything out to make them lighter. It is hard work and they can do it only because the boats are made from a single trunk. It is stony beneath the water, which comes up over the hub of a cart wheel. Another river comes to it here and there are islands in the middle, where it joins the Odra.'

If we took the steerboard up, Onund said later when I mentioned it, we could also haul *Short Serpent* over it, though there was a chance we would break its back and the keel would take bad damage.

'Since we are not bringing it back on to a real sea,' he added, with a sideways look at me, 'that does not make much difference.'

I had not mentioned such a matter, of course, but should have known Onund would have spotted it. We would never get *Short Serpent* all the way upriver and I was prepared to follow this Leo through the Bulgar lands to the Great City if he took Koll there. I said as much and Onund nodded, with no sign of remorse for all his wood-skill.

'Why all this, then?' I added, nodding at the half-carved elk-head prow.

'If we burn this ship,' he rumbled, 'I thought to burn her as the *Fjord Elk*. It is fitting – besides, I am trying to have the fame of being the shipbuilder who has lost more vessels of that name than any other.'

We laughed, though grimly; the tally of lost *Elks* was growing fearsome. I told him not to say anything to Crowbone and he grunted. That boy, however, had other matters on his mind and came up to me to air them.

'She will run,' he said, perched at my elbow like a white squirrel. 'The first chance she can take.'

I did not need to ask who and he perhaps had the right of it. I asked if his birds had told him what Dark Eye was planning, but he scowled at that, though I had not meant it as a sneer. Still, I told Finnlaith and Ospak to watch as much for the girl escaping as for visitors with their pricks in their hands as we snagged up for the night. There was some daylight left under the pewter sky, so that those who wanted to hunt could do it.

By the time darkness came we were eating duck with the horse beans, with some fresh-caught river fish and wild onions. I broached the ale, enough to put some flame in the mouth but not enough to cause trouble; by the fireglow, men laughed and sang filthy songs, arm wrestled and watched admiringly as Onund Hnufa brought an elk to life out of the ash-wood with each careful paring of his knife.

The night sang with freshening life and Bjaelfi unwrapped a harp. It was really Klepp Spaki's instrument, but he had given it to Bjaelfi before we left; neither he nor Vuokko came with us, for they had the memory stone to finish and I had no quarrel with that. So Bjaelfi bowed us a tune, which even Finnlaith and his Irishers nodded and smiled at.

'Though it has to be said,' Finnlaith added seriously, 'that while your instrument is like a harp, it is only as like a harp as a chicken is a duck.'

'For a true harp,' added one of the Irishers, a great lump of a red-haired giant who, like all of those rich-named folk, was called Murrough mac Mael, mac Buadhach, mac Cearbhall, 'is a dream of sound which comes from being strung with fine deer gut and plucked, not hung with horsehair strings and scraped, like a sharp edge on the chin.'

'They are braiding together well,' Finn noted quietly while the argument and laughter rolled on, his face blooded by fire-light and his loose hair ragging in the wind.

'Save for Crowbone,' he added, nodding to where the boy sat, scowling at the clever work Onund was making; he did not want to see a new prow on his ship, nor it renamed *Fjord Elk*.

'We will pay his price for all this by and by,' I answered and Finn nodded, then sighed as Bjaelfi bowed his harp and sang on.

Eager and ready, the weeping lone-flyer,
Frets for the whale-path, the heart lured
Over tracks of ocean. Better that from Odin,
Than the dead life he loans me on land.

Those close enough to hear grunted low appreciation and Finn's soft 'heya' was a world of praise all on its own. It came to me then that he was the most content I had seen him in a long time and the moon-shadow of the prow beast that rose suddenly behind him was no accident; Finn was where he was happiest.

Worse was, it came to me with a stab of guilt for all those I imagined labouring away in Hestreng, that I shared the feeling, if only because the Oathsworn were the only family who would not shrink from me completely on learning what I had done.

TWELVE

The wind went to the stern, or died to a whisper and let us make better time over the next few days, though it rained soft and hard, stippling the skin of the water. As Dark Eye had said, we saw no sign of life beyond the tree-fringed banks save in the far distance, but I thought it likely our presence was now well-known. I wanted to find peaceful folk to ask about a monk, a boy and a boat full of hard-faced men.

The ship, powered by all the oars, slid along so that the water creamed under the prow beast's neck and the crew had an easy pull of it. Trollaskegg would not put up the sail, for the wind was twitchy and we did not have enough sea room for mistakes; the sky veered from a faded blue to a mottled grey, where harsh clouds piled up and looked like the face of a great, grim cliff.

The men, serene as swans on this water, sang their rowing songs, where each line was repeated by the opposite side, a pulling chant that helped keep time out on the open sea, where we did not need stealth. Here, the thinking was, everyone knew we were on the river and being loud would make folk realise we meant no harm.

What do we care, how white the minch is?
Who here bothers about wind and weather?
Pull the harder lads, for every inch is,
Taking us on to gold and fame.

This last was always boomed out, rolling over the water like the wind, which whined now, a hound too long tied up. It came in strange gusts, leaping and whirling round like an eager pup, then vanishing, so that I wondered where it went. Did it bowl on and on across the long floodplain, endlessly blowing?

'Perhaps it is another type of *djinn*,' Red Njal put in when I voiced this aloud. 'Like the circling sand ones we saw in Serkland.'

'Or the snow ones we had out on the Great White,' added Crowbone, 'the ones which always came before those *buran* storms.'

The Svears, who had sailed up and down the Baltic a few times and thought themselves far-farers, looked at the old Oathsworn differently after that, realising now just where we had been and nudged into remembering the tales of what we had done. That a boy of twelve had seen and done more than them, with their tangle of beard and growling, was to be considered; like all who knew Crowbone for a length, they were coming to realise that he was not the stripling he appeared.

The thought of all these clever far-farers as oarmates cheered them, all the same, so that they sang until their throats burned.

Skanish women have no combs.
Pull, swords, pull,
They fix their hair with herring bones.
Pull, swords, pull away.

The song floated out across the water, rippling past the tree-fringed shore, out across the meadowland of the floodplain, to where deer heard it, or, I thought aloud, perhaps a herdsman who hid himself and watched, unseen by us.

'Deer,' snorted Kuritsa when he heard this. 'Not enough brush for deer.'

So far the hunters had shot five ducks, three geese and, once, a half-a-dozen fat wood pigeons, but nothing else. Further along, Kuritsa said, if the woods thicken like the girl said, we would find deer and maybe elk, too.

'We need a *strandhogg*,' Finn grunted. 'Fuck your deer – let us find a place with flour and smoked meat and ale that we can raid. Aye, and women, too, else we *will* be fucking your deer.'

> *The Varmland men have no sleds.*
> *Pull, swords, pull.*
> *They slide downhill on old cod heads.*
> *Pull swords, pull away.*

The singing stopped late on in that day, when the wind came skittering down on the prow beast again and stole our breath away with the effort of rowing against it. The sky grew too dark for it to be night and then, across the front of us like a herd of black bulls, stormclouds rolled, spitting white stabs at the earth; rain lanced the river.

We took the sail over and used some awning canvas as well, but it was a miserable wet night, despite hot coals on the ballast stones near the mastfish which gave us grilled fish and soggy bread. We drank the last of the ale and hunched into ourselves listening to the rain hiss and the night bang; the blue-white flashes left us blinking and the air was thick and heavy with a strange, blood tang.

Red Njal said that it was a pity Finn had not worked out the use of his hat and Finn told the tale of it, of how he had taken Ivar Weatherhat's famed headgear in a raid. Those who had laughed at the crumpled, stained object with the wide, notched brim now looked at it with more respect.

190

'Keep away from your ring-coats and helms, lads,' warned Alyosha, 'for when the night smells of a hot forge, Perun is hurling his axe at any byrnied warrior he can see.'

'Is that true?' demanded Bjaelfi and men hummed and hemmed about it.

'It is true, bonesmith,' Alyosha declared, 'for I have seen it and Perun is as like your Thor as to be a parted birth-brother. Once I saw a *druzhina* horseman in an autumn storm such as this near Lord Novgorod the Great. A proud man and brave, too, all splendid in brass and iron and he rode with his tall spear sticking into the rain and wind as if he did not care. Then there was a flash and Perun's axe smacked him.

'There was nothing much left but twisted metal and a black affair that might have been him. The horse had been turned inside out and we found one of its shoes in the summer, when we went to the wood a good walk away. It was stuck in a birch, half-way up the tree.'

Another flash and bang showed the white-eyed stares of the listeners and everyone hunkered deeper into their own shoulders, shifted a little away from stowed weapons.

The storm wore itself to weary grumbles eventually and I drifted to sleep, listening to the water hiss and gurgle and comforted by the faint glow of the dying coals. Men were curled and twisted into odd shapes, round sea-chests and oars, squeezed in corners and all of them sleeping as if the places they touched leached rest into them. They snored and whistled and wheezed and that was as comforting to me as the glow of coals.

I saw Finnlaith, on watch, shift slightly, a vague silhouette against the faint blood-glow of the coals; as I watched, I saw him settle and tip, like a bag of grain not set down square and I knew he was asleep. That made me annoyed, for I had just got myself comfortable and was enjoying the fire and the men snoring and the river talking quietly to itself about the storm that had blown out. Now I was going to have to lever myself up and kick his Irisher arse awake.

Somewhere a wolf ached, sharp and sorrowful, threading its cry through the night like a bone needle and I struggled and grunted out of my space, feeling the chill as the cloak spilled warmth out – then I froze, astonished.

At first I thought it was a mangy bear, waddling slow and quiet towards the boat, for they do sometimes on the travelled routes of Gardariki, seeking meat or a lick of sweetness after their winter sleep. Then I saw it was a man, working slowly, easily, down towards the ship; a shift of brief moonlight slid along the blade he held.

I almost let out a yell, then, for all the while I had been thinking it one of the crew deciding to try his luck with Dark Eye while her guard slept – but this man was coming from the shore, from further down. Besides, the naked blade told the truth of it.

Moving slowly, rolling each foot along from heel to toe as old Bagnose had taught me, placing each one carefully between sleepers and stacked oars, I crept towards Finnlaith. Beyond him, the shadowed figure with the long knife paused, then came on again.

I snapped Finnlaith's axe from his hand and flung it, even as the Irisher sprang awake with a yell. The long, heavy bearded axe spun through the air and I heard the crack and the grunt as it hit the creeping man; I leaped, hoping he was stunned at least and scrabbled for the place he had fallen, hearing Finnlaith bellowing behind me.

I landed on the man's back, driving more air out of him, sprang a forearm under his neck and gripped his other shoulder, levering his chin up until I heard the neck bones creak. He swung wildly behind him and I saw he still had the knife, flickering like a wolf fang in the watered moonlit dark.

He grunted when I grabbed for the hand, spilled me off him and we rolled now, me desperate not to let go of his knife-hand. I banged my nose and the pain of it made my whole head explode in red.

Men were yelling and the world was a whirl of grass and cracking twigs, heavy with the fetid stink of sweat and fear and fresh-scabbed muddy earth. I heard shouts, felt the thump that hit the man I struggled with; he fell away from me then.

'That will tame him,' growled a voice.

'After the other one . . . quick now. Move yourselves.'

A hand hauled me up and light flared as someone lit a torch from the coals and brought it. Finn looked me over with narrowed eyes as men thronged around, then he relaxed.

'That neb of yours is not lucky,' he pointed out, but I did not need him to tell me that, for it throbbed blindingly. Someone held the torch over a little and, as Finnlaith fetched his axe, grinning, I saw what I had been fighting.

'Sure and that was a fine throw,' he said cheerfully, 'though you are lucky it is not so balanced and only the shaft hit him, else he would be dead.'

'Sure and it is a fine thing,' I answered, mimicking his tone, 'that I did it when I did, else you would be dead and we would have to wake you to let you know of it.'

Finnlaith's grin slipped a little and he nodded wryly, scrubbing his head with embarrassment. The giant red-head, Murrough, reached down and plucked a limp figure from the bruised grass.

He was a small man, dressed in a stained tunic that might have been white once and wearing bits of fur here and there, which is why I took him for a mangy bear. His face was mole-sharp and shaved clean, though he had greasy hair the colour of old iron worked in three braids, two from his brow and one behind him. He half-hung in Murrough's grip looking one way then another with small, narrow eyes, as if to find something he could bite.

'Is this a Wend or a Sorb?' I asked. 'Does anyone speak enough to ask him?'

'Only the girl,' growled Alyosha and Crowbone appeared then, his cheeks flushed and eyes bright from running.

'The second man ran for it and we lost him in the dark – who is this one?'

'A Sorb,' grunted someone.

'Or a Wend.'

Mole-Face said nothing, but tried a smile with more gap than tooth and spread his hands, moving them to his mouth.

'Came to steal food, I am thinking,' Finn growled. I picked up the man's long knife; it was a good one, ground down from what had once been a decent sword, so that the hilt and fittings were all there and they were Norse. The likes of Mole-Face would have sold it long ago if he was so starving and I said so.

I handed it to Finn and added: 'Well, I have my truth knife and it has never failed, no matter whether we speak the same tongue or not. So string him up and we will start with his fingers, until they are all gone. Then we will move to his toes . . .'

'Until they are all gone,' chorused those who knew the way of it, laughing like tongue-lolling wolves.

'Then I will start on his prick and balls,' I added.

'Until they are all gone,' came the chorus.

'Ah, no, wait – Christ's bones, no.' The man's tongue flicked like an adder and he stared wildly from one to the other.

'That truth knife,' Finn grunted, 'seldom fails to impress me. Already we know he speaks good Norse and is a Christmann and we have not even drawn blood.'

'I know who he is,' Styrbjorn declared, bursting through the throng. 'His name is Visbur, by-named Krok, but most know him as Pall, which name he took when he was baptised and chrism-loosened. He is one of Ljot's men.'

'You may not have any food,' Finnlaith said to the mole-faced man, 'but you are rich in names.'

'Bind him,' I said and men sprang to obey; the man panted and struggled briefly, but he stayed silent, stumbling back to the ship with the press of men at his back. Once there I had them loop a cord round his ankles and then hauled him a little way up the mast, where he hung and swung like a spider's prey. I brought the truth knife out, feeling the cold sick settle in me, for I never liked this.

'Now,' I said, 'I know you are called Hook and named after a Christ-saint called Paul and that you are no Wend or Sorb.'

'True, true,' he panted. 'Let me down – I will tell you everything. Anything.'

'Who was the other man?'

'What other man? I was . . .'

He broke off, for I had grabbed one bound hand and whicked the little finger off him; the knife was so keenly sharp that he felt it as no more than a tug – then he saw the blood spurt and the pain hit him and he shrieked, high and thin, sounding like Sigrith when she was birthing her son.

'Yes, yes,' he screamed. 'Two of us. We were sent by Pallig.'

'I remember now,' Styrbjorn spat out suddenly. 'He was always at the elbow of another called Frey . . . something.' He frowned, then brightened. 'Freystein, that is it.'

The hanging man moaned and blubbered and Finn, with a scornful look, thanked Styrbjorn for his part, while wishing he had been a little quicker.

'I am sure Pall here will forgive you for the loss of his finger,' he added, 'it being just a little one.'

Styrbjorn scowled and the pair of them bristled at each other for a moment – but this was Finn, who made stones tremble and Styrbjorn wisely slunk off. I was aware of them only at the edge of my mind, for Visbur/Pall had started to babble.

It all spilled out like blood from his finger-stump, while the torch guttered in a rising wind and he turned and swung and bumped against the mast.

Pallig had sent him and three others. This Pall and the one

195

called Freystein had been dropped off when they spotted the boat; the other two had rowed their little faering silently past, the idea being to pick Pall and his oarmate up once they had done their task. They had planned to set the boat adrift, maybe even fire it if the occasion presented itself.

I sent men off down the bank and we waited moody as wet cats, while Pall swung and moaned.

'Cut him down,' said a small, light voice and Dark Eye stepped into the torchlight.

'This is no matter for you,' growled Finn. 'Go and lie down somewhere warm.'

Dark Eye studied him and most would have said she did it as cool as a calved berg, but I saw the tremble in her and, suddenly, stepped away from myself to her side and saw it as she did – a band of savage-eyed, grim men, tangle-haired beasts gathered round a pole to poke and taunt a hapless victim. She looked at me with those seal eyes and I felt shame.

'Take him down,' I said and, after a pause, Red Njal and Hlenni did so. Pall collapsed on the deck in a heap and Bjaelfi, who never liked this business, came forward and thrust a scrap of cloth at him, one of the many he had rune-marked for healing.

'Here,' he said gruffly. 'Bind the wound with this and keep it clean. Do not take it off, for the rune on it is Ul, a *limrune,* which is to say a healing rune, in case you have Christianed yourself away from even that knowledge. It invokes Waldh, who is an old healing-god of the Frisians.'

Dark Eye smiled, a small sun that flared for a moment and was gone as she moved off back to her place in the lee of the stern. Finn hawked and spat over the side.

'So thralls rule us now,' he growled and I felt a surge of anger; any less a man would have had my fist on him.

'She is no thrall,' I answered, stung. 'A princess in her own lands and as valuable to us as a queen. And no-one rules us, not even me and, for sure, not you.'

He saw the thunder in my face and realised he had gone too far. Unable to row back from what he had said, he simply turned and rolled off down the ship to the prow, pulling off his crumpled hat and scrubbing his head with confusion.

The men I had sent out came back when the birds had finished yelling at the dawn.

'They saw us,' Kuritsa said, 'just as the sky got light. We managed a shot or two, but they rowed off. There were only two.'

'My fault,' added another of the trackers wryly, a lanky Svear called Koghe. 'I am not as skilled as Kuritsa here and let them see me.'

Kuritsa waggled his head from side to side, a gesture that meant the matter was neither here nor there. He also voiced an opinion that had been in my head, too.

'It means the second man from tonight is still somewhere around.'

He had done more than well, what with this and other matters and I looked at him and knew what I had to do. Gripping him by one shoulder I bellowed it out so that everyone could hear.

'I see you.'

Men turned; a few 'heyas' went up, for they liked Kuritsa and had long since stopped treating him as a thrall – which meant not noticing him at all. Now I had declared him as noticed and had Red Njal bring my drinking horn, filled with the last scum of the ale. Grinning, he handed it to Kuritsa, who then handed it to me. I drank and gave it back to him. He drank and everyone cheered, for Kuritsa was now a free man.

In some places there is more to it, involving six ounces of silver – if the thrall is buying his freedom – and him brewing ale from three measures, which is a powerful drink to present to his former owner, but all that is colouring the cloth of it.

'Well,' Crowbone said brightly, 'now that we have no more thralls, we will have to rely on Finn Horsehead's cooking.'

Which, of course, was what we had been doing already, for Finn was known for his excellent meals, but it raised a laugh as men clattered about, sorting themselves, trying to find sleep again and mostly failing. When the light was enough to see by, the ship was shoved off from the bank, the rowers settled on to their sea-chests, slid out the oars and bedded themselves into the rhythm of it, helped by Trollaskegg's loving curses.

Dogs, he called them one minute and *maeki saurgan* the next, which strangers take as an insult, since it means 'dirty sword'. They miss the part of how such a sword came to be so stained, by proving its worth and not breaking.

I took Pall by the scruff of the neck and hauled him to where Finn sat.

'Here,' I said. 'Aim your scowls at this instead of me, Finn. This Pall might be useful yet, even if only in one of your stews.'

Finn managed a twist of his mouth, for he did not want a quarrel any more than I; Pall hunkered miserably, but I saw his thin face turn this way and that, cunning as a rat. A thought struck me and I cursed myself for a nithing fool.

'Where were you going?' I demanded. 'Before you thought to be clever with our boat.'

He flicked his adder tongue over dry lips and I reached round into the small of my back, under the cloak, which made him flinch and cup his finger-short hand in the other.

'Upriver,' he answered in a voice as whiny as the wind, then, seeing me produce the truth knife, added hastily: 'To warn the Saxlanders you are coming. Pallig wants you dead for killing his brother.'

'Dare not do it himself, all the same,' I pointed out scornfully.

'Crucify him,' Finn advised, then, remembering the Rus punishment for Christ-worshipping criminals, added: 'Upside down.'

'Christ Jesus,' moaned Pall and collapsed to the deck, no doubt believing he was on his knees to his White Christ while the reality was he babbled with his nose in Finn's boots; Finn laughed and prodded his face with a toe, while I added this latest bad cess to the growing heap of problems.

The rain started again and the wind swirled and circled, sometimes strong enough to catch the prow or the steerboard and lurch the ship sideways, like a balked horse. The current was strong, too and, in the end, I had us back at the east bank with the rowers drooling and panting. It had thicker woods nearby, so we stayed the rest of that day, sending men hunting or fetching firewood and fretting at having little food and less ale.

It gave me too much time to think, about when Odin would take me as his sacrifice, about what Thorgunna and the others at Hestreng would be doing and about the night-sneak by Pall and his oarmate.

When I had spotted it, I was thinking it one of the crew stealing up on Dark Eye, and tried to tell myself the feelings I had had were because she was valuable to us. Since then, she only took those eyes from me when she scanned the banks, as if hoping to see a face she knew. Even with my back to her I could feel the heat of those eyes.

She was young, yet old enough to grip the interest of all the crew, but she seemed like some animal fresh from a burrow in the woods, thrown into somewhere strange; I saw a hunger in those eyes, which I took to be for the woods and hills of her own place. I knew that hunger. Mine was for a fjord and misted cliffs and a distant blue line of mountain, like something seen on the inside of your eyelids when first you close them at night. I tried hard not to think of hers as another hunger and mostly failed.

That night we had a bigger blaze, just to cheer us and the glow of it fired the river and drowned the dark with blood red. I saw her, when everyone had gone to snores and grunts, a sharp profile against a sudden unveiled moon.

She turned and the firelight caught the shadow of a smile on a mouth that was neat as a hem, yet full enough for me to wonder if she knew how to kiss.

THIRTEEN

The woods seemed still until you were in them, when things moved and made noises; a brown bird flickering in a bush of berries, a fox picking delicately through the sodden edge of the meadow, rooks arguing in a tangle of trees, their new-hatched joining in with an uncertain clamour of young voices as broken as Crowbone's.

I was enjoying this, a hunt and a scout both and free of the ship and the grumbling, quarrelsome crew, even if my bow-skill was likely to shoot my own foot as something tasty for the pot.

The scouting was more important – the day before we had spotted smoke, a thread in the weak, faded blue, no more – but it spoke of fresh food and ale and perhaps even women, so here we were, Kuritsa and me, plootering as quietly as we could through the damp woods in a sudden burst of warmth which brought out the insects in stinging swarms.

For all that I was bitten and had to keep spitting them out, felt them in my hair and trying for my eyes and nose, the pests could not make me unhappy. At times, a silence fell so that I thought I could hear the new buds straining to be free on all the branches, that I could hear the grass hiss and rustle out of the ground. It was during one of these

200

moments that I caught the movement, like *alfar* at the edge of my eye.

I froze and turned, but Kuritsa had already seen it, no more than a shadow sliding in shadows – then I lost it. A curlew called, sharp and two-toned and I saw it, wings curved and gliding, so that just the tips of them fluttered; a mallard hen bow-waved out of nearby reeds, fluffing in anger and followed by a string of ducklings; the river swirled in fat, slow eddies.

Kuritsa placed his fingers on his lips and it was clear he did not like even that much shifting, so I stayed where I was in the willows and peered, feeling the sweat trickle and the insects nip; their whine became the loudest noise.

Somewhere behind, coming up with long, slow, easy strokes, was *Short Serpent*, looking to us for warning, for they were close to the east bank, the west being where the sharpest current swung downriver. And I was sure now that we were not alone here, even if only Kuritsa seemed to know that other men were about. Pallig's men? Perhaps the two who had escaped in the boat, or the one who had fled on foot.

I was offering prayers to Odin that it be them when I saw the man, no more than an arm's length away through the screen of new brush.

He was bareheaded and had dark hair done in braids, with soot-stripes down his cheeks and across his forehead, to break his face up in the brush, like the dapple of a deer. That alone marked him as no friend, for only someone trying to remain hidden from sharp-eyed men would do that, but the bow, nocked and ready with a big, barbed battle arrow, was a clear sign of what he hunted.

The curlew called again, hovering over the nest the man had gone too near and he glanced up towards the sound, knowing he had given himself away to anyone who could read the sign. Then the stripes on his cheeks dropped away as his eyes widened at the sight of me.

There was no time for a bowshot. I dropped it and leaped

ahead, crashing through the willows and trying to haul the seax out of the sheath across my front. The man grunted and tried to back off, give himself some room to shoot, but it was too late for that; I felt branches whip my face and try to snag my tunic.

He dropped the bow, flailed a wild slash at me with the arrow and I crashed on him, grabbing his hand as he grabbed mine; face to face we heaved and grunted and I tasted the onion breath and fear-stink coming off him in waves, saw the bursting beads of sweat roll darkly through the charcoal streaks.

He brought his knee up and almost caught me in the nads, but I had half-turned and he hit my thigh instead which dead-legged me. I knew I should call out, but that would bring his friends as well as mine and he had clearly worked out the same, for we fought in grunting, panting silence, straining like lovers.

I stumbled on the numbed leg, twisted myself and dragged him over on me; we crashed through the willow twigs and shrubs and my knee was up between his legs when he landed on me and I heard him cough out a grunt that turned into a thin, high whine when he lost my knife hand and knew his doom was on him.

I got the seax round then, got it right around and slid it into him, feeling the slight give and the skidding on ribs before it found the gap between and sank all the way. He freed my other hand then and I clamped it across his mouth. His eyes, inches from mine, went big and round with desperation, almost pleading, as if to beg me to take back the knife, the moment of it going in. I saw a tear pearl along the lower lashes of his right eye, then I rolled him off and scrambled back, panting.

He flopped on his back, eyes open, and kicked once or twice. The fingers of one hand moved, almost like a farewell wave from a child.

Kuritsa came up then and I whirled, panicked as a deer, so

202

that he held up both hands and stopped where he was until I saw him. I spat a sour taste in my mouth, blinking the rivers of sweat that poured in my eyes, while the insects whined and pinged, joyous with the iron stink of fresh blood welling and soaking through the rough undyed wool tunic he wore.

'Men ahead,' Kuritsa whispered, his mouth so close to my ear that the hot breath scalded. 'Hiding in the reeds in those wood and skin boats they have.'

He had eyes like a dog, the dead man, like a sad, whipped, gods-cursed dog. I should have rifled him, armpits to boots, for what he carried, though I was betting-certain he had less than an empty bag. Finn would have searched him, or Red Njal, or Hlenni, puddling in the blood and his last shit to find his riches, but I was not that good a raiding-man at this moment.

I stumbled away, dragging my bow and his war arrows, Kuritsa leading the way.

There were seven or eight boats, long fishing efforts made of hide stretched over a wood frame and each crammed with at least ten men. If we had not found them, they would have shot out of the reeds and been on *Short Serpent* in seconds and, though these folk did not look much and had no helmets or armour, they had bows and short spears and desperation enough. They might even have succeeded.

Instead, as they crouched and sweated and batted insects as silently as they could, they suddenly discovered themselves ambushed. My first shot took a man just below his rough-chopped hair, almost in his ear; his scream was as shattering as a stone in the quiet, slow-eddying river. Seconds later, he was in the river and it thrashed with bloody foam.

We shot all the big battle arrows, about ten, one after another, fast as we could and if we missed a mark, I did not see it. Then, as the men howled and scrambled and dived into the water from their boats to escape, we slid away, then ran and ran until, laughing and sobbing, we burst free of the bush and trees and saw *Short Serpent*, swan-serene, walking down the river to us on all its oarlegs.

Heads bobbed up from behind racked shields and stared in astonishment at Kuritsa and me, hanging on to each other, panting drool and spraying sweat and laughter at getting away unharmed.

Not long after, when we all came up to the place, we found one boat upturned and four or five bodies, turning and bobbing in the current. Another man lay on the bank, half-in, half-out. I did not want to splinter through the willows to find the one I had knifed.

'Well,' said Finn, 'we have found the source of the smoke we saw.'

'We have found that they are not friendly,' Alyosha pointed out. 'Even after taking the prow beast off.'

I had agreed to that, though I did not think it would matter much – *Short Serpent* was no little *hafskip*, or river *strug*. It was a *drakkar*, a raiding ship and looked as friendly as a fox in a hen coop, but the men wanted to try and appease the spirit of this land and so the prow beast came off and was stowed gently away.

'Why would they want to attack us?' Yan Alf asked Pall and that one's mole-face split in a twisted grin.

'Perhaps they think you are the sort who would string a man up and cut off his fingers,' he answered bitterly and Trollaskegg smacked him hard on the back of his head, so that he pounded forward three steps.

'Perhaps,' I added, while Pall sullenly rubbed the back of his scalp and scowled, 'someone has been telling them how bad we are. Your friends, I am thinking.'

Finn blinked as the idea took root in him, then he growled, so that Pall scurried a few steps away from him.

'No, no – they are in as much danger here as we are,' he whined.

'They think you are slave-takers,' said a soft voice and we

all turned to where Dark Eye stood, wrapped like a little Greek ikon in my cloak. 'In a ship like this, coming upriver, they will think you come to raid early.'

She had the right of it, sure enough, though raiding men with a *drakkar* would not usually come up this far – it was easier to buy such slaves cheap in Joms, having left it to the Wends to raid Polanians and the Polanians to raid Wends. Sometimes, I had heard, their respective chiefs even raided their own villages and took folk to sell if they were silver-short that year.

I was anxious for news, of Randr Sterki and of a monk with a band of Sorbs and a boy. Even so, there was more sense in rowing on and leaving the whole matter, as I pointed out. Other voices, hungry for cheese and meat and ale, wanted to see if this misunderstanding could not be put right. And one of my names was Trader . . .

Since there were scowls that made it clear this was all my fault, I did not think it clever to refuse. I dropped thirty of us, about half the crew, on the east bank, then had Trollaskegg move the ship to the opposite side, out of immediate harm.

'If you see us running like the dragon Fafnir was breathing flame on our arses,' Hlenni said, scowling at Trollaskegg, 'you had better be within leaping distance of this bank before I get to it, or matters will be bad for you.'

'If I am not, you will be dead, I am thinking,' chuckled Trollaskegg good-naturedly, 'and so no danger to me.'

'Even dead,' Hlenni yelled back as we moved off, 'I am a danger to you. Black-faced and with my head under my arm, I am a danger to you.'

Which was not, considering matters, a good thing to let the gods hear you say, as Red Njal pointed out.

It was not hard to find them, these lurkers in reeds – there were tracks everywhere and signs, like sheepfolds and marked tillage, that a settlement was close. Not that we needed them, as Finn said.

'Just follow the screamers,' he growled, trying to cuff Pall, who was dragging on the end of a rope leash like an awkward dog.

It was not surprising, I was thinking, that folk fled from us, yelling and waving their arms and leaving kine and sheep behind. One man, with scarcely a backward glance, even left a toddler, all fat limbs and wailing; Hlenni scooped him into the crook of one arm and jogged him, though the red-cheeked, yellow-haired boy only started to gurgle and grin when Hlenni took his helmet off.

'Lucky it was Hlenni and not Finn,' Red Njal chuckled, sticking out a dirt-stained finger for the boy to grab. 'To win over bairns and maids takes a gentle lure, as my granny used to say. That wean would have shat himself if Finn had taken his helmet off.'

'I think he has anyway,' mourned Hlenni, sniffing suspiciously at the boy's breeks.

'Na,' said Finn, seeing his chance. 'I am thinking that is just how Hlenni always smells.'

There was laughter and no-one thought Orm Trader could not gold-tongue and silver-gift his way out of this matter and into the smiles of the settlement. I was not so sure; we were all byrnied, helmeted, shielded and armed, moving with a shink-shink of metal, cutting a scar across their pasture and ploughland to where they perched on a mound behind a log stockade. Besides – we had just killed a lot of them; even before we had come within hailing distance, I heard the gates boom shut.

That brought us to a ragged, uncertain halt. It was a small settlement and the stockade was dark with age, yet it looked solid and the gate had a big, square tower with a solid hat of wood to cover it. Men appeared, just their heads and shoulders showing above the rampart edge. So did the points of spears.

'You are the jarl and so should speak to them,' Crowbone said and winced a little at the withering look I gave him.

'Just so,' I said. 'Hold a little. I will learn their tongue while we make a fire. Perhaps Finn can make us a stew while we wait?'

'I can,' said Finn, 'if I had water and someone found some roots and Kuritsa shot something tasty.'

'I thought we brought Pall for talking to them?' Crowbone persisted.

'Aye,' growled Finnlaith, giving the answer before I could speak, 'but can you trust what the little rat tells you is being said?'

'We brought Pall because I like him where I can see him,' I pointed out and Crowbone, seeing it now, frowned a little and nodded. It did not diminish the truth of what he said, all the same. There was nothing else to be done, otherwise we had come all this way for no reason – but I did not have to like it.

Hlenni, Red Njal, me, Finn and the leashed Pall and Styrbjorn all moved out – the latter because I did not want him out of my sight – with Finnlaith and Ospak as shieldmen in case matters turned uglier than Hel's daughters. Every step into the place where arrows might reach made my arse pucker and my belly contract. When I thought we had come close enough to be heard without bellowing at the edge of voice, I stopped and hailed them.

A head appeared, this one wearing a blue hat with a fringe of fur round it, probably what passed for the rank of riches in this place – everyone else I had seen was bareheaded. The iron-grey beard beneath that blue hat hid a mouth I knew would be a thin line.

He was hard, this headman, a nub of a man worn by toil even if he had managed to work himself up to a blue hat with fur round it; even at a distance I saw the lines on his face, etched deep by wind and worry.

'We come to trade,' I yelled, hearing the stupidity of it in my own voice, for we had just killed a half-dozen of his people, a hard dunt of menfolk loss in a settlement this size. He was not slow to point this out and I was surprised to hear him say it in halting Norse.

'It seems we will not need you today, Christ-rat,' growled Styrbjorn nastily and gave Pall a kick so that he yelped.

'Go away, slavers,' Blue Hat added, his voice carrying clearly with the faint wind that drove from him to us. 'Nothing easy is here for you today.'

'I seek a monk,' I yelled back. 'A Greek one in black. He had a boy with him.'

There was silence for a moment, while the damp warmth seeped and the insects annoyed us.

'Escape you?' came the reply. 'Good.'

I sighed; this was going to be a long, hard day.

'We can trade,' I began, trying to keep the weary desperation out of my voice . . . but Hlenni stepped forward suddenly and held up the yellow-haired boy, swung him up and into the air at the end of both of his hands so that he could be clearly seen. The boy chuckled and laughed, enjoying it.

'See?' he bellowed. 'We mean no harm.'

A woman screamed – probably the mother; I wondered how her man had explained how he had run off and left the lad.

Hlenni moved forward and someone – Red Njal, when I thought on matters later – called his name uncertainly, but Hlenni strode forward with the boy in his arms and set him down almost under the gate.

'Growl not at guests, nor drive them from the gate,' Hlenni said, grinning back at Red Njal. 'As your granny used to say.'

The boy toddled a bit, lost his balance, fell forward, crawled a bit, then rose up, wobbling. Abandoned, uncertain, he began to bawl.

'Cautious and silent let him enter a dwelling,' Red Njal muttered. 'To the heedful seldom comes harm.'

There was an argument above and a woman's voice sounded shrill, so it was not hard to work matters out.

'Your granny,' Hlenni said, turning to grin at Red Njal, 'was . . .'

Then someone hurled the rock at him from the ramparts.

A big one it was, big as Hlenni's stupid head and the crack of it hitting in the curve of his neck and shoulder was loud; louder yet was the roar of disbelief and rage that went up from us. Hlenni pitched forward on his face and Red Njal howled and leaped forward.

Arrows came over with a hiss and shunk, some skittering through the wet grass. Finnlaith caught Red Njal as he hirpled past, caught and held him, though Njal raved and struggled and frothed and Ospak stepped in front of them both, shield up against the shafts.

Eventually we dragged Red Njal away out of range, where he subsided, gnawing a knuckle and trembling, his eyes fixed on the fallen Hlenni.

The gate opened and men darted out, grabbed the bairn and took Hlenni by the heels and dragged him in, which set all the men off again until Finn and I had to crack heads and draw blood.

Sweating, we crouched like wolves after a failed hunt, panting with our mouths open, sick with loss.

'Perhaps he is alive,' Styrbjorn ventured, thoughtful as only a man who did not really care could be. 'They may regret what they have done and bind his wound.'

No-one spoke. I blinked the sting of sweat from my eyes and tried to think. In the end, though it wove itself around like a knot of mating snakes, matters came out the same way. I rose up and went back to the stockade to hail them.

I had barely bellowed when something arced over the stockade wall, smacked into the wet earth with a crunch and then rolled almost to my feet. I did not have to look to know what it was; none of us did.

Red Njal howled until the cords on his neck stood out and spittle flew, roared until he burst something in his throat and coughed blood. The rest of us did not speak for a long time and I only had to nod to send long-legged Koghe loping back to fetch the rest of the crew, for the sight of Hlenni's bloody, battered head, the rough-hacked neck trailing tatters of skin, had sealed the wyrd of this place.

Hlenni. Gone and gone. One of the original Oathsworn from long before my time, who had survived everything the gods could hurl, save a stone from some dirty-handed, skin-wearing troll of a farmer.

'I do not think,' Finn said bitterly to Styrbjorn, 'that they have bound his wounds. Or regret what they have done.'

Red Njal lifted his face then, a stream of misery and hate poured up at the stockade, his eyes cold as blue ice.

'They will,' he rasped.

I found Blue Hat, eventually. He was in the Christ hall, for these folk were followers of the White Christ and had built his temple partly in stone, thinking it a refuge for times of trouble. But they had never come on trouble like the Oathsworn, wolf-woken to revenge.

We took our time on it, too, cold as old vomit, while the rain drizzled. We took all but ten men from the boat and stood behind shields, beyond arrow range of the wooden walls, the rain dripping off the nasals of our helmets and seeping through the rings of iron to the tunics beneath.

We were howe-silent, too, which unnerved the defenders and when I sent others to cut wood, that steady rhythm of sound must have seemed, in the end, like a death drum to those in the stockade, for they stopped their taunts.

'Well,' growled Finn as men came back lugging a solid trunk, trimmed and sharpened. 'What is the plan, Jarl Orm?'

Most of the others looked surprised, for it seemed clear to them – under cover of our shields we would knock the gates in with this ram then storm the place. Apart from deciding what insults to bellow, that was usually the way and surely the way the famed Oathsworn would do it.

Finn knew me better than that and even Crowbone, stroking his beardless chin like some ancient jarl considering the problem, knew more than older heads.

'You do not care for that way, fame or not,' he said while men gathered to listen.

I admitted it then and have done since. I am like other men and desire proper respect and esteem, when it is due. In the end, though, Odin taught me about fair fame – it was a tool, an edged one that can cut the user unless it is properly used. I said so and Abjorn grunted a little.

'You do not agree?' Finn challenged and Alyosha chuckled, one jarl-hound to another, it seemed to me.

'It does not seem quite right,' admitted Abjorn, but it was Styrbjorn, all fire and movement, like a colt new to the bridle, who hoiked it up for us all to look at.

'A man's reputation is everything,' he spluttered. 'Fair fame is all we have.'

'Once I thought so,' I answered. 'Like the Oath we swear, it binds us. It weakens us, too, for it makes us act in ways we would not usually do.'

'Like charging through the gates of that place like mad bulls,' Crowbone added brightly. Styrbjorn subsided, muttering, but Abjorn nodded slowly as the idea rooted itself.

In the end, it was simple enough. I had men run forward, shields up and shouting, so that heads popped up on the ramparts and a flurry of shafts came over. No-one was hurt and we collected some.

'Hunting arrows,' Finn said with satisfaction. It was what I had been thinking; Kuritsa and me had shot off what war arrows these people possessed. Hunting arrows we could protect ourselves from.

* * *

211

The sky lowered itself like a gull on eggs, all grey and fat and ugly. Twenty men, led by Finn, went into the woods carrying bundles and axes and more chopping sounds came. This time, though, they were making ladders and the bundles held all the spare tunics folk had, which they put on under their mail, up to four of them. Then they circled, unseen, to the far side of the stockade.

I sent men with the ram against the gates, moving up under shields where there was only pant and grunt and fear. Rocks clattered on us, shafts whumped into shields, or struck and bounced, skittering like mad snakes through the wet grass.

On the far side, while the gate thundered like a deep bell, Finn slapped ladders against the almost undefended rear wall and led the others up and over. There were only twenty of them, but they were skilled men, mailed, shielded and moving as fast as their bulk would let them, fast as a shuffling trot, hacking at anything that came near and heading for the bar on the gate.

The folk in the settlement panicked when they saw such a group, iron men slicing through their meeting square, toppling the cross-pillar, scattering chickens, splintering carts, kicking buckets, some of them stuck with arrows which went through byrnie and one layer, perhaps two – but would not go through ring-coats and the padding of four tunics.

Hedgepigs in steel, they were and that broke the will of the defenders, so that they ran, screaming and throwing away their hayforks and hunting spears.

When the gate broke open, then, all I saw was a shrieking, milling crowd running this way and that and it was like mice to cats – the very act of them running in fear brought what they dreaded on them, launched the howling Oathsworn at them, flaming for vengeance over Hlenni Brimill.

Arrows flicked at the edge of vision and I ducked, for I wore no helmet, thanks to the still healing scar across my forehead and my tender nose and I could hear my father,

212

Gunnar, snort in my ear at that – if you have the choice of only one piece of armour, take a helm, he had dinned into me. Never go bareheaded in a fight.

Well, it did Koghe no good, for the arrow that flew past me hit him and there was a wet, deep sound. I half-turned; tall Koghe staggered past with the force of his own rush, the arrow through his mouth, a *fud*-hair below the nasal of his helmet. Choking on his own blood and teeth, pawing the shaft, he was dead even as he gurgled and fell.

I saw the bowman then, ran at him as another arrow was fitted to the nock, held my sword – Brand's splendid blade – in front of my body until the last moment before I got to him, for I knew what the archer would have to do.

He snapped the arrow into one hand and stabbed with it and I took it round in an arc down and right, smashed in with my shoulder and knocked him flying, arse over tip. He was still struggling like a beetle on his back when I chopped him between neck and shoulder.

Shouts and screams soaked the air, almost drowning out the high, thin sound of a bell; I sensed a shadow and stepped back sharply. A body struck the ground, the wood axe meant for my head spilling from one hand and then Styrbjorn stepped up, grinning, the seax and the hand that held it thick with gore.

'The Christ place,' he said, nodding towards the building and I realised that someone was calling the last defenders to him there. Still grinning, he let me lead the way and I realised he had probably saved my life with his handy backstab.

Blue Hat was the bellringer and he was dead by the time I got to him, through a madness that was as like Svartey as to have been its crazed brother. Men moved like grim shadows, killing. There was no plunder, no tupping women in the dust. Only killing.

I walked through it as if in a dream; Uddolf ran across my path, chasing a fear-babbling youngster up to a wall, where he ran at him with his spear, so hard that it broke and the boy, pinned, screamed and writhed like a worm on a hook. Uddolf, shrieking, beat the boy's face bloody with the broken haft.

Ospak kicked away a young woman, begging on her knees with her hands clasped round his calves, then split the head from her mother with two strokes; yellow marrow oozed from the bone of her neck.

The Christ place was dim and silent and I slumped against the painted wall, feeling the shadows and the quiet like a balm. Then my eyes grew used to the light.

Under the cross with its Tortured God, Red Njal stood on splayed legs, head bowed, panting like a bull after mating. At his feet was Blue Hat and I would not have known the man had it not been for his headgear, for Red Njal had not been kind.

'Hlenni . . .'

I followed Red Njal's glazed look and saw the body, strange with no head, but linen-wrapped neat enough. Nearby was a dead Shaven Priest in his brown robe, killed kneeling in prayer.

They had bound Hlenni's wounds after all, it seemed. Just a little late.

It was all too late. Dull-eyed men staggered, too exhausted to kill now but it did not matter for everyone was dead. No, that was not right, I saw. Every *thing* was dead, even the dogs and the goats and the hens. Everything.

I found myself in a long hall, a meeting place perhaps, for these folk did not do chieftain's *hovs*. Yet it was like one as to bring a rush of memories and I ran to them with my arms out, to try and wrap myself from what went on outside.

There was a pitfire, cold ash now, but the smell of it and the seasoned wood of the pillars flooded Hestreng back on me, a Hestreng unburned. This was the time of year when the sap shifted in everything and the sun came back, so that you could peg out furs and bedclothes and let the sun drive out the lice and fleas. Men would work half-naked, though it was

214

this side of too cool to be comfortable; there was enough food, but most of the ale was finished, so fights were few.

Summer was the lean time between harvests, so that the unlucky could starve to death eating grass while the sun poured down like honey.

There were sheep and goats to be taken to upland pastures, but not the ones reserved for the horses; sheep and goats ate the grass down to the soil, leaving nothing – but they gave wool for *wadmal*, and milk for curd and cheese and this was the time when *skyr* was made. I remembered it, thickened whey, white as a virgin's skin, lush off the wooden spoon.

But Hestreng was black timber and ash. With luck, a new hall would be up and giving shelter, the wood reeking of newness and tar, but there would be no time for *skyr* and few furs or bedclothes to peg out.

The outside noise yelled me back to a strange, cold, dead hall; someone burst in, saw me and backed out. I rose, feeling as if my legs had turned to wood, but having to move before the tale went round that Orm, White Bear Slayer, leader of the famed Oathsworn, slayer of were-dragons, tamer of the half-women, half-horse steppe creatures was sitting by himself staring at fire ash and near weeping.

Outside, those with life left in their legs and arms had started to look for plunder, moving as if the air was thick as honey; I picked my way through the litter of corpses, feeling the suck of bloody mud on my boots.

I stopped only once, in the act of stepping over a corpse, at first just one more among so many. It was smaller by far, though, with fat little limbs and yellow hair, though there was a lot of blood in it now and the little, budded, thumb-sucking mouth that had smiled at Hlenni Brimill was slack and already had a fly in it.

FOURTEEN

There were hills on either side of us, easy rolling and wooded with willow and elm and the flash of birch, thick with berry bushes and game, while the river hardly flowed against *Short Serpent* at all. But there was no singing from the oarsmen now and no joy in the stacked plunder, for all that they had snarled at the lack of it before.

We had beaver and squirrel and marten skins, *wadmal* cloth baled with grease-rich fleeces against the rain – the work of winter looms – and carded wool waiting to be woven.

Now there was mutton and lamb and beef, for we had slaughtered every breathing creature in that place. We had winter roots pickled in barrels and sweetness wax-sealed in pots. Ale, too, though old and a little bitter. There was even hard drink, like the green wine of far-away Holmgard, a clear spirit made from rye – but not enough of it to chase the sick taste of what we had done to that nameless place.

We loaded it all, stuffing it into *Short Serpent* until it wobbled precariously, as if the more we took the better the excuse for what had been done. For some of us, the only excuse was the laying out of Hlenni on a cross-stack of timbers ripped from the houses, with Koghe next to him and Blue Hat at both their feet.

216

Then we scattered all the lamp oil we could find, sprayed that expensive stuff like water, for this was not a howing-up, dedicated to Frey – this was a blaze that sped Hlenni and Koghe straight up to Odin, as was proper. A beacon, one or two muttered uneasily, that could be seen for days.

They had been our only deaths. The morose Gudmund had taken the prong of a hayfork in his belly and Yan Alf had taken the flat of a wooden spade on the side of his head – wielded by a woman, too, to add to his annoyance and shame – but he had only a rich, purple bruise to show for it.

We had slaughtered one hundred and seventy-four of them, women and bairns among them. Now there was a sickness on us, like the aftermath of a *jul* feast that had gone on too long, one where folk told you what a time you had because you could not quite recall it for yourself. One where, for days after, everything tasted of ash and your mind was too dull to work.

Worse than that, at least for me, was the feeling that there had been too much blood spilled, as if it poured into a deep, black hole in the earth, the Abyss that Brother John always warned me I was destined to descend. The same Abyss which had flowed out and into me the night I had ripped out the throat of a berserker.

I felt like the prow beast, carved in an endless snarl, unable to change my expression, only capable of nodding approval at what was done. I looked at that beast now, back where it had been taken from and rearing proudly up; there seemed small point now in appeasing the spirits of this land. I would rather have them afraid of us.

We came round the bend and into the sight and sound and smell of a big settlement, this one on the west bank of the river.

It was, said Pall, the Wend *borg* of Szteteno. He was still leashed, tied to one or other of us, or the mast when all were busy, yet he had recovered a measure of his sleekit smoothness and grinned at the sight of the place, picking the beef from his gapped teeth with a sliver of bone.

'They have no love for those on the east side of the river,' he told us. 'They will, perhaps, thank us warmly for burning those trolls out.'

'Do you believe this ferret?' sneered Styrbjorn and I looked from one to the other.

'I have a little knife that finds out the truth,' I answered, which made Pall glance at his bound hand, scowling. Styrbjorn laughed and I turned and handed him a long bundle wrapped in a square of sun-faded silk which had once been blue. He looked at it, bewildered, then took it, feeling the weight and knowing what it was. Yet he whistled through pursed lips at the silk.

'They say worms make this,' he grinned. 'I have seen worms and all they make is dung and good bait for fishing. It is something when a man hands me my sword and the wrapping on it is half the worth of the sheath.'

'The silk is something to trade, the blade will help you keep what you get. Take both, use them to go home,' I said with a growl and more gruffly than I had intended. 'Take Pall with you, for he is no more use to me than a hole in a bucket. I am thinking that what you do with him and how much you trust him is your affair.'

It was reward enough for his seax-skill at the settlement and we both knew it. When the ship slid with a gentle kissing dunt against one of the spray of wooden piers, he sprang over the side with a laugh and a wave. Pall, less skilled and more eager, scrambled after and darted away, throwing the leash off him with a last curse.

'Is that jarl-cleverness I am seeing, then?' asked Finn, appearing at my elbow as the oars were clattered down and men milled, sorting themselves out and tying *Short Serpent* to the wharf. 'Is there a plan to it? Am I follow and finish it?'

There had been enough blood over all of this to slake even Odin's thirst and I said as much. He shrugged.

'Well, there is always the Loki-luck that will see them throat-cut before they reach King Eirik again. By then, of course, you will have come up with some gold-browed words to appease Jarl Brand.'

Returning his son would be enough, I was thinking. I watched until the figure of Styrbjorn had vanished in the throng on the wooden walkways. Tall and lithe and still raw with youth, he had the look of greatness, yet something was lacking in him – I was thinking that he knew it, too, and it scorched him sullen. Still, I did not think it was his wyrd to be throat-cut.

The men spilled out of the boat and had no trouble stepping easily onto the planks of the wharf, which I noted; usually we had to scramble up half the height of a man to a planked pier such as this, but the river had risen.

'Aye,' grunted Trollaskegg, seeing me look at the rain-sodden sky. 'I can smell storm, me. Over behind the mist are those mountains and I am betting sure Thor is stamping up and down and throwing Mjollnir for all he is worth.'

'No matter,' Crowbone broke in, bright with excitement, 'for we will be snug and safe here, at least for one night.'

Those nearest agreed with hooms and heyas, looking forward to a chance to dry out cloaks and tunics and boots by a real fire, with milk-cooked food and ale enough to chase away the blood-cloud which had settled on all of us like a cloak of black flies.

I was more fretting than I showed; Pall's oarmates had escaped and he had told us they were coming upriver to alert the Saxlanders.

I had been thinking that, if we proved empty-handed with weapons and full-fisted with silver, the Saxlanders would not care overly much – yet we were alone on that wharf, the men turning this way and that, wary as kitchen dogs hunting scraps, hunched under the stares of dark doorways and the sightless eyes of shuttered windholes. Beyond that, I saw big men in leather armour and spears, with a man in front holding a staff.

'Should we prepare war gear, Orm?' Alyosha asked and I shook my head; no-one had approached us at all, neither trader nor soldier and I had the notion matters were held, like an insect in amber.

I told them to unload and stack the furs and *wadmal*, so that the sight of such a mundane task – and the profit it promised – might allay some fears. For all that, the sweat was greasy on my face and slid a cold finger down between my shoulders.

For a little while we sat and shivered in the rain of that place, the men growing more and more restive, hunched and miserable and leashed by me, for I wanted some acknow-ledgement that we were welcome before I let these growlers loose to scatter through the settlement.

It did not help that they could smell the roasting ribs and boiling cauldron snakes and hear the fishermen inviting customers to choose an eel and have it sliced and cooked there and then. The gulls wheeled and screeched – better fed, muttered Bjaelfi, than the Oathsworn.

A man started down the walkway, not looking up until he saw us and realised he was alone, having crossed some in-visible line which held everyone back; he was so startled that he took a step off the walkway into the muck and lost his shoe jerking his foot back. Cursing, he fished it out and half-hopped away.

A child ran out, laughing, hands out and mouth open; his mother raced after him, snatched him up and glared at us as if it was our fault. Even the dogs slunk, tails curled and growling.

We waited, driven mad by the smells of what we had not had in a long time, so thick we could taste them; cooking fish and hot ovens and brewing beer – and shite pits and middens. One or two grumbles went up and Murrough, in a loud voice, proclaimed that if he didn't get some fish and bread and ale soon he would eat the next dog that presented itself, skin and all.

Then the man with the staff suddenly appeared, striding down to us; men burst out laughing, nudging Murrough and telling him his meal had arrived. The man, a grey-beard dressed in embroidered red, half-shrouded in a blue cloak fastened on one shoulder with a large pin, was bewildered and bristling, so that he paused and glared.

'Welcome,' he said eventually. Up close, I saw the staff was impressively carved and had a large yellow stone set in the bulbous end.

'There will be no berthing fees for you,' he added, chewing the Norse like a dog does a wasp.

'Fees? What fees?' demanded Trollaskegg, chin bristling.

'Berthing fees,' I told him and he spat, only just missing the staff, while the messenger stared down his long nose.

'I do not pay berthing fees,' Trollaskegg declared, folding his arms.

'That is what he said,' I answered wearily and Trollaskegg, uncertain now whether he had won something or not, grunted and nodded, deciding he had the victory.

The messenger inclined his head in a curt bow and swaggered off, almost knocked over in the rush of traders who arrived in a sudden, unleashed mob, hucksters all of them, crowding round and spreading their wares out on linen or felt, dark coloured for the gem and trinket sellers.

They had combs and pins and brooches of bone and ivory, some pieces of Serkland silver set with amber and flashing stones; the Oathsworn gathered round and fished out barter-stuff and even hacksilver, for these hard, tangle-haired growlers were magpies for glitter.

The traders were good, too, I noted, even if all their gems were glass, for they had stories for all the pieces and, if they forgot which story went with which from customer to customer,

221

it did not matter much. If all the stories were true, though, each had some potent magic from somewhere which would create sure sons in the most barren womb and make men hard as keel-trees if their women wore it when they wore nothing else.

Men believe what they wish to believe, a weakness that can be used, like any other. The gods know this; Odin especially knows this.

The men milled and slowly scattered, looking for food and ale and women. I spent some time haggling a price for the *wadmal* and furs and knew I was robbed; it was too early to be this far upriver. Since we had raided all the goods, though, it hardly mattered and was all profit – anyway, I was glad to be quit of the bundles and what they made me remember.

I had just finished handseling a deal with a spit and slap when Abjorn forced his way through the throng, chewing meat on a wooden skewer. He jerked his head backwards as he spoke.

'There is someone wants a word,' he said, spraying food and I looked behind him; the grey-beard with the staff had returned. The trader I had been talking to took a sideways sidle to avoid him and clamped his lips on what he had been telling me. I had asked this trader, as I had asked others, about a Greek priest and a north boy and had nothing worth noting – they had been here, for sure, yet folk seemed reluctant to admit it.

'The merchant Kasperick wishes words with you,' the grey-beard intoned.

'Who is this Kasperick?' I asked and the messenger raised one irritated eyebrow.

'He is the one who wishes to see you,' he replied smartly and Finn growled like a warning dog.

'Then I must make myself worthy of visiting such an eminence,' I replied, before Finn decided to pitch the messenger into the river. I turned to Trollaskegg.

222

'Fetch my blue cloak from my sea-chest and the pin that goes with it,' I told him loudly and watched the scowl thunder onto his brow as he did it, slow and stiff with annoyance. He thrust them truculently at me and, before he could also tell me to fuck off and die and that he was no thrall to me, I drew him closer.

'Get everyone on board and stay there,' I hissed. 'Loosen off the lines. I will take Finn, Crowbone and Red Njal with me and if all is well, I will send Crowbone back. If not, Red Njal. If you see Red Njal, pole off to the river and row for it – upriver. Make sure the girl is safe and kept on board.'

Trollaskegg blinked a bit, then nodded. The water was up and it would be hard pull against the narrowed spate.

'Can I go ashore?' asked a voice and we all turned to where Dark Eye stood. She wore a tunic, one of Yan's for he was smallest, yet it suited her for a dress down to her calves.

I shook my head. 'Later perhaps,' I added and she drowned me with those seal eyes, making me ashamed of even that friendly lie.

'We should go armed,' growled Finn and again I shook my head, never taking my eyes off her. No sense in inviting trouble. A sword, as was proper, but no byrnie or helms or shields or great bearded axes. Finn grunted, unconvinced.

'I see no trouble,' Onund argued, looking around, while the messenger waited, tapping his staff impatiently.

We had come upriver on a raiding boat with the prows up, smoke from a burning staining the sky behind us and the warning whispers of enemies in every ear. Even allowing for the folk on the west bank not liking those on the east, traders in geegaws, along with everyone else, would have vanished like snow off a sun-warmed dyke at the sight of us. Yet here they were, lying and haggling, not in the least afraid – but it had taken them two hours and more to be so friendly.

Onund thought about it, frowning, but it was Dark Eye who dunted him gently to the centre of it.

'They have been told not to be afraid, to make us welcome,' she said, soft as the lisp of rain. 'They have been told that either we are no danger – or will be made to be no danger.'

'Heya,' Finn said, grasping it. 'It is a trap then.'

'And you walk into it like a bairn?' Bjaelfi accused, but Finn clapped him on the shoulder, grinning.

'It is only a trap if there is no escape from it,' he said.

'There is only escape if others come for us,' Crowbone added. 'What are Onund and Trollaskegg and Abjorn and the others to do?'

I looked at him and them and shrugged.

'I am thinking you may have to hold a *Thing* on that for yourselves,' I said, 'once the girl and the ship both are safe.'

'Quickly,' added Finn meaningfully to Trollaskegg. 'So you reach that part where you come to rescue us.'

The place was more than *thorp*, less than town, a fetid cluster of little log houses with steep roofs that came almost to the ground, with a shop or a workplace in an open part and sleeping benches in an attached, closed space.

Tight-herded about split-pine walkways, the houses teemed with life and smells – but the messenger who led us seemed well-known and folk moved out of our path, even those who struggled with heavy loads of fish, or barrels. In any trade town further north, the haughty messenger, stick or no, would have been kicked into the side muck, as Finn pointed out.

I was only vaguely aware of it. As we left, she had whispered, 'Come back alive,' and my arm and my cheek burned – the one where her hand had laid, the other where her lips had touched. Finn had growled like a guard hound and shaken his head. I was still swimming up from the depths of her seal eyes as we traipsed after the messenger.

The houses straggled out, became more withy and less wood, until they stopped entirely. Then there was the fortress, the approach to it lined with cages on poles and, in most of them, a dessicated, rot-blackened affair that had once been human. A few of them, I saw, were fresher dead than that.

It was a good, solid affair, ditched and stockaded, with a solid half-timber, half-stone keep on a mound – what the Rus-Slavs call *kreml* and *detinets*, though there were no Rus-Slavs here. No Wends, either, I saw and we all exchanged meaningful glances, for the leather-armoured spearholders at the gates were big, ox-shouldered Saxlanders, who stared straight ahead. The wind hissed through the cages, played teasingly with the lank straggles of remaining hair.

This Kasperick was also Saxlander, I was thinking, when we were eventually ushered into the hall, a place drifting with a mist of smoke, where people in the dim light seemed transparent as ghosts.

There was heat, but it came from a clay stove, which I had seen before in *izbas* in Novgorod. There was light, too, from sconces stuck on the pillars, metal-backed to keep the wood from scorching and most of them were clustered round a high seat, on which was this Kasperick.

He did not rise to greet us, which got a growl from Crowbone; his voice had broken completely now and our amusement with his testing of it had ebbed. The rest of us had been to the Great City and were used to these sorts of manners – but Kasperick was no Greek nor, I was thinking, was he Wend.

Saxlander then, I decided, watching his white hands flutter over documents. A ring caught the sconce light on a carved surface and played with it as I watched his square face, handsome once but running to jowl even under the red-gold beard, as neat-trimmed as his hair. I watched his eyes, too, which were watching us and not the documents he held.

I did not think he could read at all and, if he did, it was birchbark he read on and had probably brought out the parchment – and the seal-ring, the expensive, fur-trimmed robe he wore and the Christ cross round his neck – to impress us with

225

his riches and power and learning. All of it, of course, a mummer's play.

'I am here, merchant,' I said, like an iron bar dropped on a stone floor. He looked up languidly and I nodded at the document in his hands. Since parchment was too expensive to waste, both sides had been written on and the one I saw was in Latin and I could read it easily save that it was upside down. I took a chance that the side he was supposed to be reading was the same way.

'You may find that more interesting if you turn it the right way up,' I added and he fluttered his hands and scowled, a look as nasty as a black storm on the Baltic, when he realised he had given himself away. Then, in an instant, he was all smiles.

'Of course,' he said in smooth Norse, with only a slight accent. 'Forgive me . . . I am so used to overawing these Wendish folk that I forget, sometimes, who I am dealing with.'

'You are dealing with Orm Ruriksson,' I said. 'A Norse trader from Hestreng who can read runes and Latin, speaks Latin and Greek and some few other tongues and knows every sort of coin folk use in the world. Who am I dealing with?'

'Kasperick,' he answered, then chuckled, waving forward a thrall with a fat silver pitcher. 'Sit, sit,' he added, waving expansively at the benches, so we did so and the thrall poured – wine, I saw, rich and red and unwatered. Crowbone barely sipped his; Red Njal guzzled down half of his before he realised it was in a cup of expensive blue glass and fell to examining it. Finn never touched his at all and neither did I.

'Trader?' Kasperick went on, lacing his white fingers together and smiling. 'You are, I suspect, no more a trader than I am a merchant.'

'So – what are you?'

'Slenzanie,' he replied lightly. 'Saxlander to you, but I am of the Slenzanie tribe and charged with holding this place as a concern by the Margrave Hodo. You may call me lord.'

'Is that the same Hodo who got his arse kicked by the Pols at Cidini?' Finn demanded scornfully, for he had listened carefully to the talk back in Joms. Kasperick pursed his mouth like a cat's arse but, just then, Red Njal, engrossed in the lights within the blue glass cup, turned it up to look at the bottom; wine spashed on his knees and he looked up guiltily.

'There was such a . . . setback,' Kasperick replied stiffly. 'We shall make the Pols pay for that and no-one should make the mistake of thinking we are weakened because of that battle. Especially you *Ascomanni*, who think yourselves lords of the rivers because your king, Bluemouth, is humping a Wendish princess.'

'Well, now we are off to a fine beginning for two folk who are not merchants,' I answered, 'for we are trading insults well enough. It is not Bluemouth, but Bluetooth, though I am thinking you know this.'

His eyes flicked a little, but he kept his lips tight as a line of stitching.

'You are right to call us *Ascomanni* – Ashmen – for we are northers with good ash spears,' I went on into the stone of his face, 'but we are not Bluetooth's Danes. At least, not the ones you know of, from Joms, for they are mostly Wends of no account, but I am thinking you know this, too. We are mostly Svears and a few Slavs from further east and north, whom the Serkland Arabs call Rus, but I am not expecting you to know that. Perhaps a Dzhadoshanie or an Opolanie would have known that – even one of the Lupiglaa – but I make allowances for the wit-lack of the Slenzanie.'

I had been listening well at Joms, too. Two red spots appeared on Kasperick's cheeks at this and there was a sucking in of breath from the ghosts who listened and watched in the dimness at the mention of the other, rival, tribes of the Silesians.

Kasperick controlled himself with an effort, though the smile started to tremble a little. He drank to cover himself and took a breath or two.

227

'No matter who you are,' he said after a moment or two and waved a dismissive hand, 'you all appear the same to me, you Northmen. It is what you carry on your ship that matters.'

'Ah, you still have your merchant hat on, I see,' I replied and then spread my hands in apology. 'I suspect some folk from downriver have tried to mire our good name, but they are mean-mouthed nithings. We have nothing much more than some *wadmal* and a few furs. Hardly worth your time. Besides – I have handseled a deal on that.'

'You have the Mazur girl,' he answered, his voice like a slap.

Finn growled and I took a breath. How had he known that? My thoughts whirled up like leaves in a *djinn* of wind.

'Slaves?' I managed to answer. 'One slave? She is thin and you have, I am thinking, plumper girls closer to hand.'

'I like Mazur ones,' he replied, enjoying himself now he had set us back on our heels. Oiled smooth as a Greek beard he was now and Finn's scowl revealed how he did not care for it much.

'To a man used to Slenzanie women, I suppose she would be sweet,' he grunted. 'They all smell of fish, though they are never near the sea.'

The red spots reappeared and Kasperick leaned forward, his eyes narrowed and his fingers steepled.

'You are the one called Finn,' he said, 'who fears nothing. We will see about that.'

Now how had he known that? A suspicion trailed fingers across my thoughts, but Finn was curling his lip in a sneer, which distracted me.

'The Mazur girl,' I said hastily, before Finn spat out a curse at him, 'is not a slave and good Christmenn do not enslave the free, or so I had heard.'

I nodded at the cross peeping shyly out from above the neck of his tunic and he glanced down and frowned.

'This? I took this from a Sorb, one of a band I had to deal

228

with. You probably saw them on the way in, safely caged. I am a Christ follower but not one of these Greeks, who can all argue that God does not exist save in Constantinople.'

I stopped, chilled, as he brought it out and waved it scornfully – the Christ cross was a fat Greek one, plain dark wood with a cunning design of the Tortured God on it worked in little coloured tiles; I had seen it before, but not round Kasperick's plump neck.

'You are Christ-sworn yourself,' he went on, smirking, 'and I suspect this Mazur girl is not. So passing her to me is no sin.'

It was my turn to look down and frown. He had seen the little cross on a thong hanging on my breastbone.

'This? I had this from the first man I ever killed,' I told him, which was the truth – though it was truer to say the man had been a boy. I had been fifteen when I did it.

'That other trinket that looks like a cross is a good Thor Hammer,' I added. 'There is another, the *valknut*, which is an Odin sign.'

Kasperick frowned. 'I had heard you were baptised.'

I shook my head and smiled apologetically, more sure than ever about who had been whispering in Kasperick's ear.

'If your God is willing to prevent evil but not able then he is not all-wise and all-seeing, as gods are supposed to be,' I told him. 'If he is able but not willing, then he is more vicious than a rat in a barrel. If he is both able and willing, then from where comes all the evil your priests rave about? If he is neither able nor willing, then why call him a god?'

'So,' he said thoughtfully. 'A follower of Thor? Odin? Some other dirty-handed little farmer god of the Wends, one with four faces? No matter – they will help you here no better than the Sorbs I caged outside, no matter how clever your words.'

'I thought those Sorbs were good Christmenn,' I answered, trying to think clearly as I spoke. 'Like you.'

'I took this cross from them, as they took it from a Greek

229

priest they sold. They used the money to get drunk and once drunk they killed a man. So there is the Lord at work – even if it was only a Greek priest he worked through.'

I blinked with the thunderbolt of it, a strike as hard as Thor's own Hammer. I had been right about the cross, then.

'Did this Greek priest have a boy with him?' I asked. 'A Northerner – a Dane.'

Kasperick, bewildered at the way this conversation had suddenly darted off the path, waved an irritated hand.

'They sold them both to another of your sort. He was going upriver.'

Upriver. A slave dealer going upriver and buying a Greek monk and a boy. The chill in me settled like winter haar.

'The dealer,' I asked. 'Did he have marks on him, blue marks? A beard like a badger's arse?'

The conversation was now a little dog which would not come to heel and Kasperick was scowling a leash at it.

'There was such a man,' he hissed, 'but enough of this. Fetch the girl and be done with it, for you have no choice in the matter.'

Randr Sterki had Leo and Koll and one swift glance sideways let me know that Finn and Crowbone had realised it, too. So did Red Njal, who had been strange since Hlenni's death and was now starting to tremble at the edges, the way wolf-coats do when the killing rage comes on.

'Red Njal,' I said sharply and he blinked and shook himself like a dog coming out of water. Kasperick, wary and angry as a wet cat, lifted a hand and men appeared, leather-armoured, carrying spears and bulking out the light. Finn, who hated Saxlanders, curled his lip at them.

'Step out and go and fetch the Mazur girl,' I told Red Njal and he looked at me, then at Kasperick and grinned, nodded and hirpled away on his bad leg. I settled on the bench, waiting and Crowbone cocked his head sideways, like a bird and stared curiously at Kasperick.

'What?' demanded Kasperick, suspicious and scowling, but Crowbone merely shrugged.

'Once,' he said, 'a long time gone – don't ask me when – up in Dovrefell in the north of Norway, there was a troll.'

'This will pass the time until folk return with my Mazur girl,' Kasperick announced pointedly and there was a dutiful murmur of laughter from the dim figures behind him. Crowbone waggled his head from side to side.

'Perhaps,' he said, 'perhaps not. This is not a long tale, for this troll was famous for two things – he was noted for his ugliness, even by other trolls and that fame was outstripped only by his stupidity. One day, he found a piece of bread in a cleft in the rock and was delighted, for food is scarce for trolls in Dovrefell. So he gripped it tight – then found he could not get his fist out unless he let the crust go. He thought about it a long time, but there was no way round it – he had to let go, or stay where he was and he could not make up his mind. For all I know, he is there yet, with a fistful of stale crumbs, but determined never to let go.'

'Trolls are notorious fools,' Kasperick agreed sourly.

'A man should always know when to let go of something he cannot hang on to,' Crowbone countered blankly.

In only minutes, it seemed, someone pounded breathlessly in and hurled himself to the ear of Kasperick, whispering furiously. The red spots flared and Kasperick leaped up.

'Only a troll tries to hang on to what is beyond his grasp,' Crowbone announced and Kasperick bellowed as the ox-shouldered guards dragged Red Njal back in and flung him to us; there was blood on his beard and on his teeth, but his grin let us know *Short Serpent* was safe away.

'The bigger the bairn, the bigger the burden,' he said, then spat blood at Kasperick.

'As my granny used to say,' he added.

Kasperick, his face a snarl, snapped an order and the oxen Saxlander guards lumbered towards us. From the dimness, one of the ghosts gained shape, sliding forward onto the bench opposite and grinning at me as hands ripped our weapons from us.

Now I knew how Kasperick had heard so much of us. That face, with no grin on it at all, I had last seen on the hard-packed floor of Hestreng, where the hot iron that had seared the ugly scar across it and blistered one eye to a puckered hole, had started a fire on his chest. I had put it out and left him.

'Bjarki,' I said into his weasel smile. 'I should have let you burn.'

FIFTEEN

The place stank like a *blot* stone, all offal and roasted meat and was not much of a prison, just a large cage in an old storeroom strewn with stinking straw, the bars made from thick balks of timber reinforced with iron.

The cage was up against one wall of this stone room, part of the lower foundations of the keep and once an underground store for the kitchens, for the stone walls were cold. Now the place was hung with chains and metal cuffs, dark with stains and leprous from the heat of the brazier. There were two thick-barred squares to let in light and circling air but they did not do much work on either.

The Saxlanders flung us into the cage and one locked the door with a huge key, his tongue between his teeth as he concentrated on getting it right. They had taken away everything of value and left our weapons on a nearby table where we could see them, but not get to them.

When they were gone, leaving us alone in the half-light, a grinning Finn fished in one boot and brought out his long, black Roman nail.

'If those Saxlanders had any clever in them,' he said, grinning, 'it was well hidden. Unlike my nail, which they should have found even if they were looking for my money – boots, balls and armpits, as any raiding man knows.'

He went to the lock and discovered, in short order and at the cost of a bloody finger, that this prison was no little chest of treasures with a dainty lock that could be snapped. The one penning us in was huge and solid and would not be cracked open with a Roman nail, which was also too thick to use as a pick.

'That Bjarki,' Finn growled, sucking the grimy, bleeding finger as if that man had done it to him personally. He shoved the nail back in his boot.

'This is not much of a prison,' Crowbone mused, looking round. It was not, as I agreed, but it was enough of one for me; what bothered me most were the wall chains and cuffs, the glowing brazier and the thick, scarred wooden table littered with tools I did not think belonged to a forge-man, though some of them were similar.

'I did not like the look of that Kasperick at all,' Red Njal grunted. 'He has the eyes of one who likes to see blood spilled, provided it is not his own and there is no danger in it. A man who, as my granny used to say, prefers to build the lowest fences, since it is easiest for him to cross.'

'Well,' said Finn, settling down with his back to one wall, 'we will find out soon enough.'

I did not like the idea and was envious – not for the first time – of how he could sit with his eyes half-closed, as if he dozed on a bench near a warm fire after a good meal and some ale. I said as much and he grinned.

'The smell, I am thinking,' he answered wistfully. 'It reminds me of the feast we had at Vladimir's hall, the one just before we all went out on to the Grass Sea to hunt down Atil's treasure.'

'Is that the one where you threw someone in the pitfire?' Red Njal demanded, though he grinned when he said it and I was pleased to see that; the death of Hlenni had been sitting heavy on him.

234

'Not someone – the son of the advisor to Prince Yaropolk, Vladimir's brother,' Crowbone pointed out and both he and Finn laughed.

'One side of his face now looks like Finn's left bollock,' Crowbone added, 'wrinkled and ugly.'

'You never saw my bollocks, boy,' Finn countered, 'for you are not struck blind and dumb with amazement and admiration – besides, it was not for quarrels that I remember that feast night. It was for the blood sausage. I ate one as long as my arm.'

'You were as sick as a mangy dog,' Red Njal reminded him and Finn waved a dismissive hand.

'That was a swallow or two of bad ale,' he corrected. 'Anyway – I ate another arm-length after, to make up for what had been lost.'

That feast had seen great cakes of bread and fried turnips and stewed meat, fished out of pots on the end of long spits, I remembered, for Vladimir held to the old ways of his great-grandfather. But the smell of a man's face and hair burning in the fire had soured much of it for me and left us with a lasting enemy – another one, as if we did not have enough of them.

Boiled blood and spew, that's what this place reminded me of and I said as much.

Finn shrugged.

'I recall it now only because we were all in prison there, too,' he added. 'You, me and Crowbone at least. And we got out of that.'

True enough. We had been flung in Vladimir's pit-prison when Crowbone put his little axe in Klerkon's forehead, which was not a bad thing in our eyes. However, he did it in the main square of Holmgard, Vladimir's Novgorod, which had not been clever. That time, we faced a stake up our arses; now we faced a hanging-cage until we starved or were stoned to death.

'Any tales that might help?' I asked Crowbone and he frowned; it was one of his better stories that had made us all laugh and got us hauled out of the pit-prison, since laughter was not usually the sound that came from such a place.

'It would be better if I stopped telling such tales,' he answered moodily. 'They are child's matters and I am a man now.'

'Your voice has snapped,' Finn pointed out, 'which is not the same thing. Let me know when your own bollocks drop like wrinkled walnuts and then I may consider calling you a man.

'Anyway,' he added, 'I like your tales.'

Which was an astounding lie from the man who had once rattled Crowbone into the thwarts of a boat at the announcement 'Once there was a man . . .'. Crowbone merely looked at Finn with his odd eyes narrowed.

'So we die here,' Red Njal grunted, in the same voice he would have used deciding on where to curl up and sleep for a while. 'Well, not the place I would have chosen, but we wear what the Norns weave for us. Better ask for too little than offer too much, as my granny used to say.'

I was thinking we would not die, for this Kasperick wanted the Mazur girl and the profit that could be had selling her to the Pols – or her own folk, whichever paid most – but he had to lay hands on her first. He would use us to trade with the crew of *Short Serpent*.

'He is a belly-crawler,' Finn pointed out when I mused on this. 'He will not hold to such a trade and will kill us anyway.'

Then Bjarki came in, sliding round the storeroom door like rancid seal oil, his grin stretched to a leer by the ruined side of his mouth.

'Kill me now,' Finn growled when he saw him, 'rather than have to suffer the gloat of a little turd like this.'

Bjarki, who was alone, came and sat carefully out of reach beyond the bars.

'No easy death for you, Finn Horsehead,' he slurred through his twisted mouth. 'Nor, especially, for you, Orm Bear Slayer. I owe you an eye and a scar.'

'When you meet Onund,' I warned him, 'be ready to pay more than that.'

'Expecting a rescue, Bear Slayer?' Bjarki jeered.

'You should be afraid,' answered Crowbone, 'for the Oathsworn are coming.'

Bjarki curled his lip.

'You are a little diminished,' he pointed out. 'A king with no crown, a prince with no *hird*. A shadow of what you were, boy. Soon even that will be gone.'

'A shadow is still a powerful thing,' Crowbone said. 'Once there existed somewhere in the world – do not ask me when, do not ask me where – a place where the Sami learned to be workers of powerful *seidr* magic. Wherever this place was, it was somewhere below ground, eternally dark and changeless. There was no teacher either, but everything was learned from fiery runes, which could be read quite easily in the dark. Never were the pupils allowed to go out into the open air or see the daylight during the whole time they stayed there, which was from five to seven years. By then they had gained all they needed of the Sami art.'

'Ha,' scowled Bjarki. 'What a poor tale. How did they eat in all this time, then?'

'A shaggy grey hand came through the wall every day with meals,' answered Crowbone without as much as a breath of hesitation. 'When they had finished eating and drinking the same hand took back the horns and platters.

'They saw no-one but each other and that only in the dim light of the fiery runes,' he went on and Bjarki, scowling, was fixed by it. 'Those same runes told them the only rule of the place, which was that the Master should keep for himself the student who was last to leave the school every year. Considering that most folk who knew of the place thought

Loki himself was the Master, you may fancy what a scramble there was at each year's end, everybody doing his best to avoid being last to leave.

'It happened once that three Icelanders went to this school, by the name of Sæmundur the Learned, Kálfur Arnason, and one called, simply, Orm; and as they all arrived at the same time, they were all supposed to leave at the same time. Seven years later, when it came to taking the bit of it in their teeth, Orm declared himself willing to be the last of them, at which the others were much lightened in mind. So he threw over himself a large cloak, leaving the pin loose.

'A staircase led to the upper world, and when Orm was about to mount this Loki grasped at him and said, "You are mine!" But Orm ducked his head, slipped free and made off with all speed, leaving Loki the empty cloak. However, just as he reached the heavy iron yett beyond the door, it slammed shut. "Did you imagine that the Father of Tricksters would be fooled by that?" said a dark voice from the blackness.

'A great hand reached out to drag Orm back just as he saw the sun for the first time in seven years, a great blaze of light which fell on him, throwing his shadow onto the wall behind him. Orm said: "I am not the last. Do you not see who follows me?"

'So Loki, mistaking the shadow for a man, raised the yett and grabbed at the shadow, allowing Orm to escape – but from that hour Orm was always shadowless, for whatever Loki took, he never gave back again.'

There was silence and then Bjarki gave an uneasy laugh, while Finn beamed like a happy uncle and clapped Crowbone on the back.

'As I said – I like your tales. They seldom miss the mark.'

'A boy's tale,' Bjarki scowled back. 'There will be no shadow-escape for you and the Oathsworn are unlikely to be storming this fortress.'

He broke off and smeared a grin on his face, ugly as a hunchbacked rat.

'Well – here is one of your saviours coming now, fresh from this hero-saga,' he added as sounds clattered at the door. It swung open and two huge Saxlanders dragged in a slumped, dangle-headed figure. Two more men scowled their way in after them.

Bjarki moved to the prisoner and lifted his head by the hair; it was Styrbjorn and the surprise of it must have showed in all our faces, for Bjarki frowned; he had not been expecting that. His face twisted even more when one of the Saxlander guards slapped his hand free with a short, phlegm-thick curse. The other fetched the key, opened the door and slung Styrbjorn in, so that he crashed to the floor and bounced.

Bjarki sniggered, hovering by the door and the irritated guard shoved him back, so that he staggered and almost fell; one hand flew to the dagger at his belt and the guard, ring-mailed and helmed and armed with a great stave of spear looked inquiringly at him, then laughed when Bjarki saw what he was about to do and took his hand away.

'You are not as welcome here as you make it seem, little bear,' Finn said with a dry laugh. One of the men who had followed Styrbjorn into the room, bald-headed and stubbled on a sharp chin, spat at him then, which narrowed Finn's eyes.

'Your welcome is worse,' Stubble-Chin said. 'This Styrbjorn killed Pall, which is red murder. No matter what happens, he will swing in a cage for it.'

'Which one are you?' asked Crowbone. 'Freystein? I did not ever hear the name of the fourth man.'

'I am Freystein,' said the second man and jerked a thumb at the bald-headed one. 'He is Thorstein, Pall's brother.'

'Ah,' said Finn knowingly. 'Same litter – I thought I saw it, but was not sure. All rats look the same to me.'

The door opened again and the Saxlander guards straightened a little as Kasperick came in, lifting the trailing hem of his

239

robe from the floor of the place. He surveyed the scene with a satisfied smile and moved to the table where our possessions had been left, lifting Crowbone's sword admiringly.

'A fine and cunning weapon,' he said, drawing it out and swinging it once or twice. 'A little light, but perfect for a boy.'

Then he drew mine, which was Jarl Brand's and he smiled like a cream-fed cat over that one. Then there was Styrbjorn's; the silk wrapping was gone. When he drew The Godi, Finn growled, hackled like a hound on a boar scent.

'Four swords of price,' he declared. 'Not a bad day – you three can take the rest of their possessions as reward. Get out.'

Bjarki and the others blinked and Bjarki looked as if he would argue, but the two huge guards leaned forward a little and the three of them left, summoning up as much swagger as they could, which was not much.

'They expected more,' I said, 'for whispering in your ear about the Mazur girl.'

Kasperick waved a languid hand. 'They are little yaps, from that large dog Pallig Tokeson. One day, we will deal with Pallig, but his little pups are useful and of small account to me when they have barked. To each other, too, I am thinking – the death of Pall will not concern them much, save that they can now split the reward I gave them into thirds instead of fourths.'

He settled his rump on the edge of the table and looked us over.

'You will send word to release the Mazur girl,' he declared. 'In return, I will release all of you – except the one they call Styrbjorn, for he is guilty of murder.'

'Styrbjorn? What does one of Pallig's little yappers matter to you?' I countered and he nodded, a nasty smile on his face.

'Nothing,' he agreed, 'save that justice must be seen to be done – anyway, I have gone to all the trouble of lighting a brazier and started heating up instruments. I will not have all my enjoyment removed.'

The threat was plain enough and he saw it had hit home as he slid his arse off the table.

'You have until first light to think,' he added flatly. Then he swept out, followed by the two guards; the door banged shut behind them, leaving us alone in the fetid half-dark.

'One who sees a friend roasting on a spit tells all he knows,' Red Njal noted. 'My granny said so and it remains true.'

'Spit-luck for us, then, that Styrbjorn is a few wrist-clasps short of a friend to any of us,' Finn answered and prodded the luckless subject with one toe. Styrbjorn groaned and Red Njal bent briefly to look at him.

'Lump like a gull's egg and a bruise, nothing much more,' he growled, straightening. Finn took the pisspot and emptied the contents on Styrbjorn, who surfaced, wheezing and blowing.

'Better?' Finn inquired as Styrbjorn blinked into the Now of it all. The enormity of where he was crashed on him like creaming surf and he subsided.

'I thought it was a dream,' he groaned.

'If it is,' Red Njal told him, 'dream me out of it.'

'No dream,' I told him harshly. 'What did you do to Pall?'

Styrbjorn shifted, rolled over and sat up slowly, like a sobering drunk after a feast. He touched the lump on his forehead and winced.

'Pall made straight for his three friends,' Styrbjorn explained. 'We just looked for the cheapest, noisiest drinking place in the settlement and, sure enough, there they were, having already poured Pallig's poison in the ear of this Kasperick about us. Pall told them of the value of the Mazur girl, said we should tell Kasperick and he would surely reward us.'

'I said he was a rat and that releasing him was a bad idea. And you went with them,' Finn growled meaningfully. Styrbjorn held his head and groaned.

'Aye, well, I was not all that welcome there, since they

241

blamed me for much that had happened, especially the one called Bjarki – silly name for a grown man, is it not?'

No-one argued with that, so he sat up a little more and then began sniffing suspiciously at the damp on him.

'The other three went off, saying that Pall and me should watch the ship – what did you just pour on me, Finn Horsehead?'

'Healing balm,' I said, wanting him to keep to the sharp of his tale. 'What happened then?'

He blinked and made himself more comfortable, closing his eyes. I remembered a time when I had taken a dunt to the head and almost felt sorry for him. Almost.

'Then we waited in the rain for a while,' Styrbjorn went on after a moment. 'We saw the crew coming back, not all at once, but in ones and twos and seeming to be easy and light about it until they were aboard. Pall said the ship was getting ready to leave, which was clear to any sailing man; he said he was off to warn Bjarki that the prize was slipping away.'

He paused and frowned, then sniffed again.

'This is piss,' he declared accusingly.

'What happened?' I snarled and he raised an eyebrow at me, then shrugged, which act made him wince. This time I felt no sympathy.

'I thought it best not to let him,' he said. 'So I slit his throat and dropped him in the river.'

'Heya,' growled Finn admiringly and Styrbjorn smiled. I looked at the youth with some new and grudging respect; he had decided to save us and killed a man without so much as a blink – yet it was a throat-cut in the dark.

I was thinking that was what kept Styrbjorn from being the hero-king he wanted to be. He could kill, right enough, but would rather be sleekit about it than face a man in a fair fight; even his saving of me was a stab to my enemy's back.

Nor had he been sleekit enough about the killing of Pall, either, since he got caught.

242

'Aye,' he agreed wryly when I pointed this last fact out to him. 'I was making for the ship, for it was now the safest place for me to be after dropping the little turd in the water, when Bjarki and the others turned up with some armed men. They grabbed me and Bjarki asked where Pall was, so the whole matter came out in the open soon after.'

He paused, defiantly.

'If it had not been for them being so bothered with me,' he added, 'the ship might not have pulled safely away at all.'

I let him think it, even if I doubted it to be true. Not that any of that helped us here, as I whispered to Finn, drawing him a little apart from the others.

'Aye,' he answered, then grinned. 'Though there may yet be a way out of this cage. Best if we wait for dark. Best also if I keep it to myself, just in case this Kasperick grows impatient for spit-roasts and questioning.'

The thought that he had a plan when I did not was nagging enough, but the idea that he did not want to share it made matters worse. As the faint light from the barred squares in the wall faded we sat in silence; I did not know what the others were thinking, but home swam up in the maelstrom of my thoughts.

I dreamed up a new Hestreng, with soaring roof and many high rooms, grand as any king's and rich with cunning carvings. I summoned up Thorgunna in it and a fine-limbed boy and thralls and a forge and sturdy wharves where all my ships swung gently.

It was a good dream, save for some annoyances; the face of the fine-limbed son was always Koll and accusing. Nor could I place myself anywhere in this neatly-crafted hall.

Worst of all, I could not put a remembered face on Thorgunna at all and summoning up the night moments, hip to hip and thigh to thigh, languorous and loving, only brought a small, tight-muscled body and a sharp face with those huge, seal eyes.

'Well,' said a voice, cracking Hestreng apart; I was almost grateful to see Red Njal hunkered near.

'Well?' I countered and he gave me a look as glassed and grey as a Baltic swell.

'I am thinking we will not get out of this.'

'A man's life is never finished until Skuld snips the last thread of it,' I said.

'Aye, right enough – but best to search while a trail is new, as my granny told me. I can feel the edge of that Norn's shears and wish only to make it known to you and the gods that I bear no malice, for we are oathed to each other and I took it freely. I would not want to come as a *draugr* to bother your family.'

It took me a moment to realise he meant he would die because of my wyrd, which I had brought on myself with my sacrifice-promise to Odin. I swallowed any venom I had to spit at him for it all the same and thanked him nicely, though I could not help but add that it was only my wyrd to die and not his. Perhaps the gods would be content with just the one death, I told him, just to watch him brighten like a bairn who had been promised a new seax for his name-day.

'Ah, well,' he answered. 'I thought to mention it, all the same. Care gnaws the heart when a man cannot tell all his mind to another.'

'Your granny was a singular woman,' I told him, straight-faced into his delighted grins.

And all the while I felt Einar at my back, the old leader who had brought his own wyrd down on himself and whom we had cursed for it, sure he was leading all the Oathsworn of that time into their doom. Not for the first time, I knew how Einar the Black had felt.

'I do not think it is my wyrd to die here,' frowned Crowbone and that did not surprise me either; the arrogance of youth was doubled and re-doubled in that odd-eyed man-boy.

'Then you can be the one to rescue Koll,' Finn decreed.

Styrbjorn sniffed and tentatively marked out the edges of pain on his lumped forehead.

'Jarl Brand is a good man,' he agreed, 'and a generous ring-giver, it is true – but would we be plootering through the rain after him if Orm did not owe him it as foster-father to his son?'

Again my fault and I let some anger slip the leash into my voice.

'Would you not go after the boy only to save him, then?' I demanded. 'It is all your wyrd that he is taken and we are in this mire.'

Styrbjorn thought about it, frowning and serious.

'You have the truth of it being as a result of my quarrel with my uncle,' he admitted, then waved one hand to dismiss it. 'That is the way of such matters and folk cannot go putting all the blame of it on me – war is war, after all.

'As to the boy,' he went on, 'if the reward was good for me, I would go after him. For you it is losing the stain on your fame and regaining the friendship of the jarl who gave you land and a steading. Good reasons – the fame and the friendship of great men is half the secret to ships and men, as you know, Jarl Orm. The other half is silver. But there is too little fame here for me, while Jarl Brand is too small a friendship for a man of my standing.'

He was a nasty twist of a youth, this one, and his arrogance sucked the breath from you. I saw it then, clear as Iceland's Silfra water – Styrbjorn would die from his unthinking attitude, one day or the next.

'You would not try for rescue at all, then?' Finn growled, a twisted grin on his face. 'From where I look, wee man with a lot to say for yourself, you have no standing. You are sitting in piss, with a dunted head and no good fame at all.'

Styrbjorn did not answer, but Crowbone fixed him with that odd-eyed stare.

'You would go if you knew what the lad felt,' he said, in

a voice which had deepened considerably since it had snapped free of boyhood. 'If you were far from home, among enemies, treated as a thrall, thrashed and bound and starved, all that would keep you taking one breath after another was the hope that someone was coming to get you.'

We all remembered, then, the saga of Crowbone's life to this point – a fugitive from the womb, his father dead. A thrall at six, his foster-father slain, his mother the usage of Klerkon's camp, bairned by Kveldulf and then kicked to death by him. At nine, he had been freed by me into the world of the Oathsworn, which was no gentle place for a growing boy.

He looked at me and acknowledged that rescue with only his eyes. Now, at twelve, Crowbone's last foster-father, his Uncle Sigurd, was also dead and, though he had sisters and kin somewhere too dangerous still to visit, he was more alone than the moon. It came to me that this was the reason, more than any, which had made him take our Oath – any family, even the Odin-hagged Oathsworn, was better than none.

'Aye, such a wyrd would be a sore one to swallow,' Styrbjorn agreed, then beamed and slapped Crowbone's shoulder. 'Skalds would make a fair tale about someone so rescued. You have convinced me that there is, after all, enough fame in it – we will hunt down the little bairn and bring him safe home, even if Orm ends up swinging in a cage here.'

'A comfort, for sure,' I muttered darkly and he laughed.

'Where is Randr Sterki going, I am wondering?' Finn asked, frowning. 'I thought he wanted us to come to him, so why is he running?'

For the lack of men, I was thinking. He would want to find a place where there were shiftless swords for hire, for I was betting sure he was crew-light now. I said so and Styrbjorn chuckled.

'Well,' he said brightly, 'in a way you have me to thank for that.'

246

I could not speak at all, but Red Njal always had a ready tongue.

'The jarl would favour you,' he pointed out, his mildness only adding to the venom of it, 'save that it is unlikely you will survive, even if this Saxlander lord does release us for the Mazur girl. You he wants to keep and play with.'

Styrbjorn's fear slid under the clear surface of his face and he swallowed.

I could scarcely see their features now; their faces were white blobs in the dim and the glow of the brazier coals seemed brighter now that the dark had raced in like Sleipnir, One-Eye's eight-legged stallion.

'If you have a spell to snap this lock, Finn Horsehead,' I grunted, annoyed by their talk of my Odin-wyrd – and, I confess it, belly-clenching afraid of it, too. Finn chuckled and drew out his iron nail, a slash of black in the grey.

'No spell, but *duergar*-magic, all the same,' he said. 'I need your leg bindings, Red Njal.'

Slowly, Red Njal unwound one leg. Once they had been fine, green wool bindings, embroidered in red and with silver clasp-ends – but the ends had gone on dice or drink long since and the frayed ends of wool, now stained to a mud-dark with only the memory of embroidery, were tucked roughly in the bind itself.

For all that, he passed an unravel of them over sullenly, one breeks leg flapping loosely over his shoes. We all watched Finn tie one end of the wool length to his nail and swing it like a depth-line, testing weight and knot – then, sudden as a spark, the whole room lit up in blue-white light.

For an instant, everything stood out, stark and eldritch and the barred squares were etched on the far wall. I saw the faces of the others in that eyeblink, flares of fright and bewilderment and knew my own was no different.

In the utter dark that followed, we heard the millstone grind of thunder, slow and low and then a hiss of rain, faint through the high, barred squares. A storm; the darkness had indeed raced like Sleipnir for it was not proper night, this.

'I came to knowing of this thanks to the rot,' Finn said calmly, ignoring the light and noise as he adjusted the knot. 'I like this iron nail, for it has served me well from the day I picked it up. On Cyprus, as you will remember, Orm and Njal, when Orm fought the leader of some Danes in a *holm-gang*. We used nails like this as *tjosnur*, to properly mark out the fighting boundary.'

The light flared again, flicking him in an instant, frozen image, as he draped the dangling nail through the bars, swung it backwards and forwards a few times, then lobbed it out, trailing the wool binding behind it. The nail whispered through the darkness and slammed on the table, hard enough to leap everything upwards; a wooden beaker fell over on its side and rolled.

The great, rolling rumble of thunder swallowed all sounds of it, seemed to tremble the backs of my teeth and come up through my feet from the floor. Red Njal looked up, just a pale blob of face in the darkness, blooded on one side by the brazier. The brightest thing in that face was the white of his eyes.

'Thor is racing his chariot hard tonight,' he muttered. 'Plead all you please with the gods, but learn a good healing spell, as my granny used to say.'

Thor could race his goats until their hooves fell off, I was thinking, for it hid the noise of Finn's nail-madness – he hauled it off the table onto the flags of the floor and what should have been a bell-loud clatter went unheard in the grinding of the Thunder-God. Finn pulled it back to him and might just as well have been dragging it over eiderdown.

'Being iron,' he said into the silence between thunders, 'it needed careful attention, but I saw that it did not get the same rot as other things of iron. Swords, for example, and axe-heads.'

248

'Different rot?' muttered Red Njal, with the voice of a man who thought Finn addled. The light flared; Thor's iron-wheeled chariot ground out another teeth-aching rumble.

Finn swung the nail back and forth and launched it again; one more crash on the table set the cup bouncing off with a clatter. Once more the nail hit the floor with a clang and was dragged back.

'If your plan was to alarm the guards,' Styrbjorn muttered, 'it may yet succeed, despite Thor.'

'The rot,' Finn went on, as if Styrbjorn had not spoken at all, 'on most swords and every axe-head I have seen, is the colour of old blood. Everyone knows that and even the best of swords gets it. It leaches from the metal like sap from a tree.'

Thor hurled his hammer in another blue-white flare. The nail trailed its wool tail through the air and slammed into the table-top again. My bone-handled seax fell off this time – together with the key to the cell lock.

'Aha,' said Crowbone. 'Careful when you pull it off the table . . .'

He fell silent when Finn jerked the nail off the table and made no attempt to try and hook the key with it – which, I was thinking, would have been a clever trick if he could have managed it, for he would have to somehow get the nail through the ring of the key, if it was large enough even to take it . . .

'So,' Finn went on, winding his nail back to him, 'I am watching my nail for signs of blood rot and seeing none. Instead, I am finding grit on my fingers, black as charcoal.'

A cold wind through one of the barred squares set the brazier glowing enough to send up some sparks, then trailed fingers through our beards, with the smell of rain and turned earth and escape. Finn bent low and slithered the nail out, underhand, towards the key. It overshot by a few finger-lengths. Again the thunder rumbled and the blue-white scarred our faces into the dark.

'This, I thought, was also rot, so I scraped it all off first time I found it, then laid the nail down to fetch some fat to grease it with,' Finn went on, tentatively tugging the nail this way and that with the wool. 'Yet, when I came back to it, all the grit I had scraped off was back on the nail again.'

He looked up into our silent, gawping faces and grinned at the sight of them.

'It was Ref who put me right on it,' he said, giving a last tug, 'for he knows iron as a farmer knows rye. The iron that leaches red rot is made from bloodstone, which is the most common iron, the stuff you fish out as a bloom on bog-grass. The iron that made my nail is rare, from a dug-out stone, where it is found in little black studs, like pips in an apple.'

He moved the nail a last nudge; the key slid towards it, stopped, slid again and then snugged up next to it. No-one could breathe for the wonder of it and even the thunder did not seem as loud.

'Ref says,' Finn went on, half to himself as he slowly dragged his nail, the key stuck to it as tight as a resin-trapped fly, 'that this iron embraces all the other iron it sees.'

He scooped the nail and key up and grinned at us, dangling it, swinging it gently back and forth.

'Be happy this key is not made of gold.'

The lightning seared the image of us staring at him, fixed by the sight of that key, sucked firmly to the side of the nail. The Thunder-God boomed out a laugh.

'There is clever for you,' muttered Red Njal, sullenly splintering the silence that followed. 'Can I have my binding back? There is a cold wind blowing right up the sheuch of my arse.'

Thor-light flicked us when we wraithed through the door of the storeroom; an eyeblink of stark, white light showed us the long, gentle slope up to the surface, a ramp where once barrels of salted meat and ale had been rolled. That was before

250

Kasperick had taken the place over for his own sick-slathered pleasures.

At the top should have been a pair of double-doors, shut and barred on the outside and only fixed with chains and a lock when something of true value was inside. And guards, always guards, at least one against the pilferers when it was a store, two, I was thinking, now that it was something else. Yet they were more to prevent folk coming across what Kasperick did in his pleasure room rather than keep his prisoners getting out.

But the rain snaked in hissing waves and the two guards Kasperick had left had opened the doors and crept inside a little way for shelter; the startling flash showed them, crouched, draped in iron and rightly afraid of attracting Perun's eye, fixed as rabbits on the stoat of Thor-lights.

No-one had to speak; Finn and Red Njal moved up like a pair of boarhounds, almost in step with one another. Red Njal's seax gleamed briefly and one guard went sagging against him, scarcely making more than a sigh as his throat was cut.

Finn made a mess of it. Though he had done this before, his Roman nail was no edged weapon and relied on his brute strength and placing skill to tear out the voice of the guard as well as rip through the heart-in-the-throat, where life pulsed.

The guard half-turned when he saw his oarmate go down to Red Njal, a movement that put Finn's perfect thrust off by a hair; the Roman nail ripped in and blood spurted straight back in Finn's eyes. Blinded and cursing, he let the nail and the man go to sweep the gore away.

The nail clattered to the stone flags and the guard, his mouth opening and closing like a dying fish, staggered out into the hissing downpour, his hands clamped to his throat and blood spraying through his fingers. He could not yell and the air hissed and bubbled from his torn throat as he tried, but he reeled in circles in the rain – and someone saw him.

The yell went through me like one of Thor's ragged blue-white bolts. Finn scooped up his nail, still cursing and sprang forward; one thrust took the nail into the gasping guard's eye, an in-out movement that sent him backwards like a felled oak.

Too late, I was thinking as someone started smacking the alarm-iron, far too late . . .

'Row for it, lads!' roared Finn.

Make for the main gate. I heard myself screaming it like a chant and sprinted into the rain, sword out. It was not proper night and the main gate would still be open, for folk came and went on all sorts of business in a fortress such as this.

The confusion helped us. The alarm was beating, but no-one knew why, or who they were looking for and we were most of the way across the yard before I heard someone bellowing out to close the gates. I spun in a half-circle, blinking rain out of my face and saw the others closing on me. A lancing fern of blue-white fretted the dark and, in the flicker of its life, showed us to each other; the great crash that followed was a mountain falling, drowning all other sound and leaving my mouth fizzing with each ragged breath.

'Keep Crowbone in the middle,' I yelled and did not have to add the why of it; he was too small and light in a fight. Finn came to my shieldless side, Styrbjorn on the other and we splattered through the muddy yard – so close now, I could hear the creak and groan of bad hinging and wood as men put shoulders to the gates.

We passed them, slashing left and right and they scattered, unarmed for the most part. Styrbjorn gave a yelp as someone snarled out at him with a fistful of steel, but he took the blow on his blade well enough and back-slashed, hardly pausing at all and not bothering to see if he had done damage. Shouts went up behind us. Arrows whicked by my head and one shunked into the back of a fleeing gateman, so that Crowbone had to hurdle him.

252

We were through the gate, skittering on the slick, uneven log walkway and the yells were different behind us, fewer and more commanding as the garrison sorted itself out; the stark, white, flash of Thor-light sent the luckless caged leering at us as we sprinted down their avenue.

We passed two side streets; folk scattered and screamed. At the third, I yelled for everyone to go right, but I was guessing. The dark rumbled and spat white fire, while a wind sprayed rain and flattened a dying, discarded torch flame; a lantern swung and rattled.

I could not be sure and spun in a half-circle, almost falling off the walkway and the others panted up to me.

'Which way?' Styrbjorn wanted to know, jerking this way and that, brimming on the edge of panic. I chose one, a left turn which sloped down. Down was good. Down led to water.

There were screams and the distant clanging of the alarm; Finn growled at a head which stuck out of a doorway and the owner jerked it back again. I stepped off the walkway by accident, a long drop that jarred my foot and pitched me on my face in the clotted mat of rot, split by a running stream. Spitting and coughing, I clawed my way up and back onto the walkway.

'They are closing,' spat Red Njal, which made us all turn to see the dark figures moving down through the buildings. Moving fast, too.

'Fuck,' said Finn, disgustedly. 'I am running from Saxlanders.'

'Good,' snarled Styrbjorn, shoving past him and skidding on the slick logs, 'keep running.'

Finn smile was twisted, his face flared by another flickering message from Thor.

'Take the boy,' he said over his shoulder. 'I am tired of running.'

'Boy . . .' began Crowbone, shrilling it in his anger; Red Njal grabbed him by the shoulder and shoved him after the retreating Styrbjorn.

'It is not seemly,' he yelled as he pushed, 'to interrupt a man when he is dying to save you. That is not my granny's saying, but one of my own.'

The dark shapes bobbed and lumbered down the darkness towards us and Finn glanced sideways at me.

'This walkway is narrow enough for one,' he grunted. 'And high enough.'

'Just another bridge,' I answered and his teeth were white in the shadow of his face.

'Bone, blood and steel,' he grunted.

The thunder grumbled and, in the next fern of white light, I saw the Saxlanders, uneasy in their ring-coats and spears with Himself banging around the sky, throwing anger about. They milled uncertainly when the light showed two men with bright blades waiting for them.

'Get them,' shrieked a familiar voice. 'Take them alive.'

Kasperick. I hoped he would come within reach but if I knew that man he would lead from the back. I wiped rain from my face and squinted into the shadows of a day gone night. There were splashes.

'They are off the walkway,' I warned – then a dark shape was on me, panting out of the dark, slick with rain and fear. He was below me, in the mud and filth, glittering with old fishscales and stuck with feathers and hair. He sliced at my ankles with the spear, for he could not see me clearly and thought a scything blow would sweep me off my feet if it failed to cut me.

I hopped up awkwardly, landed badly and on my weak ankle, which shot fire through me. On one knee and cursing, I heard him suck in a triumphant breath and lurch forward; the spearhead, trailing droplets of water, slid past my eye and I slashed wildly, felt the edge hit and heard him scream and the splashing of him stumbling away.

'If you have rested enough,' Finn panted from above me, 'I would be glad of some help.'

254

Two Saxlanders were at him, one on the logs and one off, slithering to keep his balance, ankle-deep in clinging mud.

Finn turned from the one on the walkway, took two steps, swung The Godi up as if for a great downward cut and then kicked the Saxlander spearman in the face as he followed the arc of it, his mouth slightly open. The man hurled backwards with a strangled choking sound; one boot was left stuck in the mud.

During this, I scrambled up and took on the other man, who crabbed and stabbed and huddled behind his shield, so that the best I could do was fend him off. Then he saw Finn was coming for him and backed off into the frustrated bellows of Kasperick, urging his men on.

They were wary, but circling, dropping off one walkway, slogging through the mud and on to another; the flash of white light showed them, dark as hunting wolves and almost behind us.

That same flash showed them stop, almost in mid-step. The darkness that followed was blacker still, but Finn had seen them and stood up straight, throwing out his arms, scattering water droplets like bright pearls.

'I am Finn Bardisson, known as Horsehead, from Skane,' he roared. 'You want me? Here I come, you nithing, chicken-fucking, Saxlander whoresons.'

He hurled himself forward roaring, nail in one hand, The Godi in the other and I tried to snag him before he went, but failed. I half-stumbled on that cursed ankle, feeling the fire-ache of it and the sick, belly-dropping certainty that this was the moment Odin took his sacrifice and that I had doomed Finn with me.

The white light split the darkness again – and they fled.

The Saxlanders turned and ran, stumbling, away from the mad, wild-haired Finn and Kasperick stopped bellowing at them to get us and ran with them. I knelt, panting, bewildered, heard a noise and staggered up on one good foot, whirling round to face the dark shapes behind.

They loomed up, silent and grey-grim against the black. Then the lightning flashed again and I saw them, as the Saxlanders must have seen them, ring-coated and helmed, sharp with edges and grins, their faces streaked black with charcoal and sheep-fat.

Familiar faces – Alyosha, Finnlaith, Abjorn and the others.

'That was a good trick of Finn's,' Styrbjorn said, pushing through to the front, 'waiting until he saw us come up and then charging them. That set them running, for sure.'

Finn strolled back, The Godi over one shoulder, his nail in his teeth. He took it out and shoved it down one boot, then shouldered into the stone-grey ranks of men as we all backed off, heading for the river. I stood, trembling with reprieve.

'You are a fool,' I said to the grinning Styrbjorn, as Abjorn and Ospak helped me hirple away, 'if you think Finn noticed any of you were there at all before he ran at them.'

SIXTEEN

The Odra roared and spat like a boiling cauldron, brimmed over into the woods and growled among the trees. It slashed the higher bank, so that sections of it slithered and sighed in slow splashes and turned the water black-brown. Trees came down, too, teetering slowly with a noise like ripping linen, clawed roots tangling so that they chained to the broken shore and made dams against which other drifts piled.

We watched it all warily, for the current in the river slithered like a coil of mating snakes, first one way, then the other, breaking round *Short Serpent* and fattening out into the floodplain so that we had no idea now where the old shore had been.

The rain fell, too. It had caused all this on the slopes of the distant mountains, now unseen through the fine, misted water that lisped on us and filled the very air so that every breath came as if we held linen cloths over our mouths and noses.

'This is no time to be sitting on this river, I am thinking,' Onund observed mournfully, 'for we can neither use oars nor sail in this and if we sit here, a floater will get us, for sure.'

It was no time to be moving, either, for though we all feared the current and the clutch of water, we feared the floaters

257

most and had seen three or four already, looming out of the boil like whales with great thrashing root-limbs. Hovering for a moment in the current, they would sink from sight again and, like the bergs of the north, most of the dangerous part was unseen. One of those great earth-clogged claws would swipe in the planks of *Short Serpent*.

There was no possibility of stopping, all the same; we had to put distance between us and Kasperick, keeping to the east bank and trusting that the spate prevented him crossing. I was sure, all the same, that I had seen horsemen, faded as fetches through the rain-mist, splashing a miserable way up the west bank, appearing and disappearing as the swollen river widened and narrowed.

'Time to haul away,' Trollaskegg said cheerfully and the men groaned, for this was almost too much when added to the lack of food and ale and the soaked cloaks and blankets on a boat filmed with water.

Little Yan went up the mast with the rope and fastened it, then it was paid out and men leaped overboard, to the places where the water was shallow, or had not yet reached. Then they pulled, so that *Short Serpent*, balking like a stubborn goat on a tether, slowly moved forward; the linden-bast rope hummed and water spurted out of it, while the mast curved.

Everyone lent a hand, the strong ones pulling and staggering through the shallows or over the brush of the bank, the weaker ones using the oars as poles to fend off the drift. Even Dark Eye bailed and I did not care for that, though I told myself, and everyone else who saw my unease, that it was because it would not do for her to get sick or injured, for we might need her yet. I had already provided my good sealskin cloak for her as a makeshift shelter.

Finn, squeezing the water from his beard so that it squirted through his knuckles, had squinted from under the drooped, sodden brim of his weather-hat and smiled, a quizzical, knowing smile I tried to ignore, all the while feeling it nag me as badly as the ache in my ankle.

She had clasped me tight when we lumbered, sodden and uneasy, spilling hurriedly onto *Short Serpent* and sliding off into the dark, rain-hissing river. In the storm's searing white light, her face was raised to mine, eyes bright, streaming with rain so that she looked as if she wept. I almost kissed her then, but the corner of my eye caught Finn's scowl in that eyeblink of light and I patted her like a wet dog instead.

In the dark, we had hauled a little way upriver, all that could be managed, before settling on the east bank to wait for daylight and the storm to growl out. By then the river was mud-coloured, frothing like a mad dog in the sullen light of morning and it stayed that way for the next few days, with no sign of stopping, so there was nothing to be done but pull.

'Bank is not made for towing,' Onund growled at me, coming up with an oar to fend off something that rolled and turned, shapeless in the water.

'Nor the current for rowing, nor the wind for sails,' I answered, more sharp than I had intended, for the truth of it nagged me like a broken tooth.

'Trees down to the water,' Onund added, which was true. Once they had been the edge of a considerable wood, set back from the river, but it had spilled over and swamped them; hip-deep in it, the men looped rope over one shoulder, padded a tunic, or a cloak or a spare serk under it and hauled, stumbling and sliding. To their left, Alyosha and a handful of men, weighed with shields, weapons and ring-coats, splashed to keep up, as a flank guard.

'The mast might go,' added Trollaskegg, watching the bowing curve of it.

'Or the line,' added Yan Alf, almost cheerfully.

I wondered if anyone had something good to say and asked it aloud. No-one answered – then Kuritsa appeared, sloshing calf-deep through the water and calling out, so that men stopped pulling and braced instead, holding *Short Serpent* against the current.

He came up to where the water deepened to the river proper, stopping when it got to his waist. He had his unstrung bow in his hand and a young doe draped round his shoulders like a fur cloak, the hooves cinched on his chest; men yelled at him and grinned, for this meant good hot eating at the end of a wet misery of hauling.

It took some time, but we got *Short Serpent* closer to him, while he came out until the current threatened to sweep him off his feet. Crowbone threw him a line, he tied the deer to it and it was hauled aboard; another line drew him in like a fish, until he stood on the deck, streaming water and grinning. The rain had stopped.

'Good hunt,' I told him and he nodded, blowing snot from his nose. He pulled off his leather cap and checked that the bowstring was dry, then coiled it up again and stuck the hat back on.

'Up ahead is trouble,' he said. 'A barrier of drift.'

Trollaskegg grunted; that was a bad thing to have happen now, but you could have foreseen it without throwing rune-bones, on a river like this and weather like we had.

It was a fallen tree, undercut and ruined, a fine big oak – a keel tree, as Onund pointed out. If we had been wanting one that would be cause for grinning, as I told him; those nearest laughed, though it was a sound as grim as tumbling skulls.

Drift had piled against it, sodden birch and gnarled pine from far upriver, willow branches swollen with new buds, all forming a great dam the length of twenty men out from the east bank and solid enough that men could walk on it.

Around the end swept the water, rippling like muscle, then breaking into dirty-white foam and growling up spits of spray. The air stank with the cloy of death, for there were bloated bodies here, sheep and cattle that had drowned, bobbing and sinking and rising again as they spun in a stately dance down to the sea.

Onund and Trollaskegg and others walked, cat-careful, out onto the barrier and peered and prodded here and there, while the men stood like patient oxen, hock-deep in the water and braced to stop *Short Serpent* spiralling backwards with the flowing current.

A tree came down, with an animal on it and men yelled and shouted cheerfully; it was a water-slicked wildcat, yowling and snarling, running this way and that as the tree caught the water's flow and half-turned beneath it.

'Shoot it,' Crowbone yelled to Kuritsa, who merely shook his head.

'Not me,' he declared. 'I almost died from shooting one once and I will not do it again.'

'How could you die from shooting a cat?' demanded Yan Alf, watching the tree in case it came too close. Kuritsa, his face serious, said it was the speed of the beast that had been his undoing and Crowbone made the mistake of asking how that was so.

'I came upon one while hunting deer,' Kuritsa said. 'Suddenly, without warning. I do not know who was the more surprised – but I had an arrow nocked and shot it, straight down the open mouth.'

He paused and shook his head.

'This was my undoing, for that cat, like all of its breed, was faster than Perun's thrown axe. It spun round to run away and my own arrow shot out of its arse. I felt the wind of it on my cheek; an eyelash closer and I would be dead.'

People laughed aloud and watched the tree and the yowling misery of its passenger spin away downriver.

Then Onund hauled himself aboard, dripping like a walrus, with Trollaskegg not far behind. Their faces were gloomier than Hel's bedspace.

'It will not be chopped up this side of summer,' Onund declared.

261

'Nor will it be hauled apart,' added Trollaskegg.

There was a pause and I waited, trying to be patient. Onund grunted and shrugged, the hump of his shoulder rising like a mountain.

'We will have to pull round it,' he said and all our hearts sank at that. It meant tethering *Short Serpent* and bringing everyone on board to take an oar – then loosing the lines and bending to rowing to the west bank. We would lose way, of course, probably back to where we had started pulling that day, before we could tether on the opposite bank. Then we would have to pull all the way back again, this time with the threat of Saxlander horsemen.

It would be a long, hard pull, too, for we would have to put some distance between us and the barrier; no-one wanted to spend a night on the west side of the river, so we would have to repeat the process to take the ship to the east bank again, on the far side of the barrier – with enough room to allow for losing way that would not carry us smack into that gods-cursed drift of trees and sodden corpses in the fading light.

The black, wet misery of it settled on us as we grunted and cursed and slithered the ship to where it could be tethered. The panting, exhausted crew slackened off, the linden-bast rope was hauled in and loosed from the masthead and folk spilled wetly over the side, sloshing towards rowing ports, sorting out their sea-chest seats.

I nodded to Finn and he went round with two green-glass flasks and men grinned wearily and brightened as the fiery green-wine spirit was passed down the line. Dark Eye and a couple of others offered soggy bread and hard cheese, pungent with its own sweat; men chewed and grunted and, slowly, began to chaffer and argue, so that I knew they were recovered.

Then Yan Alf called out that there was a boat snagged in the barrier.

This time, I went with Finn and Onund and others, step-ping cautiously out onto the slick, wet tree, treacherous with stubs and broken ends, draped with crushed willow. The boat was half-swamped, cracked like an egg and ragged with splintered wood, but clearly a *strug*, the solid riverboats Slavs made. It would not have been important at all – there were lots of them and it was hardly a surprise to find one as part of the wreck of this swollen river – save for the crew it still held.

He was snagged by his own belt, hair drifting like weed, pale face fat with water and curdled as old cheese. For all that, it was a face I knew and I remembered him, stumbling back from where he had dug up my silver, showing handfuls of it to the rest of his oarmates, that bloated face bright with the wonder of it. Hallgeir, I remembered suddenly. His name was Hallgeir.

Finn nodded and growled when I told him this, peering up the river; he pinched one side of his nose and blew snot down into the wreck.

'So, Randr Sterki has met with some trouble,' he growled. 'Which can only be a good weaving for us, thank the Norns.'

I did not answer; I was too busy searching the water for signs of a small corpse, my belly sick with the thought of Koll, turning in a slow, stately dance like the sheep dead in the mucky water.

The oak finally behind us, days melted, one into the other and went unnoticed. No-one saw much else other than the red-brown water and the sucking mud as they stumbled, heads down and rope over one shoulder, through the shallowest parts they could find. The boat, that great shackle they were fastened to, fretted this way and that, the prow beast snarling and jerking.

The land changed, started to roll into short hills rising out of the flood, some of them flat-topped, others already undercut by the merciless waters. Half-drowned trees shouted out all their green buds even as they died; others huddled like herded cattle on the hills above the water.

The rain sighed itself out and the sun broke through, so that the ground steamed up a crawling mist and the insects came, bloated and fat on carrion, yet still wanting more from the living.

Gudmund died, raving and bursting sweat off him, despite Bjaelfi's best prayer-runes binding the black-rotted holes where the hayfork had gone in, so we rolled him into the water and consigned him to Ran and Aegir, which was as much as we could do in that place.

Freed from that, Bjaelfi now went to treat the ones shivering and sweating and leaking their insides down their legs from some sickness or other – probably in the water, Bjaelfi thought, or perhaps poison from the insects.

'Not good, Orm,' he told me, as if I needed him to inform me of that. He slapped angrily and cursed the stinging insects.

'Perhaps it will rain again,' Crowbone offered cheerfully, 'and drive the insects away.'

'Not as if you suffer,' Yan Alf countered gloomily. 'I want that charm you have.'

Those on board – bailing, poling, or too weak and sick to pull – laughed, but uneasily, for the way the biting hordes avoided Crowbone was too close to magic for comfort and most remembered the reputation of the odd-eyed boy.

'They do not bite him,' Finn declared, bellowing from where he leaned on the sweep, fighting to keep the prow beast snarling into the current, 'because he has no man-juice in him.'

'They do not bite you, either,' observed Dark Eye suddenly, her clear voice made stranger by the silence that had gone before from her. Finn squinted calculatingly, then grinned.

'They do, but if you look closely, you will see them falling dead at my feet,' he growled, 'since there is too much man-juice in me for those little bodies to handle. One taste is all it takes.' And he winked lewdly at her, so that I found myself bristling like an old hound and had to turn away with the shock of it, hoping no-one could see.

The next day, hungry and wet and tired as always, men looked sideways at Crowbone and at me, him for bringing the rain back, or so it seemed and me for . . . everything else. They were muttering more openly now, about forging on after this boy when there was little else in it for anyone. Yet they were fairly trapped, for they could not go downriver now, into the clutches of the waiting Kasperick. Ahead was not any more attractive.

Ahead, growling and spitting white lances and ferns, another storm fretted; the river, fresh fed, surged again the next day and the men started to stumble and fall and it was all I could do to keep them moving. We were close to the Vrankeforde now and I knew Randr Sterki would be there, what men he had as worn out as ourselves; if we were fast enough, he would not have time to find others, for when he thought he had enough, we would not have to chase him – he would come for us.

Then, so close I could almost taste the woodsmoke fires of Vrankeforde, there was a day that began under a vaulted sky of milk-silver, where the air clung to the skin and the men hauling and falling up the river, mouths open and panting, had almost lost the strength to put one soaked foot in front of another.

I saw Gunnliefr, best spearman we had, sink to his knees and weep, all his strength gone. I watched Osnikin, from Sodermannland, fall with a great splash and have to be hauled up by Murrough, or else he would have lain there and drowned.

'Orm,' Trollaskegg began and I did not need him to tell me what was best, so that my look was harsher than a slap and made him click his teeth on his next words.

'Pull, fuck your mothers,' roared Finn, seeing my face. 'Haul away, you dirty swords.'

265

She moved beside me and I felt a hand on my forearm, but when I turned, she was that little wooden carving, staring out over the river, saying nothing, looking at the distant rolling black of cloud, dragging all our eyes to it. As if, some said later, she had magicked it up.

The air tightened, twisting like the iron rods of a smith starting on a new sword. The wind rose, knotting with force, hissed stipples on the river and the dark swooped like a cloak of crows.

The storm broke on us, a great laughter of Thor howling out of the sudden new dark, his Hammer sparking blue-white with a banging that seemed to split the air and fist our ears. The men leaned and the linden bast threw up skeins of water and trembled, while the mast bowed and sang like a harp string.

'It will break,' shrieked Trollaskegg, but the wind grabbed his words and whirled them away down the river, which was a mercy for Yan Alf, since he was clinging to the top of that whipping pole, searching the river ahead while the rain drowned his eyes.

It was the end and it came swift as a secret knife. Through the sheeting veils of rain, I watched a tree blaze and heard the sky crack, looked up and half-expected to see the wheelrim of Redbeard's goat chariot breaking through the dome of the world.

Instead, there was Yan Alf, clinging to the *rakki* as the mast swung and sawed, his face a pale blob in the dark, shouting something the wind snatched away. He pointed out beyond the prow beast where, looming up like some snake-head goddess, the great tree crashed down on us, a huge ram with horns of clotted roots.

The prow beast rose up, dragging the men on the bank backwards, tearing the rope and the skin from their hands. I had time to turn, to think that all our struggle, all the days of effort to this place, hung on a thin, stretching line and the skidding crew who held it – when the linden bast spurted water, snapped and whipped back. Ospak yelped with the lash of it, spun half-round and went over the side.

The *drakkar*, locked in what seemed a raging battle, spun round; timber shrieked, planks splintered and men were mouthing bellows no-one could hear. The ship seemed to rear up like a stallion in a horse fight, right up until the stern went under and it tilted. I saw oars and chests slide away – saw Dark Eye slide away and milled my arms to try and grab her.

Water slapped me, snagged me, dragged me down and round and round, so that the silver trail of bubbles from my mouth circled me like a flock of birds.

I saw them, like pearls, like the last thought trailing from my mind – Odin would have to fight Aegir for his sacrifice offering.

Then there was only darkness.

The moon was a bright eye and an owl shrieked, a thrown chip of a cry. From the rolling charcoal of hills came the scream of some animal, high and thin and trembling with loneliness and then there was Vuokko, sitting beside me on a flat, black rock, cradling his drum.

'I can only do this because it is Valpurgis,' he said, 'when the veil between the worlds is thinnest.'

May Eve, when the Wild Hunt staggered to a halt. Einmanuthur, the lonely month. I felt the crush of it, wanted to be home . . .

'There is a loss coming,' Vuokko said. 'Keener than winter. Odin will take his sacrifice soon.'

I wanted to be home more than ever, wanted to tell the Sea-Finn, who I knew was soaring in the Other watching me die, to take messages with him, of love and friendship and last words. But when I started to speak, he hit his drum and kept on hitting it, a thundering sound that jarred me, pounding on and on and on . . .

*　　*　　*

The blood thundered in my ears and my chest ached with each huge, retching breath; my throat burned and my nose throbbed. There was the iron taste of blood in the back of my throat. Ospak peered at me long enough to make sure I had come to my senses, then stopped pounding my chest and rose up, his knees cracking.

'It is a bad habit to get into,' he declared, 'this having to be hauled out of water just before you drown.'

Dark Eye, cat-wet and scowling, glared at him and then turned a soulful look on me.

'I shall try and break it,' I managed to hoarse back at him and he chuckled at that and the slap from Dark Eye as he reached out a grimy hand towards my nose.

'That neb of yours is cursed, I am thinking,' he said and then tilted his head slightly. 'It is only straight on your face if I stand like this. And it looks flatter than it did.'

If the pain was anything to go by, I did not doubt it, but I was more concerned with what had happened. I had thought him dead, for sure, a thought I shared with him while Dark Eye fussed.

'I thought the same when I went over,' he told me grimly and showed me the blue-black welt on his upper arm. 'That rope seemed set with a life of its own and it took me a while to get clear of it.'

'Double thanks, then,' I rasped, 'for hauling me out.'

He chuckled. 'Not me. The Mazur girl did that.'

I looked at her and she smiled.

'I was supposed to save you,' I said to her and she fixed me with her seal eyes; it came to me then that we were alone, the three of us, soaked to the skin on a patch of wet barely raised above a black swamp where the mud and water oozed and new, sodden reeds stood straight up like hairs on a boar snout.

'Where are the others?' I said, sick with the possibilities and scrambling to my feet. I was weary to my bones, my head pounded, my chest burned and the whole front of my face felt seared, but I forced it off; I was ashore and the ground might squelch, but it was solid enough for me to feel safe after that muscling river. There was freshness in the air, too, as if the storm had finally gasped itself out, tangled and shredded in the branches and brush by the tiny sprigs of green. A bird sang somewhere unseen.

'Back upriver,' answered Ospak with a shrug, 'if they are still in the world at all. You and me and that girl were all tangled in the one rope, which is a strange thing. Perhaps the Norns wove it that way for a purpose.'

'Well,' I said, pushing the crushing weight of it grimly, like a bad plough, 'it seems we have a walk back to camp, then, if camp there is.'

I rose, weaving. Dark Eye straightened, wiped the palms of her hands down her sodden skirts and bent to pick up something beside me. My sword, still sheathed, the baldric loop missing a few silver ornaments.

'I hauled you ashore with it,' she said in her thin little voice. 'I had to take it off, for it was round your neck and strangling you.'

I felt the burning welt of that now, too, and fingered it, wondering at the strength in her to have managed that. I smiled and took the sword – Jarl Brand's sword. At least we still had that and I turned to Ospak and told him so, for the cheer in it.

'Aye, sure and that's a good thing, for I have an eating knife only,' he answered and then tilted his beard off to one side. 'And they were a worry.'

I followed his gaze and saw the six horsemen sitting at the limit of bow range, watching, resting easy on hipshot horses, bows out and arrows ready.

I looked back at Ospak and then at Dark Eye, whose face was a carving block.

'Magyar,' she said.

Which was hardly a comfort.

Two things happened then and it is sometimes strange how such weight as your life can hang on the thinnest thread – a voice understood and a scratch behind the ear.

Dark Eye moved two paces forward and hailed them, in her own Mazur tongue, which it was clear they understood. At the same time, a dog trotted out from the horsemen, a smooth, long-legged loper the colour of old bracken; it headed straight for me. Though smooth-coated, it reminded me of the big grey, wiry wolfhounds that had been with me not long before; we had eaten them out on the Great White and left nothing much more than the paws and I had been sorry for that later.

This one came close and sat while I moved to it, a few paces, no more. It let me scratch behind one ear.

The horsemen shifted then. The leader came forward, his hands out to either side and empty; when he got close, he halted and waited for me to walk to him. The dog followed me.

He was sallow, black moustached, with a clean chin and dark eyes over high cheeks. His hair hung under a fur-trimmed cone and was knotted in hundreds of small braids, like ropes and he wore an embroidered coat over loose breeks tucked into high boots which had what looked like silver coins down each side.

We fished for understanding for a while and found Greek. He grinned whitely at me and placed one hand on his chest.

'*Bökény fia Jutos*,' he declared, which I took to be a name. Later, I learned that he was Jutos, son of this Bökény.

'Orm,' I answered, slapping my own chest. 'Ruriksson.'

'You are *Ascomanni*, from Wolin,' he said and I put him right on that. He frowned.

'Sipos says you are to be trusted,' he answered and sounded as if that was strange to him. It took me a moment to realise he was speaking of the dog.

'Sipos,' said Dark Eye, coming up beside me; the dog licked

her hand and grinned, pink tongue lolling wetly. 'It means Piper. The Magyar call these dogs *viszla*, which means "deerhound" and they are much prized for hunting.'

'Mazur,' said Jutos, looking at her and it was a statement, not a question. Then he nodded and turned the horse.

'Come,' he said. Ospak looked at me and I shrugged. It was not as if we had much say in the matter, for the horsemen closed round us, like herders on cattle. We went a little east, away from the river which fretted me, for I thought it was further from the others and said so.

'If there are others,' Ospak answered moodily. 'That was a big tree.'

We left the floodplain for soft rolling hills and then, beside a rill that ran white between great smooth boulders until it made a large, dark pool, came up to their camp of wagons, some covered, some with two wheels and some with four. Horses snickered; smoke drifted, thick and pungent and a woman, squatting by the stream with her skirts spread for decency, took a piss and smiled at us.

The dog, wedge-head held low, snuffled and quested and answered a bark from the centre of the wagon circle with a hoarse one of its own, which seemed to be squeezed out of the red-gold body. It set ducks up off the water of the pool and Jutos laughed.

'Home,' he said and I could not disagree. We came up to a fire whose perfume was as heady as incense to me and the warmth made us all realise how chilled and cold we were.

People milled; we were given blankets to wrap ourselves and stripped of our clothes under the decency of them, made to sit down under a *wadmal* canopy and presented with bowls. A woman, grinning and nodding her head while she spoke a trill of softness I did not understand, cracked eggs in a cauldron of barley broth and meat, then filled our bowls. I ate, sopping fat chunks of bread with it, ravenous.

In the end, sated, we all sat back.

'By the gods,' sighed Ospak after a while, which said it all.

The camp moved with soft life while the sun of late after-noon slanted through the surrounding trees and Dark Eye curled up and slept with the dog, both cradled in the dry beech mast near the fire. The ducks came warily back to the pool, planing in to land with creamy wakes.

Folk passed and stared curiously, but left us alone. Ospak nodded, half-asleep; a woman came to where our clothes hung, studied them, poked a finger in a hole and tutted. Then she fetched needle and thread.

Jutos startled me from my half-sleep by looming up and squatting, face smiling.

'I have been told of others of your kind, not far. An hour's ride, perhaps more. They are by the river and their boat is badly damaged.'

That sounded like Finn and the others and I wanted to know if he knew how many. Jutos shrugged.

'Enough for my hunters not to go too near,' he answered, grinning. 'There are too many riders out on the land these days. Something has stirred them up.'

He said it in a way that let me know he thought part of that stirring was us, but he seemed friendly enough still and we talked until the shadows stretched and our clothes were dry enough to wear again.

These folk were, I found, Magyars, a trading party who travelled part of the old Amber Road, which once led to the north of Langabardaland and then down to Old Rome.

'Not now,' Jutos explained. 'Now we take it to our land and trade it on to the Bulgars and others, who take it down to the Great City, where the power and the gold now is.'

'I thought there was power and gold back in Old Rome,' I answered, to show I knew some matters of trade, 'now that Otto the Saxlander has declared himself Emperor, like his father of the same name before him.'

Jutos spat so that the embered fire sizzled.

'Best not to speak of the Ottos when my father comes,' he said grimly. 'Our *fejedelem* is Géza, who has eaten salt with the Saxlanders and Romans to gain peace. He has even taken a Christ worshipper to his household, a monk called Bruno – but friendship with the Saxlanders is not something that sits lightly with one of the Seven.'

I knew the word *fejedelem* meant something akin to 'ruling prince' and I had heard how this Géza had been forced to accept the Christ worshippers because the Great City and Otto had made an agreement. Of course, since Géza had little say in the matter, his Christ worship was not entirely full-hearted – but there it was again, that working of kings that always seemed to favour the White Christ. I said as much and Jutos grinned.

'Perhaps, after all, the Tortured God has more power,' he growled. 'It is certain our own gods did not help us when my father became one of the Seven.'

I did not recognise the reference to the Seven and wanted to know more, but Ospak bridled at this discussion, for he was an Irisher who had embraced Thor and loved him.

'This Christ has no power,' he argued. 'If you need proof of that, look at my god and him together. The Christ is nailed to a lump of wood; my god has a Hammer.'

He spat on one palm and slapped his hands together, as if he had made a good legal point at a Thing and even Jutos joined in my laughter.

Still, I did not have to wait long to find out about the Seven, for Jutos' father came to us soon after. At first he was just a tall, thin shadow against the red-dyed sky, moving slow and stooped, flanked by two other, stockier shadows who wore ring-coats and the high-crested helms favoured by Magyars and Khazars. Closer, the white blur of face resolved into features and what I had taken for a bald head was white hair, iron-streaked and dragged back.

Closer still and Ospak sucked in his breath, while Dark

Eye went still and quiet, as she always did when faced with horrors, sliding into the earth and stones, becoming invisible.

This Bökény had a face like a skull. There was no nose and he had no ears and age had shrunk the cheeks so that the skin on the knobs under his eyes looked to be splitting. Hard wrinkles marked him, deep-scored plough-lines across his forehead and great scars down the side of his mouth, deep enough to lose a finger up to the first joint. One eye was milk, the other black-bright as a crow and his hair was dragged back and tied at the nape of his neck, yet it spilled down almost to his belt.

I marked that. Finn had lost an ear long since and never tied his hair back. This man, this Magyar *horka*, did not care; more than that, he offered his face like a defiant, triumphant banner.

He squatted stiffly, and I saw his cloak, fastened at the shoulders by two discs, each marked with a bird holding a sword. That sight ran a shock through me, for the sword was a sabre and I had heard that these Magyars worshipped the sword of Attila, for they were Huns, when all was said and done. It also reminded me of something I had in my sea-chest – if I still had a sea-chest.

The old man gathered his cloak round him then spoke, while Jutos translated; it was the usual welcome and prettily enough done, so I gave him back the same.

He spoke again and Jutos answered him, then shrugged and turned to me.

'He wonders what you have to trade. You may count so far as hospitality, but if those are your men we found, they will perhaps need food and other things. Can you trade?'

Ospak grunted, for he did not like all this talk of trade, being – like the rest of the Oathsworn – a man who preferred to consider what he wanted down the length of a blade. Unless, as I told him sharply now in Norse, he was outnumbered and out-ranged, which he admitted with a scowl and another grunt.

I did not know what was left to trade and thought a salting of truth was best, so I said there had been riches enough aboard the ship before it was smashed and was sure all could not have been lost.

Jutos rattled this off to his father, who considered it for while, the blood-egg sun doing things to his face that would have sent bairns screaming into their ma's skirts. Then he spoke again and Jutos turned, almost resignedly.

'He wishes to know if you will trade the Mazur girl and what you will take,' he said. I looked at him steadily, so that he knew the answer without me having to speak. With a brief, almost relieved nod, he told his father, who grunted and muttered.

'He says,' Jutos told me, 'that you northers are hard to bargain with. He is fated to see unusual slaves he cannot get. He does not wish to meet any more of you on this trip.'

Ospak chuckled at that. 'Well, we are equal matched then,' he answered, grinning to take the sting from it, 'for this is one norther who does not wish to see a face like that again. How did he come by it?'

I closed my eyes and waited for the storm this would cause, but I had it wrong, for it was no insult to note this singular face.

'He is one of the horde of Bulcsú,' Jutos answered and the old man's head came up at the sound of that name. 'Last of the Seven.'

'Bulcsú,' the old man repeated and then began talking, in his own tongue, a great solemn, slow-rolling chant, thick as a saga tale and, though none of the three of us understood it, we were all struck by the telling of it.

He was as good as any skald versing on the giant Ymir whose skull forms the dome of the world, or of Muspell, at once burning and freezing, or of Odin and the gods of Asgard. But the old man's tale was no misted saga, but recent, from his own life and, as he poured it out, thick-voiced with remembering, Jutos translated the meat of it.

275

The old man told of Lechfeld some twenty summers before, when the Magyar, the fire of Attila still coursing in their veins, had come to take on the might of Otto the Great, the present Otto's father. The old man spoke lovingly of the clans all arrayed and the colours they wore and the myriad tiny, fluttering signal banners of the chieftains, Lél, Súr and Bulcsú.

He brayed and clashed his palms together to bring back the horns and the drums and the brass discs they struck, howled out the old warcries, showed how they were wild to fight. He stood up, no longer stiff but straddle-legged, riding an unseen horse, firing backwards as he feigned flight with all the others – twenty thousand and more – on that day.

I had heard of this battle. In the end, the bowmen on their light horses, fur hats scrugged down tight on their heads, had been mastered by the solid ranks of Saxlanders, had hurled themselves like heroes to be cut down, until only a handful were left, the chiefs among them.

Jutos, grim as a dark cliff and his eyes bright with water, watched the old man slump; someone brought him drink and it ran down the harsh grooves off his chin.

'The Saxlanders cut the ears and noses off the survivors and sent seven back to our ruling prince of that time, Taksony,' Jutos added blankly. 'They hung Lél and Bulcsú from a tower in Regensberg. Súr came back as one of the seven, and he was killed for causing such a tragedy, for he was not of the line of Arpad. The last warriors who survived that day were honoured for their courage, all the same, and my father is the only one left. The Magyar have stayed in their homeland since that day and have no love for the Saxlanders.'

'Heya,' said Ospak, his Irisher soul stirred by such a tale and the old man raised his head and nodded acknowledgement to that salute.

'Since then, we have travelled the Amber Road as traders,' Jutos went on. 'There are more of us now. All the men of this clan who rode with my father were killed in that battle, but slowly we grow stronger. One day, we will be strong enough to pay the Saxlanders back.'

I looked at the old man, milk-white in the dusk, slumped and spent now, sitting in a ring of some forty wagons, with horses, men, women and bairns. I thought of Hestreng and how we were not so far from each other, Magyar and Northman.

Horses were brought, but I told Ospak to stay with the Mazur girl. Stone-faced Jutos sat on his horse and said nothing as I climbed onto mine, flanked by a half-dozen Magyars armed with lances and bows and wearing their pointed helmets with elaborate nasals. Bökény rose stiffly and nodded to his son, who returned it. Then he hirpled away to his tent, leaving me with the vague idea that some message had passed between them.

In silence, we rode out into the dying day and, for a while, nothing more was said. That let me work on how this horse moved, for it was a rangy, bow-nosed creature, not one of the short, stiff-maned, fast-gaited ponies I knew. After a while, I felt Jutos arrive at my knee, where he cleared his throat, like the dull rumble of distant thunder. Here it comes, I was thinking.

'There is a lot of happening up and down the Odra for the time of year,' he said in a low, even voice. 'Particularly when the rains have been so bad.'

I stayed silent, feeling my stomach turn slowly, like a dead sheep in the river; I gave great attention to the sitting of my horse.

'We came past an old settlement we had visited before,' he went on, 'and found it burned out and everything dead. Everything. Children, dogs. Everything.'

He shook his head with the memory of it and I swallowed the sick rise of shame in me.

'There are riders out everywhere,' he added, 'from the Pols. A force is out and not a small one – hundreds. I have not seen so many since the Pols marched this way two summers ago, heading for war in the north against the Pomorze.'

'I have heard the Pols are swallowing other tribes,' I said, in order to say something and give away nothing at all, even though the thought of hundreds of Pols searching along the Odra was a chill knife in my bowels. I had not thought they would be so stirred by the burning of a Sorb village. I had it right – they were not and the next thing Jutos said made that clear.

'They seek a Mazur girl and a band of northers,' he said flatly and that made me look at him. Here it was, then, out in the open. I waited to see what came next, strung tight as a drawn bowstring.

'You have eaten salt with us,' Jutos went on, slowly, carefully, like a man picking his way across a marsh. 'This means you will come to no harm from us, neither you nor your band by the river. My father, of course, is more honourable than I am, for he sought to buy the Mazur girl and so save your life; I argued that it was too much danger brought on us, but he insisted.'

I saw he was not lying and was both surprised and a little shamed at my thoughts, which had been along the path of how their elaborate hospitality was more to do with fearing to tangle with a band of armed growlers like the Oathsworn. Now I saw they pitied us and regarded us as already dead, which was not a comforting thing.

'Then we will trade for food and be gone,' I answered, 'before you are made sorry for your hospitality.'

Jutos crooked one leg casually over the saddle, an elegance I envied.

'Of course,' he added, white teeth gleaming in the dusk of his face, 'our obligation ends when trading ends. Usually, we allow a day between us before considering matters.'

I rode the gentle threat and stared him down.

'We are not so generous,' I gave him back, 'feeling half that is distance enough, should one side feel aggrieved.'

The dog, Sipos, ambled over to run alongside me and Jutos widened his grin.

'He likes you,' he said. 'Perhaps you have something to trade for him?'

I shook my head, feeling annoyed at the smile of this man, bland as oatmeal and curved sharp as a sabre blade.

'I like dogs,' I answered. 'All us northers do. With some winter roots, a peck of salt and the lees of old wine they make good eating.'

Scowling, he jerked the head of his horse savagely round and away and left me staring down into the mournful eyes of the dog until I blinked and looked away.

The rest of the ride was silence until, in the gathering dusk, Jutos hissed out a command and men galloped off and the rest of us reined in. A few minutes later, a rider returned and spoke briefly to Jutos, who turned to me.

'Your men have made camp, but lit no fires,' he declared, almost admiringly. 'None of my scouts have been able to approach closely without being seen. Perhaps you should ride out and hail them before there is unpleasantness.'

I was pleased as I edged the horse forward – and not a little anxious that Kuritsa would do something rash in the twilight, for I was sure he was watching. When I could no longer see the Magyars behind me, I decided enough was enough and bellowed out my name.

The voice, soft and almost in my ear, made me leap and teeter in the saddle with the shock of it.

'I see you, Orm Bear Slayer.'

Finn slithered out of the dark, with Kuritsa close behind, arrow nocked.

'Good to find you alive,' Finn growled with a grin. 'With a horse, too. And new friends.'

'Magyar traders,' I answered flatly, as if such a thing was no more than to be expected from the likes of me. 'Ospak and Dark Eye are safe in their camp. How are things with us?'

Kuritsa shook his head admiringly.

'I had heard that if Orm Trader fell in a barrel of shite he

279

would find the only bag of silver in it,' he laughed. 'Until now, I had not believed it.'

I acknowledged the praise with a nod and a grin, but kept looking at Finn for an answer to my question.

'Four dead,' he said flatly. 'Or so we believe. They were the weakest of the sick and have not, like you and Ospak, surfaced from the river.'

'The ship?'

He did not answer, but turned away, so I rode down to the river with him, past men iron-grey in the growing dark, shields up and helms on. One or two grinned and called greetings; just as many gave me blank looks, or even scowls.

Short Serpent was snagged tight to the heavy bole of a tree, which was furred green with moss. Slimy clumps of frog eggs drifted in tattered skeins along the riverbank, while the river itself growled and spat still, a mud-brown coil like a snake's back.

Men clustered round the *drakkar*, leaping on and off her, fetching and carrying; a smaller group stood by the prow – Onund, Crowbone, Trollaskegg and Abjorn – who turned as I came up.

'Odin's arse,' Onund said, his pleasure as clear as a dog's. 'Here is a good sight.'

'Doubled,' Finn said, 'for he has Ospak safe and found us food and shelter.'

'If my sea-chest survived,' I added and Trollaskegg said that it had and a lot of gear had been saved. Crowbone, eyes bright, nudged Abjorn.

'See? You owe me six ounces of silver – I said he was not dead.'

Abjorn looked at me and shrugged apologetically.

'It was a wild river,' he said by way of excuse, 'but I am glad it did not claim you, for we have been holding a Thing on it and could not agree on who would now lead.'

'Aye, well, include me out of that now,' shouted a cheerful

voice and Styrbjorn hurled something over the side of the ship, then followed it, both splashing wetly on the bank and spraying mud, to a chorus of curses. Undaunted, Styrbjorn hefted his prize and held it out to Onund; it was his carving of the elk head, antlers proud against the wood.

'Yours,' he said. 'All that is left of this ship.'

'The ship is exactly like my carving,' Onund agreed, mournful as a wet dog. 'Finished.'

I did not need him to tell me that, for the whole proud curve of the bow was staved in and the water frothed and gurgled in and down the length of it. The prow beast, white with gouges, still snarled even though the teeth in its mouth were broken and it hung by a splinter.

'We could cut new planks,' argued Trollaskegg and looked desperately at Crowbone for support, but even little Olaf knew, with all the wisdom of his twelve years, that we could not repair his wonderful ship.

'*Short Serpent* put up a good fight against that tree,' Crowbone said softly and Abjorn picked up the elk head.

'Lash that to a spear shaft,' I told him. 'We will have new fierceness yet. Light fires in hollows where they will not be seen – these Magyars are safe enough, but others are out hunting us – then give me half-a-dozen men with drag-poles to fetch back supplies. Finn – you command here. I will go back and stay with the Magyars, for the trading.'

Their faces asked all the questions, but their mouths stayed shut. Abjorn simply nodded and went off to see some of it done, handing his armful of prow beast to Onund, who gave a grunt and sloshed off to higher ground to see to the camp, rolling in his great, bear way. Crowbone and Trollaskegg stood, twin pillars of misery, looking at the ship.

'When it is empty of everything we can use,' I said, knowing I sounded crow-voiced and that they would not realise it was from the river and not from harshness, 'cut it free and let the river take it. With luck, the Saxlanders will see it – or find it if it makes it to the opposite bank – and think us dead.'

I found my sea-chest, and Red Njal sitting on it, with Finnlaith and Murrough nearby. All the Irishers were happy to hear that Ospak had survived. Alyosha and Kaelbjorn Rog and others came up to see for themselves the marvellous event that was Orm, returned from the river with Ospak in tow. Not one of them, or anyone else, cared whether Dark Eye had lived or died, I noted.

I rummaged in the chest and found what I was looking for in the last of my treasures – a handful of hacksilver and three armrings, one of them already cut almost to nothing.

But there was a torc, too, and I took it out so that it gleamed pale in the last light of day. The Irishers were drawn to it like bright-eyed magpies and it has to be said it was a fine piece I had guarded carefully, an old necklet taken from Atil's hoard.

Not as fine as the one I wore round my neck, the torc of a jarl – even with its dragon-head ends battered and the twisted length of it nicked and cut – but a rich thing, of gold and amber-metal, which the Romans call *electrum*, with bird-head ends. It was those I had remembered, seeing the old man's cloak-pin.

Jutos' eyes widened when I presented it to him back at the camp as what I had to trade. He turned it over and over in his hands, the firelight sliding along it and folk coming up to look and admire. I saw them point to the bird-heads and heard the word *turul* repeated in awe and wonder. It turned out that I had been right – this bird, the *turul*, was worshipped by the Magyar.

Jutos wanted to know where it had come from and I gave him it straight, so he would know he dealt with more than just another trader from the north. The treasure hoard of Attila, I told him and watched his eyes grow round and black as old ice, for Attila was as good as a god to them.

Then he looked at Crowbone, who had come along because

he had never seen Magyars before, and you could see the thoughts flit across his face like hound and hare, for the distant, misted tales of the Oathsworn and the strange odd-eyed boy who was one of them had suddenly arrived at the fire where he was sitting.

So he went to the old man with the torc in his hand while we ate and drank in a dusk thick and soft as unseen smoke, with the quarrelling of women and the bark of dogs comforting as a cloak. Enough food for a night's decent meal was sent off back to the Oathsworn, so I was content enough with the start of this Thing.

Later, in the black of night, we went away from the others, to where the pool shimmered and there she moved to me. Others moved, too, so that the beech mast rustled; there was a laugh in the throat here, a groan from over there.

There was no love-talk – little talk at all between us, though she murmured soft, cooing sounds in her own tongue – nor even much kissing or hugging, but we moved as if we had known each other before and there was little need of any of the rest, for my heart was huge and urgent and in my throat and I knew it was the same for her.

She was white and thin, all planes and shadows, smelled of woodsmoke and warmth and crushed grass and there was not night long enough for us. As the dawn silvered up I lay back, with her breathing slow and even on my chest, snugged up under the same cloak.

'What will you do with me?' she asked.

'Give me a minute,' I answered. 'Perhaps two.'

She thumped me on the chest, no more than the flutter of a bird wing and I laughed.

'Will you take me back to my father?'

'Was that what this was about?' I asked, made moody by her now. She struck me again and this time it was a small, hard nut of knuckle that made me wince.

'You think that?' she demanded and her eyes were big and

round and bright in the dark. Just her eyes alone made me ashamed of it, so that I shook my head.

'If you are not taking me back,' she went on, slow and soft in the dark, 'then why am I here?'

I told her; because the Sea-Finn's drum had said to bring her. She was silent, thinking.

'Did it say to bring me to your home, after the ice-headed boy is found?'

That made me blink a bit, thinking of Thorgunna and what she would have to say about a second woman – wife, I realised with a shock, for I would have to marry Dark Eye. I was still thinking of an answer when she shivered.

'I will not marry you,' she said.

'Why not?' I wanted to know, chastened and wondering if she could read thoughts. She raised her head for a moment, then pointed out across the water of the tarn, where a mallard drake, all jewel-flashing in green and purple, swung down into the waters with a hissing splash.

'That is why not,' she said. The drake made for the nearest of the ducks and mounted her, vicious and uncaring, leaving her half-drowned and squawking.

'That is the lot of such as me,' she said, 'no matter whose I am at the time. A strange woman in a house of women. The men will all want to mount me, the women to peck my feathers off.'

Half-sick with the truth of it, I growled some bluster about what would happen to any who treated her in such a way, but she laid her head on my chest again and I could feel her soft smile.

'I do not know what path I am to take,' she answered. 'I am away from my people and cannot go back to them, since that would start a war. I am Mazur and if I am to marry I do not intend to do it in a land of ice.'

She stopped and looked into my face, her eyes looming like a doe's.

'But there will be a child,' she declared with certainty and I felt the skin-crawling whenever *seidr* presented itself to me. 'It will be a son and I can only offer it a safe place if I go with you.'

She stopped and shivered. 'Iceland,' she said. 'A country made from ice.'

I laughed, more from relief at being able to steer off the topic we had been on.

'It is not made of ice,' I told her. 'Anyway, I am not from Iceland. Onund is.'

'Somewhere as cold,' she muttered, snuggling tight to me. 'At the edge of the world.'

I liked the feeling and pulled her closer still.

'Iceland is not at the edge,' I answered, drifting lazily. 'Near the centre. North of Iceland is the *maelstrom*. You follow that star there.' I pointed to the bright North Star and she looked, squinting.

'What is the *maelstrom*?'

I told her; the place where the giant women, Fenja and Menja, turn the great millwheel Grotti, blindly churning out the last order they were given before the ship carrying them all sank – to make salt. Which is why the sea tastes the way it does. The *maelstrom* is a great whirlpool caused by them turning and turning the handle far beneath the waves.

Sleepily, she laughed. 'Good tale. The Christ worshippers, though, say the centre of the world is in Jorsalir, where their White Christ was nailed to his bits of wood.'

'What do you believe?' I asked, but there was no reply; she slept, breathing soft and slow and I began to wonder if it was not the will of the gods to bring her back to Hestreng. What other reason could the Sea-Finn's drum have had? It was never going to be possible to travel all the way across the land of the Pols to her own Mazur tribe, hunted every step of the way.

Of course, the gods laughed while we slept, were still laughing when the sun strengthened, rich and red-gold and we dressed and moved back to the others, me prepared to endure the jibes from Ospak and Crowbone.

I started to hear the gods cackling when I saw Crowbone rise to his feet, slow and stiff, as if he had spotted a *draugr* coming across the space between the wagons. But he was not staring at us, but off to our right, where I saw the old man tottering forward with his two warrior pillars and his son.

Even then I thought Crowbone had spotted the old man's face and had been stunned by it, for it was a swung stick to the senses, that face, and I was chuckling when I came up.

'He is not half as fierce as he looks,' I said. 'I would not worry over much.'

Crowbone looked at me, then back to the old man, who came up closer to us.

'Nose,' Crowbone said, pointing and I turned.

The shock of it dropped my jaw; the gods' laughter grew harsh and loud as disturbed ravens.

The old man had come in his finery, from brocaded coat to red-leather riding boots and fine-hilted sabre. Round his neck he already wore the bird-ended torc, to show he had accepted the trade and we would now haggle only over the price.

But his last piece of jewellery was what staggered those who knew it by sight. Bound by a blue-silk ribbon, carefully tied to show his lack of ears, was the final statement on his flag of a face.

Sigurd's silver nose.

SEVENTEEN

We scarred the laden drag-poles over a sodden land steaming in the new sunshine, ripe with new life and old death, thick with the smells of dark earth and rotted carcass. We scattered birds from the raggled corpses of drowned cattle and, at the end of the first day, sent up a cloud of rooks like black smoke from dead sheep the retreating waters had left hanging in gnarled branches like strange fruit.

'Why are we pushing so hard?' panted Kaelbjorn Rog, who only voiced what others thought. 'We are leaving a trail a blind wean could follow, never mind some Magyar scouts.'

I said nothing, but grimmed them on through the fly-stinging, sweat-soaked day, the sick tottering along with the shite rolling down their legs rather than be bumped in drag-poles, for it was not the Magyars I feared, nor was I entirely running from enemies. Only Crowbone shared my thoughts on why we truly scowled our way so swiftly across the land and he was still mourning the distance between him and his uncle's silver nose.

Jutos had seen Crowbone's reaction and knew something was not quite right; slowly the tale of it was hoiked up and sense was made of things that had been said earlier, of northers encountered and hard bargains being struck.

The Oathsworn had not been the first band of Norse the Magyars had met; that honour had been given to Randr Sterki and some eighteen or so survivors of his own river-wyrd, stumbling out on the floodplain, starving and thirsting, for they dared not drink the foul water they sloshed through.

'My father wanted the boy they had,' Jutos told us, 'a rare child, white as bone. Their leader, a man with skin-marks on him, offered us a Greek Christ priest, but that was no trade for us. We said to take him to the Pols, who might give them a little food, for I thought the Pols might know better what to do with a priest from the Great City.'

'Where did they go?' I asked and Jutos shrugged, waving vaguely in the direction of the distant blue mountains.

'South, this side of the Odra,' he replied. 'After he had traded this marvellous nose for enough supplies.'

He paused and grinned widely. 'If you happen to have ears that match, we will make ourselves go hungry to acquire them.'

I told him the torc was rich enough and tried to get the nose back, for Crowbone's sake. In the end, though, we got supplies only – and the only bargain in it came as we were leaving, hauling the drag-poles away on a surprising gift of three horses.

Jutos came up and thrust out his hand, so I took it, wrist-to-wrist, in the Norse fashion and he nodded.

'We part as traders,' he said formally, then paused. 'I will give you a day, then send riders to find the Pols and tell them of you and the Mazur girl. That will stop them raiding us when they find out we helped you. The horses we have given you will let you travel faster away from them.'

It was as fair as you could expect from Magyars and, at the end of that first day, I told the rest of the Oathsworn what we could expect and that Randr Sterki and the boy we had come to rescue lay just ahead. There was silence, mainly, and Finn had the right of it when, later, he demanded to know what else I had expected from the crew.

'The fact that we have enemies ahead as well as behind is not a joy of news,' he added, to which I could find no answer.

The next day we had grown used to the smell of rot, so used to it, in fact, that we stumbled into horror when we should have been warned long since.

When we came round the side of a hill and saw the *grod*, we slowed and came to halt; men unshipped weapons and shields and stood uncertainly, looking from one to another and then at me.

It was a good *grod*, a well-raised earthwork, wooden stockade surrounding a cluster of dwellings, with a big covered watchtower over the gate. It had been built on a hill above the floodplain and the rising waters had swept round it like a moat, save for a narrow walkway of raised earth and logs, which led to the gate. The watery moat had since sunk and seeped almost back to the river, leaving bog and marsh which steamed in the sun.

The gate in the stockade was wide open and there was not a wisp of smoke. No dog barked, no horses grazed. Then the wind shifted slightly.

'Odin's arse,' Finn grunted, his face squeezed up. He spat; the stink was like a slap in the face, a great hand that shoved the smell of rot down your throat.

'A fight, perhaps,' Styrbjorn said. 'Randr Sterki and his men, I am thinking. The villagers have all run off, save for those he has killed.'

Styrbjorn grunted out that this was good work from only eighteen men, but most ignored him, cheered by the idea of a whole village lying open and empty and ripe as a lolling whore – perhaps Randr and his men had left some loot, too.

Then I pointed out that Randr and his men might still be there, waiting to ambush us.

'Send Styrbjorn the Bold in,' Abjorn declared and men laughed, which made Styrbjorn scowl and go red.

I chose Finn, Abjorn, Kaelbjorn Rog and Uddolf to go with me, leaving Alyosha to organise the others into a cautious defence; when we moved to the gates, magpies and crows rose up, one by one, flapping off and scolding us.

The place was empty, just as we had hoped. Wooden walkways led to a central raised platform of wood, with a tall pole on it, carved with four faces – their meeting place, with their god presiding over it. No Christ worshippers these. At first there were no bodies either, yet the smell of death was thick as linen as we prowled, turning in half-circles, hackles up and wary as cats. A goat skipped out of an alley and almost died under Abjorn's frantic axe; a cow bawled plaintively from an unseen byre.

Uddolf poked a door open and then leapt back with a yelp; two dogs sidled out, whimpering, tails wagging furiously, tongues lolling from want of water – but they were full-bellied and the smell made my hair rise, made me breathe short and quick, not wanting to get the air anywhere deep in me.

I peered in, squinting through the gloom at the three bodies, black, bloated and chewed by the dogs. A man, his clothes tight against puffed flesh. A woman. A youngster, who could have been girl or boy.

After that we found others, one by one, two by two; a woman slumped against a wall, part-eaten, part-pecked. A boy whose face seemed to be peppered with scabs. A man with a bloated face that looked like oatmeal had been thrown at it and stuck. I grew afraid, then.

'Sickness,' Kaelbjorn Rog declared and he was right, I was sure, so I sent him back to fetch up Bjaelfi, who knew about such matters. We prowled on uneasily.

There were two handfuls of long timber houses, where kettles and cauldrons, horn spoons and looms sat, waiting for hands. There were storerooms and barns, hay in the barns

290

and barrels of salted meat in the storehouses, while the bawling cow had teats swollen and sore, being so overdue for milking. The strange stillness became even more hackle-raising.

'The livestock has been turned loose,' Finn said, nodding to a brace of chewing goats. 'So someone was alive to do that.'

Not now. We found them when we came up to a larger building, clearly a meeting hut. Here the truth unravelled itself from this sad Norn-weave.

'Look here,' Abjorn called and we went. A man and a woman lay at the door of the meeting hut, part-eaten but not as long-dead as the others. The woman had a wound in her chest, the man a knife in his throat and we circled, calling the tale of it as we read the signs.

'The last ones left alive. He stabbed the woman,' Finn declared.

'Thrust the knife in his own throat,' added Uddolf, pointing. 'Missed, but bled. Did it again by putting it against his throat and falling on it, so he could not fail.'

We wore that little tragedy like a cloak as we filtered through into the meeting hut, almost having to push again the smell. Here they were, on pallets or slumped against the walls, dead, swollen, scabbed, eaten by scavengers, brought here to be more easily cared for, though there was no care that kept them from dying.

Bjaelfi came up, the fear slathered on his face. He had seen the other corpses, but he took one look at the stabbed woman's body and turned it with his foot so that the flies rose up with the stink. One arm flopped and he pointed at the untouched, mottled flesh down her arm, where small red and white dots stared accusingly back.

'Red Plague,' he said and it hit us like a stone, so that we scrambled from the place. Fast as we were, the news of it was faster and, by the time we were hawking the bad air out of us, everyone knew.

Red Plague. We moved away as fast as we could, but I knew we would not outrun the red-spotted killer, that we probably carried it with us. I had expected to die for Odin, but the thought of thrashing out my life in a straw death, the sweat rolling off me in fat drops, my face pustuled and no-one wanting to be near me, was almost enough to buckle my knees.

We made camp at the top of a hill, in the shelter of some trees, where two fires were lit, smoking up from wet wood. Beyond a little way, bees muttered and bumbled, stupid with cold and spilled from their storm-cracked nest; men moved, laughing softly when one was stung, fishing out the combs of honey and pleased with this small gesture from Frey.

Warmth and sweetness went a long way to scattering the thought of Red Plague, as did Finn's cauldron of meat and broth, eaten with bread and fine, crumbling cheese. Their bellies no longer grumbled, but it would not be long, as I said to Finn when our heads were closer together, when their mouths did it instead.

That night one of the sick died, a man called Arnkel, who had bright eyes and a snub nose and told tales almost as good as the ones Crowbone had once given us. Bjaelfi inspected him for signs of plague, but it was only the squits he had died of and he had been struggling for some time.

'Ah, well, there's an end to truth entire, then,' Red Njal mourned when Bjaelfi brought the news of it to the fire in the dull damp of morning. 'No more tales from him.'

'Truth?' demanded Kaelbjorn Rog, his broad face twisted with puzzlement. 'In bairns' tales?'

'Aye,' Red Njal scowled. 'Told by those old enough to remember. Wisdom comes from withered lips, as my old granny told me.'

'Was this just before she told you one of her tales?' Kaelbjorn Rog persisted. 'Made up completely, for sure.'

'Only those written down,' persisted Red Njal and men

craned to listen, for this was almost as good entertainment as one of Arnkel's tales.

'You mean,' Abjorn offered, weighing the words slowly and chewing them first to make sure the flavour was right, 'that stories are only true if they are not written?'

Red Njal scowled. 'If you are laughing at me, Abjorn, I will not take it kindly. Let no man glory in the greatness of his mind, but, rather, keep a watch on his wits and tongue, as my granny said.'

Abjorn held up his palms and waggled his head in denial. Finn chuckled.

'Ask Crowbone. He is the boy for stories, after all.'

Crowbone, staring at the flames of the fire, stirred when he became aware of the eyes on him and raised his chin from where it was sunk in his white, fur-trimmed cloak.

'When you hear something told, you can see the teller of it and pass judgement. But if you read it, you cannot tell who wrote it, and so cannot say whether it is true or not.'

Red Njal agreed with a vehement growl and Finn chuckled again, shaking his head in mock sorrow.

'There you have it,' he declared, 'straight from an ill-matched brace of oxen, who cannot read anything written, not even runes – so how would they know?'

'You do not understand,' Red Njal huffed. 'There is magic in such tales and if you needed the measure of it, remember Crowbone when he told them.'

Which clamped Finn's lip shut, for he did remember, especially the one which had once snatched us from the wrath of armed men. He acknowledged it now with a bow to Crowbone and, seeing the boy only half notice it, added: 'Perhaps the prince of storytellers will grace us with the one he is dreaming of now?'

Crowbone blinked his odd eyes back from the fire and into the faces round it.

'It was not a tale. I was remembering the whale we found once.'

Short Serpent's old crew stirred a little, remembering with him and, bit by bit, it was laid out . . . on a desolate stretch of shingle beach, pulling in for the night, they had come upon a small whale, beached and only just alive. No matter that it was another man's land, they flensed it, cutting great cubes of fat, thick as peats, thick as turf sod. They ate like kings, bloody and greasy.

It was the dream of home, of north water and shingle and it fixed us all with its brightness. For a reason only Odin could unravel, I kept thinking of the patch of kail and cabbage at the back of Hestreng *hov*. Thorgunna had grown a lush crop there, using the stinking water from the boilings of bairns' under-cloths and it had survived everything, un-trampled and unburned, when Hestreng was reduced to char and smoulder.

Uddolf crashed into the shining of this, asking for men to come and howe Arnkel up. His closest oarmates went and, in the end, we all stood by the mound; as *godi*, I placed one of my last three armrings in it, to honour him, which went some way against the grey grief of his loss.

It was a cloak that descended on us all. Onund wept and when he was asked why, said it was for the black sand and milk sea of his home. No-one mocked him, for we were all miserable with similar longings.

Through it all, two figures caught my sight. One was Dark Eye, still and slight and staring at the dark beyond the fire while men sighed and crooned their longings out; it came to me that this was how she must feel all the time, yet bore it without a whimper.

The other was the fire-soaked carving of the *Elk*, proud-antlered, lashed to its spear-haft. I was thinking that a prow beast was leading us still, further than ever from where we wanted to be.

In the morning, stiff and cold, men moved sullenly in our camp on the hill, hidden in trees where the mist shredded and swirled. I was gathering my sea-chest together when Styrbjorn came up, with men behind him. Everything stopped.

'We have been talking among ourselves,' Styrbjorn said. Finn growled and men shifted uncomfortably. I said nothing, waiting and sick, for I had been expecting this.

'It seems to us,' he went on, 'that there is nothing to be gained by continuing in this way and a great deal to be lost.'

'There is a deal to be lost, for sure,' I answered, straightening and trying to be light and soft in my voice, for the anger trembled in me. 'For those who break their Oath and abandon their oarmates. Believe me, Styrbjorn, I have seen it.'

The men behind him shifted slightly, remembering that they had sworn the Oath, but Styrbjorn had not. One scowler called Eid cleared his throat, almost apologetically, and said that when they had held a Thing, as was right for *bondi* to do when they thought I was dead, it was generally understood that whoever was chosen would lead them home.

Men hoomed and nodded; I saw no more than a handful, all from Crowbone's old crew of *Short Serpent* and that, while Styrbjorn stood with his arms folded, pouting like a mating pigeon, it was to Alyosha that these men flicked their uneasy eyes.

'Now I am returned and there is no need for such decisions,' I said, though I knew it would not silence them.

'If I had been chosen,' Crowbone added defiantly, 'we would still be after the boy.'

Eid snorted. 'You? The only reason any of us are here at all is because Alyosha was sensibly tasked by Prince Vladimir to keep you out of trouble after he gave you the toy of a boat and men. If anyone leads here, it is Alyosha.'

Crowbone stiffened and flushed, but held himself in check, which was deep-thinking; if he started to get angry, his fragile voice would squeak like a boy. Styrbjorn, on the other hand, started turning red, though the lines round his mouth went white as he glared at Eid; he did not like this talk of Alyosha leading.

'Prince Vladimir gave *Short Serpent* to ME,' Crowbone answered his crew, sinking his chin into his chest to make his voice deeper. 'He gave YOU to me.'

'No-one gave me anywhere,' growled Eid, scowling. 'What am I – a horn spoon to be borrowed? A whetstone to be lent?'

'A toy, perhaps,' grunted Finn, grinning and Eid wanted to snarl at him, but was not brave enough, so he subsided like a pricked bladder, muttering.

Alyosha, markedly, stayed stone-grim and silent, with a face as blank as a fjord cliff, while Styrbjorn opened and closed his mouth, the words in him crowding like men scrambling off a burning boat, so that they blocked his throat.

'And there is the girl,' added a voice, just as I thought I had the grip of this thistle. Hjalti, who was named Svalr – Cold Wind – because of his miserable nature, had a bald pate with a fringe of hair which he never cut, but burned off and never got it even. He had an expression that looked as if he was always squinting into the sun and a tongue which could cut old leather.

'The girl is another matter,' I answered. Styrbjorn recovered himself enough to smile viciously.

'A sweetness we have all missed,' he replied, 'save you, it seems.'

I shot Ospak a hard look and he had the grace to shrug and look away, acknowledging his loose tongue and what he had seen and heard by the Magyar fires.

'Am I a chattel, then?' said a new voice and I did not have to turn to know it; Dark Eye stepped into the centre of the *maelstrom*, a hare surrounded by growlers. 'A thrall, to be passed around? A horn spoon or a whetstone, as Eid says?'

No-one spoke under the lash of those eyes and that voice. Dark Eye, wrapping her cloak around her, cocked a proud chin.

'I have a purpose here. The Sea-Finn's drum spoke it and

296

those who have heard it know its truth,' she spat, then stopped and shrugged.

'Of course,' she added slyly, 'if all it takes for such hard men to seek Jarl Orm's *fostri* is a sight of my arse-cheeks, I will lift my skirts and lead the way.'

There was a chuckle or two at that and Styrbjorn opened his mouth. Dark Eye whirled on him.

'You had all best move swiftly and catch me first,' she said loudly, 'for Styrbjorn is skilled at stabbing from behind.'

Now there was laughter and Styrbjorn turned this way and that, scowling, but it was too late – men remembered him for the sleekit nithing he was and that he had been the cause of all this in the first place. For all that, like a dog with a stripped bone, some still thought there was enough meat to gnaw.

'This chase is madness.'

His name was Thorbrand, I remembered, a man who knew all the games of dice and was skilled with a spear.

'Ach, no, it is not,' Red Njal offered cheerfully. 'Now, mark you, mad is where you chase a band of dead-eaters, who chase a thief, who is chasing a monk, and all in the Muspell-burning wastes of Serkland. That is mad, Thorbrand.'

'Aye, madness that is, for sure,' agreed Thorbrand. 'What fool did that?'

Finn grinned at him and slapped his chest. 'Me. And Orm and Red Njal and a few others besides.'

He broke off and winked.

'And we came away with armfuls of silver at the end of it. The best fruits hang highest, as Red Njal's granny would no doubt have told him.'

Styrbjorn snorted.

'That sounds like one of the tales Red Njal likes so much. Is it written down anywhere? I am sure it must be, since it smacks of a great lie.'

'As to that,' Finn said, moving slowly, 'I could not say, for reading other than runes is not one of my skills. But I can hear, even with just the one ear and I am sure you just called me a great liar.'

The world went still; even the birdsong stopped. I stepped into the silence of it.

'There is only one safe way to stop heading the way I am steering you,' I rasped, feeling my bowels dissolve, 'and that is for one of you to become jarl. And there is only one way for that to happen – what say you, Styrbjorn? You will also have to take the Oath you have so far managed to avoid.'

There was a silence, a few heartbeats, no more, where Styrbjorn licked his drying lips and fought to rise to the challenge, even though his bowels were melting faster than mine. I relied on it; I knew how Styrbjorn liked to fight and it was not from the front.

It stretched, that silence, like the linden-bast rope that had held *Short Serpent* to the bank and the fear-heat spurted from it like water.

Just before it broke, Kuritsa loped up and parted it with a slicing sentence.

'Fight later – men are running for their lives and one of them is Randr Sterki.'

They were running like sheep, all in the same direction but only because they blindly followed a leader; the water sluiced from under their feet and their laden drag-poles were flung to one side.

'They will never get away,' Abjorn grunted, pointing. He had no need to; we could all see the horsemen, big as distant dogs now and closing.

'They are heading right towards us,' Red Njal said, his voice alarmed.

Of course they were – Randr Sterki was no fool and he saw high ground with trees on top, knew if he reached it the horsemen would be easier to fight if they decided to charge in and, if they balked at that, the trees would provide cover from the arrows.

'Form up – loose and hidden,' I ordered, peering out, searching for what I had not yet been able to see.

'We are going to rescue Randr Sterki?' demanded Styrbjorn incredulously. 'After all he has put us through? Let him die out there.'

Finn spat, just missing Styrbjorn's scuffed, water-stained boots.

'*Fud* brain,' he growled. 'The boy is there.'

Styrbjorn, who had forgotten why we were here at all, scowled, while Alyosha and Abjorn slid away to give orders; men filtered forward into the trees, half-crouched, tightening helmet ties, settling shields.

'Randr Sterki will not thank us, all the same,' muttered Red Njal; I had been thinking the same myself and thought to leap that stream when we were near falling in it.

There – two figures, one half-falling, slower than the rest, stumbling. The taller one, black, stopped, hauled the little one up into his arms and half-staggered, half-ran to keep up; I could hear the rasp of his breathing from here, but I was puzzled as to why the monk should care so much to rescue Koll.

A man fell, got up and stumbled on, then fell again. Sick, I was thinking as the monk reeled past him, then let Koll slip to the ground, taking him by one hand. The pair of them ran on and the horsemen were closing fast, spraying water and clotted muck up.

'An ounce of burnt silver says that small one is first to die,' Eid muttered close to me, nudging his oarmate, one of Finnlaith's Dyfflin men.

'You never had an ounce of burnt silver,' this one replied and Thorbrand's curse was reeking.

'That small one is the boy we came all this way to get,' he spat at them.

Out on the sodden plain, the first of Randr's men had

299

reached the foot of the low hill and we could hear the desperate, ragged dog-panting of them. Randr himself stopped and half-turned, bellowing at those who lumbered past, almost on all fours, what he wanted them to do when they got the shelter of the trees. It was a good plan, but I was thinking to myself that none of his men were up for it.

The weak man fell yet again and the first long-shot arrows skittered and spat up water behind him, so that he scrambled up and weaved on, almost at a walk now. A dozen steps further on and he fell again and this time he lay there, so that the horsemen, almost casually, shot him full of arrows, whooping as they ran over him.

'The boy . . .' growled Eid and sprang to his feet. Thorbrand followed and, with a curse, so did the Dyfflin man. They roared out of the treeline, leaving me speechless and stunned with the speed of it all.

The horsemen, felt hats flapping, their bow-nosed ponies at full stretch, were heading for the bulk of the fleeing men; more arrows flew and two or three men went down. Randr himself stopped bellowing and started scrambling up the low hill towards us.

Two or three horsemen had turned off towards Koll and Leo the monk, but they had their sabres out, planning to run them down and slash them to ruin. The monk shoved Koll to the ground and then dived and rolled as the first horseman came on him, lashing out with his left hand as he did so; my heart thundered up into my throat, but the horseman missed and Leo's slap had no effect, or so it seemed, while the others over-ran the pair.

Then Eid and the other two came howling down the hill like mad wolves and the horsemen, bewildered, milled and circled. Two of them whipped out arrows; the third turned back to Koll and Leo. After that, I remember it in fragments, like a shattered mirror flying everywhere, all the pieces with a different reflection.

300

Two arrows felled Eid as he ran. Thorbrand and the Dyfflin man crashed down on the two horsemen, stabbing and hacking. The third man's horse staggered and fell as if Dane-axed, just as the rider urged it towards Koll and Leo; poison, I was thinking, even as I turned to fight. Enough in Leo's stab to fell a horse in a few heartbeats – so he did have a hidden dagger after all.

The rest of the horsemen came up the slope, slinging their horn and wood bows and hauling out that wicked curve of sabre, a long smile of steel for hacking down on the fleeing. They were Vislanians, I learned later, who wore skin breeks and felt coats and caps and could climb under their ugly dog-ponies and up the other side at full gallop.

Not in the trees, though. They reined in from a gallop; Randr Sterki's men were on their knees, frothing and gasping, with no fight in them and it looked to be easy enough for the riders – until they discovered the hornet byke they had stepped in.

Kuritsa began it by putting the last of his war arrows in the chest of one of the horses, so that it reared up and rolled its great eyes until the whites showed, pitching the rider off with a scream.

Then it was blood and shrieks and mayhem. Red Njal ran at them, hirpling on his lame leg, bellowing like a bull and his spear took one of the horsemen in the belly, so that his head snapped forward and he went over the plunging horse's arse. Red Njal let the spear go and whipped out his seax.

Axes scythed, spears stabbed, swords whirled. It was bloody and vicious and my part in it was brutal and short – I came up on the man doing the most shouting, sitting on his dancing, wild-eyed pony, waving a crescent-moon of steel and bellowing.

He saw me come at him and raised the sabre, his eyes wide and red, his black moustaches seeming to writhe as he yelled; then something seemed to catch his arm as he raised it and

I saw the shaft, through his forearm and into the shoulder, pinning his arm – a hunting arrow from Kuritsa.

The sabre fell from his fingers and he looked astonished, though he had only a few seconds to think at all, before I took Brand's sword in a whirling, two-handed backstroke at his waist. Finn and others called this 'opening the day-meal' and it was a death-blow even if the victim did not die at once, for his belly split and everything in it fell out, blue-white, red, pale yellow.

He fell like a gralloched stag – and the rest of them tried to flee.

Cut them down, I heard myself screaming, though it sounded far away. None must escape to tell of what had been found and where we were.

The Oathsworn wolfed them, snarling and clawing. The last man turned his pony and flogged it back downhill, men chasing him, screaming. Kaelbjorn Rog, panting and sprinting, fell over his feet, bounced up and hurled his axe at the fleeing back in a fury of impotent rage, but it fell well short.

The arrow hissed out, a blur of speed and the smack of it hitting the rider's back was almost drowned in the great roar of approval that went up as the fleeing man spilled from the saddle. The pony kept going and I knew, with a cold, heavy sink of feeling, that we had failed.

There was a heavy silence, reeking of blood and vomit and moans. Men moved, counting the cost, clapping each other on the shoulder in the sudden ecstasy that comes with surviving a battle, or else retching, hands on their knees and bent over.

Randr Sterki lay flat out, a great bruise on the side of his face and Onund looming over him like a scowling troll. He had made for Randr as soon as the fight started and slammed him in the face with the boss of his shield. Now Randr lay on his back, propped up on his elbows and spitting out teeth and blood.

'I owe you that and more,' Onund growled at him, touching

his chest where, under his stained tunic, the glassy scars of Randr's old burning still wept.

'The severed hand seldom steals again,' Red Njal pointed out, scowling. 'And a head in a tree plots only with the wind.'

'Your granny was never one for a boy to snuggle into,' Crowbone muttered, hunching himself against the black glare Red Njal gave him in passing.

The rest of Randr's men, cowed and gasping, sat sullenly, aware that they had leaped out of the skillet into the pitfire. As I came up, Onund handed me a sheathed sword, taken from Randr; it was mine, taken when he had me prisoner and the V-notch in it undammed a sudden, painful torrent of remembering – of my sword biting into the mast of the *Fjord Elk*, of being slammed into the water, of Nes Bjorn's charred remains, of the loss of Gizur and Hauk and all the rest.

Randr must have seen that gallop across my face like chasing horses, for he stayed silent.

There was a survivor from the horsemen, a sallow-faced scowler with blood on his teeth and still snarling, for all that he had the stump of a hunting arrow in his thigh and his left arm at the ugly angle only a twisted break would allow.

I wanted answers, but his black eyes were sodden with anger and pain and defiance. Then Dark Eye came up and spoke to him, a string of coughing sibilants. He replied, showing bloody teeth in a snarl. She answered. They shot sounds like arrows, then were silent.

'He is a Vislan,' she said. 'That tribe are all Christ worshippers.'

'All that for so little?' I answered and she sighed.

'He called me names. He calls you all flax-heads, which is what they call the Saxlanders. Barbarians.'

There was more, I knew, but caught the warning spark from her and let Finn erupt instead.

'Barbarian?' he bellowed. 'I am to be called this by a skin-wearing troll?'

'*Quisque est barbarum alio*,' said a weary voice and, turning, we saw Leo the monk, with Koll behind him and Thorbrand trailing after.

'Everyone,' Leo translated, with a wan smile at Finn, 'is a barbarian to someone.'

I gave him no more than a glance, my attention on Koll, who came up and stood in front of me.

'You have fared a fair way from home,' I said, awkward and cursing myself for not having more tongue-wit than that.

'I knew you would come,' he answered, staring up into my face with the sure, clear certainty of innocence. He was thin and his bone-white colour made it hard to see if he was ill or not, but he seemed hale enough. Yet the pale blue eyes had seen things and it showed in them.

'Well,' drawled Finn, circling the monk like a dunghill cock does hens. 'You have led us a long dance, monk.'

Leo acknowledged it with a wry smile. His hair was long and stuck out at odd angles and he had gathered the tattered ends of his black robe up under his belt, so that it looked like he wore baggy black breeks to the knee; beneath them, his legs were red and white, mud-splattered and bloody from old cuts and grazes. He reeked of grease and woodsmoke and did not look much, but I knew he had a needle of poisoned steel on him and said so.

He widened his eyes to look innocent and Finn growled at him.

'Find a rope,' Red Njal spat. 'Make him dance a new dance. The breathless tongue never conspires.'

'No.'

It came from two throats – Koll's and Finn's – and took everyone by surprise, even the pair who had hoiked it out.

'Kill him another way,' Finn growled, scrubbing his beard as he did when he was discomfited.

'Do not kill him at all,' Koll declared defiantly. 'He helped

304

me, saved me when the rest of these pigs wanted to sell me to the Magyars. Him and Randr Sterki stood against them.'

I knew why Randr would want to keep the boy, but not the monk and I said so to Leo, who shrugged.

'I took him as a counter in a game,' he said diffidently. 'He still had value.'

Koll blinked a bit at that, but I had expected not much more. I put my hand on the boy's shoulder, to show him he was safe once more – then Randr Sterki struggled weakly to his feet and growled to me across the trampled, bloody underbrush of the clearing.

'Well? Will you finish it, Bear Slayer? What you started on Svartey?'

I wondered how many of the Svartey crew were left and wondered it aloud; the answer was straight enough – only him alone. All the others had died and the men of his crew who sat, shivering and sullen, had no connection with that old *strandhogg*.

'Kill him and be done with it,' Styrbjorn said and Randr Sterki curled a lip at him.

'So much for fighting shoulder to shoulder,' he answered bitterly. 'Well done is ill paid, as the saying goes. Here is the dog who fought, the chief who led and the ring-giver who paid – only the fighting dog dies, it seems.'

I looked from Styrbjorn to Leo and back to Randr. He had the right of it, for sure – all of those who had helped the Norns weave the wyrd of what happened were here, including the Oathsworn, who had scoured Svartey in one bloody thread of it.

'Matters would have gone better for me,' Randr Sterki went on morosely, 'but for this bloody habit of slaughter you Oathsworn have. The death of that village you visited has called out an army of Pols, all bent on skewering Northmen – my bad war luck to run into them before you.'

'Truly,' agreed Onund coldly, 'when you annoy the gods, you are fucked.'

305

Finn added his own bloody growl to that by cutting the throat out of the Vislan and, while he choked and kicked, Abjorn and Alyosha counted the cost of the fight and the heads left.

There were fourteen of Randr's men left, including himself. We had two dead and four men wounded; the two dead were Eid and the Dyfflin man, whose name, I learned from Thorbrand, was Ranald. Finn could not understand what had made them charge out as they did and asking Thorbrand only brought a weary heave of his shoulders and the answer that he had followed the other two. I thought I knew, for I had felt it myself – little Koll, the prize for all that had been suffered, was in danger of being snapped up by someone else.

It had cost us, all the same and we would need Randr and his men, I was thinking and I said that to them and him. Red Njal cursed and one or two others made disapproving grunts, but I laid it out for them; we were alone and together made no more than sixty. Somewhere, hordes of Pols hunted us.

'Turn Randr Sterki and his men loose, then,' Kaelbjorn Rog offered truculently. 'Let the Pols hunt them down while we get away.'

'Tcha!' spat Red Njal. 'At least make it easy for the Pols – the foot removed cannot scurry far.'

'I am now sure I dislike this granny of yours,' Crowbone said, shaking his head, then stared his odd-eyes into the pig-squint glare Red Njal tried to burn him with.

'If the wind changes, your face will stay like that,' he added grimly. 'My ma told me that one and she was a princess.'

'It is too late for running,' I said, before matters boiled. 'The Pols will know where we all are in a few hours.'

'Why so?' demanded Crowbone, moody because he had been effectively kept out of the fight by his iron wet-nurse, Alyosha. 'We have killed all these dog-riders.'

'But not their horses,' Alyosha told him, seeing it now. 'They will track back and find us.'

It was then that folk realised some of the bow-nosed ponies had galloped off and those who knew their livestock knew what horses did when riderless. They went home. I knew it, as well as I knew we could not stay here to fight, nor run somewhere else out on the wet plain.

There was only one place we could go which would give us a chance of fighting at all and it was not one I wanted to visit. When I laid it out, the words fell into a silence as still as the inside of an old howe, which was answer enough.

Save for Leo, who always had something to say, even about stepping into a plague-ridden fortress.

'*A fronte praeciptium, a tergo lupi*,' he declared and turned to Finn, who stunned the monk even as he opened his mouth to translate it.

'A cliff in front, wolves behind,' Finn translated. 'I have heard that one before, priest. It is the place the Oathsworn fight best.'

EIGHTEEN

His breathing, as Bjaelfi took pains to tell us, was just a habit, for the fever had fired him so that his blood had boiled up into his thought-cage and destroyed his thinking entire. What was left sucked in air the way a deer kicks long after you have gralloched it.

It was a habit strong in him, for he took three days to be quit of it and, at the last, was open-mouthed and desperate as a fish. Ulf, his name was, called Amr by his oarmates, which meant Tub on account of his considerable belly. Well, it had been considerable, but in three days of vomit and leaching sweat he had melted like grease on a skillet, become a wraith, his face pocked red and white and pus yellow and his eyes gone white as boiled eggs.

Bjaelfi tied his mouth back up with a scrap of cloth and we sat back and stared; Ulf, the emptied Tub, first to die of the Red Plague and lying there with drooping hare-ears of cloth on top of his head, making him look as if he was being silly to amuse bairns.

'They are coming again,' roared a voice from outside the dim hut.

I heaved myself wearily up, took up the blood-gummed shaft of the bearded axe and looked at Bjaelfi.

'Burn him,' I said and he nodded. Then I lumbered out to war.

We first saw our enemy when they filtered out onto the soaked plain in front of the *grod* not long after we had panted our way into it and barred the gate; we made it easier for them to find us, for we burned the main hall, after tying bound cloths round our faces – for all the good it would do – and dragging all the scattered, half-chewed bodies there, where most of them already festered.

Their horsemen trotted up, spraying water up from the steaming ground, to be greeted by great black feathers of reeking smoke; close behind came foot soldiers in unbleached linen and only helmets and spears and round shields. Behind them came a knot of iron-clad horse soldiers, sporting lances with proud pennons and one huge banner with what appeared to be a wheel on it. Dark Eye said that was the mark of the Pol rulers, who had been wheelwrights until the favour of their god raised them up.

'They will think we slaughtered all the folk of this place and burned some of it,' Styrbjorn said bitterly. 'Someone should tell them there is pest here and that we are doomed. That will send them running as far from this place as they can get.'

'It would send you scampering,' Alyosha replied, watching the enemy closely as they assembled – counting heads, as I was. 'What they will do is keep a safe distance and shoot anyone who leaves with arrows. When we are all dead, they will burn it. The last thing these folk want is us running all over their land, spreading Red Plague.'

'Better they do not know we have disease here,' I said, loud enough for others to hear and spread the sense of it. 'It will mean the reddest of red war and no-one will be able to throw down their weapons and be spared.'

Finn and I exchanged looks; we knew no-one would be spared anyway, once the talking had stopped.

309

'I make it four hundreds, give or take a spear or two,' Alyosha said, coming quietly to me. I had much the same; the rest of the men, grim and silent on the ramparts, knew only that the plain in front of the *grod* was thick with men who wanted to kill us.

'Get them working,' I said to Alyosha, 'for busy hands mean less chance to think on matters. Send Abjorn to the river wall – there is a small gate in it, used by the fishermen, I am thinking. It may also be the only way to bring water in from the river unless you can find a well. We have small beer but not enough, so we will have to drink water in the end. Finn – since you can tally a little without having to take your boots off, find out what we have in stores. Slaughter the live-stock if we cannot feed them, but leave the cows until last, for they at least provide milk.'

There was more – making arrows from what we could find, ripping out heavy balks of timber and finding all the heavy stones we could to drop on heads.

Hot oil, Crowbone told us with all the wisdom of his few years. Or heated gravel where there was no oil, he added and Finn patted him, as if he was a small dog, then went off, shaking his head and chuckling. It was left to Alyosha to patiently explain that flaming oil and red-hot stones were not the cleverest things to be dropping all over the wooden gate and walls of our fortress.

Randr Sterki came up to me then, badger-beard working as his jaw muscles clenched and unclenched.

'Give us our weapons back and we will fight,' he growled.

I looked at him and the men clustered behind him. They wanted their hands on hilt and haft, were eager – even desperate – to defend themselves, if no-one else.

'We are in this leaking ship as one,' I pointed out, more for the men behind than him. 'Those dog-fuckers out there call us flax-heads, think we are all Saxlanders and will curl their lips at any man who crawls out to claim he can open

310

the gate if only he is spared. They will kill him once he has served the purpose.'

Feet shifted at that and I knew I had them; Randr Sterki half-turned to his men, then turned back to me.

'We will fight, until dead or victorious.'

It had been said in front of witnesses and was Oath enough, so I gave him my V-notched sword back, for I would not give him Jarl Brand's own. He grinned, then drew it and stood, naked blade in hand and within striking distance of me, who had nothing in his hand but old filth and callouses.

'If we survive, Bear Slayer,' he said flatly, 'there will be matters to discuss.'

I was sick of him and his matters, so I turned away, putting my back to him and the blade he held, though I felt the skin creep along my backbone as I did so.

'I would not count on living out the rest of this day,' I answered over my shoulder, going off to fetch Brand's sword, 'never mind having a cunning plan for tomorrow.'

When I was sliding the baldric over my head, Koll trotted up, followed by Yan Alf, whom I had set to guard him. The boy's white-lashed eyes stared up into mine, sullen as a slate-blue sea and he wanted to know why I had stopped him from going near the monk.

'He ran off with you,' I answered, annoyed at this. 'Is that not reason enough? Because of him we are here, a long way from home and . . .'

I stopped then, before the words 'dying for the matter' spat past my teeth; I did not want the boy – or anyone else – empty of hope.

'He saved me,' Koll persisted.

'He has done killing in the night,' I countered, 'with some strange magic.'

I broke off and looked at Yan Alf, who shrugged.

'Alyosha and Ospak stripped and searched him,' the little man said. 'The only way he could be more naked is if they

311

flayed him. They found no weapon. Ospak guards him now and he has asked to help Bjaelfi with the sick.'

Very noble and Christ-like – but Alyosha would have turned the monk inside out rather than leave him as a threat to his charge, little Crowbone, and, if he had found no weapons . . .

Yet I did not trust Leo and said so.

'Keep at arm's length from that monk,' I added and saw the hard set of Koll's lip and, worse, the dull sadness in those pale eyes. I had told him of his mother's death and he had taken it with no tears – and yet . . .

'Did your father tell how to behave as a *fostri*?' I persisted and he nodded reluctantly, then repeated the words all sons are told – obey and learn. I merely nodded at him, then had an idea and handed him Brand's sword.

'This belongs to your father and so to you. You are come early to it and it is likely too large and heavy for you to use, even if you knew how. One day Finn will show you the strokes of it – but for now you can guard it.'

The pale blue eyes widened and brightened like the sun had burst out on a summer sky. He took the sheathed weapon in both hands and turned, grinning to Yan Alf, before running off with it.

'Keep him away from the monk,' I said softly to Yan Alf as he passed me, chasing his charge. If he had an answer, I did not hear it and turned away to hunt out a seax or an axe for myself. The whole sick-slathered wyrd of it had come down to this tapestry woven by the Norns and the picture of it was clear enough – a cliff in front, wolves behind.

I would not survive it, whatever happened, for I was sure Odin had, finally, led me to the place where he would take the life I had offered him.

First, though, there were the dance-steps of the rite, beginning with horn blasts from them to attract our attention. I had seen this before, though from the other side, when we had arrived at the Khazar fortress of Sarkel with Sviatoslav, Prince of Kiev. Ten summers ago, I suddenly realised, climbing the ramp to the tower over the gate, where Finn and others waited. I had Dark Eye with me, for she was the only one who could talk to these Pols in their own tongue.

A knot of riders came slowly, ambling their horses across the wet grass and scrub to where the raised walkway led to the gate. One of them, accompanied by a single rider bearing the huge red flag with a spoked wheel worked in gold threads on it, came forward a few steps more.

He was splendid in gilded ringmail and a red cloak, his elaborately crested helmet nestled in the crook of one arm, allowing his braided black hair, weighted with fat silver rings, to swing on his shoulders. His beard was black and glossed with oil and it was clear he was someone of note, which Dark Eye confirmed.

'Czcibor,' she said softly. 'Brother of King Dagomir, whom folk by-name Miezko as a joke, for it means "peace". He makes it by fighting all who resist him. This Czcibor is the one who beat the Saxlanders at Cidini and took the Pols to the mouth of the Odra.'

I had thought Miezko meant 'famous sword', but then his enemies would have a different take on it and there was no more bitter enemy of the Pols than Dark Eye. When this Czcibor spoke, I wondered if I could even trust what she said – then scattered the thought, half-ashamed at it.

Dark Eye listened and then spoke back to him and turned to me; heads craned expectantly.

'He says you should give in, for you cannot win. It is better if you submit. I would be careful of him, Jarl Orm, for he knows Norse well enough.'

She spoke in a guarded, level voice; I looked at Czcibor, who grinned.

'Is this true – you know the Norse?'

'Of course. My niece, Sigrith, is a queen in your lands.'

Styrbjorn suddenly thrust forward, eager as a bounding pup – if he had had a tail it would have shaken itself off.

'You are Czcibor,' he declared and the man, frowning at this breach of manners, nodded curtly.

'Ah, well,' Styrbjorn went on, 'then we are related, after a fashion, for my uncle is married to your niece. I am Styrbjorn . . .'

Czcibor held up a hand, which was as good as a slap in the face to Styrbjorn. When he spoke, it was a slow, languid, serpent-hiss of sound, made worse by the mush-mess he made of the Norse.

'Styrbjorn. Yes. I know of you. My niece sent word of it down the Odra.'

I saw Styrbjorn stiffen and pale at that, which he had not been expecting.

'I shall have a stake cut especially for you,' Czcibor went on. 'And for the little monk who killed the woman Jasna. Perhaps I will make it the same one for you both.'

My stomach roiled and my knees started to twitch against the rough wood of the rampart stakes, where I had braced them. For a man with a name like a fire in a rainstorm he could summon up a mighty vision.

'An interesting idea,' I managed eventually. 'I would enjoy watching it under other circumstances. But we are all comfortable here and our arses free from stakes and a lot more dry than yours will be, by and by.'

He cocked his head sideways a little, appraising me; I had made it clear that I knew his predicament – he could not surround the *grod* completely because of the swamps on three sides and the river the settlement was practically thrust into. His own camp was on a soaked flat offering little comfort and no chance to dig even the simplest of privy pits or earthwork defences that would not instantly fill with mud and water.

All he could do was attack and be done with the business as fast as possible, which was a hard option – but this was a man come fresh from victory and unmoved by such problems. He nodded politely, put on his splendid helm, dragged out a spear and, with a swift throw and a gallop off, hurled it over the ramparts as the signal that the bloody matter had commenced. It skittered on the hard ground behind me and a few men scattered, cursing the surprise of it.

'That went well,' Finn declared, grinning, then scowled and thumped Styrbjorn's shoulder, making the youth stagger. 'You nithing arse.'

Styrbjorn had no answer to it and slunk away while others who heard about his fawning attempt to wriggle over to safety jeered him.

And Dark Eye came to me, snuggling under my arm – which gained us both a couple of scowls from those who saw a sweetness they were not allowed – so that she could whisper softly.

'He asked for me.'

I had guessed that and had made quiet warding signs to prevent him voicing it in Norse for all to hear; let the Oathsworn think they were sieged here for the settlement we slaughtered, for if they suspected Dark Eye was the cause, they would hurl her to them in an eyeblink.

Yet it nagged me, that thought, for there was a whiff of betrayal and oath-breaking in it. Worse, there was the thought that this was what the Sea-Finn's drum had spoken of, so that defying it was standing up and spitting in Odin's one eye. I thought I heard Einar's slow, knowing chuckle as I turned away, whirling with mad thoughts of how to get folk out of these closing wolf-jaws.

Them, of course. Not me. I was only offering prayers to Frey and Thor and any other god I could think of to help convince AllFather to spare me long enough to see the crew away.

All the rest of that day we worked to improve our lot, comforted by the distant sound of axe-work in hidden trees; the Pols were making scaling ladders and would not attack before that was done.

Just as the dusk smoked in and we lit fires and torches, Finn came back from where he had been checking the watchers on

315

the river wall; there were skin-boats on the river, crude and hastily made, carrying one man to row and one man to shoot.

'The ground between the river and the wall is sodden, knee-deep at least,' he added. 'It will take four, perhaps five days for the water to seep away back to the river and even then a man will be hard put to walk through it without sinking to the cods.'

We ate together, waving off clouds of insects under the awning of the sail, for no-one wanted to be inside one of the houses, as if the air was thicker with rot there than elsewhere. I made a Thing of it, once they were licking their horn spoons clean.

To get away we would have to cross the bog down to the river, go in quietly, so as not to annoy the watchers in boats, then drift downstream a way to safety. Those who could not swim should fill bladders with air to stay afloat – there were sheep and goats enough for it – and we could try this when the bog had dried out, in five days.

By then we would be ankle-deep in blood, which I did not mention, and there would have to be men on the ramparts to let the others escape, which I did.

'I will be one,' I said, hoping my voice would not crack like my courage at the thought. 'It would be helpful to have a few more, but I do not demand this.'

'I will stay,' said Crowbone at once and Koll piped up bravely on his heels. I saw Alyosha stiffen at that, so I shook my head.

'Not this time, little Olaf,' I said to Crowbone. 'I need you to make sure Koll Brandsson gets back to his father.'

'I will stay,' Koll shrilled.

'You will obey your foster-father,' growled Finn, 'whose duty it is to keep you safe.'

The white head drooped. Crowbone paused a moment, then nodded at me; from the corner of my eye, I caught Alyosha's relief.

'I will be at your shieldless side,' Finn declared and I acknowledged it; one by one, men stood up and were counted, each louder than the last and each into cheers louder than the one before. At the edge of them, Randr Sterki glowered in silence, offering nothing.

In the end, I had to turn men down, keeping ten only – Abjorn, Ospak, Finnlaith, Murrough, Finn, Rovald, Rorik Stari, Kaelbjorn Rog, Myrkjartan and Uddolf. We broke out a barrel of the fiery spirit that passed for drink in this part of the world and men fell to flyting each other with boasts of what they would do in the morning.

Later, as the fire collapsed to showers of sparks and glowing embers, Finn and I walked the guardposts, pausing in the tower over the gate to stare out at the field of red, flickering blooms which marked the camp of our enemy.

Beyond it, the night was silver and grey, soaked with the scent of a rain-wind, fresh-cut wood and torn earth; the moon, blurred and pale, darted from cloud to cloud, as if trying to hide from the all-devouring wolf which chased her.

'Will you tell them about the girl?' Finn growled and I felt neither alarm nor surprise; Finn was no fool.

'They would hand her over,' I answered flatly and he nodded.

'Aye – was this not what the Sea-Finn's drum meant? Can you stand against it? Defy that wyrd?'

I must and hoped he would not ask me the why of it, for I had no answer. Every time I thought of it, all I saw were her great, seal eyes.

He nodded again when I howked all this out.

'Is she so worth it then, that everyone here has to die? Even if both you and she get away, I am thinking Thorgunna will not be happy to see a second wife come into her home. I am thinking also that the Mazur girl is not the sort to be settled with being a second wife. If anyone makes it out of here at all – you are under the eye of Odin, after all.'

I had churned this to rancid butter night after night, after every furtive, frantic coupling we had stolen and had no answer for him.

317

'Tell Red Njal to get her away to safety when the time comes,' was all I could manage. 'Tell him to take her back to Hestreng. I charge him with that and taking Koll home.'

Finn nodded, a twist of a smile on his face. 'Aye – I wondered why you did not include Njal in your hopeless *hird*,' he answered. 'So did he – this will go some way to calming him for it.'

There was a noise and a figure that turned us; she came up the ladder to the tower, wrapped in her too-large cloak and it was clear she had heard us talk. Her eyes had vanished in the dark so that her face, pale and seemingly pitted with two large holes, looked like a savage mask.

'You will not take me home, then, Jarl Orm?'

I shook my head. It was too far and I would not be there to do it myself, for my wyrd was on me. The best I could offer was safety at Hestreng.

'In time,' I added, limping the words out, 'it may be that you could be taken back to your people. Word can certainly be sent to your father that you are no longer held by his enemies.'

She nodded and paused, head raised as if sniffing the wind.

'My father is called, in our tongue, Hard-Mouth,' she said. 'He is well-named and has a hand to match. I have two brothers and he whipped them every day from when they were old enough to walk. Every morning, before they ate, so they would know what pain was before pleasure and that such was our lot in life as Mazurs.'

She paused; a dog fox screamed somewhere far away.

'But he called me his little white flower and it was the hardest thing he did, handing me over to the Pols. He had no choice and wept. I had never seen my father shed a tear.'

Again she paused and no-one offered words to fill the silence.

'When he finds I am no longer held by the enemy,' she went on, stirring suddenly, 'he will raise up his warriors and fall on the Pols. They will slaughter him, for they are much

318

stronger now. It will take them time, for my father is skilful and folk will follow him. They will run and fight and run again – but, in the end, they will submit, when all the young men are dead. Bairns and women and old heads will die, too. The Mazur will be rubbed out, vanished like ripples on water.'

It was as bleak as an ice-field, that vision and I felt Finn shiver next to me. Then she turned and smiled whitely in the dark of her face.

'I have prepared a hut for us,' she said brightly. 'It does not matter to me whether the red sickness crawled in it. Does it bother you?'

I could only shake my head and she wraithed down the ladder and was gone. Finn looked at me.

'Do not ask what that meant,' I told him, 'for up here I am as much in the dark as you.'

Later still, weary as I was, I went to find Koll and knew just where he would be. The door of the hut was open, spilling out yellow light and letting in cool air, for here Bjaelfi moved among the sick, murmuring softly.

The monk was there, wiping the neck and chest of a man, while Koll sat some way back from him, his father's sword across his knees. Yan Alf crouched like a patient hound nearby and gave me a despairing look and a shrug when I came in, as if to say 'what can I do?'

Koll leaped up when he saw me and Leo turned his head, a twist of a smile on his face.

'I obey,' Koll said and thrust out the sheathed sword as far as he could before the weight dragged it to the beaten-earth floor with a clunk. 'I am at arm's length.'

'So you are,' I said. 'I came to make sure you had a sensible place to sleep.'

'This is sensible,' he answered uncertainly and Leo chuckled as I jerked my head at Yan Alf, who rose and propelled the boy outside.

'Do you believe I mean him harm?' the monk asked. I did not know for sure, but I knew he meant him no good and that, if he was a counter in the game, then he was my counter. Leo shrugged when I told him this.

'It is, then, a matter of bargaining,' he said and smiled. 'You are, after all, a trader as well as a slayer of white bears and a finder of treasure.'

'You are short of items to trade,' I answered.

'I have the boy,' he replied and I cocked my head and told him it was the other way round.

'You seem to wish to die here,' he said, as lightly as if passing judgement on the cut of my cloak, or the state of my shoes. 'What will happen to your men? To the boy?'

I had not thought beyond them drifting to safety and saw the mistake. Leo wiped the man's fat neck with one hand, the other resting comfortably at his side. The sick man's belly trembled as he breathed, low and rasping.

'The quickest way to safety is through the Bulgar lands,' Leo said. 'I am more of the Emperor's envoy there. In the Great City, I can provide help and aid for those who survive.'

He turned his face, less moon and more gaunt these days; life had melted some of the sleek off him.

'I can ensure the boy is returned to his father from the Great City.'

'For a price,' I spat back bitterly. Leo waved his free hand, then settled it, like a small moth, lightly back on his leg.

'What do you care – you are dead?' he replied, crow-harsh in the dim; I heard Bjaelfi grunt at that.

'I will return the boy, unharmed to this father,' he went on. 'I will make sure Jarl Brand knows that this is because of what you have done, so that you fulfil whatever vow you made. I know how you people value such vows. If there are other agreements made – what of it? The boy is still safe and your fame is safer still.'

This last was sneered out, as if it held no value at all – which, him being steeped in the Great City's way of doing things, was accurate enough. Yet there was merit in this and he saw me pause, knew he had gaffed me with it.

'What is the price?' I demanded and he waved his free hand again.

'Little enough – freedom of movement. When the time comes, let your men know you trust me to guide them, so they will take pains to help both me and the boy.'

I pondered it.

'Of course,' he went on smoothly, 'it also means you cannot carry out your plan to kill me when the enemy breaks down the gate.'

He turned his bland smile on me. 'That *was* your plan, was it not?'

It was not, exactly. I had planned to leave him tethered for the Pols to find and stake him for the red murder of Jasna and the threat to Queen Sigrith. I had the satisfaction of seeing him blink; I could feel his hole pucker from where I stood and laughed.

'How was that killing done?' I asked. He recovered and shifted wearily, then paused in his endless wiping of the man's head and neck.

'One day,' he replied slowly, 'you may profit from the knowing.'

Then he smiled his bland smile. 'Of course,' he went on smoothly, putting aside the cloth and lifting the man's limp, slicked arm up high, 'all this is moot. This one is called Tub, I believe. He is leaking a little and he is the first, I think. It may be that no-one goes home without God's mercy.'

I stared at the accusing Red Plague pus-spots crawling down the arms and up the neck of Tub and heard Bjaelfi curse as I left.

In the morning, all our enemies were at the gates.

There was no skilled planning; Czcibor used his foot soldiers like a club and they came piling across the narrow causeway, fanning out under the looming cliff of earthwork and timber ramparts, throwing up makeshift ladders.

We had one good bow – Kuritsa's – and a few more hunting ones we had found, but the horsemen had been dismounted and launched great skeins of shafts to keep our heads down, so we could do little but lob heavy stones from cover.

When the Pol foot soldiers, in their stained oatmeal tunics, finally got to the lip of the timbers, their archers had to stop firing; then we rose up and the slaughter started.

That first morning, I plunged into the maw of it, sick and screaming with fear, sure that this was where Odin swept me up and trying to make it quick.

I kicked the head of the first man who appeared, open-mouthed and gasping, so that he shrieked and went backwards. I cut down at the ladder, hooked the splintering top rung with the beard of my axe and then ran, elbowing my own men out of the way and hauling the ladder sideways; men spilled off it, flailing as they fell.

Some others had made the top rampart anyway and I plunged towards them, took a slice on the shaft of the axe, where metal strips had been fitted to reinforce the wood. In the same move, I cut up and under, splintering his ribs, popping his lungs out so that he gasped and reeled away.

Another came at me, waving a spear two-handed, so I reversed the axe and batted him off with the shaft, my left hand close up under the head – then gripped the spear with my free hand, pushed it to one side and sliced the axe across his throat like a knife.

The blood sprang out, black and reeking of hot iron, and he fell, half-dragging me as he did so, so that I staggered. Something spanged off my helmet; a great white light burst in my head and I felt the rough wood of the walkway splinter into my knees.

Then there was cursing and grunts and a hand hauled me

away; when I could see, Red Njal was standing over me, his own axe up and dripping.

'You will get yourself killed with such tricks,' he chided, then hurled himself forward, now that I was climbing to my feet.

Between us we pitched the struggling men back over the ramparts; no sooner had the heels of the last one vanished than two arrows whunked into the wood and we dived behind the timbers, panting and sweating, to listen to the drumming of others, flocking in like crows on offal. Crazily, I was reminded of rain on the canvas awning on the deck of the *Fjord Elk*, though I could not remember which *Fjord Elk* that had been.

'Five days,' Red Njal said and spat, though there was little wet in his mouth, I saw. I was thinking the same thing – these would be five long days.

The rest of it is a dull, splintered memory, like a tapestry shredded by a madman. I am certain sure that it was on the day we tied up Tub's mouth that we suffered a moon-howling loss that drove us a little mad.

It was the same as any other attack, though the ramparts by now were scarred, the timber points black and soaked with old gore, the walkway both sticky and slick. They came piling up over their own dead, threw up the ladders and did what they had been doing for what seemed years.

And we stood, we three, last of the band of old brothers, struggling and slipping and sweating and cursing, while Uddolf and Kaelbjorn Rog and others fought their own battles a little way away, for we were veil-thin on the rampart now.

Red Njal set himself behind his shield, took a deep, weary breath and shook himself, like a dog coming out of water.

'Fear the reckoning of those you have wronged,' he muttered, moving forward. 'My granny said it, so it must . . .'

The spear came out of nowhere, a vicious stab from the

323

first man up a ladder we had not seen. It caught Red Njal under the arm, right in the armpit, so that he grunted with the shock of it and jerked back. It had hooked and stuck and, even as we watched, the man who owned it fell backwards, ladder and all, as Finn smashed The Godi into his chest. Fixed to the spear, like a fish on a gaff, Red Njal was hauled over the rampart, a silent slither of ragged mail and leather.

I was stunned; it was the roof collapsing, the earth vanishing beneath my feet. I could not move for the sick horror of it – but Finn screamed, skeins of mad drool spilling down his beard and launched himself at the pack on the walkway, hacking and slashing.

I roused myself, moving as if I was in the Other, walking in a mist and slowed. Twice, I know, I held his back, stopped the crash of a blade on him, but I only came into the Now of matters when he was pounding the head of the last man on the walkway, screaming at him.

'What is it called?' he shrieked. Slam. Slam. 'This place? What is it called?'

The man, leaking blood from his eyes and ears and nose and mouth, spattered out a word, so that Finn was satisfied enough to haul him up under the armpits and heave him over the rampart.

We huddled in the lee of the black-stained points, sitting in the viscous stink and staring at each other, while the arrows wheeked and whirred and shunked into the wood. Eventually, Finn wiped one bloody hand across his bloody beard.

'Needzee,' he said slowly and my blank eyes were question enough.

'Name of this place,' he explained. 'I was thinking we should know where we are dying.'

That night, he and Kaelbjorn Rog and Ospak flitted down the rampart on knotted ropes, but it was dark and they dared not show any lights, so they could not find Red Njal in the heap, some still groaning, at the foot of our stockade.

His death was a rune-mark on matters coming to an end.

The end came two days later, when eighteen of us were rolling with sweat and babbling and twenty more had died, three from the plague. Almost everyone else was wounded in some way.

Worst of all, Koll was sick. The red and white spots started under his armpit and down his thighs in the morning and then erupted on the pale circles of his cheeks. By nightfall he looked as if someone had thrown a handful of yellow corn that had stuck to his face, each one a pustule that festered and stank.

The monk sat with him, in between tending the others, while Bjaelfi, half-staggering with weariness, moved back and forth, Dark Eye with him like a shadow, answering a whimper here, a cry there.

In the fetid, blood-stinking dark, we gathered round the fire, streaked and stained and long since too weary to wash. My braids were gummed with old blood and other, even worse, spills from the dead and my clothing stained and ripped; no-one was any better.

We carried Koll to the fire; no-one minded, for there was no escape from the pest and if the Norns wove that red thread into your life, that was it. Only Styrbjorn scowled, thinking that distance meant more safety.

Behind us, torches burned at the raised wooden platform that marked the centre of the village – Needzee, Finn had called it, but Dark Eye had put him right on that. The luckless man had gasped out '*nigdzie*' as Finn pounded his head to ruin, screaming to know what the name of this place was that we were all dying for, the place where Red Njal had gone to meet his granny.

Nowhere, the man had said in his own tongue and Finn

had thrown back his head and bellowed with cracked laughter when Dark Eye told him that.

Now Dark Eye lit torches and knelt on the wooden platform, praying to her four-faced god, while the shadows flicked and men, too tired even to eat or talk, huddled in a sort of stupor, heads bowed, watching the smoke writhe. A pot steamed on an iron tripod and the men lay in a litter of helms and weapons, slumped with shields as backrests, crusted ringmail puddled like old snakeskins at their feet.

When Dark Eye wraithed herself back to the fire, a few heads lifted and dull eyes took her in. Styrbjorn, always ready with his mouth, curled his lip.

'Praying for rescue?' he asked.

'Only the fearful pray for rescue,' she replied, pooling herself into a comfortable squat. Styrbjorn stirred uncomfortably, for everyone could see that promised stake up the arse occupied most of his waking hours.

'The man who says he is not afraid in this matter is a liar,' he responded.

'Tell Finn that,' Uddolf chuckled harshly. 'He is well-known for having no fear.'

'Perhaps he can tell you the secret of it, Styrbjorn,' Onund added with his usual bear grunt. 'Then we will be quit of your whine.'

'As to that,' Finn said softly. 'Since we are all about to look our gods in the face, it may be that you want to know the secret of having no fear.'

Now men were stirring with interest, me among them.

'When I was young,' he began, 'I did matters which were not agreeable to certain men in Skane and, when they caught me, there was no Thing on it, no outlawing. Justice was rougher in those days and none rougher than Halfidi. He was as white-haired as any kindly uncle and as black-bowelled as a *draugr*. *Slátur*, men called him.'

There were chuckles at such a fine by-name – *Slátur* was

326

a dish made by stitching pungently strong black-blood sausage into a lamb's white stomach.

'They kicked and beat me,' Finn went on, 'and starved me for a week, which was to be expected. Each day Halfidi, or one of his sons, would dish out the meat of a whipping and take delight in telling me when I would hang. At the end of that week, they took me to the top of the cliff they used, where a rope was fastened to an iron ring. They put the other end round my neck and tied a cloth round my eyes. Then they spun me and pushed me to walking, so that I did not know where the cliff edge was.'

Men grunted with the cruel power that vision brought.

'Three days they did this,' Finn said, soft, lost in the dream of it. 'On the second day the shite was running down my leg and I was babbling promises not even a god could keep if they would let me go. On the third day I did the same, only for them to let me see.'

He stopped. Men waited; the fire flared a little in a wet night wind, throwing up a whirl of sparks.

'On the fourth day, they were careless with the bindings and I worked one hand free, so that when they came to prodding and pushing, I tore the cloth from my eyes. There were eight of them, who all saw I had one hand free and so they came at me with spears.'

He paused, a long time this time, until Styrbjorn – that child would never learn when to put his tongue between his teeth – demanded to know what happened next.

'I went over the edge,' said Finn. All breathing stopped at the dizzying vision of that, of what it had taken to do it.

'And died, of course,' sneered Styrbjorn. 'I heard this tale when I was toddling.'

'I did not die. I went over the edge and, when I hit the end of that bast rope it snapped clean through. I should have had my neck cracked, but had my free hand taking a deal of the strain, so I was spared that. I hit the sea and got through that, too.'

327

Men were silent, for such a matter was a clear intervention of the hand of some god. Frey, suggested one. Odin himself, another thought and those who favoured Slav gods offered their own thoughts on the matter.

'I have had no fear since,' Finn said. 'It was snapped from me by that bast rope. Nothing and no-one since has made me drip shite down my leg through terror.'

'That is why you did not want that Vislan hanged,' I said, suddenly seeing it and Finn admitted it.

'And why you follow the prow beast,' Kaelbjorn Rog added. 'Since you cannot return to Skane while Halfidi and his sons are waiting.'

Finn said nothing.

'They are not,' I said softly, staring at him, rich with sudden knowing. 'But you can still never go back, can you, Finn Horsehead?'

Finn stared back at me, black eyes dead as old coals. 'I went to their hall in the night. That same night. I barred all the doors and fired it. No-one got out.'

It might have been the wind, or the trailing finger of that horror, but men shivered. The burning of a hall full of his own kind was the worst act a Northman could do and he was never forgiven for it.

It was cold, that burning revenge, for there were women and weans in it. It came to me then that humping a dead woman on the body of a dying ox was neither here nor there for a man such as Finn. I had been wrong, telling Brother John bitterly that I was leading the charge into his Abyss, for no matter how hard I ran down that dark, steep way, Finn would always be ahead of me.

'Heya,' growled Rovald. 'That was a harsh tale – what did you do that so annoyed this Halfidi?'

We expected robbery, dire murder or killing his ma – or all of them, after what we had just learned. Finn stared at the fire, leaned forward and stirred the cauldron.

'I fished his river,' he answered. 'Fished it once by moon-light for the salmon in it. He was not even sure it was me that one of his men saw.'

No-one spoke for a long time after that – then Onund suddenly leaped sideways with a curse and lashed out. Folk sprang up, hands on weapons and Onund looked at them back and forth for a moment, then grunted sheepishly.

'Rat,' he said. 'Ran over my hand. I hate rats. They come out for the raven's leavings.'

Crowbone's new voice was still more of a clear bell than others and heads lifted when it spoke.

'Pity the rat,' he said. 'It was not always as you see it now.'

He shifted his face forwards, to have it dyed by embers. His odd eyes were glinting glass chips.

'In the beginning of the world,' he said. 'When Odin was young and still had both eyes and so was more foolish than now, he was more kind-hearted. So much so that he did not like to see folk die. So one day he sent for Hugin, Thought, who was his favourite messenger from Asgard to men. He told that raven to go out into the world and tell all people that, whenever anyone died, the body was to be placed on a bier, surrounded by all the things precious to it in life and then freshly-burned oak wood ashes were to be thrown over it. Left like that on the ground, in half a day, it would be brought back to life.'

'A useful thing to know,' Styrbjorn announced. 'Find some oak ash and we will have our own army round these parts by tomorrow's rising meal.'

'Not now,' Crowbone announced sorrowfully. 'When Hugin had flown for half a day he began to get tired and hungry, so when he spotted a dead sheep he was on it like a black arrow. He sucked out the eyes and shredded the tongue and made a meal of it. Then went to sleep, entirely forgetting the message which had been given him to deliver.'

'After a time,' Crowbone went on, looking round the rapt,

329

droop-lipped faces, 'when the raven did not return, Odin called for the smallest of his creatures – the rat. It was not a skulker in sewage and darkness then, but a fine-furred beast, even if he had no discernible use other than sleeping. Odin, in his foolishness, sought to raise the rat in life and sent him out with the same message.'

'Odin sounds very much like every king I have ever heard of,' Onund Hnufa rumbled, 'while his rat reminds me of every royal messenger I have ever seen.'

The laughter was dutiful, but so weak it dribbled out like drool from a sleeping mouth and scarcely made Crowbone pause.

'The rat was, as you say, a poor messenger,' he went on. 'He fell asleep, went here, went there – and, though he eventually remembered the message, forgot what it was exactly; so as he went about among the people he told them that Odin had said that, whenever anyone died, they should be set on an oak bier, surrounded by all their prize possessions and burned to ash. In half-a-day, they would be brought back to life.'

Crowbone stopped and spread his hands wide.

'Well – by the time Hugin woke up and remembered he had a message, it was too late. He flew around furiously yelling at people to stop setting fire to their dead and telling them of the message Odin had given him – but folk said they already had a message and it was all too late.'

'And so,' Crowbone said, 'the Odin dead are always burned to this day; the god in a fury rescinded the secret of resurrection and went off to find the sort of wisdom that would stop him making any more mistakes like that.

'Now no-one trusts a raven when it speaks – and the rat is hated for the false message he brought.'

Folk shifted slightly as the tale came to an end; Rovald shook a mournful head.

'Think of that,' he said, nudging his neighbour, who happened to be Styrbjorn. 'If the raven had not stopped to eat – folk would all still be alive.'

330

'Blame the dead sheep for dying, then,' snarled Styrbjorn.

'Or having tasty eyes,' added Ospak moodily.

Koll stirred and moaned, came awake into his nightmare.

'Moonlight,' he said and a few folk looked up; like a pale silver coin, it seemed to drift across the sky between clouds.

'Rain on the wind,' muttered Thorbrand.

'This place is famous for it,' Ospak growled and that raised a weak chuckle or two.

'The same moon,' Koll whispered, 'shines on my home.'

It was a link, right enough and the tug of it brought every head up briefly. Styrbjorn wiped his mouth, gone dry with the thoughts that flitted nakedly over his face – home was there, under that silver coin in the sky and just as unreachable. He would die here. We would all die here.

'Tell me of your home,' the monk asked gently and Koll tried, in his shadow of a whisper, a thread of sound that stitched all our hearts. Of running barefoot on the strand's edge. Hunting gull eggs. Playing with his dog. Fishing. A bairn's things that, to these hard raiding men, were as far removed as that same moon – yet close enough to be remembered, to make them blink with the sudden rush of it. A man grunted almost in pain as Koll lisped about sliding on the frozen river on goat-bone skates. Then the boy's voice faded – mercifully – to sleep.

'What of your own home, monk?' I harshed out, eager to be rid of the pangs of Koll's memories, sure that tales of Miklagard would be more diverting, since most of the men here had never been to it more than once and that only briefly.

'The city walls rise like cliffs,' Leo said obligingly, 'and the towers and domes blaze with gold. In the morning, a mist hangs over the roofs, there is smoke and ships . . .'

He stopped and I was surprised to see his eyes bright. Murrough shifted his big frame and coughed, almost apologetically.

'I have heard they have women of great beauty there,' he

grunted, 'but veiled, like the Mussulmen women. I thought you were all Christ believers in Miklagard?'

'Veiled, unveiled, beauteous and plain as a cow's behind,' Leo answered with a small smile. 'All manner of women – but you are asking the wrong man, since they do not bother me. I am a priest of Christ, after all.'

'I had heard this,' Randr Sterki answered, frowning. 'It is a great wonder to me that a man can give up women for his god.'

'It is a great wonder to me that a god would ask it,' added Onund and men laughed now. I relaxed; this was better. Even Randr Sterki seemed to have covered the sharp edge of himself.

'Worse than that,' Finn growled, 'these Christ folk say you should not fight.'

'Yet they do it, all the same,' Myrkjartan pointed out. 'For these Pols we are killing are Christ men, or so I have been told – and there is no greater army than the one of the Great City itself, yet they are all Christ followers.'

Leo smiled indulgently.

'They are told not to kill,' Murrough corrected, 'according to all the canting Christ priests of my land. Perhaps it is different in the Great City. I have heard they follow the same Christ, but in a different way.'

'The rule,' Leo said slowly, picking his words like a hen does seed, 'is that you should not kill. A commandment, we call it.'

'There you are, then,' Finn muttered disgustedly. 'The Christ priests command the army not to kill and the chiefs command the opposite. It is a marvel that anything is done.'

Leo smiled his gentle smile. 'Actually, the original gospel commanded us not to murder, which is a little different and not too far from what you northers believe.'

There were nods and thinking-frowns over that one.

'This is what happens when such matters are written,' Ospak declared, shaking his head and everyone was silent, remembering Red Njal.

'Then confusion will be king,' Leo answered, 'for the Mussulmen have some similar rules written down in their holy works.'

'Are you Mussulman, then?' asked Crowbone, knitting his brows together. Leo shook his head and his smile never wavered; another priest of Christ would have been outraged.

'I wonder only,' Crowbone said, 'because I met a Mussulman once and he had sworn off women. He ate like you did, too, with one hand only.'

He looked at me when he said it, but just then Finn leaned forward, sniffed the pot, lifted the ladle and tasted it. Then he fished out his little bone container of emperor salt and poured generous whiteness into it.

'Salt,' he declared, sitting back. 'A man should eat as much salt as he can. It cleans the blood.'

There was silence, while the fire crackled and the cauldron bubbled and men sat slathered and crusted with other men's salt-cleaned blood and tried not think about it. Then Koll woke and managed to whisper out to Finn, asking him what he missed of his home.

Finn was silent and stared once out at the dark ramparts where our guards huddled and watched; I thought his head was back in Hestreng, was full of thoughts of Thordis and Hroald, his son.

I should have known. Thordis and he would never trade vows and Hroald was a boy ignored as much as acknowledged; Finn showed the truth of it all when he stretched out one long arm and pointed to where Onund's elk carving perched on the gate tower, slanted slightly, but still upright and proud, a symbol that the Oathsworn were here and not leaving in any hurry.

'I am home,' he growled.

NINETEEN

We had left it too late; Czcibor had more men and bigger boats on the river; it cost us three dead to find that out and Styrbjorn came staggering back from the little river gate, clutching his bloody arm and ranting with the fear howling in him, for we were trapped.

That was the day we started burning corpses in a mad, desperate fear-fever that sought to try and scour the Red Pest out before it killed us all.

That was the day they brought up the ram and smashed in the gate.

They had tried fire, but lacked oil for their arrows and we had water enough to soak the gates and timbers where they tried it. Then we saw men hauling back a good tree, sweated out of the river further down, where it had lodged. It was, as Finn pointed out, as good an oak for a ram as any he had seen.

We had to watch it being crafted, too, for there was no place to hide out on that plain and every hammer and axe-stroke that shaped it rattled us to the bone, for we had no way of stopping such a beast. Their archers would keep our heads down – it was almost impossible to put your head above the timber-teeth of the rampart now, unless there were enemy climbing over it – and the ram would come up to the gate and splinter it to ruin.

'Barrier the inside of the gate,' I suggested and Alyosha nodded, then grinned.

'Battle luck for you, Orm Bear Slayer, that you have skilled men here. Better than a barrier is our wolf-teeth.'

Alyosha and the Rus were old hands, having fought in sieges on both sides of the ramparts and they knew what was needed.

They had a house demolished for the great timbers of the roof-tree and lashed them together like a cradle. Then they gathered up spears and split the heads from them, or cut the shafts short, so that they were fixed to the cradle, all odd lengths and all deadly.

After that, it was shifted to a point just beyond where the curved groove of dirt showed how far the gate opened inwards.

'Wolf-teeth,' Alyosha said, when his chosen men had sweated it into place; they beamed with satisfaction. Finn and others strolled round it, eyeing it with a professional air, for we were raiders, when all was said and done and avoided anything that looked like this bristling terror.

'A place to hang their cloaks and hats when they come,' Finn said eventually, which was admiration enough to make Alyosha beam.

'Growl not at guests, nor drive them from the gate,' Ospak added, 'as Red Njal's granny would say.'

'No more on that,' Finn growled. 'Without it coming from his mouth, I would sooner see Red Njal's granny laid to rest.'

Ospak merely nodded and smiled, twisting his dirt and blood-crusted face into a hard knot.

Not long after, hidden watchers peering through slits on the gate tower announced that the enemy were coming again.

I stood behind the barrier with Finn at one shoulder and Ospak at the other, fetid with fear and old blood, rot-red with rust. My bowels curled like waves on the shore and the first great boom of the ram on the door almost loosened them entirely.

On the ramparts, Finnlaith and Alyosha and others hunkered down and heaved the last of our stones as well as spike-studded timbers down on the heads of the ram party; we heard them clatter and bounce off the roof of shields, though there was an occasional scream to let us know they were not having it all their own way.

We sweated and shivered behind the wolf fangs, while the gate rang like a bell and heaved in another little bit with each blow, the bar on it creaking and dancing in the locks. Great gouts of muddy slurry spurted up from the hinges.

Crowbone slid up to the tower steps with a party bringing up more timbers, manhandling them up the ladder, with the gate bulging in right at their ears. Alyosha, his helmet flaps up and laced across the top of his head so that his ears were free and he could hear better, saw it and bellowed out something, lost in the mad din. Crowbone merely waved at him and Alyosha, scowling, half-stood to make his way to the steps and tell Crowbone to go away.

The arrow took him in the neck, just under the ear; if he had had his helmet flaps down it might have saved him, but they were up like little birdwings and the arrow went in one side and out the other. He jerked and pawed at it, a puzzled look on his face, then reared up; blood came out of his mouth in a great, black gout and he fell sideways and clattered down the steps to Crowbone's feet.

The boy howled – but someone grabbed him just then, dragging him back and under the cradle of wolf fangs, just as the gate crashed open with a splintering rend of wood and hinge.

The first man through was a mad-mouthed frother, black hair flying, lunging in with a spear up and a leather helmet askew on his forehead; he had time to see what he was running at, time to skid to a halt – then the ones behind crashed on him and he was shot forward, shrieking for his ma, to be impaled like a shrike's breakfast.

The first half-dozen ended up like that – there were longer blades with two and three bodies on them; some of the shafts snapped under the weight.

Those behind realised something was up when they were brought up short and found they could go neither ahead, nor to the side, while those in the gate tower above were hurling slabs of spiked wood down on them.

I hacked and stabbed and cut and slashed; the wooden cradle started to shift and slide back under the press, so men put their shoulders to it on our side and shoved, while others elbowed for room to fight. There was a fine haze of steam and stink and misted blood, a great bellowing shriek of fear and dying; the earth under the gate tower churned to a thick broth of muddy blood.

I saw Finn take a jaw off with a wild stroke. I saw one of Randr Sterki's men eat the point of a spear and go down, gargling. Arrows whirred and shunked and men from both sides screamed and died; the Pols were shooting through the open gateway, heedless of who they hit.

Yan Alf went crazed then and leaped up on top of the wolf-fang cradle and its smother of hanging bodies, then hurled himself, screaming, into the middle of the pack; I never saw him alive again. Finnlaith, screaming 'Ui Neill' and spittle, followed him, leaping off the top of the watchtower and I saw him once after that, rising through a frothing sea of enemy like a breaching whale; then he disappeared.

That broke them. One minute I was slashing and stabbing, my breathing high and shrill, my arm aching, seeing the blood curve off the end of the axe blade in fat, greasy spray – then I was slumped against the scarred, gouged cradle where bodies writhed and groaned. The Pols backed off through their own arrows and Finn yelled out a warning as the full weight of shafts fell on us.

337

Shields up, we stood there until men brought up some thick timber doors torn off the houses and used them as shelter. In the end, the arrows stopped and men went out to heave corpses aside and shut the gates again, though they were so badly splintered that they could not be barred.

I know I shouted instructions for some of this, for Finn told me. I know I helped carry Alyosha away and consoled a weeping Crowbone, while the crew of *Short Serpent* – what was left of them – stood, covered in gore and grim silence while Alyosha was shield-carried to a pyre. Ospak and Murrough, the last Irishers left, stood like dumb posts, unable to go out and find Finnlaith; in the end, Onund whacked their shoulders and gave them work to keep their minds off the loss.

I know all this, but was aware of none of it. I only came back to life later, when Bjaelfi was binding up my ankle – the old injury, which burned like fire. I had gone over on it, according to folk who saw, and limped about for a long time until Bjaelfi and others managed to pin me down and tend my wounds.

I had a scratch down one cheek, my ribs ached from a blow I did not even know I had come by and my nose thundered with pain and trickled new blood, so that Finn, unharmed and grinning through the stains on his face, shook his head.

'That neb of yours will not last much longer if you persist in getting it dunted,' he noted and Ospak, staggering past with an armful of timber to be spiked with spear and arrow points, stopped long enough to look and tilt his head almost onto his shoulder.

'Every time I look at it,' he said, 'I have to stand at more of a list to steerboard than before, just to keep it straight on your face.'

Then he laughed, a shrill, high sound. They all laughed, those that were left, hair stiff with clotted filth, armour red-rusted and weapons stained with gore. They moved as though their legs were wood – yet they moved, getting ready for the next attack.

Finnlaith was dead, Yan Alf was dead. Thorbrand was dead. Hjalti Svalr had the Red Pest, had lost most of his right hand and was groaning and babbling of home. Others were stacked like winter wood, their weapons bound to cold hands. And those who were left mourned with laughter, like wolves.

I had no belly left for laughing. As the shadows lengthened and weary fires sprang up, Bjaelfi came to me, his face scored with misery, carrying a limp little bundle which he laid at my feet like an offering. It was so small, that bundle, yet it broke us all like a falling tree and men groaned and bowed their heads; some even wept, leaving wet white streaks through the filth of their cheeks.

Koll. He was wrapped warmly and his face was so swollen his father would not have known him but for the bone-white of his hair. One hand rested on his chest under the warm wrap, but one had flopped free and the blue veins on it stood proudly out, so proud it was hard to believe that blood did not pump through them. The rest of the hand was pale, the shrinking flesh spatterered with white pustules.

Bjaelfi looked at me, waiting to take the small body to the burning; men stopped and made Hammer signs for mourning and not just because Koll was dead. He was what we had struggled all this way to get, had fought for, had watched oarmates die for – and we had failed.

I tied his little hands round the hilt of his father's sword and gave him to the Odin-fire. It was like the death of hope itself, watching that small, wrapped body smoke up into the dark.

That night, Dark Eye came to me, silent as a summer breeze, yet when I reached for her she was limp and slick-sheened with sweat, hot as embers in my arms. To the question in my

339

eyes, she simply slithered from her shapeless tunic-dress and raised her arms; even in the dark, where her silver shape glowed, the red spots on her thighs and under her arms were clear, almost as big as the tender tips of her hard breasts.

She shivered and sweated.

'In the morning,' she said, 'I will go to them.'

I argued. I swore. I ranted. I babbled. In the end she pressed hot, cracked lips on mine to silence me.

'This is my wyrd,' she said, her breath fetid on my cheek. 'This is best. I am what they want – let them take me, for it will be their own doom. This is what the Sea-Finn's drum saw.'

I saw it, then, hot in her eyes, with a coldness deep in my bowels. It was her wyrd – at one stroke she saved us, saved her people and would spread the red, ruinous pest through Czcibor's army.

'It must be done in the morning,' she said, 'before I am too weak to pretend.'

I nodded then, still frantic with the loss of her, with the sight of those great, liquid seal eyes already filming blue-white with sickness. I held her most of that night, leaving her only long enough to take a stained, unbleached linen scrap and wrap it round a shield.

There was not enough dark in all the world that would keep back the creeping dawn.

When it spilled up, staining the rampart, making it like the jaw of some snarling prow beast, men stood, shaking and weary, beards and hair stiff with filth, eyes bright with the knowledge that today they would stand before their gods – and were amazed to see me walk Dark Eye to the gate.

I handed my axe to Finn and left Dark Eye with him while I shoved through the splintered ruin, stepping over the bodies and through the bloody crust of mud. I held the linen-wrapped shield high, hoping it was white enough to be noticed as a truce-sign. I paused only once to look Randr Sterki in his red-rimmed eyes. His grin was a curve of snarl.

Picking my way through the festering dead, I stumbled out to where Czcibor sat on his horse; he looked more gaunt now, I was thinking and I wondered if the Red Pest had already reached his army.

'Be quick,' he said harsh and haughty, so I was.

'Is she trade enough for our lives?' I asked and he looked over my shoulder to the small figure in the broken gateway, having to look across the heaped bundles of his own dead men, having to see the spears and blades still defending the rampart, the cradle of wolf-teeth gleaming just inside the gate.

When he looked back at me, his eyes were hard and cold and bleak, which did not bother me much – I knew he would agree, for he could not stay here longer. He ached to stake us out, but the cost was high and he was too much of a good commander to let his hate ruin his army and his ambition.

What stabbed me to the bone was the rest of his look, the bit just behind his eyes which curled a sneer at me for giving up this slip of a woman to save our lives.

Perhaps it choked him, perhaps he was too tired to do more – but he nodded, which was enough.

I walked back to the gate and took my axe back from Finn. Dark Eye, impassive as a carving, wrapped the tattered cloak round her and walked out, the way she had always walked, as if she had gold between her legs, into the maw of the Pols. She did not look back.

I came back into the faces of those who knew the business was finished and that they would not die today. Yet there remained, hovering like a waiting hawk, the knowledge that it had been the girl the Pols had wanted all along – but no-one who saw my face wanted to bare their teeth on that, all the same.

Save one, of course. There is always one.

'You fuck,' yelled Styrbjorn, trembling with the nearness of that fearful stake. 'It was the girl. All this time. We died so you could have a hump while the . . .'

I hit him with the haft of the axe, a wet smack in his face that sent him crashing to the ground, where he lay and snored out bubbling blood and teeth. Uddolf moved to him, turning him over so that he would not choke.

I was cold with it all, cold and sick. A little shape was burning on a pyre, another was staggering away to die among enemies and both had held skeins of my wyrd in their hands; with their loss, I could not see one more step in front of me. I was almost on my knees, begging Odin to take his sacrifice and I half-turned to where Randr Sterki stood, silent and watchful, almost willing him to make his move.

'Good blow,' said Bjaelfi after a swift look at Styrbjorn. 'Though I am thinking it would have been better to have used the edge. A head hacked off cannot conspire, as Red Njal's granny would say.'

Finn shifted slightly and cleared the rheum from his throat.

'Make that the last of Red Njal's granny,' he growled, so that everyone could hear, 'and be content that our Orm used the shaft and not the edge. He was always the one for leaving folk alive who should be dead, yet is known for a man who can fall in a bucket of shite and come up with a handful of silver. Perhaps there is worth in Styrbjorn yet.'

He frowned down at the groaning Styrbjorn, then hefted The Godi and clawed everyone with his gaze.

'This needs cleaning. Then we can quit this Nowhere place.'

There were twenty of us quitting, no more; the rest were dead, and those who were not, we killed for mercy's sake and then burned them, with all their gear and even their sea-chests, the black feathers trailing accusingly into a sullen sky behind us as we moved across fresh green and birdsong.

For most of that first day we moved grim and fearful, a scar on the land, always looking over one shoulder, for no-one trusted the Pols and we were on their side of the Odra now, heading for a tributary river called Notec, which we would

342

have to cross. After a while, when it seemed as if we had, truly, escaped, men began to look round at the green tips and buds, to turn to where a raven harshed, or a small bird peeped.

They took deeper breaths of spring air and started to grin at each other – except the sick, who staggered or were carried, babbling. The Red Pest stayed with us, tagging along like a dog that could not be sent home and still they grinned at each other, as if they had thrown particularly good dice.

I was the only one not exulting in survival, not cheered by avoiding the cliff and the wolves, moving like a man already dead and waiting, waiting, waiting, for Odin to strike. I was a scowl on the face of their cheerfulness and men avoided me, all save Finn and Crowbone – and the monk, strangely, who strode out alongside me now and then, the uneven dagged ends of his black wool robe flapping round his calves.

Eventually, because I knew he was waiting for me to do it and would never break the silence first, I asked him what he wanted.

'To knit you back, like the broken bone you are,' he said, easy enough with the words and looking ahead at the trail. Crowbone loped past us, an old bow in his hand and three arrows in the other.

'I am going hunting,' he declared and I knew it was to take his thoughts off the dead Alyosha, so I fought for words to rein him in and yet not make it seem so, for his nursemaid was gone.

Kuritsa appeared and slapped Crowbone manfully on the shoulder.

'Nothing with legs is edible when you kill it,' he declared. 'You gutshoot it and the meat is bitter when it runs. I will go with you and teach you how to hunt.'

He shot me a look over one shoulder, a reassuring grin with it, then the pair of them moved off ahead of the trail, with men chaffering them, pleased that there might be more than old bread and oats that night.

'I do not need your Christ for my salvation,' I told the monk and he nodded.

'Then I do not offer him. But you need something.'

I was wondering why he cared and said so.

'I need you to get me back to the Great City,' he said, which was truthful enough, if not exactly the warm spirit of caring I had imagined. I laughed, the sound echoing as if my head was in a bucket and he smiled.

'See? Now matters are better.'

'What happens when we do get to the Great City, monk?' I demanded. 'It comes to me that taking such a dangerous man as yourself back to the place where he is powerful and we are not is foolish. Perhaps we should kill you here; it is no more than you deserve.'

Leo walked in frowning silence for a while, then smiled suddenly, bright and wide.

'You will just have to trust me,' he said. 'I will be more use alive in the Great City than dead in a heap out here.'

'So I will not have to offer some jewelled cross for our lives, then?' I offered wryly. 'Now that your bargaining counter is burned to smoke?'

'Jesus died on a wooden one,' he answered and I had no answer to that and felt suddenly washed with weariness, so that we walked in silence through the wood, which seemed never to end – so much so that I remember saying so and asking how far we had to walk into it.

'Only half-way,' Finn answered, peering at me, 'then we are walking out of it, as any sensible man will tell you. You look like eight ells of bad cloth, Trader. Perhaps you should rest.'

The day had slithered into grey twilight, where the *alfar* flickered and I was only vaguely aware of Finn calling a halt for it seemed that the grey light smoked round me, so that I saw and heard them as if in a mist.

344

There was a steading. Once, it had been a substantial *hov*, a shieling of some note, built low to the ground, but it had fallen to ruin, so that the moss had reclaimed it to a mound of green; grass hung, dried and withered off what was left of the roof, drooping like the bodies of the dead on the ramparts we had so recently left.

I woke to find myself under the shelter of the only roof-space left, sharing it with groaners with sweating, plaguey faces, or wounded from the fight, or moaning with belly-rot and boils. Fires were lit, the rest of the men huddled outside, under the stars and what cloaks they had, sharing them with those who had none.

Kuritsa and Crowbone had returned, the big archer with a buck over his shoulders and it was jumped on, gralloched, cut up and spit-roasted; the smell of meat sang round the house like a memory of better times.

They brought me slivers of succulent deer, bread softened and savoured in the blood-juices of it, but I had no hunger, which I found strange and even the bit I forced down tasted like ash. Bjaelfi came and peered at me and it was then I realised, with a shock, that I was sick.

For a time, I lay and listened to the men mutter softly and start in to weaving themselves together; straps were repaired, weapons cleaned, men tried to sponge the worst stains from clothing and cloaks.

They dragged out combs – all of them had them, good bone ones and, even if some of those implements grinned like gappy old men, they still dragged them through clotted, raggled hair. Bjaelfi produced shears and some of the worst matting was cut off; beards and hair were trimmed and Leo shook his head with wonder, for he had not realised that norther warriors are more vain than women.

In the end, I drifted off in my jarl-bed under the roof with the murmuring sick, listening to the gentle shift of Bjaelfi and the monk, moving like soft, clucking hens.

345

I moved into a dream of smoke and water, where familiar people and places shredded mistily away when I looked at them, living only at the edge of my dream-sight, like *alfar*. When I surfaced from this, it was like breaching from the ocean, whooping in air and shivering, blurred and blinking. Sweat rolled off me and I shook; I knew what ate me.

I got up and the place heaved gently as if I stood on a deck in a swell; my feet seemed too far below me and did not even seem to be mine as I moved, slowly, like an old, blind man, out past the soft glow of the fire, the snorers and farters, out to where a man stood on watch in ringmail and helm.

He looked at me and I stared blankly back at him; it took long seconds for me to recognise Ospak, by which time he had come close enough to give me his concern.

'You should go back to the fire, Jarl Orm,' he said flatly. I wanted to tell him to leave me alone, that I needed a shit – which was a lie, of course. What I needed was privacy to find out what I already knew in my heart.

All that I croaked out of me, all the same, was 'shit'. He nodded slowly, and turned back to his guard duty. I struggled on, to where the dark ate the fireglow and beyond, to where only the half-veiled moon gave light.

I dropped my breeks, bent my head to look. I saw the red spots crawling out of my groin and on to my thighs like embers from a forge-fire. I touched the burn of them, knew the truth and either it or the fever swam my head, so that I half stumbled and nearly fell.

'Steady, Bear Slayer,' said a voice, cold as quenched iron. 'I would not wish you hurt. That is my pleasure alone.'

Randr Sterki moved blackly out of the dark to stand in front of me, where I could see him if I could raise my head. I could do that only a little but the blade he held gleamed like an old fang in the moonglow. Naked from the waist, the white of his body seemed eaten by whorls of darkness, which I slowly realised were his Rus skin-markings.

346

The stupidity of him made me laugh and I saw myself as he saw me – swaying, head-bowed, breeks around my ankles. It only made matters funnier and the laughing choked me, so that I suddenly found myself with my arse on the wet grass.

'Get up,' he hissed angrily. 'Or die on your knees.'

On my arse, I wanted to correct. I am on my arse here and dying of the Red Pest and whether you slit me here or wait for me to die makes no difference and will not bring any of the ones you loved back again. Odin takes his sacrifice-life – in the cruelest way, of course, that being the mark of One-Eye.

But all that came out was 'arse'. Which, given the moment and the matter, was not gold-browed verse likely to sway him from his path.

He grunted, moved like a lowered brow, black and angry and the sword silvered through the shadows, seemed to leave a trail behind it as it moved, like the wake of a ship on a black sea. My sword, I noted dully; I could see the V-notch in it, as if the dark had taken a bite from the blade.

'Hold, Randr Sterki,' growled a voice and a figure scowled out of the shadows and grabbed Randr's arm. 'Do not kill him. We need him . . .'

Randr yelped with the shock of it and we both saw it was the monk, black-robed and tense as coiled wire, his hand gripping Randr's sword-arm. Randr, with a savage howl, flung Leo away from him and cursed in pain as he did so.

'Get away, you Christ-hagged little fuck,' he snarled, rubbing his forearm and scowling. 'Once I deal with this dog, you will be next.'

Leo rolled over and came up to his knees. Strangely, he was laughing through the blood on his mouth. Behind him, I saw Finn sprinting forward, The Godi in one fist, nail in the other.

'You *nithing fud*,' he shrieked, but it was desperation, for he knew he would never make it. I knew he would never

347

make it, watched the slow, silver arc of my own sword curl on me like a great wave. I smelled crushed grass and new earth, heard Odin laugh – though it may have been Leo. This way was better, I was thinking. Quicker than the Pest, praise be to AllFather after all.

The laugh sounded softly again as the wave of that silvering sword cracked and broke; Randr's hand faltered, seemed to lose the strength to grip and the blade fell from it, tumbling point over haft to land in the crushed grass. He stood, shook his head a little, looked like a bull which had just butted a rock.

'I . . .' he began and rubbed his forearm with his spare hand, the forearm where Leo had gripped him so tightly.

'Itches,' said Leo gently and spat a little blood from his mashed lip. 'Those scratches are deep.'

I almost felt Randr Sterki nod. He stood like a *blot* ox waiting for the knife, one which had been fed enough mash to still it, so that it barely managed to hold the great mass of its own head up.

Finn arrived in a rush and skidded to a halt, panting, uncertain, as Leo held up one hand to stop him striking Randr.

'Kill,' said Randr, blinking and dull-voiced. 'You. All.'

'I do not think so, Randr Sterki,' Leo said flatly.

Randr staggered two steps and then fell toward me, toppling like a great wind-blown oak; his head bounced at my feet.

There was silence for a moment – then shapes moved in the dark, sliding easily to the side of the stunned Finn, armed and ready and alerted by Ospak.

'It would be better, I am thinking,' said Crowbone, 'if someone were to help me with Jarl Orm. You, Styrbjorn, since you brought all this on us.'

Styrbjorn licked his lips, looked from one to the other and back again and could have been on the edge of pointing out how it had been Crowbone's bloody vengeance that had brought all this. He stayed silent and stared, finally, at the toppled giant that had been Randr Sterki, the fear of *seidr* magic washing off him like heat from a sweating stallion.

There was no magic here, as Crowbone pointed out.

'Battle luck for you, Jarl Orm,' he said, stepping past where the monk still sat, working the jaw Randr had hit, his left hand sitting quiet as a white spider on one knee. Crowbone picked up my sword, handed it to a bemused Finn and looked at me with chiding sorrow.

'You should have paid more heed when I told you how the monk ate his food,' he added.

I blinked like a light-blind hare; then it came to me. Leo ate with his right hand – like a Mussulman, Crowbone had said. In fact, he did everything with his right hand. I had never seen Leo use his left hand at all, save to strike with. We had all wasted our time looking for a cunningly hidden needle.

The monk shrugged and held up the white spider, where long nails on thumb and forefinger, both splintered from use, gleamed balefully in the light.

'I have no idea how much is left,' he said, 'after so long without renewing.'

Enough to kill Randr Sterki dead as a flayed horse, I thought but could manage no more words. I watched Leo smile his bland smile, his face wavering as if he sat under water, while Bjaelfi and others pounded up, shouting.

'You are strong,' he said to me, though he seemed to be receding, growing pale as mist. 'With God's help and some simple skills, we will all get safe to Constantinople.'

'Aye,' said Finn, flexing his fingers on both sword hilts and glancing at the poison-dead Randr Sterki. 'You have saved our jarl for sure, monk – but forgive me if I do not grasp your wrist in thanks over it.'

HESTRENG, high summer

The rock was old and stained from use. Just a stone on a hill, flat here and hollowed there, small enough for a tiny body. It was here, then, that Odin had claimed the life I had offered him and there was nothing left to show for it after so long, for the birds and the foxes had picked it clean and scattered the remains.

A long, hard birth, Aoife told me, weeping with the memories of it. The bairn – a boy – had arrived with a head too big and a leg too short and the little chest heaving for breath, so that Aoife knew, as they all knew, that it was broken inside as well as out.

It was the last of Thorgunna's womb, too, and she must have known that wee crippled mite was all the bairn she would ever have, all the son she would ever give, for a man she did not even know would come safe home.

Yet it lived, so Thorgunna did what all good wives did when a bairn was born who would never be whole. She stumbled with it up to this place, offered *blot* to the gods to wrap it safe and warm in their hall and left it there, naked on the rock.

She had never been back to it, Thordis told me, even after she had been brought from the brink of death herself.

Not, she added with bitter accusation, in all the time I had been away.

Yet the bairn on the rock lived in front of Thorgunna's eyes every day, so that she could see nothing else and sat, staring. She left her own life on that rock, all that she was, all that she would ever be and Thordis took a long, hard time telling me how she had gone off with a Christ priest and others who followed him. West, Thordis said, to Jutland, perhaps even to Saxland or beyond, for the god of the White Christ, it seemed, did not condemn twisted bairns to the wind and rain and cold.

A hand on my shoulder; I knew it was Finn, his eyes doglike and round. The others were there, too, standing awkwardly as you do when you see someone you care for so stricken and not able to offer anything other than mumbles of sympathy.

I climbed to my knees from that stone and looked up at the sky, that great, cold, blue eye of Odin that watched all I did and regarded me now as I worked out the measure of what I had offered as sacrifice. It had been a puzzle, intricate as a secret box, when I recovered from the Red Pest with only a few pockmarks to show for it. Down on the strand, a *knarr* with our battered elk prow crudely tied to it rocked heavily, fat with flagons of olive oil and bales of silk; our rich prize from a grateful Leo. I had lived and prospered and did not understand why Odin had spared me and taken little Koll.

I heard Aoife calling on her son and turned, knowing what I would see.

The pale of him, the bone-white of little Cormac running in and out of the tide-shallow as men splashed back and forth. Laughing, with his hair like spume on a wave, he brought back the crushing sight of Brand when I had told him his son was dead.

He was already a wasted man, the muscle and bulk burned off him with wound-fever so that his knees and elbows were big as galls on an oak, while one side of his face was a scarred horror. I told him his son, my *fostri*, was dead and sent to Odin with his sword. I told him his enemy, Styrbjorn, lived.

He said nothing, but when I left I knew there would be no more visits from him and that what friendship we had was ended. Soon, he would ask me for the boy Cormac and his mother, too, in a way that could not be refused, even if I had a mind to. Not long after that he would find a way to take Hestreng back.

One-Eye had been cold and cruel and wolf-circling as ever. He had taken the life I offered as surely as if he had struck me down with the spear Gungnir – Dark Eye, Thorgunna, my son, Hestreng, all made as dust, so that there was now nothing for me in the world save the Oathsworn of the *Fjord Elk*.

I looked at Finn and Ospak, Kuritsa and the others – Crowbone, his odd-eyed stare bland and cool and Onund Hnufa, his face strange, a cliff that set itself hard against the terror of old memories. I saw his unnatural, crooked shoulder and the way he stared at the flat, hollowed, stained stone and knew, with a shock of understanding, that this should have been his wyrd, yet somehow he had avoided it. I wanted to ask him how he had done it, but he caught my look, held it until it was me who looked away, sliding from gaze to gaze until I was back at the hollowed stone, feeling the eyes of the Oathsworn rest on me.

The Oathsworn, still bound one to another tighter than the ties of brothers – and now the only family I knew. In the bleak dark of me, a small ember glowed warmly.

'Heya, Jarl Orm,' Finn said softly and stared out to sea, his eyes narrowing against the glare. 'I am told that raiding has started again in the lands of the Englisc. Good pickings to be had, I hear.'

'Vladimir will want us in Novgorod, for sure,' Crowbone countered, with a glare at Finn. 'To fight for him against his brothers.'

352

'Anywhere but back to the Wendish lands,' added Ospak and looked meaningfully at me. 'I hear red sickness rages there.'

There was a long pause which the wind filled with a mournful, gentle sigh. I looked at them, one at a time, finally settling back on the grim-faced hunchback.

'We will need a new *Fjord Elk*,' I said to Onund Hnufa.

Down on the blue-grey water, the prow beast rocked, nodding as if satisfied.

HISTORICAL NOTE

The Odra – the Oder – in the tenth century was a boundary river and has stayed that way for a thousand years, marking the frontier between Germany and Poland – or, in A.D. 975, the Saxlanders of the Holy Roman Empire and the Slavs to the east, chief among them the Pols.

The Holy Roman Empire saw itself as a bastion of Christian civilisation against the heathens from the east and that view persists even to the twenty-first century, no matter what political correctness dictates – any manifesto of the right-wing parties of Europe is worthless unless it includes a diatribe against the economic migrants beyond the Oder.

Dealing with the tenth century along the Oder you can see the same strains, the same hatreds, the same divides, the same naked warfare not far from the surface of any meeting. Scores of small tribes clutched the last of their lands on both sides of the river, swearing allegiance to whichever of the major powers held most sway at the time. Like the river itself, politics were fluid in this region.

Yet this was a trade route of some note, part of the Amber Road, that lesser-known son of the Silk Road and the Silver Way, which led from the Baltic to the north of Italy when Rome was more of a power and that capital city the centre of the world. In the tenth century, the Ottos of the Holy Roman Empire, father and son aspiring to be as great as the Emperor in Constantinople, had revived the fortunes of the city of Rome and trade was on the move again.

New breeds were straddling the tenth-century Amber Road, too, turning the Balkans into the forge-fire it has remained to this day – the Magyars, only recently brought to a stop in their westward expansion, were now settling in what would become Hungary and had been forced to become Christians though they, like everyone else, quickly saw the benefits of belonging to that club.

The Bulgars would bump against the Byzantine Empire with a friction so irritating that, in the end, one of the best of Byzantium's emperors would be known as Bulgar-Slayer.

The last thing such a delicate thread of a trade river needs is a boatload of pagan warriors snarling their way up it and scowling at everyone who gets in their way. The last thing a boatload of pagan warriors would want to do is go up it at all – so why would Orm and the Oathsworn?

Because of Koll, Jarl Brand's heir and, more importantly, Orm's foster-son. The importance of the *fostri* in Norse lands of the time is not so hard to work out – how many reading this would entrust their son with another family for the formative six or seven years of his life, trusting that he is brought up properly? If that son represented all the hopes and dreams for the future of a dynasty? Think of a public school – I mean a real one, not some limp-wristed Hogwarts – with one pupil and an ethos of edged weapon sport and you might get some idea.

The one so entrusted had a supreme responsibility from the moment the child was declared a *fostri* – not least for the safety of the boy – and this was doubled because accepting the task also acknowledged that the foster-father had bound himself to the real father, accepting a degree of fealty as well as admitting that his status was slightly better than your own.

355

To lose such a boy was the worst stain on your fame. Since 'fair fame' then was all that truly mattered, worth more than any amount of gold, retrieving such a reputation was worth any hardship, any risk.

As ever, I have tried to weave real people into a fictional tale. Queen Sigrith is real, as is King Eirik the Victorious and the babe that Orm fought so hard to defend went on to become King Olaf, called Skotkonung, the Lap King. Styrbjorn is also real, as is Pallig Tokeson – though his brother Ljot is fictional – and their subsequent fates are no part of this tale.

Leo is also real – Leo the Deacon is the prime historical record for this era in Byzantium, but I have almost certainly maligned the man by making him into a combination of Moriarty and George Smiley.

Real, too, of course, is Crowbone, Olaf Tryggvasson, and the relationship between him, Queen Sigrith and King Svein Forkbeard might have been different if Sigrith had been nicer to a teenage boy. In later years, the widowed Sigrith tried to interest Olaf in marrying her and he took advantage of it, enjoyed the fruits and then, at the last, cast her aside in revenge for the slights she gave in his youth.

Enraged, Sigrith then had more luck with Svein Forkbeard and worked at turning that king against his former ally and friend. In the end, Olaf went under the swords of all his enemies, brought together by Svein as much for Sigrith's revenge as any gain in lands.

Crowbone's stories of Dyl U'la-Spegill are my take on the origins of the later tales of the trickster Till Eulenspiegel, or Dyl Ulenspegl – the name translates, roughly, as 'mysterious owl-mirror' – although the original Low German is believed to be *ul'n Spegel*, which means 'wipe the arse' and altogether is a more satisfying soubriquet for a character who so viciously ripped the pith out of the venal and pompous in society.

Till Eulenspiegel's social satire tales are almost certainly older than the tradition that has him born in 1300. Since the same tradition has him dying in the sixteenth century, I have no trouble assigning him to an altogether darker time, before his tales were sanitised for children and turned into a tone poem by Richard Strauss in the nineteenth century, thus bringing him to the attention of an English-speaking culture.

As ever, this tale is best told round a fire against the closing dark. Any mistakes or omissions are my own and should not spoil the tale.

ACKNOWLEDGEMENTS

As ever, the list of people who made this book possible is enough to crew a longship – but, at the head of it stand the real Oathsworn, the members of Glasgow Vikings (www.glasgow vikings.co.uk) and the rest of the Vikings, national and international (www.vikingsonline.org.uk) who provide entertainment and education in several countries as well as striking fear into publicans everywhere.

Treading on their heels is Clare Hey, my editor at HarperCollins, a delicate fragrance of a woman whose skill in spotting how a story should be is matched only by her bloodthirsty love of the Oathsworn.

As ever, all the Oathsworn raise their swords to my agent, James Gill of United Agents for without his vision they would not be being enjoyed at all.

My wife, Kate, deserves all the silver of the world for putting up with muddy Vike boots, a litter of swords and my endless absence at a computer with indulgent patience.

Finally and most importantly of all – the dedicated band of Oathsworn fans who actually buy the end result. More power to you for your praise, criticism, comments and unfailing humour. I hope this one pleases you as much as the others seem to have done.

358